PAT STRODA

DEFENDING

The

HILLFARM PUBLISHING GROUP

Foreword

Dear Reader,

Protecting the Lady Fossil Hunter is a historical adventure novel set in Kansas in 1867. It was a turbulent era. Some of the incidents included in this story were inspired by actual events and people but adapted by my imagination into the scenes you read here.

The railroad reached Salina in 1867, a flood that summer wiped out much of Ellsworth and badly damaged Fort Fletcher, which was moved and became Fort Hays.

Major Sternberg was a surgeon at Fort Harker in 1867 and battled the cholera outbreak that year which took the life of his wife. He later became Surgeon General of the United States Army. Sternberg was a fossil collector, but his brother Charles earned fame as a paleontologist. The family founded what is now the wonderful Sternberg Museum of Natural History in Hays, Kansas where the famous "fish within a fish" fossil is displayed.

Attacks by Cheyenne warriors and Dog Soldiers wreaked havoc along the stage lines, settlements and railroad west of Salina for several years in a futile attempt to stop the flow of white men into their traditional lands. I am not an expert on Cheyenne customs and culture, but I spent many hours studying about them and their way of life. I worked hard to portray these remarkable people in a realistic fashion, but these scenes came wholly from my imagination. Some may find the language I used offensive and for that I'm sorry. I tried to be true to the era.

Patricia Stroda, author.

Chapter One

Salina, Kansas, June 1867

"Before I met you, Dev, I didn't know what the inside of a jail looked like."

Stretched out on a lumpy cot in the next cell, Devlin Elder suppressed a grin at Buck Murphy's forlorn tone. Devlin raised the black hat covering his face and glanced at his young friend. The gangly blond youth sported a black eye, split lip and a nasty bruise on one cheek.

Judging by the soreness of his jaw, Devlin suspected he looked about the same. "It's not like I planned it."

"Gosh darn it, Dev, this is the third time we've been locked up this year. Why'd you start that fight, anyway?" Buck's thick Tennessee drawl held only mild censure.

A good brawl was an easy way to blow off steam, but the fight that landed them in jail four days ago had been different. "You didn't have to join in."

Buck snorted. "What kind of friend would I be if I let you take on those rowdies by yourself?"

"One that wasn't locked up."

"This ain't nothing to joke about." Buck leaned back with a huff and fell silent.

Devlin stared at the dust motes floating in the shaft of afternoon sunlight pouring through a small, barred window set high in the stone wall. The slow crawl of the light across the rough floor was his only means of telling time inside the dank cell. Beyond the window came the sounds of hammering, yelling teamsters and the tinkling notes of a piano from a saloon down the street. The railroad had arrived in Salina a month ago. The town was booming.

A brown wren landed on the window ledge, resting a moment before flitting away. Devlin tamped down a fierce longing to follow. He needed fresh air and to feel the sun on his face. The cell reeked with the fetid odors of old urine and vomit from the previous occupants. He hated being closed in, but his years among the Sioux and Cheyenne had taught him to endure any discomfort in silence. A few days in jail was nothing compared to life as a seven-year-old Sioux captive.

Buck rose and paced across his cell. "There were four other fellas in that fight. So how come you and me are the only ones locked up? Sheriff Wilson sure has it in for you. What'd you do to rile him?"

Devlin settled his hat over his face to hide his smile. "Don't rightly know."

The taste of Clara Wilson's pouting, whiskey-flavored lips, her body pressed against his, made it easy to forget the past for a time. Hell, she almost made a week in here worthwhile. Almost. He'd been careless on their last night together.

The sheriff had been watching the room Devlin had rented behind the saloon. Fortunately, Devlin spotted him before Clara stepped out. Leaving her alone in the room, he'd started the fight as a diversion to draw Wilson away so Clara could slip out unseen. He hadn't intended the brawl to land him or Buck in jail. That was all Wilson's doing. The man must be getting wise.

Devlin's smile faded. Wilson might suspect him in the disappearance of a few whiskey barrels or some crooked gambling, but if he ever had proof his wife spent her lonely nights with Devlin while he was on duty, Devlin's life wouldn't be worth spit. Wilson was a mean, jealous man.

"Elder, you got a visitor." The sheriff's bellow made Buck jump. Devlin remained still. With an indifference that belied his curiosity, he pushed his hat brim up with one finger. A petite blond woman stood beside the towering, beefy sheriff. The top of her head barely reached the star pinned to Wilson's broad chest.

She looked to be in her teens, but Devlin realized her size gave that impression. When he met her gaze, he knew she was no giddy girl. Intense, dark blue eyes behind round spectacles studied him without wavering. A tingle raised the hairs at the nape of his neck. He had a sixth sense about trouble and never ignored it.

Her gray traveling dress was dusty and stained, but it was the height of fashion. More fashionable than anything he'd seen since before the war. He'd bet his last dollar it came straight from a dressmaker in London or Paris.

Hooked over her arm was a folded parasol in matching gray and white stripes. Its long-pointed brass tip gleamed faintly in the poor light. Soot peppered her clothes, her tightly braided hair and the crown of a ridiculous little gray hat with a short veil perched forward on her head. The woman looked as out of place as a peacock's feather in a Cheyenne war bonnet. Who was she?

He'd heard the train whistle an hour ago. Whoever she was, she'd wasted no time hunting him down. Why?

Pulling a scrap of white lace from her sleeve, she held it to her nose. The soft scent of lavender wafted to him, reminding him how long it had been since he'd had a bath. Too long.

With deliberate slowness, he rose to his feet, leaving his hat settled low on his brow to shadow his eyes. "Ma'am."

She looked him over with critical appraisal. "Are you Mr. Devlin Elder of Fort Harker?"

"I've been a scout there."

She returned her handkerchief to her sleeve. "I am Lady Wilhelmina Smith of Silsby Hall, Bedfordshire, London and lately of Philadelphia."

She obviously expected him to recognize her name. He didn't. Her accent was British and cultured. He touched the brim of his hat out of respect. "Pleased to meet you, Miss Smith."

One dainty eyebrow rose a fraction above the rim of her glasses. "It is Mrs. Smith. Are you implying you do not know who I am?"

Something in her voice said she'd judged him and found him wanting. He didn't care for the feeling. The high-buttoned neckline of her dress was prim enough for a preacher's wife, but it didn't hide the fact she filled it out nicely. Very nicely. As his gaze settled on her chest, she flushed a pretty shade of pink.

A sudden desire to see exactly what lay under all that fancy clothing sent a curl of heat through his blood. He leaned his shoulder against the bars, giving her a brazen smile. "I'm sure I would have remembered if we'd met, darling, but if you say otherwise, I must have been real drunk. I'm flattered you came chasing after me."

Anger flared in her eyes. "We have not met, but I believe you know my husband, Arthur Pendragon Smith."

So this was Artie's wife. Other than being a short blond, she didn't resemble Artie's description of "a mild, stout-hearted girl, but not much to look at." Winged brows arched delicately over her wide, intelligent eyes. High cheek bones and a rounded chin gave her face near perfect proportions, but her pert nose kept her from being a classical beauty. As far as Devlin could see, there was plenty to look at. Course, clothes hid a lot. Maybe she had ugly legs.

He'd liked Artie a lot, but the man had been a damn fool in more than his business affairs if he'd thought his wife was plain.

Pushing aside his physical awareness of her, Devlin speculated on a more important issue. How much did she know about his dealings with her husband?

He took his time answering. "Smith's a common name, but Arthur Pendragon, that doesn't ring a bell."

She studied him for a long moment, then her eyes narrowed. "You're lying."

He straightened, surprised more by the fact she saw through him than by her accusation. "Out here you can't go around calling a man a liar."

"I just did," she snapped, glaring at him.

Buck moved to stand at his cell door. "I know who she means, Dev. She's talking about that red-headed English fella who came out here to collect Indian stories and weapons. You remember. Called himself Artie Smith."

Devlin forced the tenseness from his shoulders and relaxed against the bars. "Sure, I remember Artie. Can't say I ever heard his full name."

"Is that so?" Her tone conveyed doubt.

Was he slipping? Women always believed his lies.

Buck grinned. "I remember because he said his father named him after some fella with a round table."

"King Arthur of Camelot," Devlin said, pleased to see a change in the lady's expression. For once, he was thankful for the rigorous education Father Benoit had pounded into a wild teenage boy. "Are you impressed I know Malory's *Le Morte D'Arthur?*"

Her eyes narrowed. "I will admit to some surprise, but impressed? No, Mr. Elder, you have not impressed me."

"Stick around, I will," he said with a wink.

"I intend to 'stick around' as you so quaintly put it. I shall inform you the instant you impress me, so your vanity doesn't suffer a moment longer than necessary."

He tipped his head toward her. *"Joli coup."*

"Un petit coup." She inclined her head ever so slightly, too.

Buck looked confused. "What'd she say?"

"She said it was a small hit," Devlin translated, enjoying the verbal sparring. "Does that mean you have something bigger in store for me?"

"Oui, si besoin est," she replied, her voice tart as green apples.

"If need be? That almost sounds like a threat." Did she think she could intimidate him?

"Take it as you will, sir."

His gaze traveled up and down her again. *"Une dame raffinée ne aurait jamais menacer un homme."*

Her chin lifted a fraction. "I doubt you have encountered enough 'refined ladies' to judge if one would threaten a man or not, *monsieur*."

Devlin suppressed a smile. She had spunk. Damn, if she wasn't the most interesting woman he'd met in years. What would she be like in bed? A spitfire. Or would she lie there like a piece of wood the way ladies were expected to behave?

"It's too bad Artie got himself killed." Buck's words broke the connection between Devlin and the intriguing Mrs. Smith.

He heard her quick intake of breath as she turned to Buck. "Are you certain my husband is dead?"

Buck shook his head. "Can't say for sure, but nobody's seen hide-nor-hair of him in eight or nine months. As I recall, he never came back for the stuff he collected. War clubs, bows, lances and such. I'll bet they're still out at the fort."

It took her a long moment to reply. "No. Major Sternberg, the fort surgeon, was kind enough to send Arthur's things to me."

She pinned her stare on Devlin again. "Mr. Elder, do you believe my husband is dead?"

"I do." He knew it for a fact but wasn't about to admit it with Sheriff Wilson listening.

Mrs. Smith leaned forward, grasping the bars as she stared into Devlin's eyes. "He is, isn't he?"

Her look of superiority gave way to sorrow. She bowed her head. Devlin couldn't suppress a pang of sympathy. "I'm sorry."

Her gaze snapped up and locked with his. All traces of grief disappeared as her haughty expression returned. He recognized it for what it was. A mask.

"Do you have proof?" she demanded.

None he cared to share. "No, ma'am."

"Until I have proof, I shall not give up searching." She turned to the sheriff. "How much is Mr. Elder's fine?"

"That'll be up to the circuit judge. Elder broke up near fifty dollars' worth of tables, chairs and good whiskey at Cutter's place."

"That's not true," Devlin piped up.

When she looked at him, he grinned. "It wasn't good whiskey. It was rot-gut swill."

She leaned toward him. "I detect a grain of honesty in your words, at last. You must endeavor to speak the truth more often."

Turning to the sheriff, she opened her handbag. "If I pay the damages Mr. Elder incurred, might you release him?"

Wilson scowled at his prisoner. "No."

Devlin brightened. If the little lady wanted to get him out of here, he'd let her. "I'm sure old man Cutter will drop the charges if he gets paid."

Wilson's mouth twisted into a snarl as he scowled at Devlin. "This weasel belongs behind bars, ma'am. The longer he stays here, the safer my town is."

With the wave of one hand, she dismissed his objection. "I can relieve you of that worry. If I secure Mr. Elder's release, it will be on one condition."

"And that is?" Devlin asked.

"That you come to work for me."

"Doing what?" The hairs on his neck started prickling again.

"Retracing my husband's last journey into the Chalk Hills."

"Nope." He stepped away from the bars. "Not a chance."

Her eyes widened. "You prefer to remain in jail?"

Dropping onto his cot, he leaned against the stone wall. "At least in here I'll keep my scalp."

A scowl marred her pretty brow. "Surely the dangers of native attacks are exaggerated. I'm told wagon trains go west from here almost weekly."

"*Large* wagon trains, with lots of *armed* men," Devlin said.

She crossed her arms over her generous bosom. "Assuage your fears, Mr. Elder. I intend to ask the army for assistance. I have a letter from Professor Joseph Leidy in Philadelphia, your country's leading expert on fossils, to Major Sternberg at Fort Harker asking him to assist me in my quest to locate my husband and his immensely important fossil discovery."

"A fossil?" Devlin snorted. The army had enough to do guarding the railroad workers, the stage line and hordes of wagons filled with greenhorns heading west in search of gold. The fort wasn't likely to have a detachment to escort Mrs. High-and-Mighty on her fool's errand. Not with Standing Bear's Cheyenne Dog Soldiers raiding in the area.

Devlin wasn't about to venture into those hills again. Even now, unless he was dead drunk, when he closed his eyes, he could still see Artie's terrified face and hear his screams.

"Yes, a very important fossil." Unfolding her arms, Mrs. Smith grasped her parasol and jabbed the tip into the floor with a resounding thud. "Well? Do you wish to stay here, or become my guide?"

Artie had claimed to be fossil hunting too, but that had been a lie. Devlin considered her offer. Sitting in jail until the circuit judge showed up wasn't appealing. If she had money to pay Cutter, maybe he should let her. Besides, he wanted to find out why she had come looking for him—and he didn't want Wilson to hear that conversation.

He stared at the floor, not daring to meet her eyes. "Can you afford my fee? I'll want payment up front before taking you to Fort Harker."

"In addition to paying for your damages? I think not, sir. You will work off what money I pay Mr. Cutter before collecting any fee."

He shrugged. "Okay."

"Excellent." She spun to face the sheriff. "Will you kindly direct me to Mr. Cutter's place?"

Wilson scowled. "You're making a mistake."

"I have traveled across Europe, Africa and Asia. I shall find Mr. Cutter with or without your help."

Heaving a sigh of resignation, Wilson nodded. "Yes ma'am, I expect you will."

Chapter Two

Lady Wilhelmina Smith, Mina to her family, couldn't believe her good fortune at locating Mr. Devlin Elder so quickly. The stationmaster knew exactly who he was when she inquired. A gambler, drifter, sometimes Army scout and a womanizer. She'd been warned to steer clear of the man. Having met Mr. Elder, she understood the stationmaster's concern.

Elder looked to be around thirty, younger than she expected. He wasn't physically large, but he had a commanding presence. Dressed in a faded gray shirt and dark blue trousers, he lounged on the bunk at the back of the cell, regarding her from beneath the wide brim of his hat.

Something in his shadowed gaze reminded her of a caged wolf. Watching, waiting for a chance to attack or escape. Perhaps it was his shaggy brown hair and piercing gray eyes, or the fresh bruises the stubble on his cheeks couldn't hide. Whatever it was, she experienced a moment of trepidation about setting him free.

Buck, with his blond curls and friendly blue eyes, seemed almost angelic in comparison. He couldn't be much over twenty. Dressed in a red shirt and well-worn trooper pants, he was less intimidating, but it was Elder's cooperation she needed. He had been Artie's guide and possibly the last person to see him before he disappeared. Elder's assertion that Artie was dead had nearly undone her. She thought she was prepared to hear those words. She wasn't.

Artie had been missing in the American west for nine months. Mina had loved him since she was twelve, married him at eighteen and loved him still—even if he couldn't love her the way a husband should. Was he dead or had he deliberately disappeared to start a new life? She'd once overheard him tell his lover he wished for that very thing.

Sorrow gripped her, but she pushed it aside. Grief, like any intense emotion, clouded one's thinking. She had allowed Devlin Elder to glimpse her feelings in a moment of weakness. She would not repeat that mistake.

He knew where her husband had traveled on his last trip. It was possible he knew the location of the fossil itself. The prospect of seeing and touching a completely new prehistoric species raised her spirits. If she could recover Artie's bird and discover more fossils, she could start a serious excavation. Artie would get credit for this discovery, but other finds would carry her name alone.

Mina followed the Sheriff Wilson to the street. He pointed out Cutter's saloon. She snapped her parasol open against the bright sun and raised it overhead. "If word of my husband should reach you, please telegraph his father in Philadelphia. I shall leave his direction at the telegraph office."

"Yes, ma'am." He tipped his hat and went inside.

With determination born of pure will, she started down the dusty street, feeling as if her corset was the only thing holding her upright. The weeklong train trip had worn her to the bone, but knowing she'd found the man she needed renewed her strength.

Elder was a skilled liar. He might have convinced her he barely knew Artie if she hadn't read her husband's last journal entries, yet he was an intriguing man none the less. His knowledge of literature proved he was educated. She needed him, but she would not trust him.

The sounds of hammering echoed from both ends of the prairie town. The dirt streets of Salina sported new businesses being built at a rapid rate, but no one had bothered with boardwalks. No one bothered with street sweeping, either. She stepped around piles of horse manure, wrinkling her nose at the odor of dung and rotting garbage. It was a far cry from the broad tree-lined avenue in front of the London townhouse, but she had seen worse places.

Near the end of the road, in front of a ramshackle building of half-timbered walls and a canvas roof, Mina considered her next move. Her eccentric journeys around the globe had been frowned upon by members of London's polite society, but the company of her husband had guarded her reputation. He wasn't with her now. Nor was her maid. The foolish woman had fainted at her first sight of buckskin clad natives in St. Louis and refused to travel onward. Mina had sent her back to Philadelphia.

To enter a saloon unaccompanied would place her beyond the pale of polite society if it became known. Her father-in-law Vincent Smith would be horrified. To him, reputation was everything.

Folding her parasol, she took a deep breath, pushed open the door and entered the dreary room. A half dozen tables and chairs sat in the middle of the trodden dirt floor. Several long planks set atop a pair of barrels served as a makeshift bar. Off to one side, a stack of chairs with broken legs and smashed tabletops lay piled in the corner. The pungent smell of whiskey and tobacco smoke stung her nose. To her dismay, the place wasn't empty.

Two soldiers sat at a nearby table with cards spread out between them. One, little more than a boy, stood and pulled his hat from his head as he gaped at her in astonishment.

Slouched at the far end of the bar, a bearded, grizzled man in tattered buckskins leered at her. "*Trés bon*. I see a tempting sweet."

His overly familiar appraisal made her skin crawl. She ignored him.

The young soldier approached. "Ma'am, I'm afraid you've made a mistake."

If she wasn't so tired, she might have appreciated his gallantry, but she wanted to finish her business and leave. "Is Mr. Cutter about?"

"This is Cutter's place, but you shouldn't be in here. This is a saloon."

"I am aware of that. Please ask Mr. Cutter to have a word with me."

"*Monsieur* Cutter," the man at the bar bellowed in a thick French accent. "You 'ave a customer!"

He pushed away from the bar and sauntered toward her. "Are you looking for work, *ma petit*? I 'ave money. For you, I would part *wiz* much of it."

He stopped so close the stench of his unwashed body and greasy buckskins made her stomach roil. The urge to run made her grip her parasol handle tightly. Projecting a courage she didn't feel, she looked him over, from the top of his thin, stringy, gray hair to his muddy, moccasin-clad feet.

"There is not enough gold in the world to impel me to 'work' for you. My business is with Mr. Cutter." She moved around him, sweeping her skirt aside to keep it from touching his no doubt vermin-ridden person.

"Not so fast." He grabbed her arm.

The young soldier took a step toward them. "Unhand her."

A knife flashed in the ruffian's other hand, aimed straight at her would-be rescuer's midsection. "*Zis* is no business of yours, blue belly."

With a deft twist of her arm, Mina broke the man's hold then drove her brass-tipped parasol down on his instep. Yelping in pain, he hopped backward.

Swinging up the sturdy handle, she knocked the knife from his hand. A kick of her boot sent the blade spinning out of his reach.

"Whore! I make you pay." The man's eyes burned with hatred as he gripped his arm.

"That's enough." The ominous click of a gun being cocked caused them to look at the bar. A bald man in a checkered vest stood with a sawed-off shotgun raised at chest level.

"The whore break my hand. You would let a woman do *zis*?"

"Seeing as it ain't my hand, I reckon so. Git out of here, Frenchy, before you find yourself in real trouble."

Frenchy spat on the floor. "I don't want none of your stinking whiskey, anyway." With a venomous glare at Mina, he said, "You, I do not forget."

Quelling her racing heart, she raised her chin. "While I shall not give *you* another thought."

Frenchy sneered and limped out the door.

Clutching her skirt to hide her shaking hands, Mina fought to keep her voice calm as she addressed the man at the bar. "Mr. Cutter, I presume?"

"I am." He lowered his weapon.

"Thank you for your timely assistance. You also, young man." She smiled at the soldier.

He grinned. "My pleasure. Not that you needed any help. That was mighty fancy work."

"Yes, a most useful maneuver taught to me by the concubine of a Chinese warlord in Shanghai."

Mina bit her lower lip to stop babbling. Something she did far too often when she was flustered. This would never do. She couldn't let a scuffle with a drunken tramp put her off now that she had come so far. "I digress. Mr. Cutter, may I have a few minutes of your time?"

"Ma'am, I'm at your disposal."

Fifteen minutes later, her purse lighter by twenty dollars, not fifty, Mina left the saloon with a paper signed by J. T. Cutter stating he dismissed all charges against Devlin Elder. Sadly, neither the soldiers nor Mr. Cutter knew anything about Artie's whereabouts, but they promised to inform the sheriff if they heard anything. At the jail, she laid the paper on Wilson's desk and waited as he read it.

"Well?" She tapped her foot.

He continued to study the document. "It seems in order."

"I assure you it is."

"Once I let him loose, what makes you think he won't hightail it out of here, leaving you stranded or worse?"

Folding her hands over her parasol handle, she straightened to her full height. "I understand your concern. I am armed and I know how to protect myself. If he flees, I have the means to have him tracked down."

"That doesn't make me feel better."

"I will not be deterred, sir."

A look of defeat crossed his face. He rose from behind his desk and led the way to the cell. At the door, he inserted the key but paused. "Elder, it galls me to let you go."

"Legally you cannot keep him incarcerated," Mina prompted.

"No, I can't. Mrs. Smith, I want you to send me word the minute you reach the fort."

She nodded. "Very well. It's the least I can do."

"If I don't hear from her, I'll hunt you down myself, Elder. One of these days, I'm going to hang you."

"You can try, Wilson. You can try." Elder's reply held a hint of anger, perhaps even a warning. Once again, Mina questioned the wisdom of freeing him.

"What about me, Sheriff?" Buck looked hopeful.

"You can go, too."

"That's just dandy, ain't it, Dev? Thank you, ma'am."

The sheriff's fierce scowl dimmed Buck's enthusiasm. "I want you both out of town—as fast as you can saddle a horse. Understood?"

Buck nodded vigorously. "Oh, we got it, don't we, Dev?"

"I expect that's up to the boss." He rose from the bunk with a surge of feral grace, smiling at Mina without a trace of humor in his dark gray eyes. "Are we leaving as fast as Sheriff Wilson would like, Lady Smith?"

"My proper title is Lady Wilhelmina, as my father was the Marquis of Silsby. Or you may call me Mrs. Smith, but not Lady Smith, as my husband was—is a commoner." Mina clamped her lips closed on her useless babble about titles. Why did Elder unnerve her?

"Yes, we shall depart with all due haste." She spun on her heels and led the way.

Maintaining the upper hand with a man like Elder would not be easy. She'd have to keep her wits sharp. At the sound of his footsteps behind her, Mina raised her chin. "Come along, gentlemen."

She left the building and set off down the dirt street towards the livery stable without looking back.

*

Devlin waited for the sheriff to hand over his gun belt, Colt revolver, knife and money pouch. He counted the contents to show Wilson he didn't trust him, but his few coins were still inside. Stepping out of the jail, he strapped on his gun and slipped his knife in its sheath as he watched the woman march ahead, taking a moment to admire the way her bustle dipped and swayed with each step. She was small, but a fine figure of a woman, even so. Fetching she might be, but he was damn sure she wouldn't scratch the itch she stirred. Maybe he could visit Clara Wilson before he left town.

The prospect wasn't as tempting as it should have been. Clara smelled of whiskey and sweat, not lavender. Why the distinction bothered him now, he didn't know.

At the livery stable, Mrs. Smith went directly to a box stall at the back of the building and held out her hand. "Come, Sabiha Amira. Are you glad to be off that terrible train?"

A soft whinny answered her. A white horse with a shimmering mane arched its neck over the top board to nuzzle her palm.

Buck moved to stand beside them. "Gosh, I ain't never seen a horse as pretty as this one."

Mrs. Smith smiled. "Few people have. She's an Arabian mare from the Bedouin people who roam the deserts of Arabia."

"What did you call her?" Buck reached out to stroke the mare's neck but jerked away when she tried to bite him.

"Sabiha Amira. It means Morning Princess."

"We'd best get going before Wilson changes his mind." Devlin crossed to the stall that held his black and white pinto and lifted his bridle off the peg. The gelding perked up his ears, looking eager to be off.

Buck went to the next stall, where a bay with a white blaze stood with his head down and one hip cocked. "Old Sunday is gonna feel real plain walking beside that filly, aren't you, boy?"

Lady Wilhelmina chuckled. "Why do you call him Sunday?"

"Because he thinks every day ought to be a day of rest." Buck grinned and blushed.

Smiling, she turned to Devlin. "I had a black and white pony as a child. What is the name of your piebald?

"Horse," Devlin answered flatly.

"Out here folks call them Indian ponies or pintos," Buck said.

She nodded. "Spanish for painted. Very appropriate."

Turning to the burly blacksmith who ran the stable, she asked, "Would it be possible to hire a conveyance and team for a trip to Fort Harker? I shall see it returned promptly."

The fellow nodded. "Five dollars. In advance."

"Excellent." She pulled the money from her purse.

"Can I saddle your mare for you, Mrs. Smith?" Buck asked.

"No, I'll ride in the wagon."

She then held out a twenty-dollar gold piece for Devlin. "Secure my horse and purchase the supplies we will need for a four-week trip. I expect a strict accounting of my funds. Meet me at the train station in half an hour. The rest of my luggage is there."

"Yes, Your Highness. Right away, Your Highness." Devlin tipped his hat and took the coin from her outstretched hand.

She lifted one eyebrow, making him feel foolish. Handing him the lead rope of her horse, she spoke to the mare. "Sabiha, allow him." Then she walked out of the livery.

Buck settled their bill while Devlin tied the mare to the wagon the blacksmith brought out front. Then he finished saddling his horse, mounted and rode out of the barn into the bright sunlight. It felt amazing to be free of that stinking jail and on horseback again. He watched as the annoying Mrs. Smith continued down the street. The woman got under his skin faster than a chigger. She might give orders where she came from, but out on the prairie, it would be a different story.

She was halfway to the station when a man rode into the street from an alley. He pulled his horse to a stop, blocking her path. Devlin recognized Frenchy Dubois. What the hell was he doing here?

"Filthy whore, I gonna make you sorry!" Frenchy slapped a riding whip against his leg. The pop made his horse flinch and roll his eyes back.

Mrs. Smith slowly lowered her parasol. "Allow me to pass, sir, or you are the one who will be sorry."

Frenchy's nervous horse shuffled sideways. He yanked its head around and pressed toward her. "You ain't got no blue belly to 'elp you now." He raised his whip.

Devlin kicked his pinto into a run.

Chapter Three

Mina shrieked and sprang toward Frenchy's horse, snapping her parasol open and shut quickly. The ballooning, flapping fabric sent the animal rearing in fright. Caught off-guard, Frenchy toppled from the saddle, hitting the ground with a bone-jarring thud, one foot still caught in the stirrup. His fear-crazed horse bolted down the street, dragging the screaming man alongside.

Elder pulled his mount to a sliding stop beside Mina.

She leaned on her parasol handle as her knees threatened to fold. Her breath came in short, ragged gasps. Glancing up, she noted Devlin's fierce scowl, the first glimpse of genuine emotion she'd seen from him. His prompt rush to her aid revealed several important things. He was quick to act, and he wouldn't allow a woman to be beaten.

Adjusting her spectacles on the bridge of her nose with trembling hands, she struggled to appear unperturbed. After straightening her hat, she met his gaze. "Please catch *Monsieur* Frenchy's horse before the man breaks his neck."

"Frenchy Dubois deserves worse."

"Perhaps, but I'd prefer not to have the man's blood on my hands."

A flicker of unease appeared in his eyes. Why? Surely, he was no stranger to violence. Whose blood was on his hands? Her husband's?

Such speculation accomplished nothing. She needed his help, but she would not trust him. Pointing at French's fleeing horse, she said, "Go! What are you waiting for?"

Leaning forward in the saddle, he fixed his gaze on her chest. "You might want to cover up before you go parading through town."

Mina looked down and gasped. The top buttons of her dress had come undone during the vigorous use of her parasol, giving Elder an excellent view of her cleavage. Heat flared in her face. She covered the gap with her hands.

Amusement softened his features. He tipped his hat, then spurred his pinto after the fleeing horse.

What an odious man, taking delight in her discomfort. Mina did up her buttons, letting her anger push aside her embarrassment.

Elder easily overtook Frenchy's horse and freed the man. Unable to hear their conversation, she was relieved when her assailant remounted and headed west at a fast clip. Satisfied Frenchy wouldn't trouble her again, she continued toward the train station.

Inside the new rough plank building, the scent of fresh sawdust made her nose itch. After giving instructions to have her luggage and crates loaded when the wagon arrived, she picked up a quill to compose a telegram to Vincent.

Arrived Salina, Kansas without incident. Hardships of travel exaggerated. No word of Arthur. Have located Mr. Elder. He is eager to assist. Will travel to Fort Harker today.

She reread her words carefully. Nothing was an outright lie, merely a stretching of the truth. No point in upsetting Vincent's frail health by including unpleasant details of her trip or her encounter with a violent local. She handed the paper to the clerk.

Remaining in the tiny office until the telegram employee finished sending the missive, she then walked outside where Buck stood waiting to help her onto an open wagon. They made one more stop at a general store where Elder stood with a stack of supplies. He handed over her change and a carefully written voucher.

She totaled the sums in her head and nodded. Other than the outrageous prices of tea and coffee, everything seemed in order. "Very good. Let us be off."

"It's a long trip. We're getting a late start. Are you sure you don't want to spend the night in town?" Elder asked.

"I wish to be underway now." She climbed onto the wagon seat and opened her parasol.

"Yes, milady. As you wish, milady." Elder tipped his hat. She didn't miss the smug smile he suppressed before swinging effortlessly onto his horse. His silent mirth irritated her, but there was nothing to be done about it.

Once outside town, their wagon jolted along the road as it cut through a seemingly endless expanse of grass. Mina clung to the hard wooden seat with one hand and held onto her parasol with the other as the wind threatened to tear it away. It soon became an unpleasant jaunt. She should have ridden Sabiha, but that would have meant a delay to change clothes. To be on her way was worth the discomfort.

Buck cast sidelong glances at her, but seemed reluctant to speak. Elder rode next to the wagon, his gaze constantly sweeping the broad valley and hills around them.

Were they in danger this close to the town? Mina took her cue from someone who knew the country, remaining silent and watchful.

For several miles, the road ran along the newly laid railroad tracks that extended westward. She watched with interest the dozens of laborers unloading massive wooden ties and rails from flat cars at the very end of the line. The choking stench of hot tar filled the air as men painted the lumber to preserve it before setting it onto the gravel bed. Beyond the tracks, men shouted to teams of mules pulling heavy road graders, while sweaty men with pickaxes broke up the sod. Mounted guards armed with rifles kept watch.

Soon, the ring of hammers striking steel, the shouts of men and the braying of mules fell behind. The hoofbeats of the team, the jingle of their harnesses and the creaking wagon were the only sounds except for the constant whistling and sighing of the prairie wind.

Mina let her gaze wander across the vast open land. Rich green grass dotted with clumps of wildflowers in bright colors stretched as far as she could see. Overhead, clouds like puffs of cotton drifted in the bright blue sky while their gray shadows raced across the grassland up and down the treeless hills. Stark yet strangely beautiful, the immense country seemed to pull at her soul. Here was the essence of freedom on a limitless ocean of waving grass. The sight lifted her lagging spirits.

After three more hours of riding along the rutted track, Mina shifted her weight again on the hard bench but found no relief for her aching backside. She scanned the unbroken prairie ahead. The only sign of human presence had been a stage station with a small cabin and a large corral holding six horses they'd passed an hour back. Buck had informed her it was a swing station, meant only for changing teams with no accommodation for stage passengers.

The sun hung low in the sky now. There was no sign of the fort. Her delight in the wide-open vista paled. "Buck, how far is it to Fort Harker?"

"Near about twelve miles."

She looked at him, aghast. "Twelve miles?"

"More or less."

"Do you mean we won't reach it tonight?"

"Nope."

Mina clutched her parasol handle. "How far is the next settlement?"

"The fort *is* the next settlement," he said.

Mina gritted her teeth in frustration. She had been in such a hurry to start the last leg of her journey she'd disregarded the most important part of travel. Planning.

A glance at Elder revealed she'd given him a reason to laugh at her once more.

His insolent gaze swept over her. "Guess you'll have to spend the night with me, milady. I'll do my best to make it an experience you'll never forget."

Instead of stirring the revulsion she expected, the look in his eyes sent a wave of warmth across her skin. His voice, soft as silk, stirred images of forbidden things.

She pushed those feelings aside and concentrated on what needed to be done. It had been foolish to rush headlong out of town without ascertaining how far she needed to travel. From now on, she would make sure she had her facts straight. One thing was certain. She refused to leave Elder with the upper hand.

She smiled brightly. "Do you cook, sir?"

His grin disappeared. "I manage."

"Excellent." She gave him her sweetest, false smile. "It will indeed be a memorable night if I do not have to attempt cooking over an open campfire."

"Dev is a passable cook. A lot better than me," Buck said.

"I am pleased to hear it. I look forward to sampling his *culinary* offerings." She stared boldly at Mr. Elder, refusing to look away. He tipped his hat, but his steady gaze said he wasn't defeated.

"Mrs. Smith, how'd you know?" Buck asked.

She glanced at her young companion. "How did I know what?"

"That your sunshade would spook Frenchy's horse?"

"It was a simple deduction. Frenchy did not appear to be a person who frequents the company of genuine ladies. Therefore, his animal was unlikely to have been exposed to the sight of a parasol being furled and unfurled."

"Yeah, but what if it had been?" Buck asked.

Mina allowed her parasol to spin in the wind like a whirligig for a second before snapping it shut and thrusting it in the air like a saber. "I would have jabbed the animal with the brass tip, thus inducing it into retreat, giving you, or Mr. Elder, time to come to my aid. The frame is sturdy. With it open, I don't believe his whip would have injured me."

Elder guided his horse closer. "What would you have done if Frenchy had a gun?"

She regarded him intently over the rims of her glasses. "The outcome would have been the same for me as for any unarmed man. I would have been shot."

His expression didn't change. "You say that calmly."

"One must endeavor to remain calm in a dangerous situation. I am sure you will agree."

Elder leaned toward her. "I find it best to avoid dangerous situations."

She arched one eyebrow. "Are you a coward, sir?"

"Dev ain't no coward, Mrs. Smith. Why, he once faced down a dozen Pawnee with only a knife and an empty gun."

Buck's leap to his friend's defense was admirable, but it was Elder's reaction she wished to judge. "Is that true?"

"No. I always have one bullet left." He moved his horse closer to her. "Exactly what are you doing out here?"

His abrupt question surprised her. She met his penetrating gaze as a shiver of excitement traveled along her nerve endings. No doubt caused by expectations of another verbal sparring match. Yes, that had to be it. At twenty-seven, she was well past the age of schoolgirl flutters. Elder, with his dark good looks and witty tongue, was the type of man who made women do foolish things. She was not a fool.

Folding her parasol, she laid it across her lap. If he wished to engage in plain speaking, then so could she. "I've come to find my husband. Or his remains. Tell me where he is."

She had hoped to catch him off guard. His expression didn't change.

His eyes bored into hers. "If the Tenth Cavalry couldn't find him, what makes you think you can?"

"Because I know where he was going," she answered smugly.

He blinked once. "And how do you know that?"

Had she rattled him? "My husband kept meticulous journals. When they arrived with the rest of his effects from Fort Harker, the last entry told me his intentions."

"Which were?" he prompted.

"To return to the Chalk Hills with you as his guide. He planned to recover important fossils he'd seen on his first trip there."

Devlin scanned the area around them and moved his horse a few steps away. "That was his plan, but it didn't happen. We parted ways in Ellsworth. Didn't he mention that?"

"As I said, it was his last entry."

Mina pressed her lips together tightly. She didn't believe Elder, but she had no proof. "My husband sent back an amazing charcoal rubbing. Do you know anything about fossils?"

Buck chuckled. "Sure, my brother lives at a place called Fossil Creek. They find all kinds of stone shells, rocks with fishbones imprinted on them, even a huge turtle shell."

Mina smiled at him. "This area was once covered by a shallow sea millions of years ago."

"How can you tell?" Buck asked.

"From the marine fossils found here and the chalk in this area. Recent theories suggest chalk is formed from the bodies of tiny marine animals that sank to the bottom of the sea when they died. Over hundreds of centuries, they built up into hills. When the sea dried up, the chalk remained. The White Cliffs of Dover in England were formed the same way."

"Sure is amazing you know this stuff," Buck muttered in admiration.

Mina smiled at him. "The specimen my husband found was the fossil of a bird, about the size of a pigeon, but with a long snake-like neck and head. The jaws were lined with teeth. It's an extremely important discovery."

"If it is so special, why didn't he send the bones instead of a drawing?" Elder asked.

She looked at her hands. "Artie was unable to extract the fossil due to a fall. He broke his leg and returned to Fort Harker."

Buck gave her a funny look. "I thought he collected native weapons and stories."

"Yes, his primary field of research was anthropology, the study of people, but he and I had collected fossils in many countries. He knew what he'd found was special."

"Did he." Devlin's tone said he didn't believe her.

Mina ignored him. "My father-in-law Vincent Smith presented Arthur's charcoal rubbing to a collection of scientists in London. They scoffed at it, laughed and called it a feeble hoax. I know it is real. I intend to prove it and clear his name."

"Dead men don't care what people say about them." Elder's terse comment brought her attention back to him.

"I am not convinced Arthur is dead. However, even if that is the case, his father and I care deeply about his reputation. We will not see his name mocked."

Devlin leaned on his saddle horn. "If his father cares so much, why did he send a girl to do his work?"

"I am hardly a girl. However, your question is valid. My father-in-law suffered a brain seizure two summers ago and has not regained his health. I stayed in England to nurse him. That is the reason I did not accompany Arthur on his last expeditions. By proving to the world Artie made a major discovery, Vincent can take pride in his son's accomplishment."

"If he's feeble, you should git back to England and take care of him," Buck said.

"He is waiting for me in Philadelphia, where I arranged a suitable housekeeper and nurse. I did not undertake this journey lightly."

Vincent was in capable hands. Mina had interviewed dozens of women before settling on Mrs. Worthington, a middle-aged war widow with two grown sons, as the best person to care for him.

"This country's no place for a lady. It's dangerous," Buck said. It was easy to believe he had her best interest at heart.

"I can take care of myself." Her life with Arthur prior to Vincent's illness had been one of travel and adventure. He and Vincent had seen to it she knew how to use guns.

Elder's scowl deepened. "Your fool's errand will get you killed."

"That would make things easier for you, wouldn't it? No more awkward questions. No one to point out you were the last person to see him alive." She scrutinized his face.

Devlin turned his horse and spurred toward the crest of a nearby bluff. Mina followed his progress with more interest than she cared to admit. He rode with the fluid motion of a man born to horseback. His black and white gelding made the climb easily. Like its owner, there was more to the horse than first met the eye.

"You shouldn't try to rile Dev," Buck chided.

"Is that what I was doing?" Mina kept her focus on Elder as he paused on the hilltop.

"Kinda sounded like it to me." Buck slapped the reins to speed up the lagging team.

"Then I shall apologize."

Devlin Elder was a puzzle. If he knew what had happened to Artie, why hadn't he come forward?

Because he has something to hide.

From what she'd seen, he was very good at hiding what he thought.

Chapter Four

Devlin reined in his horse at the top of the butte and let his temper cool. Damn the woman! Pretty she might be, but she could be a thorn when it suited her.

So Artie kept journals. What had he written? What did his wife think she knew? Unless the man's ghost was visiting her, she knew nothing for sure. She was guessing, but she wouldn't catch him off guard. He'd learned to keep his emotions hidden from a very young age.

He scanned the distant horizon. A few pronghorns dotted a ridge to the south. Their calm grazing told him there was nothing worrying beyond. Their eyes and ears were better than his. He turned his attention to the wagon moving across the prairie below. The flashy white mare prancing behind it managed to reach down and tear up a quick bite of grass every few steps. Artie's wife turned in her seat, laughing at the horse's antics. The wind carried the musical sound to him.

He didn't need the hairs on the back of his neck to warn him. He had a white woman with a horse every brave and half the white men on the plains would be tempted to steal. Trouble wasn't a strong enough word for the pair. They had all the makings of a disaster. He couldn't get rid of them fast enough.

Devlin nudged his horse into a trot along the ridgeline. Right now, jail didn't seem like such a bad place.

*

Just before sunset, Mina stepped down from the wagon with a sigh of relief and walked about to ease the ache in her backside. Elder had found a sheltered spot beside a bend in the Smokey Hill River to set up camp. As soon as the wagon had rolled up, he disappeared into the dense trees lining the bank.

With Buck's help, Mina pitched her tent and retired inside to change into more comfortable clothing. Once she had loosened her corset, she donned a simple dark green blouse and a skirt of plain gray calico, then she plaited her hair into a braid and left it hanging down her back.

She removed a small derringer from her handbag and slipped the gun into the pocket of her skirt and added a bar of her favorite scented soap to the other. Then she picked up a towel. The chance to wash after a week of endless traveling sounded like heaven, even if she had to wash in river water.

She emerged from her shelter to find Buck had a small fire going. Elder sat across the clearing on a fallen log cleaning two large catfish. He looked up, and his gaze lingered on her far longer than necessary.

Determined to ignore the acceleration of her pulse and unsettling sensations he aroused, she smiled warmly at Buck. "How may I be of assistance?"

"You can sit by the fire and look pretty." He blushed, then stared at his boots.

"Nonsense. I intend to pull my weight."

Buck smiled shyly. "I was just gonna rub down the team and take them to water. Your mare reared straight up and wouldn't budge when I tried to untie her."

"I'm sorry. I forgot to tell her it is all right."

Buck followed as Mina crossed to where Sabiha waited, her head held high.

"Sabiha, allow him." Mina said firmly, then handed the lead rope to Buck. "She will always go with you now. Just not anyone else."

"If you say so." He looked dubious but led the mare away.

Pulling a large handful of dry grass from a nearby clump, Mina began rubbing down one of the sweaty horses. By positioning herself near the black gelding's head, she had an unobstructed view of Elder. His knife flashed as he made quick work of skinning the fish.

He was out of earshot, but she spoke quietly anyway when Buck returned. "Have you known Mr. Elder long?"

Buck tied up Sabiha and began wiping down the other horse. "About two years, I reckon. He was a scout at the fort then."

Her curiosity got the better of her. "Where is he from?"

"Never heard him say."

"Does he have family here?" The thought that he had a wife and children waiting for him didn't set well.

"Never mentioned any." Buck stepped to the other side of his horse.

"He speaks with a slight accent I cannot place."

"Guess I never noticed, Mrs. Smith."

Was she being too obvious? "My family calls me Mina. Where are you from, Buck?"

"Tennessee. After the war, there wasn't anything left of our home. My brother and I stayed in the army and got sent out here. When our enlistment was up, we started looking for a place to settle down."

"Does your brother live nearby?" she asked.

"He and his wife work for the Butterfield stage line west of Ellsworth. Dev and I got enough cash together to buy us a little ranch outside of Abilene. It isn't much, but it's got good grass and a spring-fed creek. Once we git a little more money together, we're gonna buy some cattle and finish fixing the cabin."

She continued rubbing the horse's neck as she covertly studied Elder. "It sounds nice. Was Mr. Elder in the war?"

"I reckon you should ask him if you're so curious."

She began brushing with renewed vigor. "I am not curious about him. I was simply making conversation." When Buck didn't reply, she glanced up to find him watching her with a speculative stare. "What?"

"Nothing. I'll take them down to water before you rub all the hair off that one's neck."

He led the pair away. Mina dropped the grass and brushed her hands together before moving to sit on a large stone near the fire. Elder suspended the fish from two green willow branches over the low flames. The silence became unbearable.

"I did not see any fishing gear, Mr. Elder. Did you use a spear? I have seen the natives of many countries fishing thus. Or do you carry a hook and tackle in your saddlebag? I imagine a pole could be constructed of any long branch, but a hook would be difficult to make." Mina bit her lower lip. She was babbling.

"I didn't use a pole or a spear."

"Then, pray tell, how were you able to land two large fish so quickly? A net perhaps?"

"I tickled them."

He was laughing at her again. Her pride rushed to the forefront. "Really sir, I may be new to your country, but I assure you I am no idiot."

"I'm not joking. I tickled them."

"And they laughed so hard they flipped out of the water and landed at your feet."

He cocked his head slightly. "You don't believe me?"

She folded her arms over her chest. "I do not."

He stood and held out his hand. "Come on. I'll show you how it's done."

She hesitated.

"Are you afraid, milady?"

Mina shot to her feet. "Certainly not. Let it not be said I hesitated to add to my education. Lead on and demonstrate how one tickles a fish into the pan."

He walked past her. Mina cursed her lack of self-control. She'd risen to his baiting faster than any hungry trout. Still, she couldn't allow him to believe she was afraid. Buck would surely come to her rescue if she screamed. Using that reasoning to quell the butterflies in her stomach, she followed Elder into the darkening woods that lined the river. As he moved along the bank, she watched him warily.

"Well," she demanded.

"First, you find the right water. Catfish like to lie in deep pools or under fallen logs. An undercut in the bank is another place they like."

"Then what?"

"You wade into the water quietly, or you can lie down on the bank and reach in with your hand."

He chose a place where an enormous, uprooted tree lay partially submerged along the bank. Walking out onto the log, he lay down facing Mina and slowly extended his arm into the murky water.

"Okay, here's one." He inched backward and motioned for her to join him.

Mina hesitated, then gathered her skirt in one hand and moved to lie stretched out on the log. She wouldn't give him the satisfaction of seeing how nervous he made her.

"Reach down to the bottom of the log and feel under it."

"How do you know if it's a fish or some other river animal?"

"By the bite mark it leaves."

She paused with her hand above the surface.

He grinned. "Slip your hand in slowly. When you touch a fish, move along its body until you locate the mouth."

The evening air smelled of mud and damp decay by the river's edge.

Mina dipped her hand into the warm water, feeling along the moss-coated bark of the log. She wrinkled her nose in disgust, but excitement replaced her nervousness when her hand touched a slick, soft body. "I think I feel one."

"Take it easy, don't scare it."

"It's so soft. Ouch!"

Mina scrambled to her knees and pressed her thumb into her smarting palm. She glared at Elder. "It bit me!"

He rose and helped her to her feet. Taking her hand, he tilted her palm to see it better. "You didn't get bit, you got finned. Catfish have sharp spines on their backs. Sometimes, they have poison on them."

He squatted and pulled her down with him. Cupping a handful of water, he washed her palm, then raised it to his mouth and sucked at the stinging spot.

A shiver raced through Mina's body that had nothing to do with fish poison and everything to do with the man whose warm lips were pressed against her skin.

He spat off to the side. She tried to close her hand, but he held it open and pressed his lips there once more.

"I believe that is fine, now, thank you." She rose to her feet, careful to keep her balance on the log.

He rose as well, pulling her a step closer. His piercing gray eyes scanned her face. Mina waited, as mesmerized as a rabbit before a deadly snake.

"You have soft, dainty hands," he whispered.

"Please, release me."

"That's a rarity out here," he continued. "Most women have hands scarred and callused by hard work."

"I assure you I'm capable of physical labor. Now, let go of me." Somehow, the confidence of her demand became lost in the breathy quality of her voice.

"This country will leave your pretty skin baked, weathered and brown. I'd hate to see that happen."

"Which is why I keep my parasol handy. To protect me."

A slight smile lifted the corner of his mouth. "You don't have it with you now."

"The sun isn't shining."

"No, but you do need protection." He held her wrist in a firm but not painful grip.

"I demand you let go of me at once." Mina jerked hard just as he released her and lost her balance, flailing to stay upright.

He grabbed her again, pulling her close while his other arm slipped around her. "Careful. I don't want you to fall," he whispered. "You'd better hold on to me."

Mina found herself pressed along the hard, lean length of him as he held her without effort. She would be no match for his strength, but the reassuring weight of her pistol in her pocket bolstered her courage. She relaxed against him, determined to put him off guard.

"I think you're right," she murmured. If he expected a weak-willed woman, she could pretend to be one.

Fluttering her lashes, she sent him what she hoped was a sultry glance. The grip on her wrist slackened. She uncurled her fist and pressed her hand to his chest. Slowly, she let it slide up to his shoulder and then down the length of his arm where it rested at her waist.

"You're just full of surprises." There was genuine amazement in his voice. Before she could form a reply, he leaned in and kissed her.

Mina's plan flew out of her mind. The whisper of the stream flowing by, the drone of insects, and the rustling of the trees in the wind all faded away, leaving her alone in the arms of a powerful, seductive man. Only when he pulled away did the sounds of the night and some of her thought processes return. She slipped her free hand deep into her pocket.

"We can finish this back on the bank," he whispered.

She withdrew her gun and stuck the barrel against his ribs. "We are finished now."

Stepping away before he could attempt to disarm her, she cocked the gun. "This is a .41 caliber double-barreled derringer. Not accurate beyond ten feet, but deadly at this range."

His silence told her he was assessing the situation. She raised one eyebrow. "Now you agree I have the upper hand, yes?"

"For the moment." The steely bite of his words gave her pause, but she didn't let the prickle of fear deter her.

"Get in the water." With a slight swivel of the barrel, she motioned him over.

"I can't swim."

"How sad. Will you fare better with a hole in you?"

"Artie was right. He said you were a cold-hearted bitch."

Now she knew Elder was a liar. Artie would never say such a thing about her. "Keep that in mind. You will not be the first man I've shot with this gun." It wasn't true, but that didn't matter. "Get in."

He dropped off the log landing waist-deep in the river.

"How fortunate. It seems you will not be required to swim after all. You should remember Sheriff Wilson is waiting for word that I've reached Fort Harker safely. If he doesn't receive my message, he and his men will come looking for you. It is in your best interest to see I remain unharmed. Do I make myself clear?"

When he didn't reply, she reached into her other pocket. Her gun didn't waver. "Since you're already wet, may I suggest you bathe and wash your clothes. You stink."

She threw the soap at him and fled toward camp.

*

Devlin caught the bar and considered throwing it back at her. Since she still held a loaded gun, he thought better of it. As she disappeared through the trees, his anger faded. So he stank, did he? He sniffed his shirt. She was right. The soap smelled like her. Like lavender.

He hadn't intended to kiss her, only scare her, but her soft body and seductive scent stirred his senses when he held her close, and his body took over from his brain.

No matter how prim she appeared, she wasn't made of stone. Devlin had kissed a lot of women in his time, but he'd never kissed anyone like her. At first, her mouth was hard and tight beneath his. Then the softening of those lips had him primed and ready for her faster than he could have imagined.

It wouldn't happen again. She'd be out of his hair tomorrow and good riddance.

He pulled off his shirt and set to work, removing the sweat, grime and jail stench from his body and his clothes. Then he climbed out of the river and let the warm breeze dry his skin. His boots would need more than the night air to dry them. With everything bundled under his arm, he strode back into camp.

She was seated on the rock across from the campfire. He had an excellent view of her face when she caught sight of him. Her eyes widened, and her jaw dropped. In a swirl of petticoats, she bolted into her tent.

29

Buck, seated with his back to Devlin, looked over his shoulder. "Dev, you can't come walking into camp naked when we got a woman traveling with us."

"Sure I can. It was her idea." Walking past the fire, he stopped at the front of her tent and thrust his arm through the flap. A small shriek followed. He grinned and dropped the bar, knowing she wouldn't take it from his hand. "Thanks for the loan of your soap."

She'd learn she couldn't pull a gun on him and get off scot-free. "I'm gonna hang my clothes to dry by the fire. Are you sure you want to retire this early, milady?" Not even a squeak in reply.

Chuckling, Devlin moved to where he'd dropped his saddle and loosened the ties of his bedroll. Pulling the blanket off, he wrapped it around himself and returned to the fire. "Pour me a cup of coffee, Buck. It sure smells good."

"It ain't the only thing. You smell sweeter than a whorehouse at Christmas."

"I'm sure milady would share her soap if you asked nicely."

"Nope. I took a bath last September. It ain't healthy to git wet all over more than once a year."

"If I come down sick, you let milady know it was her fault."

"How's come you keep calling her milady instead of Mrs. Smith?"

Devlin fell silent. Because he hated thinking of her as Artie's wife. Hated thinking of her as the woman who loved the man he killed.

Chapter Five

Growing daylight slowly illuminated the inside of Mina's tent. Sounds of movement and Buck's muted voice told her the men were up.

She contemplated remaining on her bedroll for the rest of the day. Fatigue from her journey and a sleepless night were part of the reason, but mainly, she loathed the idea of confronting Mr. Devlin Elder.

She couldn't remain hiding indefinitely. That was probably what the insufferable toad hoped she would do. Instead, she dressed for another day of travel in a simple brown split skirt and blue blouse. She left her hair in a long braid down her back and tied the blue ribbons of a wide-brimmed straw hat under her chin.

The delicious smell of cooking bacon and her rumbling stomach convinced her to leave her sanctuary. She raised the tent flap and stepped out. The first thing she saw was the amused look on Elder's face. It took a good deal of willpower not to scurry back inside.

"Hungry?" He turned a sizzling side of pork in a blackened skillet.

She wanted to deny it, but she was starving. "A little."

He moved the pan to the side of the coals. After lifting a dented coffeepot from a flat stone beside the fire, he poured some of the steaming liquid into a tin cup and offered it to her. "You should have stayed up for the catfish last night."

She took the cup, being careful not to touch his fingers. "Something spoiled my appetite."

His exhibition might have driven any thought of food from her mind, but it hadn't lessened her curiosity. Her fascination with him both puzzled and worried her. Artie had often teased her about her inexperience with men, but she recognized Devlin Elder's attraction. Something told her he was used to women giving in to that attraction, but she wasn't gullible enough to make the same mistake again. Elder was a tool to help her locate the world's most important prehistoric avian discovery to date. And Artie, of course.

Elder was the means to an end. She would master her body's peculiar response to him, as she had learned to master other aspects of her life.

"I have decided not to let unpleasant experiences prevent me from enjoying my travels. I like my bacon well done, but not crisp, my toast lightly browned with marmalade, and I take my coffee with milk and sugar. Can you manage that?"

He scowled. "Where the hell do you think I'll find milk?"

Mina glared at him. "Do not curse at me. Canned milk is a common military ration. I'm sure it must have been available in Salina. I gave you money to buy supplies. Had I known you expected me to travel without the barest necessities, I'd have done the shopping myself."

He pulled the skillet from the fire and plunked it on the ground. "We don't have toast or marmalade. We have plain biscuits. If you want *milk*, go catch a female buffalo. If that spoils your trip, I'll be happy to take you back to Salina soon as I hitch up the team."

She crossed her arms. "It will take more than a lack of jam and your bad manners to make me abandon my quest."

"My bad manners? What do you call sticking a gun in a man's ribs? Is that socially acceptable behavior in London?"

"You said this is dangerous country. I was protecting my virtue."

He snorted. "Virtue, ha!"

"I didn't quite catch that." She glared at him.

"You two sound like an old married couple arguing before breakfast, the way my grandpa and grandma used to do." Buck came up behind them from the river.

Embarrassed to be discovered exchanging insults with Elder, Mina turned to the younger man. "I apologize if I sound out of sorts. It has been a trying journey."

Elder muttered something, but she pointedly ignored him and applied herself to sampling his culinary offering. The coffee was tolerable, even without milk. The bacon was excellent, as were the biscuits.

When she finished, she rose to her feet. "Shouldn't we be on our way? I want to reach Fort Harker today."

Elder didn't reply, but he set about breaking camp.

"We'll git there 'bout noon." Buck said, pouring the last of the coffee on the fire and kicking dirt on the remaining coals.

Mina rode in the wagon with Buck again. She questioned him about the countryside as they traveled along. His company was less vexing than Elder's, but her eyes were drawn constantly to him as he rode ahead.

By noon, the valley had narrowed. The heat became oppressive. Thin bluffs with toppled outcroppings of brown sandstone boulders littering their fronts pressed close. The only trees she saw hugged the thin line of the river as it snaked its way between the rugged hills to the south.

Elder moved close to the wagon. Mina noticed he never stopped scanning the horizon. She fell silent, keeping a watchful eye on their surroundings, too. Only when the fort, such as it was, came into view did he relax.

Buck drew the wagon to a halt before a two-story brownstone building with a broad white veranda and climbed down from the seat. "The place is looking mighty fancy these days."

"Is it?" Mina saw a few squatty brownstone buildings, rows of tents, and several shanties plunked down in the middle of nowhere. No barricade of logs or stone walls separated the buildings from the vast prairie. Row after row of white tents stretched beyond the few buildings, showing the troops lacked permanent housing. It was a far cry from fancy and difficult to reconcile the word "fort" with the rag-tag structures.

Buck helped her down. "You should have seen the first fort. It was nothing but shallow caves dug into the high banks along the river and fronted with logs. In my barracks, you could sling a skunk through the cracks in the wall without getting stink on them. One winter was enough to convince me the army would do fine without me."

Despite its defensive deficiencies, the area teamed with activity. Men marched past in formation lifting a small cloud of dust while others cared for horses and mules in the large corrals. Obvious signs of new buildings being raised showed the army planned a large presence on the gentle rise overlooking the grasslands.

Stretched out along the river south of the fort, two dozen covered wagons stood in a long line, their white canvas tops a bright contrast to the stark landscape. Beside the wagons, women cooked over open fires while men gathered in groups and children played around them.

Mina turned to Buck. "Since you are familiar with the post, perhaps you can tell me how to locate Major Sternberg."

"I reckon the Major will be over at the hospital if he ain't out looking for them bones he collects." He pointed to a long, one-story stone building across the parade ground.

Mina turned to Devlin. "If you will see to the horses, I shall speak with Major Sternberg and discover how soon a group may be formed to accompany us on the rest of our journey. Buck, will you have the wagon and team returned to Salina?"

"Sure thing. I'll be heading back to our ranch first thing in the morning, so I'll drop it off."

She drew a letter from the bag hanging from her wrist. "Please make certain Sheriff Wilson receives this."

Buck took the paper. "What is it?"

She cast a sidelong glance at Elder. "A letter telling the sheriff I have arrived safely. Mr. Elder is eager to see it delivered. Now, I must find the Major."

"Good luck," Devlin called out. She didn't believe for a minute he was sincere.

At the hospital, she gave a soldier on duty her card. She didn't have long to wait before he returned and showed her to the surgeon's office.

A tidy man of medium height with wavy, dark hair and intense dark eyes sat behind a scarred oak desk. He looked up from a stack of papers and rose to his feet. She was pleased to see an assortment of fossils on his desk and the bookshelves along one wall. He appeared to be a serious collector.

"Mrs. Smith, I am pleased to make your acquaintance. I only wish it could have been under happier circumstances."

She took his extended hand. "Arthur spoke highly of you in his correspondences, Major Sternberg. Please forgive my interruption of your work."

"I'm glad of anything that takes me away from the army's paperwork. What can I do for you, Mrs. Smith?" He pulled a straight-backed chair away from the wall and placed it in front of his desk. She sat down and he returned to his seat.

Mina leaned forward. "I intend to mount an expedition to retrace my husband's last journey. I'm here to request the Army's assistance. It shouldn't take over two or three weeks."

His eyebrows rose in surprise. "Mrs. Smith, I sympathize with your loss, but we have no way of knowing where Arthur traveled after he left here. Our patrols scoured the hills looking for any sign of him. If you are holding on to the idea that you may find him alive, let me gently dissuade you. This is a harsh land. Only savages and a few lawless men can survive unaided."

Mina looked at her hands. "I cherish the hope my husband is alive, but I accept it is unlikely. I am here to excavate the fossil he discovered."

She opened her bag and withdrew a piece of paper. Unrolling it carefully, she spread it on the major's desk. "Arthur made an astonishing discovery. As you know, he broke his leg before he finished excavating it." It was a small lie, but it didn't change what needed to be done.

"I remember when his guide brought him to us back in July. He made a swift recovery and left again in September."

"Arthur intended to return and complete the work. This is a charcoal rubbing of his find. I discovered it when his things arrived in London tucked inside his journal."

Major Sternberg studied the sketch she laid out. "Most unusual. The body is a bird, is it not? But the skull surely belongs to a species of reptile. Very unfortunate the bird's body wasn't intact, but then fossils seldom are. I believe only two Mesozoic bird fossils have been discovered to date. In France, wasn't it?"

"Germany," Mina corrected. "The skulls of both those specimens were missing. Look closely, Major. See the way the neck articulates back on the body? I believe this *is* an entire skeleton."

"The jaw is clearly lined with teeth, Mrs. Smith. Birds do not have teeth."

She carefully stowed the drawing in her bag again. "That is precisely what Professor Owen said when Arthur's father attempted to present this sketch to the Royal Society of London. They scoffed at him."

Sympathy filled the doctor's eyes. "I'm sorry your father-in-law endured unkind treatment."

Mina lifted her chin. "Vincent is a very proud man, Major. It was a deep blow. I speak frankly when I say Arthur did not live up to his father's expectations of what a son should be. But this discovery is of *enormous* significance. I intend to recover this fossil and prove my husband right. You must help me."

She pulled open her handbag once more. "Arthur left a detailed map. It shows his camp site north and west of here. I'm sure with your help, we can locate it."

"I'm afraid that won't be possible."

She didn't look up as she pulled out Artie's last journal. "I do not require many men. Five or six. If any of them have experience in fossil hunting, that would be helpful."

Major Sternberg came around to her side of the desk and closed his hands over hers. He waited until she met his gaze. "This post cannot spare men for such an expedition. I'm sorry."

All the pain and effort it had taken to come this far—was it to be for nothing? It couldn't end here.

Mina allowed anger to fill the void opening before her. "What do you mean, sir? It is the army's job to assist civilians. I require your assistance!"

"This is a dangerous time in Kansas. Indian raids are increasing as more whites pour into the country. Our job is to protect the stage line, the wagon trains and the railroad."

Regret deepened the furrow between his brows. "We are only a thin line of men in a territory stretching for hundreds of miles. It is our job to keep the peace. It is not our job to assist a young woman to carry out a fool's errand."

She shot to her feet. "This is important scientific research."

"No fossil is worth your life. Surely you see that."

"Arthur may have died trying to recover this unique specimen. I have a letter from Professor Leidy in Philadelphia assuring me, as a collector of fossils yourself, you would understand the importance of this."

"Truly, I'm sorry, Mrs. Smith. I can't help you."

Mina pressed a hand to her chest. "You left my husband to lie dead and forgotten somewhere in this God-forsaken wasteland. Now you'll deny me the chance to make his death stand for something. I cannot accept that. I will not!"

"Mrs. Smith, I won't assist you in committing suicide. If my plain speaking has upset you. I apologize."

"I can abide plain speaking, sir. Your words don't offend me, your lack of support does. If you will not assist me, I shall manage on my own."

She had to press on. She simply could not go back empty-handed.

"And how do you propose to do that?" he asked gently.

"I shall do as Arthur did. I already have a guide."

"It's no longer safe to venture into the Chalk Hills, even for large parties. Stop this nonsense."

"Good day, Major." She turned and left the office.

Chapter Six

Outside the hospital, Mina stopped to allow her raging emotions to settle. Pulling her glasses off, she carefully cleaned them with a handkerchief. Once she was certain she would neither burst into tears nor begin screaming like a madwoman, she replaced her spectacles.

This was a setback, to be sure, but it would not deter her. Snapping open her parasol, she set off across the parade ground. Devlin Elder, still mounted on his horse, met her halfway. She ignored him as he rode beside her.

"I told you what would happen." His smug tone brought her anger roaring back.

"I'm sure you enjoyed saying that, but you are too hasty."

"Nope, I was right. The army hasn't got men to spare to track down old bird bones."

She whirled to face him. "It is also my husband I am trying to find. But you don't want to look for Arthur, do you, Mr. Elder? No, you would much prefer I go back to Philadelphia. Why is that? I think it's because you're afraid. Because you know exactly what happened to Arthur and where he is. What transpired between you and my husband after he hired you to guide him out into those hills?"

"I don't know what you're talking about." His features didn't change. Not so much as a flicker of his eyelid hinted she was on the right track.

"Arthur was a disappointment to his father in many ways. He wasn't the brilliant scientist he believed himself to be, but he excelled in one aspect of scientific work. He kept meticulous records. Shall I tell you what he wrote in the final entry of the last journal he sent? He wrote he had hired Devlin Elder to lead him into the Chalk Hills. He paid you the sum of fifty dollars plus supplies, and he detailed the cost of each and every item. I'll spare you the lengthy list. He wrote that you and he planned to leave this fort on Sept 20th."

She stepped closer, laying a hand on his horse's neck. "You were the last person to see him alive. Where is he? Tell me!"

*

Devlin studied Mina's angry features. She was close to the truth, but she knew nothing for sure.

"Your husband hired me, that's true. We left here together, but if he was such an excellent writer, I'm sure he wrote about how we parted ways in Ellsworth the very next day."

She looked flustered by his admission. "As I said, it was the last entry in his journal."

"And there aren't any more journals, are there?"

Her eyes narrowed as she glared at him. "If there are, they remain where my husband left them. One more reason I am determined to retrace his steps. Why did you part ways? If you did?"

"When we reached Ellsworth, the driver of the eastbound stage came in with the bodies of two station workers and four passengers from an overdue stage. They'd been tortured, killed and scalped. The station manager escaped by hiding in the woods near the buildings. He listened to the screams of those people for two days before they died. The leader of the war party was a half-breed named Standing Bear. He's ruthless."

"What does this have to do with Arthur?"

"I told your husband it was too dangerous to head into the area until the army had run Standing Bear down. Your husband wouldn't listen. He insisted on going anyway, so I gave him back his money. I told him to get himself killed without my help. I reckon that's exactly what he did. So you're right, Mrs. Smith. I am responsible for your husband's death because I didn't drag him back to this fort by his hair."

Her defiance crumpled at his admission. Whatever inner demon was driving her seemed to wither away. She swayed on her feet. Devlin dismounted and took hold of her elbow. He hated causing the pain he saw in her eyes, but she needed to accept the truth, or as much as he could share.

"No one can tell you where your husband went after he left Ellsworth," he said gently. "There's a million square miles of grass out here, thousands of places where his body could be lying. You could pass within a dozen feet of him and never know. You're not going to find him. Go home."

She jerked away. "I will not give up. I know where Arthur was going. I have a map."

"A map?" She was just full of surprises.

"Yes. Something the U.S. Army didn't have when they went looking for him—if they looked at all. I had hoped for an escort, but since they have denied my request, I shall improvise. It may be more difficult, but I am not a person who shies away from difficulties. We'll proceed to the nearest town in the morning and hire local men."

He'd had enough of her foolishness. "No."

She looked stunned. "I beg your pardon?"

"*We* aren't going anywhere."

"Are you forgetting I paid a goodly sum of money to get you out of jail? You agreed to guide me."

"To Fort Harker." He spread his hands wide. "Here you are."

"You mean to desert me the same way you deserted my husband?"

"I'm giving you the same advice I gave him. Go home."

"I don't need your advice. I need your knowledge of the Chalk Hills. You must help me."

He wanted to shake her. "You have got to be the stubbornest woman on the face of the earth! I won't take you out there!"

She glared at him for a long moment, then closed her eyes and bowed her head. "I had hoped it wouldn't come to this."

She didn't sound like a woman giving up. She sounded like someone with an ace up her sleeve. The urge to jump on his horse and ride out crept up his spine. "Come to what?"

Reaching into her bag, she withdrew a thick folded paper. "This is a warrant for your arrest issued in Philadelphia, Pennsylvania."

"My arrest? For what? I've never even been to Pennsylvania."

Her face could have been carved from stone. "For the murder of my husband, Arthur Smith."

His stomach dropped. "You're joking."

"Not at all," she said calmly.

"Then why get me out of jail in the first place?"

"As I said, I need your expertise as a guide. You leave me no choice. You will take me west or you will hang."

Was she bluffing?

"Lest you think you can run." She rattled the paper at him. "You should know my father-in-law will post a five-hundred-dollar reward for your capture. Dead or alive. At a word from me to our attorney back east, every town and hamlet in the state of Kansas will be flooded with wanted posters featuring your name. In fact, I don't have to do anything. If my attorney doesn't receive a telegram from me by the end of this week, the same thing happens. You'll have a hard time hiding from men who will hunt you for such a fortune."

"Whether or not I'm innocent?"

She regarded him with an unblinking stare. "Do you take me west, or do I turn this information over to the authorities?"

Devlin stared into her earnest blue eyes. He was about to take a gamble that could cost him his life. "Milady, you can go to hell."

She shook the paper in his face. "With this price on your head, I have every confidence you will precede me."

"You're bluffing."

"I can assure you this paper is entirely legal."

He gathered his reins and swung effortlessly into the saddle. "It may be legal, but you won't turn it over to anyone."

She looked baffled. "What makes you so certain?"

"Because you're not sure Artie is dead. You don't want a man's blood on your hands. Remember? Not that scum Frenchy Dubois and not mine."

He stared at her until her hand dropped to her side. Smiling, he tipped his hat. He'd won.

"If you won't guide me, I shall find someone who will!" There was desperation in her voice now.

"I doubt it, but if you do, it won't be my concern. Goodbye, milady. Can't say it was a pleasure knowing you."

Chapter Seven

Mina stamped her foot in frustration as Devlin Elder rode away. He didn't even look back.

He was right. The warrant in her hand was a bluff. She'd had it printed in Philadelphia, but it wasn't legal. There were no wanted posters waiting to be plastered over the countryside. Vincent could afford the reward and more, but he didn't know about her plan.

Was the infuriating Mr. Elder innocent or simply a better gambler?

Going home was out of the question. She could never face Artie's father and tell him how miserably she had failed.

She could, however, make good on part of her threat. Using her husband's journal as proof the two men left the fort together while only Elder returned might be evidence enough for a judge to grant a warrant for his arrest. She had more than enough of her own money to put up a bounty. Then she would have the pleasure of seeing the odious Mr. Devlin Elder thrown back in jail.

Having him arrested would make her feel better, but it wouldn't serve her purpose. Until she was certain Artie was dead, she would not set that chain of events in motion. With Elder and the army unwilling to render assistance, she had to find another guide.

A sudden chill in the afternoon air caused her to seek the source. Dark gray clouds were piling up in the west, obscuring the sun. A storm was moving in. The distant rumble of thunder reminded her she still didn't have a place to stay. She set about locating the fort's stables and found Buck pitching hay to her horse.

He tipped his hat when he caught sight of her. "Major Sternberg sends his compliments and asks that you stay with him and Mrs. Sternberg while you're here."

"Thank you, Buck. Where will you stay?"

"Dev and I can camp down by the river."

"I'm afraid Mr. Elder rode out a while ago." She couldn't hide the bitterness in her voice.

Buck was unfazed. "I reckon he's gone over to Ellsworth. The town's a couple of miles west. He'll be back."

"I doubt it. He and I came to a parting of ways."

Buck eyed her closely. "He told you he wasn't taking you any farther."

She leaned on the stall door and watched Sabiha nibble at the hay. "Both he and Major Sternberg seem to think it is too dangerous for a woman."

"Could be they're right." He threw another forkful to the mare.

Mina cast a sidelong glance at Buck. He knew this area. He'd been stationed at this very fort. Could she persuade him to help her? She wasn't above using a few womanly wiles to get what she wanted. She sighed heavily and allowed tears to form in her eyes.

"I simply don't know what I shall do." Her forlorn tone wasn't difficult to fake.

He leaned on his pitchfork, regarding her with sympathy. "I wish I could help."

She gave him a wide smile and laid a hand on his arm. "What a wonderful offer. I don't know why I didn't think of it sooner. You can be my guide."

"Me?" he squeaked.

"Why not? You know the country. I have a map. I'll pay you fifty dollars for a month's work."

"Gosh, Mrs. Smith. I don't know."

"Very well, a hundred dollars." She was desperate.

"It ain't the money."

Biting back her frustration, she said, "Then perhaps, like Mr. Elder, you're afraid."

"I ain't a coward, and neither is Dev. It's just too risky for a woman."

"You underestimate me. I have traveled through some of the most remote and dangerous places on earth."

"Dev would skin me alive if I took you out there."

"Then you leave me no choice. I shall find a scout myself."

She addressed a young soldier leading a pair of mules out of a nearby stall. "Excuse me, sir. Where might I hire a guide for a trip west?"

He motioned with his chin. "There are usually a few scouts looking for work down at the wagon camps. How big is your party?"

"Only me, it seems."

"Then I wouldn't count on finding anyone. The Cheyenne are raiding all along the trail. No one is going to risk traveling alone."

"We shall see about that." She started in the direction he'd indicated.

"Wait." Buck came after her. She ignored him even when he fell into step beside her.

"Mrs. Smith, you don't know these men."

Mina opened her parasol, effectively blocking Buck from sight.

"Dang it, what you're doing is crazy."

"Do not swear at me, Buck. If you won't help me, I must help myself."

As she neared the first campsite, four grubby men squatting beside a fire eyed her with obvious curiosity. She stopped and addressed them. "Gentlemen. I am looking to hire a guide to take me into the Chalk Hills."

The men rose slowly to their feet. One, the tallest among them, dressed in fringed and beaded buckskins, spat a stream of tobacco juice into the fire. "Is that so?"

A chill crept over Mina as he ogled her. Quelling her uneasiness, she faced them with an unwavering gaze. "Are any of you interested?"

"I might be." He stepped closer. "It'd be a rough ride. But then, maybe you like it rough?" His cohorts chuckled and snickered.

"Mrs. Smith, please," Buck pleaded.

Mina ignored him. "This is strictly a business proposition. I will not tolerate rudeness or slacking of any kind. Is that understood?"

The smallest man in the group looked her up and down. "How much are you paying?"

Buck muttered a curse, then said, "All right, I'll do it."

She cocked her head in his direction. "I'm sorry. What did you say?"

"I said, I'll do it."

Waiting a moment until she could contain the triumph she knew was written on her face, she took a deep breath and nodded to the rag-tag group of men. "It seems I won't require your services after all, gentlemen. Good day."

She turned to Buck. "Thank you. You can't know how happy this makes me. We'll leave as soon as we can purchase pack animals and load them."

Defeat showed in his face and drooping shoulders. "Yes, ma'am. I'll take care of it."

Slipping her arm through his, she began walking back to the fort. "Can you please find someone to deliver my letter to the sheriff and return the wagon?"

"I reckon."

"This will be a wonderful adventure, Buck. When we return, you'll have more than enough money to buy cattle for your farm."

"I won't git to spend it."

She squeezed his arm. "Nonsense. Of course you will."

"No, cause if the Cheyenne don't git us, when Dev finds out, he's gonna nail my hide to the wall."

*

That evening, Mina enjoyed dinner with the Major and his charming wife Louisa. Mina learned the major's younger brother, Charles, was also an avid fossil collector, currently on an expedition to the Black Hills of the Dakota territory. The Major shared some of his brother's letters. Charles wrote about the abundance of fossils in the Black Hills, leaving Mina astonished and eager to explore more of the American West.

Early the next morning, she followed Buck as he rode out of Fort Harker with a pair of heavily loaded pack mules in tow. A beautiful morning surrounded them as they crossed the vast prairie with larks and blackbirds singing from their perches on the tall grasses. The air smelled fresh after the previous night's rain. Well rested, Sabiha pranced along, arching her tail and tossing her head, making her long mane ripple in the sunshine. Clumps of blue and yellow flowers scattered among the grass added charm to the scene.

Mina wore her mauve riding skirt and a frilly white blouse with embroidered roses decorating the sleeves in a ribbon of color and a mauve hat with peacock feathers curving around the brim. The rich colors suited her mood. She liked pretty clothes but had practical outfits as well.

Her elation at starting the last phase of her journey kept her spirits high for the first hour, but they soon fell oddly flat. Admitting the cause did not improve her mood. She had left the fort without a glimpse of Devlin Elder. Why it should matter, she couldn't fathom, but it did.

Mina urged Sabiha up beside Buck. "How long do you think it will take to reach my husband's last campsite?"

"I reckon it'll take four, maybe five days."

"That long?"

"Maybe longer. Your map ain't real specific." They had reviewed it together the previous evening.

"But it shows we should turn north at Fossil Creek Station. After that, we need only to find the landmarks my husband drew. It shouldn't be difficult. How far is Fossil Creek?"

"Two days if it doesn't rain again and keep us from crossing the creeks between here and there. My brother Jim and his wife run the station."

"I shall be delighted to meet your family. I must think what I can give as presents." She would wear her best outfit to impress his family. Perhaps she could give Buck's sister-in-law one of her hats.

"They have a little boy, too. His name is Caleb. I've only met him once. It'll be good to see them again. They're the only kin I have left."

As they topped a rise, a group of buildings clustered alongside the riverbank came into view. Mina drew Sabiha to a halt. "Is that Ellsworth? Do you think Mr. Elder is still there?"

"Yup."

It would be enormously satisfying to show him how well she had managed without his help.

"What makes you so sure?"

"Because I know Dev," was Buck's sour answer.

He urged his horse forward. Once they reached the town, he stopped at a hitching rail in front of the dry goods store and dismounted.

Mina remained on her horse but glanced around, hoping to spot Devlin. "I don't understand why we're stopping here. We have all the supplies we need."

"I gotta find Dev."

"So he can talk you out of taking me farther?"

Buck scowled at her. "I gave my word. Dev will understand."

Several men came out of the store. They stood on the boardwalk and gawked as if they had never seen a woman before. She unfurled her sunshade and raised it overhead. "Do hurry, Buck. I've no desire to be an object of curiosity a moment longer than necessary."

"Try not to cause trouble while I'm gone."

She sat up straighter. "I do not cause trouble."

He rolled his eyes and walked away.

One of the men stepped forward. "Ma'am, that's sure a fine-looking filly you're ridin'."

"Thank you, sir."

"Would you be interested in selling her?"

"I would not." She strove to ignore the man as she watched Buck enter the wide double doors of a livery stable at the end of the block.

"Your horse could be worth a lot of money," the stranger persisted.

"I'm aware of my mare's value. I still have no interest in selling her. Good day to you."

The would-be horse buyer scowled. "I'm only trying to make polite conversation."

She gave him a stiff smile while hoping Elder would appear. "It should be painfully obvious I do not wish to converse. Please go about your business."

"She's a snooty one, ain't she, Gerald?" one of his friends called out.

"Real hoity-toity," Gerald answered.

Another man snickered. "Could be she's the Queen of England here for a visit? I heard some rich English folks are coming to shoot buffalo. Who else is gonna be riding a fancy piece of horseflesh like that?"

"She ain't the Queen," Gerald scoffed.

"I am not the Queen. I am Lady Wilhelmina, daughter of the Marquis of Silsby and the Queen's cousin." She bowed ever so slightly. Sabiha arched her neck, pawed the ground, and tossed her head in showy style.

A young boy of about ten joined the group in front of her horse. He stared at Mina with wide eyes. "Glory be! Are you a real princess?"

"She ain't, no such thing," Gerald jeered.

Mina gave him a frosty stare. "When I see Her Majesty, I shall report this country is full of rude men."

"We ain't all rude," the boy insisted.

She looked at the growing crowd. "Indeed? Where I come from, a proper gentleman does not stare, and he bows when introducing himself to a lady."

"Like this?" The boy clapped one hand to his stomach and bent forward with a quick jerk.

She hid a smile. "More slowly, young man."

He tried again. Mina returned his bow with a slight inclination of her head. His wide smile nearly split his grubby face.

Mina chuckled. "I shall tell Her Majesty I met one perfect gentleman in America."

Still grinning, the boy took off at a run down the street. He stopped a couple near the hotel and pointed toward Mina, then rushed on.

After looking at each other, several of the men standing before her gave sketchy bows. She acknowledged each of them in turn. A sheepish Gerald followed suit.

Just then, a commotion across the street captured everyone's attention. A man flew out of the saloon doors and sprawled face down in the dirt. Slowly, he rolled over and sat up. The saloon door opened again. Devlin Elder stepped out with his arm draped over the shoulders of a woman in a scarlet dress. He held a brown bowler hat in his free hand.

"Never let me hear you talk to a lady like that again." Devlin's slurred voice carried a heavy dose of menace. He tossed the hat to the man on the ground.

"But Nora, I done paid for my time with you," the man whined.

"Don't fret, Billy," Nora said. "One of my gals will take care of you."

She spoke to someone inside the saloon. "Send a bottle up to my room. Make it two." She tugged on Elder's arm. "Come on, handsome. I need to thank you proper-like for defending my honor."

She steered him toward the stairs at the side of the building. He climbed with unsteady steps, his arm still draped over her shoulders. They disappeared inside a door at the top of the landing.

A moment later, Buck appeared at Mina's side and untied his horse. "I left a message for Dev at the livery stable. Reckon that's the best I can do."

"I have located him."

"Where?" Buck glanced around.

She pointed across the street. "He has just gone into the establishment above the saloon."

Buck stared in the direction she indicated. A dull red stain crept up his neck and engulfed his face. "Oh. Well—I ain't gonna interrupt his— ah, rest. I left a message for him."

Her intense curiosity about Elder prompted her to study Buck's reaction closely. "What's wrong?"

"Nothing. I thought you were in a hurry."

"I am, but I want a word with Mr. Elder first." She started to dismount, but Buck stopped her by grabbing her arm.

"You can't go up there. Please, Mrs. Smith."

Mina scanned the building. Two scantily clad women leaned out open windows on the second floor, displaying an indecent amount of cleavage. A sign above the stairs leading up the outside of the building read, Boarding House, Nora Perry Proprietress.

Like a splash of cold water, it hit Mina. It was a brothel.

She pressed her lips together. "I see exactly what kind of rest Mr. Elder is engaged in. I should not be appalled. From the moment I met him, I knew he had the morals of a toad. Let us be on our way."

So what if he was spending time with a woman of ill repute? Mina couldn't decide if she was angrier with him or with herself for caring.

Turning Sabiha, she headed out of town. Her mare, eager to be off, pranced with high steps, tossing her flowing mane. Along the way, two women curtsied while several men doffed their hats and bowed.

Buck caught up with her. He looked at the gawking townspeople, then at Mina. "Why are people bowing to us?"

"They think I'm royalty."

Taken aback, he stared at her in amazement. "You told 'em you're royalty? Are you?"

"I'm a noblewoman but not of royal birth."

"You lied?"

"I did not lie, I simply elaborated. My great-grandfather was a third cousin, twice removed, to Maria Theresa, Queen of Hungary, Croatia, Bohemia, Lodomeria and Galicia. If these people think I meant I'm related to the Queen of England, I can't help that."

"You can't go around pretending to be something you ain't," he scolded.

Mina pressed her lips into a hard line. She'd spent the last eight years pretending her marriage wasn't a sham, pretending it didn't break her heart she would never have children, pretending the past didn't haunt her. Pretense wasn't second nature to her. It was her nature.

With her head held high, she urged Sabiha into a gallop. As unlikely as it seemed, she hoped the despicable Mr. Devlin Elder was watching.

Chapter Eight

Devlin woke with a pounding headache. His mouth felt like someone had stuffed it with dry buffalo grass. He chanced opening one eye.

He lay face down on a bed in an unfamiliar room. The pale light coming through a crack in the drapes at the window told him it was daylight. But what day?

A soft sigh let him know he wasn't alone. Carefully turning his head, he made out the figure of a woman with blonde hair lying beside him. She was naked.

He focused on her face and tried to figure out who she was, but it didn't seem worth the effort. Concentrating made the pounding in his skull worse.

"Morning, love. How are you feeling?" she whispered.

"Like a mule that's been dead three days."

She giggled. "I'm not surprised. You drank a lot of whiskey."

"I was making up for lost time." He sat up and swung his feet to the floor without his head rolling off. The room spun like a demented top. He clutched the edge of the mattress.

"How long have I been here? And where is here?"

"This is my boarding house in Ellsworth. You've been holed up for two days." She rose to her knees behind him, slipped her arms around his neck and pressed her warm body against his back.

"Are you ready to get down to business?" she purred in his ear before nipping his lobe playfully.

The scent of her cheap perfume made his stomach heave. "Sorry, I've forgotten your name."

"It's Nora."

"Nora, I'm played out."

"We ain't played yet. I got a bar of lavender soap like you wanted." She plucked the bar from the bedside stand and waved it under his nose. He took the soap from her and stared at it. Visions of Mina's face swam before his eyes.

"I got Kitty to loan me her spectacles. I promised they wouldn't get broke. It'll take me a minute to braid my hair like you wanted. I can give you a bath as soon as I heat some water. I like a man that's clean."

Still holding the bar, Devlin propped one elbow on his knee and dropped his aching head onto his hand. "I asked you to braid your hair, wear spectacles and give me a bath with lavender soap?"

"Men ask for stuff like that all the time, honey. You don't remember?" She began massaging his shoulders.

"No, and I don't want to." He shrugged her off and rubbed his aching forehead.

She leaned down to whisper in his ear. "I'm ready to get started if you are." She let her hand slide around him and trail down his belly.

He stopped her. "You mean we didn't?"

"Nope."

"Not even once?" He'd never been too drunk to perform. What had that damn little witch done to him?

"We can do it now," Nora whispered and planted a kiss on his neck.

He tilted his head away. "I don't think so."

"Ah, come on. I'll show you a good time."

"I said no, Mina."

"It's Nora!" She sat back with a huff.

"Where are my clothes?" He stood and staggered a step as the room spun wildly before settling down. If only his stomach would do the same. His clothes lay folded over a chair in one corner. His boots sat next to them.

Nora reached toward him. "Don't rush off. It's raining out. Come back to bed."

"Did I drink all the whiskey?"

"All four bottles."

"Then I'm leaving."

He stuffed the soap in his saddlebag, got dressed without falling over, and left her pouting but counting the money he tossed on the bed.

Outside, he turned his collar up against the rain and walked carefully down the stairs. The wind rose in a damp gust that helped clear his head. Pausing at the street, he tried to remember where he'd left his horse. Buck would be waiting for him at the fort.

Mina was most likely back in Salina by now. Good riddance. She'd been trouble from the start.

Crossing the muddy street, Devlin headed toward the edge of town. He found his horse at the second livery stable he tried. The burley blacksmith pumping the bellows of his forge didn't pause as he looked Devlin up and down.

"Reckon ya had a fine time over at Nora's."

"How much do I owe for the pinto's keep?" Hopefully, not more than he had left in his pocket.

"Yer friend took care of it."

Puzzled, Devlin eyed the big man. "My friend?"

"Young fella. Had a pair of pack mules and a woman with him riding the sweetest prancing white mare I ever laid eyes on. He left a message for ya. Said he was taking the woman out to find her husband. Said you'd know what he meant."

"Damn!" Buck had better sense. How had Mina talked him into it? "When were they here?"

The smithy stopped pumping. "Day before yesterday. Left around noon, with half the town gawking and bowing at the woman, declaring she was some kinda princess. Pure foolishness if ya ask me."

"She's no princess. She's a pain in the ass."

They had a two-day lead, but he could catch them. He didn't have pack animals to slow him down. It was one thing to insist on getting herself killed, but Buck deserved better than to get scalped because of her. She had no idea what she was getting into.

Devlin saddled his horse, donned his yellow oilskin slicker, then rode out, ignoring the rain dripping from the brim of his hat. At the edge of town, he watched a wagon train straggle past.

The lure of riches and land drew men to give up everything and make the dangerous overland trip. Some of them would never reach the mountains, but that didn't stem the flow pouring across the plains without regard for the land or the native peoples who lived there.

Mina wasn't after something as practical as gold. She was after bones so old they'd turned to stone. Damn her stubborn hide!

Devlin turned his horse west and galloped around the wagons. If he had to, he'd bring her back at gunpoint. Maybe she'd resist, and he could hogtie her to her fancy horse.

No, that would be too easy for Lady Wilhelmina Smith of Silsby

Hall, Bedfordshire and London. Since she was hell bent on making his life miserable, the least he could do was return the favor. If she didn't talk him to death first. The thought of using her hair as a gag gave him a few moments of satisfaction. He'd think of more suitable punishments for putting Buck in danger when he caught up with them.

All day, he crossed the grassland in the pouring rain, pausing only to rest his horse briefly. Each chilly, soaking mile gave him time to think of another way to repay Mrs. Smith for his misery.

At night, he made a cold camp. Rolled up in his bedroll under a hastily constructed shelter of cedar limbs, he slept, but his dreams took an erotic turn. In them, he found plenty of sensual ways to exact his revenge. Waking hard and stiff and unable to ease that hunger gave him one more reason to curse the blond witch.

The second morning dawned without rain. Weak sunshine peeked through scattered gray clouds. The break from the steady downpour was a welcome relief. Devlin saddled up. A few hours later, he topped a rise and spotted his quarry.

Below him Lost Creek ran bank full a mile above where it emptied into the Smokey Hill. Mina was easy to spot. She wore a yellow riding costume and a yellow hat with a white feathered plume curving around the wide brim. Was she trying to attract the attention of the Cheyenne? At least she was riding astride and not on one of those ridiculous sidesaddles.

Buck, mounted and leading two mules, had almost reached the opposite bank of the creek. Both heavily laden mules were having a tough time against the churning brown current. Devlin held his breath as he watched them struggle out of the water. Buck should have known better than to cross in a flood.

Mina had reached mid-stream when her mare balked and fought the bit, refusing to swim. Mina might have coaxed her across, but the carcass of a dead buffalo drifted around the bend and came bobbing and spinning toward them. Her terrified horse reared and fell backward, taking Mina under the rolling flood waters.

Chapter Nine

Devlin kicked his horse into a run down the steep hillside. He saw Mina's head break the surface of the water as she began swimming. Thank God she knew how. The current carried her away from her mount as the riderless animal splashed back toward the bank.

Devlin raced beside the creek, jumping fallen logs and dodging trees as he tried to keep Mina in sight. Twice she went under but came up sputtering with the damn feather dangling in her face. Knowing the current would rapidly sap her strength, he looked for a place to get into the water ahead of her before the swollen creek swept her out into the raging river ahead.

At the next bend, he spurred his reluctant horse into the swift water. It was then he saw Mina wasn't making for the riverbank. She was swimming closer to the buffalo carcass.

"Smart woman," he muttered when she got a hand on the hairy body. He turned his horse back to solid ground and headed downstream. Not far ahead, the creek made a wide bend that would bring Mina close to his side of the shore.

Clinging to the bloated animal, she kicked and paddled her makeshift raft out of the swift current. After nearly a quarter of a mile, she'd worked herself to the water's edge. When she found her footing, she stood, still hip deep in the muddy water, and slogged toward the bank, letting the buffalo drift downstream.

Devlin drew his horse to a standstill. Mina's glasses dangled from one ear. Mud, debris and buffalo hair clung to her wet gown. A few steps from land, she stumbled and fell. Her ruined hat flipped forward over her eyes. The rank smell of rotting buffalo reached Devlin. He smiled. He couldn't have come up with a better punishment if he had tried.

Mina pushed her hat back and settled her glasses on properly. Her eyes narrowed when she saw him. Without a word, he turned in the saddle, pulled the soap from his pack and tossed it toward her. It splashed into the water in front of her and bobbed to the surface. "Since you're already wet, I suggest you bathe and wash your clothes. You stink."

Fury darkened her eyes.

Laughing, he turned his horse and rode away.

*

Mina struggled the last few feet to dry land. On solid ground, she gathered the hem of her riding habit and wrung it out. Under her breath, she muttered every vile name she had ever heard in any language. How dare Devlin Elder laugh at her!

She yanked her sodden hat off and stared at the mangled mess. In a fit of anger, she sent it sailing out into the muddy water and watched it sink from sight.

The knowledge she could have easily joined her hat in a watery grave gave her pause. She shivered as a gust of wind cut through her wet clothing. Buck had told her the current was too fast to cross, but she had insisted on making the attempt. What she hadn't counted on was her desert-bred mare's reluctance to swim.

Mina trudged with squishing steps to a nearby fallen log, sat down, clasped her arms across her bosom and tried to stave off another shiver. The roar of the rushing flood waters filled the air. The sun came out briefly but offered little warmth before being swallowed by gray clouds again. Her teeth began chattering. Hoofbeats approaching made her look up.

Devlin had returned with Sabiha. "Cheer up, milady. You're alive."

"No thanks to you."

"You and old Stinky seemed to do fine."

"Enjoy your mirth, Mr. Elder. Someday I shall return the favor."

She stood, surprised to see the water had risen almost to the base of her log. She took Sabiha's reins from his hand. "Can we go now?"

"Where?"

"Any place dry."

"That's gonna be a problem."

"So I've noticed. What fool called this the Great American Desert? It's done nothing but rain since we left Fort Harker."

"It'll be hotter than Hades' front door in a few days. You'll wish for a rain then."

"I'm sure you are right, but for now, all I want is to get out of these clothes. Please tell Buck to set up camp."

"Tell him yourself."

Why did this man have to thwart her every request? She pulled herself into the saddle, too tired to fight. "Very well. Where is he?"

Devlin pointed over her head. She turned and spied Buck waving from across the widening expanse of muddy water.

"Bloody hell!" The words popped out before she could stop them.

Devlin chuckled. "Might be three days or more before he can cross back. If the rain stops."

Three days without a tent, without her clothes, without camping utensils? Mina shivered again. She faced Devlin, reluctant to give him the upper hand but knowing she had no choice. "It seems I must rely on you for assistance."

"Not me, milady. I don't owe you a thing. Enjoy your wait." He turned his horse and rode away.

"Yes, go," she shouted after him. "Obviously, you're the sort of man who would leave a defenseless woman to fend for herself. Wouldn't your mother be proud of you?"

He whirled his horse and charged up so fast Sabiha backed in fright. Mina saw anger blazing in his eyes.

"Never speak about my mother. Not ever! You're sniveling about wet clothes while she endured a life of pain and humiliation you can't imagine without a whimper."

"I… I'm sorry." The anger in his eyes faded, replaced by a coldness that chilled her far more than her wet clothes.

Devlin nodded toward the south. "We'll make camp on the bluff above the river. I wouldn't mind leaving you for the wolves. They wouldn't stand a chance against your sharp tongue, but I'm not gonna ride off and leave Buck out here alone. When the creek goes down, I'm taking you back to Fort Harker if I have to drag you there by your hair. And I will enjoy doing it."

He spurred his horse to the top of the rise, leaving Mina to follow once her heart dropped out of her throat. It seemed the enigmatic Elder had a chink in his armor, after all. She had pierced it with her comment about his mother.

He led the way toward the Smokey Hill river. Mina followed, quietly shivering. At the base of a steep bluff, he dismounted near a stand of large cedar trees and pulled his rifle from its scabbard.

"Stay here," he commanded without looking at her. He pushed his way through the thick branches.

To her relief, he reappeared a few minutes later. Gathering up his reins, he led his horse through. Another few minutes passed before he emerged again. "What are you waiting for?"

"You told me to stay here."

A huff of frustration escaped his clenched lips.

"You did," she insisted. "I'm simply doing what you told me. You said to stay. I stayed. If you want me to follow, give some indication."

"Shut up and get in here before I shoot you."

A gust of wind sent a deep chill racing through her body. "There is no call to be rude. I am quite happy to follow now that I know you wish it."

He turned back with a muttered oath. Dismounting, she led Sabiha through the dripping branches and discovered a shallow cave extending fifteen feet into the hillside behind the cedars. Debris, bits of fur and the bones of small animals littered the floor, but it was dry.

They unsaddled the horses in silence and left them tied to a cedar limb near the entrance. Devlin propped his saddle on end near the back of the cave. Mina did the same after unstrapping her parasol and opening it to dry. Then she unpacked the contents of her saddlebags.

Devlin soon had a small fire going. Mina gratefully crouched beside it to warm her hands, but the fire's heat didn't penetrate her soaked clothing. Her shivers became more frequent, although she tried hard to stifle them.

"You need to get out of those wet things." His gruff voice startled her.

"An excellent suggestion. Unfortunately, I have no other attire."

He flipped open his saddlebag and tossed her a bundle of cloth. "Put these on."

She held up a shirt and pair of pants. "I can't possibly wear men's clothing. It's indecent."

"Take off those wet things, or I'll take them off for you. Your choice. I will not be stuck with a sick woman." The hard glitter of his eyes convinced her he wasn't joking.

"Very well, but you must wait outside." Her attempt to sound in charge was foiled by her chattering teeth.

He picked up his rifle. "Make it quick."

The moment he was out of sight, she did exactly that. The wet laces of her corset refused to cooperate, but she finally loosened them enough to wiggle out of it. She worked off her boots and sodden stockings, then pulled on his pants. They were too large at the waist, but they fit well enough over her hips. She rolled up the pant legs to keep from tripping on them and stared distastefully at her bare feet. It couldn't be helped. She wasn't about to stick them back into wet boots.

"Are you finished yet?" His impatient call came from beyond the trees.

"Almost." She pulled on his shirt. It fell to her thighs, but the buttons strained where she tried to close them over her breasts. She might be covered, but she was hardly decent. Quickly, she took down her hair and unbraided it.

*

Devlin crouched beneath an evergreen outside the entrance, scanning the countryside without leaving cover. Nothing moved in the rain. Glancing upward, he saw the smoke from his fire dissipating a few feet above the trees. The rain would keep the smell from traveling far. If only he could wash that woman out of his mind so easily.

He knew exactly what she was doing behind the screen of greenery. She was stripped naked and drying her pale body before the warmth of the flames. The glow of the fire would highlight her curves and valleys. She would slip her arms into his shirt and pull the front closed over those full, tempting breasts. He tried to think of something, anything else, but it was no use.

"I'm finished," she called.

"I'm going hunting," he yelled back.

"In the rain? That's not very sensible."

Oh, yes, it was. Taking a stroll in the pouring rain was the most sensible thing he'd done since leaving Salina with Lady Wilhelmina Smith in tow. He rose and started toward the river.

An hour later, he returned with a plucked sage hen in hand. He pushed his way through the cedar branches and stopped short.

She was bent over with her back to him, sweeping the stone floor with a bundle of evergreen branches. His pants hugged her sweet little derriere as she swayed to the rhythm of her work. He considered going back out into the rain but knew it wouldn't help. It was going to be a long night.

A small stack of firewood proved she had been busy while he'd been gone. She'd arranged her belongings along the floor where she had unpacked her saddlebags. He gave the tools and other items only a cursory glance because he saw his rope stretched from a twisted root growing out of the back of the cave wall to the tree nearest him. Her bedroll and clothing hung over it, including her undergarments. The whole place smelled like lavender. He reached out and touched the delicate lace edging her chemise.

Yup. A very long night.

Best not to dwell on what he couldn't have. "What do you think you're doing?" he snapped.

She shrieked and spun around. "You startled me!"

He stood dumbfounded at the sight before him. Her hair hung loose down the front of her in rippling, pale gold waves reaching to her waist. It glinted in the firelight and beckoned to be touched. He wanted to wrap his hands in it and pull her close. He wanted to bury his face in it, brush it aside and explore all the beauty it was hiding. She touched a strand self-consciously.

He forced his gaze away. She wasn't his for the taking, even if she stood naked in front of him. "You're lucky I wasn't a Cheyenne brave. You should have been keeping a lookout, not keeping house."

She tossed her makeshift broom aside. "I'm sorry. I wasn't thinking."

"No, you weren't. That will get you killed."

"I'll do better in the future. I see you were successful in your hunt. Come and dry off. I'll cook, unless, of course, you prefer to do so."

He held out the bird, and she took it. Did the fire give her cheeks such a rosy flush? Or was it something else? Desire? Had she been without a man since her husband left her? Would she give in with a little persuasion?

Squatting before the small blaze, she built a tripod of limbs. "Thank you for the loan of your clothes. I hope you don't mind my using your rope as a clothesline. I found a place where the rainwater was pouring off the rocks into a pool on the side of the hill and washed my things. They should be dry by morning. It took a lot of scrubbing to get the river mud and the smell of buffalo out of my dress. I never thought I would say this, but thank you for the use of your soap."

She flipped her hair back to keep it out of the fire and he saw why she had let it down. His shirt barely buttoned across her breasts. The thin white fabric left little to his imagination.

*

Mina bit her lower lip to stop her pointless chatter. She was in trouble, completely at the mercy of the wolf she had set free.

The hungry look in his eyes made her tremble, not with fear, but with some unexplained emotion. Did he find her desirable? Or would he look at any woman the way he had been looking at her? Had he looked at Nora like this in the room over the saloon?

She smoothed her hair with her free hand, pulling it forward again. Determined to maintain a calm demeanor, she drew a steadying breath. "Could you see how Buck is fairing?"

Elder turned away. "Buck's fine. He knows to sit tight. I'm gonna take the horses down to water and let them graze for a while," he said in a rush, unlike his usual cool drawl.

Mina frowned as he led the animals away. Did he enjoy spending time in the chilly rain? Maybe he wanted to avoid being alone with her. Her self-esteem sank. Maybe she repulsed him. Artie had disliked seeing her undressed.

Without Devlin's dominating presence in the small cavern, she relaxed and finished setting the bird to cook over the coals. Then she sat on the floor, listening to the rain trickling off the ledge over the entrance. The drip, drip, punctuated with the occasional hiss and pop of the cooking fowl soothed her. The smell of roasting sage hen and the fragrance of wet cedar filled the air. She looked around the cave and realized how lucky they were Devlin had found such a snug shelter.

Along the back wall, a smooth irregularity in the otherwise jagged limestones caught her eye. She rose to investigate. Her pulse quickened at what she saw.

*

When Devlin led the horses back inside the cave, the first thing he noticed was the smell of burning sage hen. The second was Mina standing on a narrow ledge of stone at the back wall, chipping at something over her head with a small mallet and chisel.

"What are you doing?"

"Devlin, come see this!" Excitement filled her voice. "I've found a fossil. It's a type of Plesiosaur skull. I'm almost sure of it. Devlin, this is wonderful!"

He liked the way his name sounded in her proper British accent.

After rescuing their scorched supper, he laid the bird on a piece of bark Mina had apparently found for that purpose before moving to stand behind her.

"Can you rig some kind of torch so I can see how to extract it properly? Never mind, I think—yes!"

The stone came loose. She spun around, holding it aloft. "I've got it!"

She lost her balance and flailed. She would have fallen if he hadn't stepped forward and caught her by the waist. His hand touched the bulge of her derringer in the pocket of her pants. He put her down and deftly relieved her of the gun. She was too excited to notice his overly familiar touch. Which was good because she was armed with a substantial chunk of rock. She ignored him and hurried to the fire.

"This is thrilling. Specimens like this have been discovered at the cliffs of Lyme Regis in England. My dear friend Mary Anning found a nearly complete skeleton in 1823. Long before I knew her, but she told me about it when I was a little girl. This may well be the first of its kind discovered in the Americas. Do you know what this means?"

Her eyes sparkled with enthusiasm. A delighted smile curved her full lips. The firelight glinted in her unbound hair, and the only thing he saw was how beautiful she looked.

He forced himself to ignore the fact and slipped her gun into his pocket. "It means you burned our supper for a rock."

"No, no, no. This is a fossil. The petrified bones of a creature who roamed the seas millions of years ago. My first major discovery in the Americas."

"You can't eat it, milady."

She seemed to recall where she was. She looked at him, then at the blackened bird. "Oh. I did burn it, didn't I? Well, it doesn't look completely ruined."

"Not completely," he agreed sarcastically.

Her gaze moved once more to the fossil in her hand. "It's a small price to pay for such a discovery. I so wish Artie could see this. He doesn't share the same feelings I have for fossils, but he would grin, kiss my forehead and make some funny comment about my love of old bones."

The wistful tone of her voice sent a stab of pain straight through Devlin's chest.

He sat down, pulled out his knife and started carving the crispy bird. The outside was charred, but the rest of it was passable. "What makes you so crazy about fossils?"

She laid the skull carefully on the ground and took the meat he offered. "When I was six, my mother insisted on spending the summer at the seashore where some of her friends were staying. Father remained in London. Mother spent all her time making social calls, so I was left on my own. One day, I wandered along the seashore looking for pretty spiral rocks, actually they were ammonites, fossil sea creatures. I found a lovely one inside a small cave in the cliff. I didn't realize the tide was coming in until a woman waded through the rising water and carried me to safety. It was Mary Anning. She scolded me, but she was as delighted as I was with my ammonite."

A faraway look of sadness filled Mina's eyes. "Mother was furious I had ruined my dress, and horrified I had associated with someone of an inferior social class. She threw away my 'filthy rock' and sent me to my room."

"Where you stayed the rest of the summer, I'll bet," he said dryly.

Mina laughed. "Not exactly. I found ways to slip out of the house and tag along fossil hunting with Mary. There was a garden shed where I would change into old clothes so as not to give myself away."

"I can see you doing that."

"It was a wonderful time. Thankfully, my mother insisted we return the next summer. I learned much later she had been meeting her lover there. Anyway, the summers in Lyme Regis were the best of my life. It was Mary who taught me to love discovering ancient and wondrous creatures and how to sketch them. Sadly, she passed away the following spring."

Mina took another bite of meat and studied him while she chewed.

"What?" he asked when he couldn't take her scrutiny any longer.

She licked her fingers before she answered. He wanted to lick them, too.

Don't think about bedding her. Think about something else.

She smiled, clasping her arms around her up-drawn knees. "I believe I owe you an apology."

"Just one?"

"Please, let me continue. I accused you of not trying to help me today. I saw you racing alongside, trying to get into a position to aid me."

"You saved yourself."

Her grin widened as she tipped her head closer. "Yes, but one cannot always count on having a dead buffalo handy, can one?"

He stifled a smile. "Reckon not."

"What I'm trying to say is you were right about the dangers. I foolishly goaded Buck into helping me and bullied him into doing what I wanted. The flood water could have swept him away as easily as it did me. I would never have forgiven myself if that had happened."

Just when he thought he had her figured out, she surprised him. There was a lot to like about this woman. When he wasn't tempted to strangle her or bed her.

"Does this mean you're going back to England?"

She picked up the skull and touched the pointed teeth lining the jaw. "If you had asked me earlier today, when I was soaked to the skin and stinking to high heaven, I might have wavered. But now? No, I'm not going back. I accept this will be more difficult than I imagined, but I cannot quit. Not when there are important discoveries waiting to be found."

"Are they more important than your life?"

"I'm not eager to reach my grave, if that's what you mean, but I owe someone a very great debt."

"I knew your husband. He didn't strike me as the sort of man who'd want a debt paid in blood."

"Poor Arthur. You are right. The debt I owe isn't to my husband."

"Then who?"

She looked away from him into the fire. "It is such a long, boring story."

He wanted to hear it. He wanted to learn more about this remarkable woman. "I've got nowhere to go."

She glanced up with a rueful smile. "After what I've put you through, I expect you have a right to know the reason."

"So tell me."

She stared into the empty eye socket of the skull for a long time, but Devlin had the feeling she was seeing something else altogether.

She spoke in a low voice. "Growing up, I lived a life of privilege. I had everything money and servants could supply. Our home was a mansion in the country. We had another house in the fashionable part of London. I had the best tutors, a pony, the prettiest dresses, dozens of dolls."

Of course, she had led a pampered life.

"However, my parents all but ignored me. Mother was busy with her society, Father with his business. I seldom saw them. They seldom saw each other. When they were together, there was trouble between them. Fights. Awful silences. Mother's affairs became more blatant. Father's drinking got worse. When I was ten, my father came home from his club, locked himself in the study, and put a bullet in his brain."

She fell silent. A stab of pity struck Devlin, but he turned it aside. Life was seldom a fairytale.

Casting him a sad smile, she said, "It turned out our lives were nothing more than a flimsy house of cards. My father was a gambler whose luck had run out. It was discovered he had embezzled the money we enjoyed from his business partner, Vincent Smith, Arthur's father. My mother wasn't sad, she was furious. She had gone from society's darling to a pariah. The party invitations stopped. People no longer came to call. They crossed the street to avoid us. Tradesman stopped selling to us and began demanding payment for goods already delivered."

"So you were left with your father's debts?"

"My father owed far more than our possessions were worth. I know because I was there when they carted away every piece of furniture, my dolls, my dresses, everything. Mother was too ashamed to show her face to the tradesmen. I'm sure they took more than they were owed, but I was a child. They didn't heed my pleas."

She leaned forward and added another piece of wood to the fire. "When they took my pony, I broke down and went crying to Mother. I found her packing. With no reason to go on pretending to be a model of society, she had thrown herself on the mercy of her lover. I still don't know who he was. She said she would send for me. Promised the servants would take care of me until she did. She left, and I never heard from her again."

Not the life Devlin had assumed.

Mina glanced at him. "When no one paid the servants, they left, one by one. Only Stanley, our butler, remained. I had no other family to turn to. A few more months went by. Stanly fell ill and was taken away. A man came with a piece of paper and said the house belonged to the bank. That's how I found myself out on the street."

She stood, brushed off her hands and faced the back of the cavern. "I'm convinced I may find more of this fellow's skeleton in the wall. Buck has my excavating equipment. I have only the small tool set from my saddlebags."

"What happened after you lost your home?" he asked gently.

She glanced at him over her shoulder. "Why, it wasn't long until, like you, Mr. Elder, I found myself incarcerated."

Chapter Ten

Devlin stared at Mina in astonishment. "You went to jail when you were ten years old?"

"Eleven by then, but yes."

"For what?"

"Oh, the most heinous of crimes. I stole a hen. Unfortunately, the shopkeeper that caught me had a large unpaid bill left by my father. He also had a brother who was a constable. The magistrate sentenced me to five years in the girl's reformatory after I had been in adult prison for three months awaiting trial."

"Five years for stealing a chicken?"

Mina cast him a half smile. "It was a very plump bird."

She tried to make light of it, but he saw a tremor shake her. Remembered horrors darkened her eyes.

"What happened?" He asked gently, trying not to imagine what could befall a young girl in such a desperate situation.

Her smile faded as she stared into the fire. "When I was first taken before the magistrate, a solicitor in the courtroom recognized my father's name. He ran into Vincent about a year later and mentioned the incident. Vincent had been in Philadelphia at the time of my father's death. The havoc Papa's crimes created in the company took Vincent months to repair. When he finally arrived in London, he found mother and I had vanished. He assumed we were together. If not for the solicitor's off-hand comment, I believe I would have died in that place. It wasn't a school. It was--"

Her voice trailed off as she fell silent, staring into the flames. Devlin waited.

Finally, she said, "You can't imagine the shame I felt when I looked up from the filthy mattress in the corner of my cell and saw my father's friend, the man he had betrayed, standing in the doorway. Without a word, Vincent took off his coat, wrapped it around me and carried me out of that pit. He saved my life."

"And in return, what did he want?"

Anger filled her eyes. "Vincent has never asked for anything. Papa's death was truly distressing for him. Vincent cared for my father as a friend, almost a brother. He believed he had failed Papa by not seeing the signs of trouble before it was too late."

Devlin looked down. "Sorry."

She drew an unsteady breath. "Anyway, Vincent became my legal guardian. He lavished me with care and attention, treated me like a beloved daughter. Saw to it my father's share of the business was put in my name. I came to love him as a father. Artie treated me as a cherished sister. Vincent found Stanley and had him cared for, then bought my former homes and reclaimed my belongings."

She fell silent. Devlin suspected she was weighing her next words carefully.

"I fell deeply in love with Artie. We were married when I turned eighteen. Together, we traveled the world on scientific expeditions. Then Vincent suffered a brain seizure. I remained in London to nurse him."

"Artie didn't?"

She shook her head and looked away. "He and a fellow scientist had already planned a trip to the Amazon. They went ahead with it, but the other man was killed. Artie came here and made a tremendous discovery. His name will be honored when it becomes known. Vincent can take pride in what his son accomplished. It is for Vincent's sake I must find Arthur's bird fossil. Only by doing so can I repay even a small portion of the debt I owe."

She drew herself up to her full height and thrust out her chin, not realizing the move made her generous breasts strain the buttons of his borrowed shirt. Devlin half-hoped they would give way, but forced his gaze back to her face.

Fierce determination sparkled in her eyes. "I will not stop trying. Even if it takes the rest of my life. Even if it kills me."

He'd seen such a look of resolve on only one other woman's face. His mother. He recognized a will that would not be broken, would not bend to hardship or pain. Mina would go on with her quest no matter what.

She'd get herself killed within a week without him.

Resignation pulled his shoulders down. He owed a debt, too. He owed it to Artie to see that his wife stayed alive. If she wouldn't go back,

Devlin knew he had to go with her. It was the only way he could help her find what she was looking for without finding too much.

"Once you have the bones Artie found, what will you do?"

"If I am convinced my husband is dead, I will return to Philadelphia. When Vincent is strong enough, we will depart posthaste for London, where I will present Artie's discovery to the British Museum. You will never see me again."

The thought didn't cheer Devlin the way it should.

She moved to sit beside him and gripped his arm. "Please, Mr. Elder. Will you help me?"

The touch of her small hand sent heat spiraling through his body. "You called me Devlin before."

"Will you help me, Devlin?" she asked softly.

"I should tie you to your horse and haul you back east myself."

"If you did, I would only return. Please?" Her eyes pleaded with him.

It was insane, but he was going to do it. "We need to get one thing straight. I'm in charge. What I say goes. If I say hop, you'll hop like a jackrabbit until I say stop. Disobey me, and you're on your own."

She pressed her palms together. "I understand perfectly. I won't be a bit of trouble."

He snorted. "Yeah, and fish don't swim."

"You won't regret this, I swear it." She beamed at him.

Caught unprepared by the radiance of her smile, he basked in its glow until the memory of Artie's face returned. No matter what she promised, Devlin knew he'd regret this decision. Hell, he regretted it already. He knew where to take her, but he couldn't let her know that.

Rising abruptly, he said, "We're not going anywhere for a few days. It'll take that long for the creek to go down if the rain stops. You mentioned a map."

"Yes. It is in Arthur's journal in my saddlebag. I keep it tightly wrapped in oiled silk. It wasn't damaged. I checked."

"May I see it?"

At her hesitation, he wondered if she knew more than she had let on about her husband's business. Several long seconds later, she arrived at her decision. "Yes, you may."

She rummaged through her things and returned with a packet clasped tightly to her chest. "It makes sense to let you look at it. After all, you're familiar with the territory. Perhaps you even know the location my husband marked."

"I might." He held out his hand.

Still, she hesitated.

"I can't say one way or the other until you let me look at it, milady."

"It's silly, I know, but this is the last thing I have of him. The last words he wrote. I haven't shared them with anyone."

Devlin's gut clenched. He didn't want to read Artie's words of love written to his wife thousands of miles away. What he wanted to do was kiss her. Hold her close and breathe in the freshness of her. He wanted to lay her down and make love to her until she forgot any man but him.

And that kind of thinking had to stop!

Lady Wilhelmina Smith wasn't for the likes of him. She was born and bred to London high society no matter what had happened in her past. She might be eccentric, but she wasn't the sort of woman to bed a randy plainsman. Besides, if she knew what he'd done, she'd likely kill him herself.

"Keep it." He tossed a stick on the fire and dropped to sit cross-legged beside the flames.

"No, you should look at it." She unwrapped the bundle and opened the journal to the page she wanted before handing it to him.

He took the book and leaned closer to the fire, tilting it to see the writing more clearly. The crudely drawn map was detailed enough to see Artie had pinpointed the location of their camp.

Mina kneeled to peer over his arm. Adjusting her glasses, she pointed to a wide, wavy line. "This is the Smokey Hill River. Each symbol with a box around a coach must mean one of the way stations. See, he has written here, Fossil Creek. Buck's brother runs the station there. I'm hoping he will remember when Artie was there and tell us which way he went. What I don't understand is this symbol. It looks like a pile of logs along this small creek. Artie doesn't give it a name. Perhaps it refers to some kind of landmark."

Devlin knew but didn't share the information. So her plan was to travel to Fossil Creek. He and Artie had gone northwest without stopping at the station. No one had seen them together.

He handed the book back. "There are lots of creeks in those hills. It'll be hard to know if we're on the right one. After this much rain, even the dry gullies will run full of water and look like streams. We could end up traveling miles in the wrong direction."

She sat back on her heels. "I know it may be difficult, but I refuse to believe it is hopeless. If we can establish the exact direction he took after leaving the stage line, we'll be able to locate which creek he followed. If the proportions of the map are correct, he couldn't have traveled over thirty or thirty-five miles north and west. All we must do is locate this place." Her finger tapped the log pile sketch.

All Devlin had to do was keep her away from that spot. With a little luck, he could lead her in a roundabout fashion to where Artie had copied her damn bird bones and get her safely back on the train to Philadelphia. Or he might get himself hung or scalped, too.

Devlin leaned back on his elbows and stretched his legs out beside the fire. "We should turn in early. Do you want to make up our bed or shall I?"

*

A jolt of surprise shot through Mina at Devlin's words. She nearly dropped her book in the fire. He lay sprawled at her feet, watching her. What was he implying? Surely not what she was thinking. Although she found him increasingly attractive, she would not abandon her morals.

She moved back to her saddle, feeling his eyes watching her every move. His scrutiny made her nervous. She re-wrapped Arthur's journal and replaced it carefully. When she returned to the fire and her overcooked bird, Devlin had risen. He stood at the entrance, staring out into the night. What was he thinking? She longed to ask but didn't dare. He turned around and caught her staring. He scowled at her. Now what had she done to earn his ire?

She clasped her arms tightly over her chest as she watched him stride across the small space to his saddle. He pulled off his bedroll, carried his saddle back to the fire and spread his blankets out a few feet away from her. "What are you doing?"

"Making our bed." He lay down and flipped the blanket across his legs before settling back.

"We'll be spending the night here? Together?"

"Unless you want to sleep out in the rain?"

"No, of course not." Mina crossed her arms. "But I can't sleep in the same bed with you."

He paused in the act of adjusting his saddle to pillow his head. "Don't think of it as a bed. Think of it as a dry blanket on a cave floor."

69

She raised her chin. "I require separate sleeping arrangements."

He placed his hat over his face. "You've got the side closest to the fire. What more do you want?"

"Privacy!"

He lifted his hat. "You want me to sleep in the rain?"

"It isn't proper for us to share a bedroll. Besides, I need to wash up before retiring."

He placed his hat over his face. "I thought you washed earlier."

"My clothes, not my person. After all, I had no idea when you would return."

"So go to bed dirty."

She stamped her foot. "I will not."

"Then wash."

"Not with you in here."

"I won't look." The leer in his voice sent a shiver down her spine. He was deliberately trying to unnerve her.

The fact it worked only made her angrier. With a huff of disgust, Mina spun away from him. To think she had unburdened her soul to this oaf. No doubt, he would use her confessions against her in the future. Well, she wasn't going to play the cringing, helpless woman for his benefit. And she certainly would not hop into bed with him because of a little thing like a damp blanket.

She resisted the urge to kick his booted foot so temptingly near and instead strode to the rope she had strung earlier. She ducked underneath it and moved her drying blanket to block him from view. Peering over the top of her dubious screen, she watched him for a long time. He never moved.

He had agreed to help her find Arthur's dig, but he wasn't trustworthy. Something she shouldn't forget, no matter how attractive she found him. She moved her parasol within quick reach.

A check of her clothing showed her dress and chemise were still damp. Even if she could wash, she'd be forced to put his clothes back on. She itched for a proper bath, but he was right. It would simply have to wait.

Taking her hankie to the cave entrance, she contented herself with using it and a trickle of rainwater to wash her hands and face. Frequent glances over her shoulder proved Devlin hadn't moved, but she felt sure his eyes followed her.

Returning to her side of the screen, she lay on the limestone floor and carefully set her glasses aside. Her saddle and saddle blanket were too wet to use as a pillow, leaving only her arms to cradle her head.

Less than a minute later, her eyes popped open. Muttering in annoyance, she sat up and used her hands to sweep away several offending pebbles. With that accomplished, she lay down again and stared at the reflection of the firelight flickering on the ceiling.

The drip of rain outside and the pleasant smell of cedar and wood smoke helped to soothe her over stretched nerves, but sleep was nowhere near. She turned to her side, put her glasses on and lifted the corner of the blanket to peek underneath.

Devlin lay exactly where he'd deposited himself earlier. Light from the fire cast his body half in glow, half in shadow. It was an accurate representation of the disturbing man.

There was the part of Devlin Elder she could see and a part she couldn't yet guess at. While she had poured out her early history, she still knew less than nothing about the handsome and mysterious man laying a few feet away.

He was good-looking when he wasn't leering or scowling, but she sensed something more beneath his rough appearance. His loyalty to Buck was unquestionable given the way he'd pursued them for days through the pouring rain. He might treat her like a nuisance, but he had tried to rescue her from the swollen stream. She didn't doubt he'd have ridden his horse into the flood waters if she hadn't stayed afloat with the dead buffalo. Had he shown the same loyalty to Artie?

Staring at him wouldn't garner her answers. She sighed as she let go of the blanket and turned to her back. The cold from the dirt floor soon penetrated her clothing, while none of the heat from the fire reached her. She shivered and considered pulling the blanket down to cover herself, but it was still wet. She might be cold now, but wrapped in it, she would soon be chilled to the bone. A second, stronger shiver coursed through her body.

Mumbling an Arabic curse, she curled onto her other side, drew her knees up and laced her arms across her chest. It was no use. The cold crept over her from all directions. With a groan of frustration, she turned over and peeked under the blanket. Devlin lay sleeping peacefully by the fire while forcing her to shiver on a cold stone floor.

The red glow of the coals and the faint crackle of the fire promised warmth. If only he had been a gentleman and let her sleep near the fire, she wouldn't be freezing her nether parts off while he slept in apparent bliss. He certainly was no gentleman. How had she ever considered him attractive? With a huff of frustration, she let the blanket fall back into place.

She folded her arms across her chest and stared at the ceiling again. She had what she wanted. A guide, but a niggling worry wormed into her restless mind. Was she unwise to accept his capitulation at face value? Until tonight, he'd been determined to dissuade her from following in Arthur's footsteps. She wasn't convinced her tale alone had changed his mind. She shifted restlessly and swept away another pebble.

Still, if Devlin meant her harm, he'd had plenty of opportunities. It wasn't her physical safety that worried her. Emotionally, the man was an enormous distraction.

She lifted the blanket to check on him again. He stirred slightly. She dropped the wool material and scooted away, listening for further movement. When she heard nothing, she slowly lifted the edge of her screen again. The scuffed toe of his boot was only inches from her face. She looked up to see him frowning at her over the top of her blanket.

Snatching up her parasol, she pointed it at his face. "If you come any closer, you'll be leading me west with only one eye. How dare you invade my privacy!"

"This isn't privacy. It's lunacy." He grabbed the tip of her sunshade, jerked it out of her grip and tossed it toward the front of the cave. The clatter spooked the horses. They shifted uneasily.

Mina scrambled to her feet. "Remember, I still have my pistol."

"No, you don't."

"I most certainly do." She shoved her hand into her pants pocket only to encounter empty cloth. Why hadn't she noticed?

"You stole it! You've left me unarmed and defenseless. How dare you! Well, I warn you, sir, I shall not submit to your perverted molestation without a fight. I can kick and scratch and bite—"

He shoved aside the blanket separating them. Before she knew what had happened, he grabbed her and slung her over his shoulder. Shrieking and kicking, she pummeled his back to no avail as he walked to the fire.

"You don't need a gun. You can talk a man to death."

"Brute! I'll see you hang for this. You had better kill me because I will cut out your liver with your own knife. I'll… I'll stab burning sticks into your eyes. I'll… I'll… I'll—"

"You'll shut up, that's what you'll do." Abruptly, he set her on her feet, but held on to her wrists.

She struggled against him. "Unhand me, you villain."

"Promise not to poke burning sticks in my eyes."

"I promise no such thing." She tried to drive her knee into his groin. He blocked it.

"Stop it. I'm not going to hurt you."

"Ha! You're a liar and a despoiler of women!" She fought harder to free her hands.

He let go. Mina fell backward, landing in an undignified heap on his bedroll.

"I've never taken an unwilling woman in my life! I damn sure don't intend to start with you." The cold calm of his voice quelled some of her fear.

"Then what was the purpose of this display?"

"The purpose was to get some sleep without listening to you huff, mutter and moan all night. You will sleep on my dry blanket by the fire and to hell with the proprieties."

"I did not moan."

"Oh, for God's sakes, woman, must you argue about everything?"

"I'm not arguing. I merely corrected your mistaken impression."

A muscle in his tense jaw quivered. Mina fell silent. It was much warmer by the fire. Perhaps discretion was the better part of valor.

She adjusted her spectacles and smoothed her hair. "Your concern for my well-being is appreciated. In the future, however, it might be wiser to simply state your case. I am not an unreasonable person."

"Argh!" He spread his fingers wide as if to strangle her.

She ignored his threat. "If I'm to have your blanket, where will you sleep?"

"On my half of it." His tone dared her to object.

"Oh." Her voice didn't squeak. She was proud of that as she considered the thick wool beneath her fingers, then glanced at the cold dirt beyond.

"Any objections, milady?" he drawled.

"None I care to share."

"Good. Then scoot over and maybe we'll both get some sleep before dawn."

She scooted, with as much dignity as she could muster, to the very edge of his blanket. Lying on her side, facing him, she willed her jumpy nerves into submission. He tossed another piece of wood on the fire, then lay down less than a foot away and once again covered his face with his hat. Except for the sound of the rain and the crackle of the fire, silence reigned. Determined not to fall asleep, Mina tried to quiet her breathing and remain still as she kept a wary eye on him.

After a quarter of an hour, Devlin muttered, "Will you go to sleep?"

Startled, she said, "I was."

"No, you weren't."

"And how would you know?"

"I can feel your eyes boring holes through me."

"Nonsense. A person cannot feel the gaze of another. Besides, I was sound asleep until you spoke."

"You haven't even taken your glasses off. You're a poor liar, milady."

She opened her mouth to protest but snapped it shut when she realized she couldn't very well argue she was an excellent liar.

He raised his hat and looked at her. His dark eyes glinted dangerously in the fading light of the fire. Warmth swept over her that had nothing to do with the temperature in the cave. Her pulse accelerated until her heart felt as if it would jump out of her chest. A flutter of unknown sensations stirred in the depths of her body.

She swallowed hard. "I warn you, I'm a very light sleeper. If you attempt to ravish me while I slumber, I will know it and you won't succeed."

For the first time, she saw astonishment on his face. It disappeared as his eyes narrowed. "How long were you married?"

She frowned. "Arthur and I were married for eight years before he disappeared. Why?"

"And in all that time, how often did he make love to you without waking you up?"

"That, sir, is absolutely none of your business." She rolled over. "I'm going to sleep now. Stop disturbing me."

*

Devlin clenched his teeth in annoyance at her superior tone. She had a way of speaking that needled him like a handful of prickly pears. The sooner he found her damn bird bones, the sooner he could put her on a train and get rid of her. Then his life would get back to normal.

Only, what would normal be like after Lady Wilhelmina Smith was gone?

He could go back to drinking himself into a stupor. Bedding women who didn't care if he was still there when they woke up in the morning.

Starting bar fights to blow off steam. None of them carried the appeal they once did.

Buck had his dream of a cabin with a porch where he could look out over a little ranch with fat cattle grazing on the hillside. In a whiskey induced moment of weakness, Devlin had agreed to become the boy's partner, but looking at the same hillside for the rest of his days held no attraction when he was sober. Whenever he had tried to settle down, his itchy feet had pulled him out to roam the vast prairie, just as he had done in his boyhood.

But now, it wasn't the grasslands that drew him. It was the sweet curves of the woman lying only a foot away. He wanted to turn her over and make love to her until any thoughts of fossils or her husband were driven out of her mind.

The bitter irony was he might be able to make Mina forget, but he knew he would always see Artie's face, twisted into a grotesque mask of terror and unendurable pain.

Mina's breathing gradually grew deep and even. He knew she slept despite her fear. Sometime before dawn, he woke to find her curled against his side, her sweet rump pressing against his hip. The cave had grown colder, and the fire was mere embers glowing under gray ash.

He had two choices. He could get up and feed the fire or he could stay where he was and enjoy the warmth of the woman beside him. The desire to see her blue eyes charged with indignation when she woke allowed him to make up his mind.

He turned to his side, fitting his body to the curve of hers. Carefully, he worked one arm under her cheek to provide her with a bit of comfort, then pulled the blanket up to cover them both. With a little murmur, Mina relaxed against him.

Gritting his teeth, he blew out a deep breath and tried to think of anything but having sex as he rested his chin on her soft hair and settled down to sleep with the most pleasant armful of woman he had ever held and not made love to. Then she rolled over. Her arm snaked across his neck while her ample breasts pressed against his chest.

Easing onto his back, he tried to put some space between them, but the sleeping vixen draped her thigh across his, inched closer and laid her cheek on his shoulder. He groaned inwardly. Lord, it was going to be a long night.

Chapter Eleven

Mina resisted the urge to open her eyes. What would it hurt to rest a few minutes longer? She snuggled her cheek into her firm pillow and tried to recapture her unremembered but pleasant dream. Nestled in a cocoon of warmth, she drifted for a moment on the edge of sleep, but the arms of Morpheus would not open for her again. The Greek god of slumber had deserted her.

Little by little, her senses came awake. Birds cawing and chirping made merry morning sounds. The smell of rain-washed air overlaid a deep, sensual, masculine scent and the smell of wood smoke. Slowly, the memory of her dream returned.

She recalled the feel of a man's strong arms around her, his breath stirring the hair at the nape of her neck. She never saw his face, but she knew it wasn't her husband as she turned and moved into his embrace. The dream was gone now, but a sense of rightness lingered.

The warm pillow beneath her cheek rose and fell in a slow, steady rhythm. She smiled. How odd. Her pillow was breathing.

Mina's eyes snapped open.

Without her spectacles, the world was a soft blur, but it took only an instant to recognize the row of small white objects in front of her nose were buttons. She followed their path upward and made out Devlin's face in the pale morning light. Thank God his eyes were closed.

With growing horror, she realized she lay sprawled across him in the most wanton fashion imaginable. He appeared to be in the same position he had assumed last night. Sometime in her sleep, she must have rolled next to him.

Humiliation sent a flood of heat to her face. Mina prayed he wouldn't wake up and discover her behaving no better than the sordid woman he'd dallied with in Ellsworth.

Gingerly, she raised her head and lifted her arm from across his chest. Then, with delicate care, she moved her leg from where it rested on his. He stirred slightly. Mina froze with her arm and leg suspended in mid-air.

He gave an odd choking snore, then turned on his side away from her. His body quivered ever so slightly. To her relief, he soon resumed his slow, steady breathing. She let out the breath she was holding. The sudden rush of air sounded like a hurricane in the still morning.

After inching her way back to her side of the blanket, she located her glasses. Keeping an eye on Devlin, she rose to her feet, crossed the cave floor on tiptoe and pulled her now dry clothing from the line. With one last glance at Devlin to make sure he was still sleeping, she slipped out to change.

Screened by the thick cedars, she dropped the trousers Devlin had loaned her. In London, she had often argued women deserved more rational dress than the corsets and petticoats fashion dictated. She refused to wear hoops. A few like-minded women agreed with her. They believed women were equal to men. They deserved the same rights and respect, including the right to vote and hold positions in the government. It made no sense women were denied those rights when the country, the entire empire, was ruled by Queen Victoria.

Arthur had agreed with Mina, but Vincent waved such remarks aside as foolish. Women in trousers, he had said, would lead to depravity. He'd been right. At least where she was concerned. Trousers and the company of Devlin Elder brought on frequent, depraved thoughts.

She kicked his pants aside and pulled on her riding habit. Properly dressed, she once again became a lady.

*

When Devlin heard Mina push her way through the trees, he risked opening one eye to make sure she was gone. He stifled another chuckle at the wildly waving branches she left in her wake. For a second, he wished he had looked to see her face when she discovered exactly where she'd chosen to sleep. But for some unknown reason, he let her escape with her pride intact. He mulled over why it seemed important to spare her feelings.

The truth was hard to swallow. He was starting to like her. A lot.

Besides, letting her slip away saved him from another one of her tongue-lashings. She was irritating, bossy, wrongheaded and more stubborn than anyone he'd met, but there was something special about her, too. Unspoiled and naïve, she acted more like a virgin than a woman married for eight years. His suspicions about Artie's sexual preference may have been true.

Some homosexual men married to hide their inclinations. Some even had children and kept their secret from their wives. Then there were men who were unable to have sex due to war wounds or illness. He didn't know which was the case with Artie, but it was pretty clear he'd never bedded his wife. How any man could resist her enticing body while sleeping next to her was beyond Devlin's understanding.

In the growing light of day, he reconsidered his offer to take Mina to Artie's last campsite. He had allowed his emotions to override his better judgment last night, and he didn't like the feeling.

Lady Wilhelmina Smith was turning out to be a dangerous woman—even without her damn sunshade.

"Good heavens!"

Her exclamation of surprise brought him to his feet with his rifle in hand, battling down the urge to rush forward. He edged out of the shelter and quietly made his way around the cedars. He caught sight of her standing on the hillside beyond the trees. She appeared unharmed. His pounding pulse settled back to a normal pace.

She had changed into her own clothes. The yellow riding habit made her stand out like a beacon against the green grass. The high-buttoned jacket with its long sleeves made her appear every inch the grand lady she was. It was something he needed to remember. She wasn't meant for a man like him.

After scanning the area for signs of danger and finding none, he moved out of the trees and saw what had caused her astonished outburst. The Smokey Hill River was out of its banks with a vengeance. It spread out in a churning torrent half a mile wide. Only the tops of the tallest trees waving in the rushing water marked the course of the riverbed.

Devlin moved to stand beside Mina. She glanced at him, her eyes wide with concern. "Do you think Buck is okay?"

"He's a smart kid. He'll have headed to higher ground."

"There's just so much water. It's amazing, frightening and fascinating all at the same time. Do you think we should move to higher ground, too? I can't believe how close it got to us in the night."

He moved downhill to the water's edge. "Looks like it has already crested. See how the grass is flattened? The water got this high, but it's receded a few feet already."

"Well, you certainly have one more thing to thank me for." She directed a bright smile his way.

"And what would that be?" He couldn't think of a single thing he needed to thank her for.

"By prompting you to follow Buck and myself, I may have saved your life."

"How do you figure?"

She waved her hand toward the broad expanse of water. "If you had remained in Ellsworth, you would be under, oh, about ten feet of water by now. When I first saw the town, I thought it was built much too close to the river. I do hope Nora Perry Proprietress knows how to swim."

She gave him a strange, self-satisfied smile before she turned and walked back to the cave.

*

Over the next two days, Mina contented herself with working to uncover more of her Plesiosaur and trying to ignore Devlin. Both were difficult tasks. The back wall refused to give up any additional fossils, and ignoring the man watching her chip away at it was like trying to walk with her shoes on the wrong feet. Possible, but not at all comfortable.

He rarely said a word, which only made things worse. To fill the quiet, she babbled constantly about fossils, about the countries she and Arthur had visited, about Vincent Smith and life in England. Devlin listened, occasionally giving her a hand with her work if she asked. He disappeared outside for hours at a time, and just when she thought she could concentrate on the task at hand, she would sense a change in the very air. Turning around, she would find him watching her once more. A person really could feel the eyes of another boring into them.

At night, sleeping on her side of the campfire on her own dry blanket, she couldn't escape his presence even then. She dreamed the most unsettling dreams about the man. It was enough to make her want to scream.

Early on the third morning, the waters had receded into the riverbanks, and Buck appeared on the opposite shore of the creek below them. His shouted hello filled Mina with relief. She shouted back and waved gaily. Devlin joined her, and she sensed his relief, too, though he refrained from any outright demonstration.

Mina set her prized skull on a stump near the water's edge. "Will we be able to cross soon?"

"Maybe by tomorrow afternoon."

"Must we spend another night here?"

He arched one eyebrow. "I thought you were having fun digging a second room in the cave."

She stared in disgust at her grime-encrusted hands. She had discarded her jacket and wore her white blouse with the sleeves rolled up. "It is more fun when one actually finds fossils. So far, the skull seems to be all that remains of my friend. Perhaps the rest of him lies further back inside the hill. However, without a major excavating team to move several tons of dirt and rock, I won't be able to locate him."

The sound of a gunshot from over the hill caused them to turn. Devlin pushed Mina toward the trees. "Stay here. I'll check it out."

He headed for the crest of the hill at a run. After only a glance at the grove of cedars, Mina hiked up her skirt and followed him.

Near the top, he dropped into a crouch, then worked his way up the last few feet on his belly. Breathless, her blood churning with excitement, Mina crawled up beside him. "What is it? What's going on?"

His answer was a fierce scowl.

"Yes, yes," she whispered to forestall his scolding, "I know you told me to stay put, but I wanted to see for myself if we are in danger."

"Lady, you wouldn't know danger if it bit you in the ass."

"I knew the gunshot was from a rifle and it came from quite a distance, not close at hand."

A second and a third shot broke the still air. She rose to look over the thick grass. "Can you see who fired?"

"You little fool." With one hand, he shoved her head down and held it pressed to the ground. "They're buffalo hunters. Most likely from the fort."

A great rumbling began beneath her ear and grew louder. "How odd. Is this area prone to earthquakes?"

"Damn it to hell! Run!"

"Really, sir. There is no need for such language."

He sprang to his feet and jerked her up. "I said, RUN!"

She looked over his arm. An ocean of enormous black beasts came rushing toward them.

Devlin pushed her toward the river. "Go!"

"A most excellent suggestion." She hiked her skirts to an indecent height and bolted down the hill with Devlin close behind.

Halfway down, the first great wooly buffalo thundered past them. Mina stumbled, but Devlin grabbed her arm and pulled her on.

"Make for the cave," he shouted.

She didn't need further urging. A glance back showed a solid wall of animals pouring over the hilltop. The ground shook beneath her feet as she rushed headlong toward the trees. As more animals hurdled past, she knew they would never make it around to the front of the cavern.

Devlin yanked her toward the rock ledge that formed the roof. He didn't pause as he leaped from the stone rim, pulling Mina after him. Her scream was cut short as she crashed into the dense prickly cedar branches. Momentarily winded, she didn't have time to assess whether she was still in one piece before she was jerked out of her nest.

"Get the horses to the back," Devlin yelled in her ear. She nodded and rushed to free Sabiha's bridle, moving both frightened animals as far back as possible. Rocks and dirt rained down from the shaking ceiling.

Devlin collapsed when a chunk of limestone struck him. Mina flew to his side and threw her arms up to cover her head as she bent over him, trying to shield him from further harm. Light from the opening was cut off. Was their haven to become their tomb?

After a few moments, she realized it wasn't the falling stone darkening the entrance. It was buffalo. As the massive stampeding herd poured over the hilltop, some animals had no choice but to leap or be pushed over the edge by those behind them. Dozens of the mammoth beasts spilled down into the trees. Some rose and ran on. Others lay still and were buried as more bodies piled up.

Gradually, the rumbling died away, to be replaced by the bellowing and grunts of the animals heaped in front of the cavern. By ones and twos, most of them untangled themselves and limped after the herd.

Devlin groaned and cursed. Mina's heart rose in sudden joy. "Thank God you're not dead. Are you seriously injured?"

"I don't know yet." He held both hands to his head. Blood trickled from between his fingers.

She helped him sit up. "You must let me see your wound. Scalp lacerations often bleed profusely. Tell me your name."

"What the hell for?" he growled.

"To see if you are lucid. To see if the blow to your head has addled your senses."

She pulled one of his hands away from his face. He looked up, then grasped her wrist in a painful grip. "Be still."

A loud snort echoed in the confines of the cavern. Mina glanced over her shoulder. A young buffalo, confused by the fall, staggered into their shelter. He stopped a few yards away and lowered his head in a menacing gesture.

Mina rose, stepped in front of Devlin and pointed. "That is the way out, you stupid beast, now get."

The buffalo raked one hoof back and shook his shaggy head. His curved black horns glinted with menace.

Grabbing her skirt, she raised it and flapped the fabric sharply. "Shoo! Do you hear me? Shoo! Shoo!"

The fluttering fabric proved more than the animal's shaken nerves could bear. He took a step back, then broke toward the entrance, scrambling over the remaining bodies on his way out.

To Mina's amazement, her knees gave out, and she collapsed beside Devlin. "Oh, my goodness gracious."

"Are you okay?" he asked.

She took a moment before replying. "Nothing hurts unduly."

He reached out and pulled a sprig of cedar from her hair. "Are you sure?"

She stared at him for a long second. "I can't believe I just did that."

"Well, you did, Lady Wilhelmina Smith of Silsby Hall, Bedfordshire and London." He grinned, the first genuine smile she had ever seen from him, one that reached all the way to his eyes, crinkling the corners into tiny crow's feet. Despite the blood coating one side of his face, he was remarkably handsome. He stood and extended his hand toward her.

"The *hotoa'e* must be your spirit animal. First, it saves you from drowning, then it turns aside when you say shoo. I think I will call you *Hotoa'hehe*."

She took the hand he offered and allowed him to pull her to her feet. "*Hotoa'hehe*. What does it mean?"

"It means Buffalo Woman in the language of the Cheyenne."

"You speak Cheyenne?"

His smile faded. "Some."

He still held her hand, but she was reluctant to remind him of the fact. She cherished the feeling of warmth and strength that seemed to flood her body from his firm grip. "French and now Cheyenne. You are quite the linguist, Mr. Elder."

"Do me a favor."

"Certainly, if I can."

"Call me Devlin."

The heat of a blush crept up her neck and she was glad of the poor light. "Very well, sir. But only if you promise not to call me Buffalo Woman. As names go, it is even less flattering than Wilhelmina. You may call me Mina."

A ghost of his smile flashed across his face. "It's a deal, milady."

The sound of voices outside surprised her. She gripped Devlin's arm. "Who do you think is there?"

"My guess would be the hunters who started the stampede."

"Well, I certainly intend to give them a piece of my mind. Of all the reckless endeavors. They could have killed us."

She let go of Devlin and marched toward the entrance. Stepping over the legs of a dead buffalo, she ducked under a broken branch of a cedar. Much of the stand of trees had been completely leveled, and the smell of crushed cedar mingled with the overpowering musky smell of the animals heaped about her.

She came to a halt, stunned by the extent of the carnage. For hundreds of yards in every direction, the grass had disappeared, churned into nothing but a wide muddy swath by thousands of hooves. Dozens of dead animals lay piled in front of the cave. Near the creek's edge stood two mule-drawn wagons. Beside them, four men worked at hacking the hide from a dead buffalo.

"You there," Mina called, "I wish to have a word with you."

They all stared, frozen by the sight of her.

"Gentlemen, and I use the term loosely, your extreme carelessness nearly cost me and my companion our lives. Did you not think to ascertain if anyone was camped in the path of these beasts before you drove them to frenzied flight?"

No one answered. They continued to gape. She thrust her hands upon her hips. "Well? Don't you have anything to say for yourselves? Do you speak English?"

Devlin strolled past her and stopped in front of a gray-bearded man dressed in fringed buckskins. "Howdy, Nat."

Nat blinked. "Howdy, Dev. It's good to see you still got yer hair. What happened to ya?"

Devlin wiped the blood from his face with the back of his sleeve. "It's nothing. Are you hunting for the fort?"

Nat peered over Devlin's shoulder toward Mina. "Naw, fer the railroad. They're paying real good wages if you're looking for work. Do you got a white woman with you?"

"I do."

"Well, glory be! I was worried there fer a second I was having one of them hallucinations."

"She's real. Looks like you're gonna make a good haul today. There must be thirty head here."

"Yup. This drop off was a lucky break. Otherwise we'd had to chase them woolies down and shoot um on the run."

He nodded in Mina's direction. "Yer woman looks kinda irate."

"I am not his woman," Mina snapped.

Devlin brushed some of the dirt from his clothes. "She's had a rough time of it. We were on top of the rise when the stampede started. We took cover in the rocks."

"You is mighty lucky, Dev. You coulda been killed."

"Did I not just say that?" Mina shouted, miffed at being ignored.

She checked around and realized her precious skull and even the stump where she had set it had been pulverized and trampled into oblivion by the herd. "No, it's gone!"

"Is she mad at us?" one man asked.

Devlin nodded. "Yup."

"What fer?"

Mina's mouth fell open. "What for? Besides nearly killing us? Now my Plesiosaur skull is gone!"

Nat scratched his bearded chin. "Her what?"

"Some old bone," Devlin explained.

"How come she's mad at us? We didn't take it."

"She thinks you ran the buffalo this way on purpose."

Nat pulled his tattered hat from his head. His bald dome shone white in the sunlight. "I'm real sorry you had such a scare, ma'am. But a body can't tell which way a herd is gonna run. Why, sometimes they just stand there and let us shoot um one after the other."

Mina opened her mouth but closed it again when she realized she would not get more of an apology. As the men continued to stare at her, she realized she must present quite a sight. No doubt, she looked as bedraggled as she felt.

Nat stepped away from the carcass and motioned for his men to continue. "Dev, I ain't one to butt into another man's business, but what in tarnation are you doing with a white woman out in these parts?"

"She's looking for fossils. Old bones have turned to rock," Devlin explained.

"I know what they are, but I sure can't imagine a gal wanting to risk her scalp to find some. Did ya know Standing Bear and his renegades are raiding out this way again?"

"Are you sure?" It was his worst fear.

"Yup. I ran into Swift Fox and his band a week ago. He's having a hard time keeping his young bucks from joining Standing Bear. Most of the Cheyenne Nation is at war."

"After Sand Creek, can you blame them?"

"There's been bad things done by both sides, but that don't make any of it right. Besides, Standing Bear was a bad egg even before Sand Creek. You'd know better than most."

Devlin's gaze locked with Mina's. "You're right."

She didn't understand the look of pain deep in his eyes.

Nat pulled at his long beard for a second, then said, "Swift Fox asked about you. I reckon you'd still be welcome in his lodge."

"It'll be a cold day in hell before I go back there."

The anger in his voice shocked Mina. He spun on his heels and walked back into the cavern. A minute later, he led his horse out, then swung up bareback. With a slap of the reins, he urged the paint into a reckless gallop up and over the hilltop.

Mina turned to the buckskin clad hunter. "Who is Swift Fox?"

"He's the chief of a small band of Cheyenne. Until she passed two years back, Dev's ma was his wife."

Chapter Twelve

As afternoon progressed to evening and Devlin still hadn't returned, Nat and his party made Mina comfortable with the loan of a tent and some buffalo robes to sleep on. She insisted her camp be placed upwind of the slaughter grounds. Once the tent was set up, she stayed inside. Watching the men engaged in the grizzly task of skinning and butchering the enormous beasts under a cloud of flies was more than she could abide. The buffalo steak they brought her for supper remained untouched on her plate.

Long after dark, she lay near the open tent flap, watching for Devlin's return. Eventually, she fell asleep without seeing him.

The next morning, she rose, brushed out her hair, and pinned it up in her usual tidy coil as best she could without the aid of a mirror and minus a few hairpins. A quick check of her arms and legs revealed a multitude of bruises and scrapes. Finding none that needed tending, she dressed and stepped out of the tent. Devlin was standing in front of it with both horses saddled and ready.

He tossed a biscuit at her. "Creek's low enough to cross. We should get going."

Without waiting for her reply, he mounted and headed down to the water's edge. Mina regretted the loss of her usual morning coffee but chose not to press the issue. Instead, she stuffed the biscuit in her pocket for later.

She gathered her saddlebags and parasol from inside the tent and strapped them behind her saddle, then she mounted and rode to where the plainsmen continued their job of butchering the remaining buffalo.

"I wish to thank you for your hospitality, gentlemen."

Nat tipped his hat. "Are ya sure ya won't change yer mind about going on? Yer welcome to ride back to Fort Harker with us."

"Thank you, but I must continue my journey." With a nod at them, she turned and rode down to the creek where Devlin waited.

She looked him over carefully. "How is your head?"

"Fine." He urged his horse into the muddy current. She followed. The water barely reached the horse's bellies now, and they made the crossing without incident. On the opposite shore, Buck waited with both mules.

Mina stopped beside him. "It's good to see you safe and sound. I wish to offer my sincere apologies for insisting we cross the creek when the water was so high. In the future, I shall give your words of caution much more weight."

A slight smile curved Buck's lips. "Good to know."

Devlin sat looking at the mules. "We're going to unpack these crates before we go another step."

"Why?" Mina demanded.

"Because I want to know what I'm hauling, and I don't want the mules overloaded. Empty the crates. We're only taking what we need."

She scowled at him. "I only brought what I require. Therefore, everything I have, I need."

Devlin swung down from his horse. "I'll be the judge of that."

Mina considered standing her ground but decided against it. She would let him have his way. Then he would see she knew what she was doing. "Very well, sir. Unpack and discard anything you think we can do without."

With Buck's help, they soon had all the boxes opened. Devlin inspected each of them and supervised their repacking. He ordered a few tools, half her clothes and a dozen bags of plaster of Paris left behind.

"I need the plaster," Mina insisted. "Fossils are brittle. The plaster is used to encase them and transport them safely."

"I'll let you keep enough to pack one fossil. That's all you're after, right?"

"It's impossible to know what other important discoveries I might make. I may need all of it."

"One bag or all of it stays."

She glared at him. "Four bags. It's the least I'll consider."

"Two bags."

She pursed her lips, then nodded. "Very well, three bags."

"Wait, I said two."

"And I said three. That is my last offer."

Devlin frowned but didn't argue further. After repacking the mules, he mounted, kicked his horse into a gallop and rode out far ahead of them.

Mina stayed beside Buck and stuffed an additional skirt and a blouse in her saddlebag when Devlin was out of sight. "Where is he going?"

"To scout ahead."

"I believe I'll give Sabiha a little gallop. We'd both like a chance to stretch our legs after being cooped up for so many days. If you will excuse me?"

She remounted and nudged her mare into a lope without waiting for Buck's answer.

After about half a mile, she reined in beside Devlin on the crest of a hill overlooking a wide valley. He didn't speak, yet he didn't seem opposed to her company. She pulled off her hat, drew in a deep breath of pure air and patted Sabiha's neck. "The view is quite spectacular, isn't it?"

"If you like grass."

A strong breeze fluttered the horses' manes and tugged at Mina's hair, threatening to pull it free of her pins. "I expect one either loves or hates this place. At first glance, there is nothing remarkable here, and yet all this vast openness is simply extraordinary. It leaves one feeling as if one owns the wind and the sky."

He cast her a speculative look. "Does it?"

She felt a blush heat her cheeks. "I expect I sound silly to you."

"Most people don't feel that way about the plains."

She leaned closer. "Ah, but then, I am not 'most people'."

"No, you're not."

The way his gaze lingered on her face caused a tingling sense of awareness to ripple through her. She looked away first. Nudging her horse into a walk, she was happy when Devlin fell in beside her. "Do you like the plains, Mr. Elder?"

"I thought you agreed to call me Devlin."

"So I did. Do you like the plains, Devlin?"

"More than any place on earth. I've traveled down to the Gulf of Mexico, even across the sea to France and England. Cities and mountains, they hem a person in. If the plains weren't here, I'd stay at sea."

"I can see why you feel that way. Did you travel to those faraway places with your family?"

"No."

He didn't elaborate. For a time, they rode side by side without speaking. Covertly, Mina studied the complex man who had captured her interest.

No, it was more than her interest. She felt drawn to him in a way she'd never experienced before. It surprised her how invigorated, how alive she felt, simply being near him. She longed to know more about him. To know everything about him. Yet she sensed he would not reveal himself easily.

"What happened at Sand Creek?"

He pulled his horse up sharply. "What?"

"Yesterday, I heard you tell those men they shouldn't be surprised the Cheyenne are at war after Sand Creek."

He nudged his mount forward and stared straight ahead. "Sand Creek was a massacre. Two years ago, the Cheyenne and Arapaho Chiefs: Black Kettle, White Antelope, Yellow Wolf, War Bonnet, Bear Man, and others sought a peace treaty with the army in Denver. They were told to take their people and camp at Sand Creek outside of Fort Lyon and wait. They did. At dawn, a man named Colonel Chivington, without orders, led close to seven hundred men in an unprovoked attack on the village. Over two hundred old men, women and children were butchered by his troops."

Mina listened to his story with a growing sense of dread. "But why attack a peaceful village?"

"Because they were Indians. Because Chivington saw becoming a great Indian killer as a wise political move. He had ambitions of running for public office."

"Surely it must have been some kind of mistake."

Devlin shook his head. "There was no mistake. Black Kettle had been given an American flag to fly from the top of his lodge in case he should meet with any troops out on the prairie. The flag was there, along with a small white flag of truce tied under it. Chivington knew exactly what he was doing."

"You're saying it was murder?"

"More than a hundred men, women and children as young as two months old were trapped by the troops under a cutout in the river's bank. The troops climbed to the top of the bank and shot everyone below them. What would you call it?"

She gaped at him in horror. "They shot the babies?"

"Yes, and they didn't stop there. They mutilated the bodies. The victorious troops rode into Denver with the scalps and severed breasts of the women as trophies and decorations."

Mina pressed a hand to her throat. "How horrible!"

"They were greeted as conquering heroes. The Cheyenne and Arapaho who escaped spread word of the white man's treachery."

"But Colonel Chivington is only one man. Not all whites are capable of such butchery."

"Tell that to the men whose wives and children were slaughtered. Is it surprising they want revenge?"

"Was Standing Bear one of them?"

"Yes. His pregnant wife and two sons were among the dead."

"Is that why he's leading others into war?"

"Standing Bear's hatred of the whites goes back a long time. He's a half-breed. His father was a white trapper. Standing Bear is a Dog Soldier, a member of a Cheyenne society of warriors. War is what they do. A man's worth is measured by how many men he has killed in battle."

She hesitated but couldn't contain her curiosity. Not when he was speaking so freely, something he rarely did. "The buffalo hunters mentioned your mother was married to a Cheyenne. Is that true?"

He rode in silence for a long time as she waited for his answer. Had she blundered by asking him a personal question?

Finally, he said, "Yes, it's true."

"To the chief, Swift Fox?"

"Yes."

"How is that possible? I mean, I've heard of white men taking native wives, but for a white woman to marry a native?"

"My mother was traded to Swift Fox for three ponies."

"I don't understand."

He stared at her for a long time. Had she made him angry? She looked away. "I'm sorry. I shouldn't pry. Please forgive me."

When he spoke, his voice was low. "I was seven when mother and I were taken captive in a Sioux raid on our homestead in Iowa."

The admission surprised her. "How awful! What about your father?"

"He wasn't home. He'd gone into town for supplies."

"How did you escape?"

"We didn't. We were captives of the Sioux for a year. I used to think my mother might have gotten away if she hadn't had me to worry about."

He related the tale with no trace of emotion in his voice. Only a quiver at the corner of his mouth betrayed the pain of his memories.

"I'm so very sorry." Mina's heart ached for the little boy who believed his mother's captivity was his fault.

"Later, we were traded to the Cheyenne. It wasn't an easy life, but it was better than being a Sioux slave, especially for my mother. She worked as hard as the other Cheyenne women did. They treated her with respect. I lived with the Cheyenne on and off until I was twenty-five."

"Thank you for telling me this."

Whatever memories she had stirred up seemed to cast a pall over him. She sought a way to lighten the mood. Her mare pranced in a little sidestep and pulled at the reins. Mina patted her neck. "It seems Sabiha is eager for more of a run. Do you think it is safe to do so?"

Devlin cocked one eyebrow at her. "You're asking my permission?"

She leaned toward him. "It comes as a shock, I'm sure, but yes, I am."

A ghost of a smile tugged at his lips. "A run will be fine if you don't tire her. Leave her enough steam so you can cover the same ground back as fast or faster."

"Thank you. Will you join me?"

At his hesitation, she added, "Might I suggest a short race between us to see who rides the faster horse?"

Afraid he would decline, she added, "I am not above placing a small wager on the outcome."

"You want to bet money your horse is faster than mine?"

"Indeed."

Devlin shook his head. "It wouldn't be fair."

"I shall give you a head start of one hundred yards. Will that do?"

"I meant it would be unfair to you."

"Oh, I see. You think Sabiha and I aren't up to the challenge? Ha! I am a tolerable rider. Shall we say, a small wager of five dollars?"

"Five bucks may be a small amount to you, but I'm broke."

"I'll accept an I.O.U."

"Let's wager for something other than money."

"Such as?"

"If I win, I claim a kiss."

Heat rushed to her face. "I think not."

"Afraid of losing?"

Her hackles rose as she glared at him. "There is no finer horse on the face of the earth than my Arab. When I win, you will do the camp chores for a week."

"Suits me." Buck shouted with a grin as he approached with the mules.

Devin scanned the horizon. "See that lone tree in the valley?"

She adjusted her glasses and squinted in the direction he pointed. She could just make out the green canopy half a mile away. "I do."

"From here around the tree and back to Buck. Agreed?"

"Agreed. I shall be the one to start us. Go!" She slammed her heels into Sabiha's sides, and the mare sprang forward.

Leaning over her mare's neck, Mina rose slightly in her stirrups. Urging her mount on, she listened for the sounds of pursuit. She didn't have long to wait before Devlin's sturdy pinto closed the gap between them, and the race was on.

The thrill of her powerful horse beneath her, the wind whipping her eyes to tears, the thunder of pounding hooves and the pure feeling of freedom caused a shout of laughter to well up and spring forth from her lips.

Sabiha jumped a ditch without breaking stride. Mina's heart swelled with pride. A rocking chair would have provided a rougher ride than the back of her flying steed.

At the tree, Mina leaned into the turn and let Sabiha have her head as she gathered speed, racing back the way they'd come. A glance over her shoulder showed Devlin had fallen behind a few paces. Perhaps he was saving his horse for a sprint at the end. It wouldn't make any difference. She knew Sabiha had plenty left.

Charging over the bright grass, Mina soon saw Buck waiting for them. A moment later, Devlin drew alongside. He touched the brim of his hat and sent her a cocky grin as his horse pulled ahead.

She let him gain a bit of ground, then she crouched lower and shouted, "Now, Sabiha! Show him what a daughter of the wind can do!"

Like a genie popping out of an uncorked bottle, the white mare shot forward. In a few strides, she passed her rival, and by the time she plunged past Buck, she was a good ten lengths in front.

Laughing with sheer joy, Mina drew up her blowing horse and turned to Devlin. "Well, sir, have we impressed you?"

He reined his horse in beside her. "I will admit to some surprise, but impressed? No, milady, you have not impressed me."

She was decidedly pleased to have her words echoed by him. "Stick around and I will."

He touched the brim of his hat. "I'm beginning to believe that. She's one the best horses I've ever seen?"

"Thank you." Mina adjusted her glasses on the bridge of her nose and discovered her hair had come undone when the wind blew a strand into her mouth. "Oh, dear. I seem to have lost more of my hairpins."

Devlin leaned over and plucked one about to fall from the ends of her tresses. "You should leave it down. It's pretty."

She treasured his offhand compliment. "That would be most impractical. The wind would quickly turn it into a bird's nest. I prefer to keep it confined."

Buck trotted up to join them. "That was some fine riding, Mrs. Smith."

"Thank you, Buck, but the credit goes to Sabiha. She is truly a daughter of the wind, as the Arab's call them." Mina patted the mare's neck. Sabiha pranced and pulled at the reins, signaling her desire to continue her run.

"She's got speed," Devlin admitted. "But does she have endurance?"

"She does, sir. She could run for many more miles without tiring. I don't hesitate to say she would run until her heart burst for me."

His smile faded. "Let's hope you never have to put her to the test."

*

Devlin turned his horse and noticed a faint smudge of dark blue on the western distant horizon. A ripple of unease moved over him. He glanced at Mina. "Now I know you can ride, can you shoot?"

She twisted her hair up and tucked it under her hat. "As you well know, I go armed with a pistol at all times."

"Do you know how to use a rifle?"

"I do. I'm sure you saw the two packed with my belongings."

"Get them both out where you can get your hands on them in a hurry."

She looked at him in surprise. "Do you mean now?"

"What is it?" Buck asked, following Devlin's gaze.

"Maybe nothing, but it looks like smoke."

Mina shaded her eyes, peering into the distance. "I don't see anything."

"It was there," Devlin said.

"Could be a prairie fire or smoke from a wagon train camp," Buck offered.

"Could be. We'll know soon enough." The hair on the back of

Devlin's neck was sending prickles of warning down his spine. Whatever it was, they were heading toward it.

"With the wind so strong from the south, we won't be in any danger from a fire to the west of us," Mina said.

She was right, but the stiff wind would also keep the smoke low and scatter it. He didn't like riding toward trouble without being prepared.

He swung down from his horse. "Unpack your rifles and ammunition."

When Mina stood in front of Devlin with her carbine, he said. "Shoot something."

She checked the gun had a round in the chamber and said, "What would you like me to shoot?"

She handled the gun with assurance. Seeing that made him feel a little better. Artie had hated guns. He hadn't been able to hit squat with one. The only weapon Artie had used was a blowgun and darts he brought back from some jungle. He'd hunted birds and squirrels with it, even a deer once. It was an effective way to kill game, but a blowgun would be a useless in an actual fight. It was a stealth weapon, meant to be used at close range. A rifle could kill an enemy before they got close enough to kill her.

Devlin scanned the countryside, then pointed to the south. "See the jackrabbit watching us from beside that large rock about fifty yards out?"

"I do."

"Shoot him."

"Do we require the meat?" she asked sweetly.

He frowned. "I need to know you can hit what you aim at."

"I don't kill an animal unless it poses a threat or unless I need meat. The jackrabbit does not look dangerous. Are they ferocious creatures?"

Why was she so stubborn? "Don't argue with me."

"I am not arguing. I'm stating a principle."

He pointed. "Shoot it!"

She glared at him. "I will not."

"For God's sakes, woman!"

"Oh, very well." She adjusted her glasses, raised the rifle to her shoulder and fired. Her horse barely flinched, proving the mare had been well trained.

He looked toward the rock and saw the rabbit hightailing it across the grass. "You missed."

"I did not. To the right of the rock, you will find a small cactus. It has a hole about two inches down from the top. The rabbit seemed harmless, but the plant looks quite vicious."

She slipped her rifle into its scabbard at the front of her saddle and waited.

Buck paced off the distance, then squatted beside the rock. "It's like she said," he called back.

She faced Devlin. "Are you satisfied?"

"What if it had been a man?"

"I know men can be far more dangerous than rabbits or cacti. I will do what I must, never fear."

"Good. But always remember to save one bullet."

"What for?"

"For yourself."

A look of speechless shock spread across her face. He knew she understood his meaning. A quick death by her own hand would be a thousand times better than what awaited her as a captive of Standing Bear.

When Buck rejoined them, they moved out together, heading westward. As the day wore on, the sun overhead grew hotter. By mid-morning, Mina unfurled her parasol. By midday, even the horses and mules were feeling the heat, moving with lagging steps and lowered heads. Only Sabiha seemed unaffected by the soaring temperature. She moved alertly with her head and tail held high.

Devlin wiped a trickle of sweat from his forehead with the back of his sleeve. He briefly spotted a thin column of smoke on the horizon again before the wind picked up and it vanished. This time Buck saw it, too, and the men exchanged worried glances.

"Think it's from the station at Fossil Creek?" Buck asked, keeping his voice low.

"Could be. We can't be more than two miles from there."

"Maybe Jim is burning brush or something."

"Maybe." Devlin didn't point out the past week of soaking rain would have made brush burning almost impossible.

Mina mopped her brow with her hankie and fluttered it briefly in front of her face. "I can't believe I would ever say this, but I miss our cave. I had no idea it could get so hot."

"This ain't nothing," Buck said. "I've known it to be over a hundred in the shade out here in the summer."

"What shade?" The trail had taken them away from the river. Since morning, the only tree they had passed was the one they'd used to mark their racecourse.

"Ready to turn back?" Devlin asked.

"Certainly not. Buck and I were merely discussing the weather."

"It won't get any cooler," Devlin warned.

"I doubt it gets as hot as it does in Giza."

"Is that near London?" Buck asked.

She smiled and shook her head. "It is in Egypt where the great pyramids are located."

Buck motioned toward her mare. "Is that where you got your horse?"

"Near there. We were touring the pyramids when a local man convinced Arthur he knew the location of another tomb filled with treasure. For a handsome fee, he would guide us there. Heedless of my warnings, for I didn't trust the scoundrel, Arthur purchased the man's information and set out on an ill-conceived expedition. Needless to say, we soon became lost in the desert after our well-paid guide vanished."

Mesmerized by the tale, Buck pressed his horse closer. "What happened then?"

"Fortunately, when were we nearly out of water, we encountered a tribe of Bedouins. They're a nomadic people who roam the Arabian desert, raising sheep, camels and beautiful horses. Their horses are so highly prized they may not be bought or sold."

"How'd you git yours?"

"She stole her," Devlin suggested, just to see the look of outrage he knew would follow.

"I most certainly did not!" Mina exclaimed.

He hid his smile.

"So how did you git her?" Buck asked.

"She was a gift. The Sheik, the tribe leader, had a young son who was very ill. I was able to successfully treat the boy with our medical supplies. As it turned out, he was the man's only son. In gratitude, we were given an escort back to Cairo, and I was given Sabiha as a gift. I prize her greatly."

"So will a lot of men," Devlin added.

"She is well trained. She will not be easy to steal."

"You haven't met many Cheyenne. Young boys practice stealing mounts almost as soon as they can walk. It's a great honor to steal an enemy's horse. A man whose son did so would give a feast and invite everyone in the village to hear the tale of his son's deed."

She met and held his gaze. "Did Swift Fox give such a feast in your honor?"

An old, familiar coldness crept up from his soul. Did she think less of him now she knew how he and his mother had lived? It was a prejudice he'd faced often, but somehow it was more painful coming from her.

"Many times," he replied without flinching.

She sent him a sudden, unexpected bright smile. "Excellent. Should my mare be stolen, I shall depend upon you to steal her back. It's good to know one's companions have skills. I, myself, am an excellent seamstress and a passing hand at whist and poker. Buck, what talents do you possess?"

Devlin pulled his horse to a stop and stared as she and Buck continued on. Did she really see horse stealing as a talent akin to playing cards? He couldn't figure her out.

A sudden shift in the wind brought the smell of smoldering wood and something more ominous. He hurried to catch up with Buck. The mules smelled it, too. He could tell by the way they laid back their ears and pulled at their lead ropes. Devlin drew his rifle and motioned for Buck and Mina to stay behind him. For once, Mina followed his directions.

He rode ahead slowly, alert for danger or signs of ambush. Beyond the bend, the remains of the stage station came into view. The stone chimney poked out of the charred ruins of the house. On a clothesline, white sheets fluttered in the breeze as if it were any ordinary washday. Just beyond the house, a stagecoach lay on its side. Its broken front axle and shattered wheel gave mute testament to how it had overturned. The horses were gone.

The large barn had one scorched side but remained intact. It may have been too wet to burn. The doors stood open. The corrals were empty. In the yard between the house and the barn, four bodies lay staked to the ground.

Chapter Thirteen

"Oh God, it's Jim!" Buck's voice cracked with anguish. He dropped the mules' lead ropes and started forward.

Devlin caught hold of his reins. "Buck, wait. It could be a trap."

"That's my brother out there." Buck spurred his horse forward, forcing Devlin to let go.

Dismounting, Devlin dropped to one knee and raised his rifle to his shoulder. "Cover him."

"Those people may need our help." Mina was still trying to make sense of the scene.

"Those people are dead."

"You can't be sure of that."

"Unless you want Buck dead, too, do as I say!"

She dropped from her horse and assumed the same position as Devlin. Her rifle barrel wavered as her pulse pounded in her ears. She scanned the grisly scene, looking for movement in the dark interior of the barn or the trees along the creek beyond.

"Easy, Mina." Devlin was rock still beside her.

His calm voice settled her. She took a deep breath and steadied her gun. Buck's life might depend on her accuracy.

The distant sound of hoofbeats sent her pulse rate higher still. She looked past the station. It wasn't a war party returning. A Cavalry troop approached from the road from the west, but they were still a half mile away. The surge of relief she felt left her lightheaded. She lowered her gun and leaned on the barrel to stay upright.

Buck's tormented cry cut through her fog of dizziness. She looked up to see him on his knees beside one of the still figures and knew he had found his brother.

Staggering to her feet, she started toward him. Devlin's tight grip on her arm stopped her.

"Don't go down there."

She didn't want to go, but she had to. "Buck needs us."

"You don't want to see what was done to them."

Did he think her a weakling? She stiffened her spine. She wasn't, and she wouldn't allow him or anyone else to treat her as if she were. "I am a grown woman, Mr. Elder. I have seen death before."

"Not like this, you haven't."

"You don't need to coddle me. I'm not frightened."

"You should be," he shouted, jerking her close. His fingers dug painfully into her arm. The face she had found so handsome seemed to belong to a stranger. His eyes glinted with some powerful emotion. Whether it was anger or fear, she couldn't tell.

"You're hurting me," she said, struggling to keep her voice calm.

His mouth twisted in a grimace, and he pushed her away. "Go then. See exactly what will happen to you if you persist in this hairbrained quest. But know this, Mrs. Smith. I'm not taking you one step further."

He turned his back on her and loosened the ropes on the pack mule.

Mina scowled at him. "What are you doing? Those supplies belong to me."

He pulled a shovel from the pack. "Relax. You'll get it back when I've finished the graves."

He shouldered past her, and she reluctantly followed. The closer she got to the bodies, the more overpowering the smell of death became. With lagging steps, she approached the first corpse. It lay spread-eagle on the ground, naked and horribly mutilated. As her eyes took in the torn flesh and blood-soaked ground around it, her brain finally recognized the body at her feet was a woman lying on the tattered remains of a red dress dotted with tiny white flowers.

Mina clamped her hands to her mouth, but she couldn't stop the bile that rose in a gush. She turned aside and staggered a few feet away before she sank to her knees and retched until nothing was left.

Gasping for breath, she leaned forward on shaky arms and let her head hang down until the queasiness passed. After a few minutes, something cool touched her cheek. She looked up to see Devlin squatting beside her. He raised her chin and wiped her face with a damp cloth. Grateful, she took it from him and pressed it to her lips.

He left her, and she heard the flap of cloth. Daring to look, she saw him spread a clean white sheet over the woman's body.

Mina swallowed hard. "Please tell me she was dead before they did such horrible things to her."

"She lived for hours and when she wasn't screaming, she could listen to her husband screaming as they tortured him."

Mina pressed her hands to her ears. "Stop it. No more, I beg you. What kind of men could do this?"

Devlin grabbed her arms and forced her to look at him. "A Cheyenne half-breed named Standing Bear and his followers. Now, do you understand what you're risking? Is this enough to make you give up?"

The sound of a dozen horses thundering into the yard told Mina the Cavalry had arrived, much too late for the people here. Devlin released her and walked away.

A fresh-faced young officer drew his mount to a halt beside her. "Madam, are you all right?"

She nodded mutely.

He swung down from his horse, took her arm and helped her to her feet. "I am Lieutenant Olson at your service. Can you tell me what happened here?"

"I am Lady Wilhelmina Smith. I don't know what transpired, Lieutenant. We just arrived ourselves."

"Then you weren't a passenger on the stagecoach?"

"No."

"Please stay here. Sergeant," he barked. "Take a detail and check the barn and woods."

Mina looked toward Buck and saw Devlin at his side. Devlin carefully spread a sheet over the body beside Buck. As he covered the man's face, Buck grabbed his hand and cried, "Cut him loose first."

Drawing his knife, Devlin severed the bonds holding the body outstretched. Only then did Buck allow Devlin to cover his brother's face.

Mina turned away and moved toward the clothesline. A tub and washboard sat on a stump beside the gaily fluttering clothes. The reminder of a simple, homey task seemed bizarrely out-of-place amid the death and destruction surrounding her. She reached out to touch a small garment and realized it was a nightshirt for a child. None of the bodies she saw were children.

Looking toward the smoldering ruins of the house, she shuddered. She crossed to where the young officer stood in conference with his men.

"Lieutenant, I fear your men will need to search for the body of a little child as well."

He nodded and gave the order. Rather than watch them searching through the charred remains of the house, Mina went to Buck.

She laid a hand on his shoulder. When he looked up, she saw such sorrow etched on his youthful face she nearly broke down. Choking back tears, she said, "I'm so sorry."

"Them stinking, murdering savages. I'll kill them all if it takes me to the end of my days. They didn't have no call to do this. Jim never hurt nobody." His voice cracked as he wiped his eyes with his sleeve.

"He's at peace now, Buck. They can't hurt him anymore. Try to take comfort in that."

"Jim was all the family I had left. We made it through the war and came west together. You should have seen him when he met Anna. He couldn't stop grinning for days. Married her quick as a flash, but she didn't like being a soldier's wife. When the chance to run this station came up, he jumped at it. I wish to God he'd stayed in the army. I wish to God we'd gotten here one day sooner."

Unable to find words to comfort him, Mina remained by his side, her hand resting on his shoulder.

After the soldiers had finished checking the area, a burial detail was formed. Devlin joined the men in digging the graves. Buck knelt by his brother, unmoving. When the graves were finished, several of the soldiers took the bodies and lowered them into the ground. The young officer pulled a small book of psalms from his saddlebag and read from it. Mina bowed her head as Devlin returned to her side. He didn't touch her, but she gained comfort from his nearness.

The young officer finished reading and came to Mina's side. "My men found no sign of a child's body."

At his words, Buck's eyes lost some of their haunted appearance. "My brother has a son. His name is Caleb. He's three."

"It's possible the Indians carried him off as a captive. My men will follow and overtake them. If they have the boy, we'll get him back."

"No!"

Everyone turned to look at Devlin. He stood apart from the group. For the first time, Mina wondered just which side of this terrible war he was on? Had he done savage things like this when he lived among the Cheyenne? She shivered and crossed her arms.

Buck moved to stand in front of Devlin. "If they've got Caleb, we have to go after them."

Devlin laid a hand on Buck's shoulder. "This was the work of Standing Bear and his renegades. They wouldn't take the boy."

"He isn't here. They must have him."

"Even if they do, you'll never get him back alive. Say your goodbyes to your brother and let it go."

Buck shoved Devlin's hand away. "Not when there's a chance I can save my brother's son."

The lieutenant spoke up. "We'll head out soon as you're ready. They have a day's start. Mr. Elder, I understand you've scouted for the army in the past. We could use your help now."

Devlin shook his head. "You won't catch Standing Bear's band. They've got fresh horses and too much of a head start."

"Are you saying you won't help?" the lieutenant asked.

*

Devlin met Mina's gaze. He saw the disbelief in her eyes slowly change to disgust. Hell, let her think he was a coward. Why should it matter what she thought, anyway?

It mattered, but it didn't change what he had to do. "No, Lieutenant, I won't go with you."

Buck spat on the ground at Devlin's feet. "And I thought you were my friend."

Devlin caught Buck's arm as he turned away. "If they have the boy and you catch up with them, they'll kill him to slow you down, or they'll use him to bait a trap and kill you. If you don't chase them, they may leave him with the next village they visit. It's a chance."

"I can't ride off and pretend Caleb doesn't matter." Buck jerked away from Devlin and crossed to the graves.

Mina joined him there. With a voice that wavered but didn't break, Buck recited the Lord's Prayer, then bent to grasp a handful of dirt. As he tossed it onto his brother's body, he said. "Every one of them will pay for this, Jim. Every last one."

The burial detail filled in the graves. Within the hour, the column had remounted. The lieutenant rode to where Devlin and Mina stood with the mules.

"Ma'am, my advice to you would be to return to Fort Harker with all possible haste."

She frowned. "I thought Fort Fletcher is closer."

"The fort was heavily damaged in the flood last week. We're moving everything to Fort Hays, but it will take time. There has been more raiding to the west. In my opinion, going east will be safer for you."

"I understand. Please be careful, sir. I wish you Godspeed."

He touched the brim of his hat, then rode to the front of his men. With a wave of his arm, he set them in motion. Buck waited until the last of them left the yard, then he turned his horse and followed.

When Buck was out of sight, Mina spoke. "Would the Indians really kill the boy?"

"Most wouldn't. The Cheyenne love and value children. Standing Bear would do it in a heartbeat if it helped him escape or if it made one white man suffer."

"How is it you know him so well?"

Devlin looked at her, his face impassive except for some emotion deep in his eyes. Instinct told her it was pain.

"Standing Bear and I were raised in the same lodge. I considered him my brother."

He took the mare's reins from Mina's hand. "We'll camp here tonight and start back in the morning."

He led the stock into the corral. When they were unsaddled and the supplies safely stowed in the barn, he carried Mina's bedroll up a wooden ladder leading to the barn's loft.

"You can sleep up here," he called out. "I'll bed down outside."

She didn't relish the idea of spending the night with four new graves a stone's throw away, but didn't voice her misgivings. Devlin would take it as a sign of weakness. Her gaze was drawn to the mounds of dirt marking the final resting places of Buck's family and two strangers. Did the stagecoach driver and his unlucky passenger have a family?

She leaned against the rough log wall of the barn. Was there a wife somewhere waiting anxiously for her husband to return? How Mina wished she could spare that woman the days and painful nights of frantic worry as hope faded but never truly died.

At least these men had a Christian burial and a grave to mark the place they were laid to rest. Had anyone buried Arthur, or did his bones lie scattered over the endless expanse of grass? Would she ever know? She walked to the rear of the barn so the graves were out of sight.

She would go back now and wait until the army had quelled the native attacks. One day, she would return to prove Arthur had made a brilliant discovery. Vincent could face the world proud of what his son had accomplished, see his son's name recorded in history. One day.

She would resume her study of fossils and perhaps make a great discovery of her own. This vast land might promise freedom, but it could crush the soul with floods, heat and dangers she hadn't imagined. Even so, she would come back.

A faint whining caught her attention. It came from behind her. She turned in puzzlement to stare at the barn wall. At the back corner, a mound of fresh dirt indicated where an animal had dug out a space beneath the logs.

She heard the faint whimper again. Kneeling in front of the opening, she tried to peer into the den-like cavity, but it sloped upward. She stretched out flat on the ground and found herself face to face with a large mongrel.

She had only a second to note the blood on its muzzle and the feathered tip of an arrow protruding from the animal's chest before the dog bared its teeth and growled deep in its throat.

"Nice doggy," she crooned as she inched backward.

She heard another whimper from behind the dog. The animal never took its eyes off Mina.

"Mama?" The single word sent Mina's heart soaring.

"Caleb?" She started forward again, only to stop when the dog snarled, and half rose. Backing away, she waited until the animal settled down.

"Caleb, you can come out now," she called softly.

"I want Mama."

"I know you do, sweetheart, but you have to come out of there."

"Taffy won't let me." A grubby, small arm circled the dog's neck from behind and tugged, but the dog didn't budge.

"I'm thirsty. I want Mama."

"You can have all the water you want and something to eat, too, if you just come out from under there."

"Are the Injuns gone?"

"Yes, dear."

"They shot Taffy. She's got an arrow in her." Caleb's voice broke on a sob.

"Can you squeeze past her?"

"No, I tried lots of times."

"All right, Caleb. I'm going to get help."

"Don't leave," he begged.

Her heart squeezed in sympathy. "I'll be right back, I promise."

She wiggled out from under the barn and shouted for Devlin.

He was beside her in a reassuringly short time with his revolver drawn. "What's wrong?"

"I've found Buck's nephew. He is under here."

Devlin slowly holstered his gun. "I'm sorry."

"No, he's alive! He's in a small space between two of the logs, but he can't get out. There is a rather large dog under there with him. The creature probably saved the boy's life. However, she is wounded. She doesn't seem to know the difference between friend and foe and won't let the boy out or me in. See for yourself."

As she had done, Devlin lay down and wormed his way under the barn. The growling escalated into ferocious barking. Neither his coaxing nor his stern commands had any effect on the animal. Mina could hear Caleb crying now.

Afraid the dog would attack, Mina tugged on Devlin's belt. "Come out, you're scaring them."

He inched backward and rose to his knees beside her. "You're right, she won't budge."

"Perhaps we can tempt her out with food or water?"

"Try it. I'll look and see if we can get to the boy through the floor inside."

Mina drew a pail of water from the well, grabbed some jerky from the supplies, and placed her offerings just inside the opening. Devlin soon rejoined her.

"Buck's brother built one hell of a barn. The tack room floor is planked, but I think the boy is between the damn walls of the tack room and the supports for the hayloft."

"I have asked you to not swear, sir. Can you get through the floor?"

"Not where he is. There isn't enough room to swing a *damn* axe."

Ignoring his deliberate jibe, she said, "Perhaps the water will draw her out."

Mina knelt. "Caleb, we've put some water here for Taffy. When she comes out to drink, I want you to come out, too."

"I'm thirsty and hungry."

"I know, sweetie. Try to get Taffy to come out." She rose and pulled on Devlin's arm. "We need to get back where she can't see us."

"She doesn't have to see us. She can smell us. Let's hope she's thirsty enough to risk it."

They moved to the end of the corral and waited. Devlin squatted on his heels while Mina shifted from one foot to the other in growing impatience.

After half an hour, Devlin rose. "This isn't working."

"I agree, but what else can we do?"

He stared hard at her. "You stay here."

Walking back to the den, he drew his revolver and lay down.

Mina's tired brain slowly grasped what he had planned. He was going to shoot the poor animal.

"Devlin, don't. She's only trying to protect the child. You can't kill her for that."

"With an arrow in her, she'll die anyway. This is quicker and humane. Caleb won't have to suffer along with her."

"But what if you hit the boy? Devlin don't do this. We'll think of something."

He inched his way under the barn. In desperation, she grabbed his foot and pulled. "No, please. I'm begging you."

"Mina, stop it."

"I won't let you do it." She pulled harder, then fell on her rump in the dust with his empty boot in her hands. She looked from the worn leather to his foot and saw a small hole in the heel of his sock. It needed mending. She burst into tears.

*

Devlin rolled over, sat up, and stared at Mina. Had she gone loco? She sat clutching his boot to her chest, sobbing like a demented woman. "What in hell are you doing?"

"Don't swear at me," she shrieked, and threw the boot at his head. It missed but not by much. A look of shock crossed her face. She pressed her hand to her mouth.

"Look what you made me do," she mumbled between sobs.

Picking up his boot, he yanked it on. "I didn't make you do a damn thing."

The sound of her weeping cut into his soul. Reluctantly, he rose and crossed to where she sat. Squatting down, he gently lifted her chin until she looked at him. "It's only a dog."

"There has been so much killing. This place reeks with the smell of blood. The ground is soaked with it. It has to stop. Please make it stop."

He pulled her close. "I wish I could."

She wound her arms around his neck and buried her face against his shoulder. He stroked her hair and sought words to comfort her. This was so far from his normal life Devlin wasn't sure where to start. Then he thought about his sister. Namid had had a puppy she loved when she was five. One day, she found it dead outside the lodge. Her sobs, like Mina's, had been heart-breaking.

He patted Mina's back tenderly. "Please don't cry. It's a mercy to put the dog down. You don't want her to suffer, do you? You don't want Caleb to suffer any more than he has already, do you?"

As he spoke, it was Artie's face he saw twisted in pain.

"Not if it's hopeless," she whispered at last.

It had been hopeless for Artie. Devlin knew that.

Mina loosened her hold on him. "I'm okay now."

Her voice was stronger and filled with the determination he respected, even when it annoyed him. He should let go of her, but he didn't want to. All she sought was comfort, but he wanted more. More time with her in his arms. Something he didn't deserve.

She sat back and wiped her tear-stained face with both hands. "I'm sorry. I'm not usually such a watering pot. Do what you must."

He nodded, not trusting himself to speak. She had a right to her tears. Few women could have endured a day like this without breaking down. He wanted to tell her how much he admired her strength, how much he was coming to care for her, but he didn't. Instead, he turned back to the barn and worked his way under again.

The yellow dog bared her teeth and growled as she faced him. He aimed his pistol at a spot between her eyes. "Caleb, I want you to move as far away from Taffy as you can."

"Why?"

"Because I said so, boy. Now do it!"

"Yes, sir."

He listened to the sound of the child moving backwards. The dog looked over her shoulder and whined once. When Devlin cocked his gun, she pinned her gaze on him and snarled.

He looked down the barrel and slowly closed his finger over the trigger. Behind him, he heard Mina's muffled crying. The dog stopped growling and grew silent. She laid her head on her paws and watched him—as if she knew what he had to do.

Chapter Fourteen

Devlin's hand wavered. The dog was ready to die to protect her boy. He took his finger off the trigger and dropped his head on his outstretched arm. He couldn't do it.

The blasted woman was making him soft.

Squirming backwards until he was clear of the building, Devlin stood up. Mina sat where he'd left her, her face buried in her hands, her shoulders shaking with each sob she tried to stifle. Ignoring the desire to pull her into his arms again, he holstered his gun and walked to the front of the barn.

Inside, he cut a long length of leather from one of the hanging harnesses. Then he grabbed his blanket and wrapped it tightly around his arm. Satisfied with the thick pad, he picked up a rope and went outside. He stopped in front of Mina and dropped one end of the rope and the leather strap on her lap.

"When I give the word, I want you to pull on the rope."

Astonishment filled her eyes when she looked at him. "What are you going to do?"

"Probably get my face bitten off, but I think I can get her out of there." If there was a reward for stupidity, he'd win hands down. The gorgeous smile Mina gave him just might be worth the pain of a dog bite.

Crawling under the barn again, he pushed his padded arm in front of him and held an open loop of his rope in his other hand. The dog watched him, growling low in her throat, but with less menace than she'd shown before. Maybe she was getting used to the smell of him. Or maybe she was getting weak from loss of blood. Either way, it might make it easier to move her.

"Good girl," he crooned, inching closer. "I'm not gonna hurt your boy. I just want to get both of you out."

She lunged without warning, sinking her teeth into his blanket-covered arm, twisting and shaking it in a crushing grip. The narrow space made it nearly impossible to move, but he pushed her backwards until he could slip a loop over one front paw.

Releasing his arm, she snapped at the rope. Working free of the blanket, he threw a fold over her head and wound the rope around her neck to hold it in place. The determined dog freed herself enough to bite his hand. Ignoring the pain, he covered her with more blanket and added a second loop of rope to her head.

"Now, Mina!" He wormed backward as the rope tightened and grabbed the line when he was out. Together, they pulled the thrashing dog free of her den.

Once she was out, Devlin laid his full weight on her. "Bring that strap. We'll make a muzzle."

Mina raced to do as he asked. Slowly, he uncovered the dog's head. Mina looped the leather strip over the dog's nose. Whatever fight she had vanished. She lay still except for her rapid panting.

The arrow he thought buried in her chest had lodged between her shoulder blade and her ribs. It hadn't penetrated her chest. The iron tip protruded just behind her elbow. Caleb's guardian wasn't doomed, after all.

Mina darted under the barn and emerged with Caleb, dusty and covered with cobwebs. She offered him a drink from her canteen. He took several long gulps.

"Not too fast. It will make you sick." She took the water away and grinned at Devlin. "You see, it wasn't hopeless. I knew you'd find a way. Bless you."

He'd never been a hero in anyone's eyes.

Caleb looked at Devlin. A fierce scowl crossed his small face. He launched himself at his rescuer with fists flying. "Don't hurt, Taffy!"

Mina saw Devlin couldn't fend off the boy's blows and hold the animal. The dog, hearing the boy's agitated voice, struggled to join the fight. Mina intervened by picking Caleb up and carrying him away. "Hush now. He isn't hurting Taffy. He's trying to help her."

"I want Mama!" Caleb wailed and began sobbing.

"I know you do." She held his small, warm body close. He wrapped his arms around her neck and held on tight. How could she make a child so young understand what had happened? Realizing she didn't know where to start, she kept silent and carried him into the barn, then sat down on a wooden box still holding the child. The smell of charred wood filled the air. Outside, she heard a loud yelp from the dog, then silence.

"I'll bet you're hungry," she said, hoping to distract Caleb. At his nod, she smiled. "Good. You sit right here, and I'll get you something to eat."

She tried to pull his arms loose, but he tightened his grip. "It's all right, Caleb. I won't leave you. I promise."

His grip didn't slacken. Instead of trying to pry him off, she lifted him and opened a bundle of her supplies with one hand. "Do you like peaches? I have a can right here, but you'll have to let go of me so I can open it."

Still, he refused to release her. Each time she tried to pull his arms down, his grip tightened until she was nearly choking. At a sound, she looked up to see Devlin standing in the doorway with the dog in his arms. The animal wore her makeshift muzzle. Subdued and no longer trying to bite, she stared at Mina with pleading eyes.

"Look, Caleb. Here's Taffy. She's fine. Mr. Elder has removed the arrow from her."

"He did?" Caleb loosened his grip enough to look.

"I think she'll be good as new in a few days." Devlin carried the dog into the stall and laid her on the straw. The dog sat up and gave a feeble wag of her tail.

"I want Taffy," Caleb said, letting go of Mina and struggling to get down. Once released, he threw his arms around the dog and hugged her tightly. She whined and licked his face.

Mina massaged her chafed neck. She glanced at Devlin and noticed blood dripping from his hand. "You're hurt."

"It's nothing. I'll live."

"A dog bite can easily become infected. You'd better let me have a look." She took his hand and moved to where the light was better. She sucked in her breath when she saw the three-inch jagged tear across the back of his hand.

"It's not as bad as it looks," he said.

"Nonsense. I can see exactly how bad it is. Wait here. No, better yet, go wash it with fresh water from the well while I find my medical kit."

"Don't fuss."

"I am not fussing. I'm being practical. I refuse to be stranded in the wilderness with a child, a wounded dog and a guide who is sick out of his mind with fever from a poorly treated bite all for the lack of a small amount of iodine and an excessive amount of male pride."

He leaned down and kissed her firmly on her mouth.

The touch of his lips robbed Mina of coherent thought. Her emotions spiraled out of control, making her dizzy. When he pulled away, she could only gape at him as her world slowly righted enough to think.

A hint of a smile lifted the corner of his mouth. "Did anyone ever tell you how cute you are when you're angry?"

"No," she uttered weakly.

He gave her a lopsided grin and pulled his hand from her grip. "Hard to believe."

Mina watched him walk toward the well and pressed her fingers to her mouth as if to hold on to the feelings he evoked. How was it possible to be so affected by a simple kiss?

It took several seconds for her scattered wits to settle into order. When they did, indignation flared.

The man was becoming entirely too familiar. It had to stop. She took a step in his direction to set him straight but changed her mind. It wouldn't do to look as though she were running after him. Better to collect her scattered wits and face him with some semblance of control. She needed to confront him with rational behavior.

After checking on Caleb, who still had his arms wrapped around Taffy, she gave the boy his promised treat of peaches and left him sharing his feast with his dog. She then retrieved her medical kit and crossed to the well.

Devlin had his shirt off. As she watched, he poured a bucket of water over his head, shook the excess from his hair and sluiced off the rest with his hands. Instead of chastising him for his earlier behavior, she found herself intrigued by the play of his muscles under his tanned skin. His bronze color proved he went shirtless often. It was hard not to wonder how the rest of his body looked.

He was beautiful but not flawless. On his upper chest, matching puckered lines below his collar bones looked as if they had been carved into him. A round scar on his left arm appeared to be a bullet wound.

Her initial impression of him came back to her. He was a dangerous man. One who had kissed her, not once, but twice.

A man did not kiss a woman without declaring his intentions. Not unless the man was a cad or the woman a light skirt.

She certainly didn't qualify as a woman of easy virtue. *How dare he treat her like one!* "Mr. Elder, I must speak with you."

"I'm listening." He turned away and reached for his shirt. Faded pink lines crisscrossed his back. He'd been brutally whipped in the past.

She stood up straight and clasp her hands together. "I insist you refrain from kissing me."

He casually leaned his hip against the stone well, his smile much too smug. "You didn't like it?"

"That is hardly the point, sir."

"So you did like it?"

"Yes. No. What I mean is that you must strive to curb your male impulses."

"Why?"

"I am not a woman to be trifled with, nor a woman to be taken advantage of." She set her medical supplies on the stone ledge.

He moved closer and held out his injured hand. "But you are most certainly a woman."

She arched one eyebrow. "And to think how hard I tried to disguise the fact. What gave me away?"

Her sarcasm worked. His smug smile slipped. She took his hand and dabbed at the faint trickle of blood with a clean cloth.

"I noticed you were a whole lot of woman the first time I laid eyes on you. Too much for that prissy husband of yours. I can make you forget him."

She dumped a liberal amount of iodine on his hand. It had to hurt, but the only sign she saw was his tightly pressed lips.

"My husband may still be alive. If he's not, I will never forget him. I don't intend to discuss this further. I have asked you not to kiss me. Do I have your word you will behave yourself?"

He pulled his hand away and blew on it. "Don't worry, milady. You made your point."

"Excellent."

Yet, as she watched him walk away, it didn't feel like a victory. It felt as if she had lost something precious rather than winning a confrontation. She wasn't a woman of easy virtue. She never could be. Yet, she couldn't help wondering what it would be like to go willingly into Devlin Elder's arms.

*

Devlin delayed entering the barn as darkness fell. He told himself it was to keep watch, but it wasn't. She was in there, tempting him, but completely out of reach. He should have known better than to kiss her, but the impulse had been too strong to resist. He wanted her in the worst way.

Her rebuff made it all too plain how she felt. Too bad it didn't erase the memory of her soft, yielding lips. Thinking about the sweet taste of her only made him want her more.

The sound of soft singing drifted to him on the night breeze. It was a tune he'd never heard before, but it was soothing. He moved from his spot beside the well to stand in the shadows just outside the doorway. It was a black, moonless night. Clouds hid even the stars.

The glow of a lantern lit the narrow confines of the stall where Mina had moved her bedding. Caleb lay beside Taffy with his arm over the dog's neck. Caleb wouldn't be parted from the dog. Taffy couldn't climb into the loft, and Mina wouldn't be parted from the child. Now, she sat beside the sleeping boy and combed her fingers through his hair as she crooned a song asking a woodsman to spare a tree.

Devlin smiled as he listened. Lady Wilhelmina Smith, the ardent protector of jackrabbits, wounded dogs and little boys. So why not a tree?

Would she protect a man who'd lost his soul?

Watching her comb her fingers through the boy's hair, Devlin yearned to be a part of the scene. He wanted Mina to run her fingers through his hair, touch his face with tenderness, to lean down and kiss him gently.

He'd been with plenty of women over the years, but none had touched him with kindness, only with lust.

Any chance he had for a life with Mina would depend on keeping a lie. He couldn't coax her into his bed and make love to her with her husband's ghost forever between them.

Until today, he thought she would give up, accept Artie was dead, but her words by the well proved that wasn't true. She still held on to hope, much the way his mother had held on to hope long after she should have accepted her fate.

Mina deserved the truth, but he wanted to protect her from it. He didn't want to see the horror in her eyes when she learned the circumstances of Artie's death. He didn't want her to have that memory. No, it was better to let her hopes die gradually. She would go back to her world of social privilege, and he would stay on the plains. It was better this way.

Better for who?

His little-used conscience pricked at him, and he struggled to ignore it.

The dog raised her head, growling softly. Mina stopped singing and turned to stare. "Devlin, is that you?" she whispered.

He stepped into the light. "Sorry if I scared you."

Taffy bared her teeth but remained beside the boy.

"She doesn't trust you," Mina said.

"Smart dog."

Mina grinned. "She certainly is devoted to Caleb."

"You seem pretty attached to the boy yourself."

She stood and moved closer to Devlin, keeping her voice low. "Do you think he saw any of what happened?"

Devlin shook his head. "He must have been playing under the barn when the attack happened, and the dog kept him there."

"Still, he would have heard the screams. I know she must have screamed and screamed."

"Try not to think about it, Mina. Even if he heard, he couldn't know what it meant."

"I pray you are right."

"You and Artie never had kids?"

"No." She looked toward the sleeping child. "My one regret. I would have loved to have a babe."

"You're still young. You might remarry."

"I won't."

"You'd spend your life mourning him? In service to a sick old man, working to make his son appear greater than he really was?"

"Arthur was a fine man."

"You forget I knew him."

She raised her chin. "By your own admission, you didn't know him long. Arthur was a kind husband and a wonderful son."

"Out here, it doesn't take long to see what a man is made of. Your husband was an arrogant fool."

Mina opened her mouth as if to protest further, but she didn't. Instead, she closed her eyes and sighed. "I know Arthur was no saint. You must think me an arrogant fool, as well."

Devlin fought the urge to hold her close and comfort her. "I don't believe I'll answer until I'm sure you're unarmed. Where's the parasol?" He leaned sideways to look behind her.

She grinned. "Tied behind my saddle."

"And the iodine?"

"In my medical kit." Chuckling, she pushed her spectacles higher on the bridge of her nose—a gesture he found endearing.

"Your pistol?"

She patted her pocket. "Right here."

"Thought so."

"Does this mean you won't answer my question?"

"You've got a pistol and a dog that hates me. I wouldn't call you unarmed. In fact, I'd say you are a formidable woman."

"Formidable. I suppose that is better than an arrogant fool, is it not?"

"Like I said, I'll answer when you're unarmed."

He gestured toward the lantern with his chin. "Put out the light. I don't think Standing Bear will be back, but there is no sense advertising we're here."

"Of course." She turned down the wick, plunging the interior of the barn into darkness.

Gradually, his eyes adjusted. He could just make out her pale hair and face when she spoke. "What is your plan now, Devlin?"

"I expect the army patrol and Buck will come back this way. We'll wait here for a few days. After that, we'll leave a message saying we found Caleb and head to Fort Harker."

"What will happen to the boy if we can't contact Buck?"

"You mean if Buck gets himself killed?"

"Please, don't say that," she whispered.

"We'll find someone at the Fort to take Caleb in."

Devlin enjoyed talking to her in the dark. Hearing the soft sound of her voice, relishing the fact he didn't have to hide how he felt. She had him tied in knots. It wasn't just sex he wanted. He was falling for her and falling hard.

Mina sighed heavily. "Does Buck have relatives? I hate to think of Caleb going to strangers."

"Are you thinking of keeping the boy yourself?"

"The idea crossed my mind."

"Buck and I have a little ranch outside Abilene. He'll be back there sooner or later. You could stay there with the boy until he does." Maybe he could stay with them.

Foolish thought. Why torture himself even more?

"Will you be going back to the ranch?" she asked softly.

"No."

"I thought the reason Buck took this job was to earn enough money to buy cattle for your place."

"That's what Buck wants."

"And what do you want?" she asked.

What did he want besides the impossible? He wasn't sure anymore. "My freedom, I guess. Maybe I'll hunt buffalo for the railroad. I hear the pay is good. Or I could just go see what's over the next hill."

"You'll become a drifter?"

"I'd get to see some mighty fine country."

"It sounds like a lonely life," she whispered.

Yes, it did. Now more than ever.

"What was it like? Living with the Cheyenne, I mean. Did you…" her voice trailed away.

"Did I what?"

"Never mind, it isn't any of my business."

His anger rose in a heated flash. "Did I torture and kill my enemies the way Buck's family was killed? After all, if I lived among savages, I must have *been* a savage. Isn't that what you're asking?"

"No, that's not what I meant at all."

"I killed my share of men in battle. Pawnee, Kiowa, white men intent on killing me, but I didn't torture anyone."

She laid a hand on his arm. "You mistake my intent."

"Do I?"

"In my clumsy way, I was trying to ask if you have family among the Cheyenne. A wife or children?"

His anger drained away, leaving him shaken and empty. The touch of her hand was all that kept him from running away. That and knowing the darkness hid his face.

He took a deep breath. "I don't have a wife. Not the marrying kind, I guess. My freedom matters to me. A wife would tie me down. I'd come to hate that."

"What was your time with the Cheyenne like?"

He snorted. "The tale of my life doesn't make a good bedtime story."

"I'm not the least bit sleepy. Besides, after the gruesome things I saw today, I doubt I will ever have a peaceful night's sleep again. Why did they have to torture them? Why not just kill them?"

He searched for the right words. "It's hard to explain. To understand, you must understand the Cheyenne way of thinking. Bravery is the highest virtue. Never show fear. When a Cheyenne man is captured by an enemy, he knows he'll face torture. He will endure it, brag about his accomplishments in battle, sing his death song until the very end to show the enemy how powerful his spirit is. A man who does this will earn the respect of his enemy and can even take away their power. In a way, they were offering Buck's brother a chance to prove his spirit was strong."

"You're right. I don't understand it and I never will."

How could she? "The natives here didn't invent torture. History is filled with examples in every culture. The reasons may be different: religion, land, gold. Everywhere people have walked, they have tortured and enslaved the weaker."

"I know. It's one thing to read about it and another thing to witness it."

"I should go." He turned away.

"No, please, talk to me. Tell me about how you came to live with the Cheyenne."

He wanted her to know about his life, to understand him. Maybe even one day to forgive him. If it wasn't for the cover of darkness, he knew he wouldn't be able to do it.

"I already told you the Sioux took my mother and me in a raid when I was seven."

"You were captives?"

"Slaves. During our time with the Sioux, mother constantly assured me my father would find us. I believed her. As often as she could, she left signs for him to follow, her name scratched on a rock, branches on the ground pointing the way. Her signs were sometimes discovered. She was beaten, but she never stopped trying. In secret, she taught me to read and write and to cipher."

"She sounds like a very brave woman."

"I think the Sioux warrior who took her admired her spirit, but his wife hated us. They beat us a lot. The more I cried, the more it hurt my mother, so I learned not to cry. I think the woman was glad to be rid of us when Swift Fox offered to buy us."

"Was your life better among the Cheyenne?"

"It was. Swift Fox is a just man. We were treated with respect and kindness. He had a sister named Singing Grass who took us under her wing. Singing Grass was married to a white man, a trapper named Pierre Benoit. He didn't live with the Cheyenne. He only came to trade with our band every year or so. Singing Grass had a son who was a year younger than me. We were as close as brothers."

"Standing Bear?"

"Yes."

Devlin grew silent, pulled into the memory of those long-ago years.

"Didn't the trapper try to free you and your mother?"

"When Pierre came to the camp, my mother and I were kept hidden, as we were anytime white men came near. Swift Fox had no intention of losing my mother. He loved her. While Pierre was there, Singing Grass was so happy. When he left, she was sad. I think she felt close to me because I reminded her of him. He had brown hair and gray eyes. The same color as mine."

"Yes, I've noticed their unusual shade."

"Have you?" Devlin wished he could see *her* eyes. He wished he could see what she was thinking.

"Indeed." She cleared her throat. "Does Standing Bear resemble his father?"

"No, he looks like a full-blooded Cheyenne. Over the next few years, he grew increasingly unhappy with his mother's attention to me. Everything became a competition between us. When I was about thirteen, Pierre came again, only this time he discovered we were in camp."

"Did he try to help you?"

"By that time we'd been with the band for years. Swift Fox wanted to marry my mother, but she refused him. She still believed my father was searching for us. Pierre persuaded Swift Fox to let us go."

"But you said you lived among the Cheyenne until you were twenty-five?"

Bitterness welled up in Devlin. "Pierre took us to St. Louis and eventually back to our farm in Iowa. Our welcome was less than cordial. My father had never gone looking for us. He assumed we were dead and remarried within a few months and had a new family. He spit on my mother for daring to show her face after she'd been an 'Injun whore'. At that moment, I was glad I was a Cheyenne brave. I drew my knife and if it hadn't been for Pierre, I would have killed him."

"Your poor mother. What did she do then?"

"We tried settling in town, but everyone knew what had happened to her. We were treated like filth. She couldn't get work. We were starving. My father came to see us once. He offered to take me. Said he could beat the savage out of me. I think he wanted a farmhand he didn't have to pay.

"Mother refused, but the law agreed with Father. The sheriff had to hog tie and gag me, then he dragged me to my father's farm. The first chance I got, I stole two horses, went back for my mother, and headed to St. Louis. We found another trapper who brought us back to Swift Fox."

"I see," Mina whispered.

Did she understand what his mother had faced among her own people? "You think it was the wrong decision?"

"That isn't for me to say."

"The tribe greeted us as long-lost loved ones. By then, Mother had her own reason for wanting to stay with the Cheyenne. It was a hard life, but for her, it was the right choice. She married Swift Fox. She was… content with him, I think. When I was seventeen, Pierre brought his brother, a French Jesuit priest, to the camp. Mother saw how I hated whites and didn't want me to make war on my own kind. She had been a schoolteacher before she married my father and wanted me to see more than the plains and an Iowa farm. She begged Father Benoit to take me back to France with him. Somehow, she convinced Swift Fox to let me go."

"What a wise woman she was."

"I hated the idea, but I couldn't add another disappointment to her life. I knew I'd be back. Pierre and Father Benoit took me to the gulf coast and eventually to France. I spent four years in Europe. Father Benoit educated me, saw to it I read the classics and learned geography and history and how to use a fork. I didn't do quite as well with his lessons on humility or God."

"Did Standing Bear travel with you?"

"No. Pierre knew his son would never be accepted in white society. He thought he was protecting his son."

"Instead, he made the boy feel inferior."

Devlin nodded, even though she couldn't see him. "I think that's true."

"Is that why he hates whites?"

"The Cheyenne have more than enough reasons to hate white people."

"Yet you remained in the white man's world."

"I went back to my tribe for a time, but I had already seen their way of life was doomed. When my mother died, I left and never went back. I chose the winning side even if I didn't believe it was the best one."

"Thank you for telling me these things."

"And you, Mina? What is your story?"

"I told you already." He could hear the retreat in her voice. The closeness of the last few minutes began slipping away.

"You've told me part of it, but not all. What is it you're hiding?"

"My good sir, I am not hiding anything. I shall retire unless you wish me to keep watch." Indignation and something else reverberated in her clipped words. The closeness between them vanished. She was once again the aristocratic lady.

He was sorry he'd chosen to share his past with her. Like the dog, she still didn't trust him. Maybe it was for the best. "I'll take the first watch. Try to get some sleep. I'll wake you in four hours."

"Very well. Good night, sir."

For the next two days, they stayed at the way station, waiting for Buck's return. Devlin watched Mina spend every free minute with Caleb while she avoided spending any time at all with him. She dodged him at every turn unless she was issuing orders like he was one of her servants. He decided she was trying to pick a fight, but he refused to give her the satisfaction.

He was at the corral fence late one afternoon when Buck and the detachment of troops rode back into the station yard looking haggard and worn.

Buck pulled his horse to a stop beside Devlin. "I thought you'd be gone by now."

"We would have been, except for one small bit of trouble." Devlin nodded toward the barn. Mina stood in the doorway with one hand on Caleb's shoulder. Taffy limped out of the shadows to sit beside the boy.

"Thank God!" Buck slid from the saddle and rushed to gather the boy into his arms.

Caleb protested. "Yer squishing me."

"I'm just so darn happy to see you. I'm your Uncle Buck."

"When are Mama and Daddy coming home?"

Buck's eyes glistened with unshed tears. "We'll talk about that later."

"We found him hiding under the barn," Mina said. "Extracting him and his Cerberus proved difficult."

Buck glanced at her. "His what?"

Mina patted the dog's head. "It's from a Greek myth. Cerberus was the dog who guarded the gates of the underworld. Taffy proved to be an effective watchdog for young Caleb. You have her to thank that the boy is safe and sound." She related the entire story.

Still holding Caleb, Buck squatted and ruffled the dog's head. "Good girl, I'm gonna see you eat beef steak for the rest of your life."

Lieutenant Olson came over, his tired, dirty face wreathed in a bright smile. "My men and I have been looking everywhere for you, my lad."

"I wasn't lost." Caleb frowned at the strangers crowding around him.

The lieutenant laughed. "I guess you weren't. Sergeant, have the men dismount. We'll rest the horses for two hours."

"Buck, what are your plans now?" Mina asked, stroking Caleb's hair.

"I don't rightly know."

"I thought perhaps you might wish to remain here and take over your brother's business."

Buck shook his head. "No. The boy's mother has a sister in Cañon City, Colorado. I think she would want me to take him there."

"You're welcome to travel to Fort Hays with us," the lieutenant said. "You can catch the next westbound stage from there."

"Thanks. We'll do that."

Two hours later, Devlin shook hands with his friend and watched him ride away, with Caleb seated in the saddle in front of him and Taffy limping along beside them. As the column rode out of sight, Devlin turned and looked for Mina. Expecting to find her in tears, he entered the barn and was surprised to see her saddling her mare. She didn't look at him.

"Come, Mr. Elder. We have delayed long enough. I find I am eager to return to civilization."

Chapter Fifteen

"You're giving up?" Devlin asked.

Did he sound disappointed? Mina wanted to believe that but continued saddling her horse. "Yes."

"Now you're being sensible." Devlin grabbed the packsaddles and left the barn.

"I don't wish to be sensible," Mina whispered to Sabiha.

With Buck and Caleb gone, she both dreaded and yet strangely hungered for the coming days and nights when she would be alone with Devlin on the trail. The closeness she felt toward him when he had revealed his past had not lessened. Each day, it became increasingly difficult to pretend indifference toward him. Despite her growing attraction, she knew nothing would come of their relationship unless she betrayed her marriage vows.

It isn't a betrayal if Arthur is dead.

No. It wasn't Arthur she would betray if she gave in to her growing passion. Her marriage to Arthur had been a sham from the start. She would be betraying her own moral values and Vincent's trust. She had foolishly promised to discover what happened to Artie and find his fossil. Instead, she had ended up here, surrounded by a sea of grass and deadly danger.

As soon as she reached Fort Harker, she would telegraph Vincent and apprise him of her situation. He would insist she return to Philadelphia. Doing so would mean she'd never see Devlin Elder again. She fought the tears that sprang to her eyes.

She'd never look across a campfire and see the way the flames lit the planes and angles of his face. Never again feel the undeniable surge of happiness when the man smiled at something she said. She wouldn't again savor the rush of her blood singing through her veins when his gaze met hers or feel her heart pounding like Sabiha's galloping hooves when he kissed her. How could she give that up?

Why should she?

Why couldn't she have a chance at happiness for once?

"Did you change your mind?"

Startled, she spun around to stare at Devlin. "What do you mean?"

"Are we going to ride out now or wait until tomorrow? Ten minutes ago, you were in an all-fired hurry."

Now was her chance to say something, to tell him how she felt. "Are you in a hurry?" she countered.

His gaze softened for an instant before turning remote again. "Have you got a bottle of whiskey hidden away you'd like to share?"

"Of course not."

"Then I'm in a hurry. A man can die of thirst in more ways than one."

What had she been thinking? She might lust after the man, but they had nothing in common. At least she had come to her senses before she admitted she cared for him. She turned away. "Call me when you have finished loading the mules."

"You could help, milady."

"I am sure I would only impede your efforts. I will be outside until you are ready."

With that, she led Sabiha out and tied her to the corral fence. Time away from Devlin was what she needed now, time to school her wayward emotions into order.

Her lagging steps carried her to the four mounds of freshly turned earth. During the first night, Devlin had placed a simple cross at the head of each one. Mina kneeled beside Anna Murphy's grave and smoothed the soil with one hand.

"I wish I had met you and your husband, Anna. If he was anything like Buck, he must have been a good man. Buck will take wonderful care of Caleb. I am sure you know that."

She sank onto her heels in silence and listened to the wind sighing through the grass. Her gaze traveled across the horizon. To the north, a line of covered wagons trekked slowly westward, and she watched them until they were out of sight. Would the hardships of this beautiful land cost some of them their lives as well? Even if it did, it would not deter the rest of them from going after their goals.

It was the danger, not to her life, but to Devlin, that made her see how foolish she had been. He could easily have easily lost his life the same way Buck's brother had met his end. The thought was unbearable. She had wanted to find Artie's bird fossil so Vincent Smith would live his last days happily, knowing his only son had won the respect and acclaim his father had so fervently desired for him and to prove her own worth as a paleontologist. None of that mattered against the life of the man she had grown to care about. She had changed because of him.

She'd spent her married life shielding Vincent from the heartbreak of Artie's true nature. And she had done her job exceptionally well. She had made her own bed. Why complain now about the lack of happiness it had afforded? At least with Arthur gone, there would be no new rumors to cover up. Devlin made her feel like a woman for the first time in her life. Made her question the path she had chosen. And that was why it would be better to part company with him as soon as possible if she wanted to keep what was left of her heart intact.

Hearing Devlin approaching, she let the dry earth atop Anna Murphy's grave trickle through her fingers. The hot wind blew away the dust of this family's dreams. He stopped beside her and waited silently.

She smoothed the dirt of the grave with one hand. "Do you think their spirits will find peace lying here together?"

"Who can say?"

"I pray they will. Despite how horribly they died, the goodness of their lives is what will live on in Caleb."

"Are you ready to go?"

She rose to her feet, dusted her hands together and squared her shoulders. "I am as ready as I'll ever be."

*

They covered the first few miles of their return trip in silence. Devlin couldn't help but wonder what was going on in Mina's head. She barely looked at him. When he caught her eye, he thought he detected a sadness that seemed at odds with her usual bossy and determined nature. It troubled him.

The other thing troubling him was the groups of two and three wagons stopped in the distance. It wasn't normal for the trains to split up and stop moving in the middle of the day. He made note of their locations but otherwise avoided them.

Later, when he saw a single wagon off the trail by itself, he pulled his horse to a stop.

Mina stopped, too. "Is something amiss?"

"This is the third time today I've spotted wagons not with a train."

"Is that unusual?"

"Very."

"Perhaps they have stopped for repairs?"

"It's possible, but not likely. The only safety they have is traveling in large numbers. The rest of the train would wait on them."

"Do you wish to investigate?" she asked.

"No. It's none of our business."

"Then let us proceed. We have a long way to go." Mina nudged her horse into a trot and left him to follow along.

Not that he minded the view of her trim form bouncing in the saddle ahead of him. She rode English style, posting up and down with the movement of the horse. She did so with an ease that let him imagine her riding him the same way. Sweat broke out on his brow.

Determined to ignore her tantalizing horsemanship, he yanked on the lead rope of the mules. He had about as much chance of persuading Mina to share his bed as he did getting the mules to fly.

As soon as they made camp, Mina pitched her tent and vanished inside, coming out only to eat a meager meal then retreating without a word. If he'd been a stinking skunk, she couldn't have made it plainer she wanted nothing to do with him.

The other night in the barn she had listened with sympathy and understanding, things that had been missing in his life for a long time. Today, she couldn't seem to get away from him fast enough. She had him tied up in knots. He wanted her in the worst way, but even if that happened, Artie's ghost would always be between them.

He tossed another buffalo chip on the fire, then rolled up in his blanket with his rifle and pistol close at hand. A light sleeper, he could depend on the mules to warn him if anyone tried sneaking into camp. Sleeping with one eye open wouldn't be difficult. Sleeping at all with Mina lying only a few feet away would be the problem.

Above him, a million stars glittered in the inky blackness. Devlin watched their slow trek across the dark sky until long into the night.

*

To Mina, it looked as if Devlin hadn't slept any better than she had when she emerged from her tent the following morning. He didn't speak as they broke camp and headed east again. The silence weighed on her. They had traveled less than two miles when both the horses and the mules began acting edgy. They all faced south with their heads up and ears pricked forward.

She rose in her stirrups. "What is it?"

"Buffalo. Can't you smell them?"

She tested the air. "I smell dust."

"And?"

She sniffed again, trying to sort through the scents of the horses, the grass and the earth. "I smell something musty." The memory of buffalo pouring over the hill came back in a rush. Casting a sidelong glance at Devlin, she brought her collar closer to her nose. "Of course, it could be my clothes. Then again, it could be yours."

Her little joke was rewarded with a faint smile from Devlin. How she enjoyed being able to coax one from him.

I shall miss his infrequent smiles the most.

He nudged his horse toward the long line of low hills to the south. "Come on. You should see this."

"I've seen more than enough buffalo, thank you."

"Not like this."

She followed him, absurdly happy for an opportunity to halt their headlong journey toward Fort Harker. He said nothing as they made their way to the top of the ridgeline. Once there, words failed Mina.

An ocean lay before her, a sea of brown-black bodies and curls of gray dust stretched for endless miles from horizon to horizon.

She dismounted and stood in awe of the sight before her. "My God! How many are there?"

"Who knows," Devlin said. "Half a million, maybe more. But not as many as there used to be."

"I can't imagine more. Where are they going?"

"They're migrating to fresh pasture. The herds travel north in the summer months, then back south ahead of the snow."

Mina moved toward a rocky outcropping for a better look. "You are right. This is a sight not to be missed. What majestic animals they are."

She lifted her skirt to step up onto a flat stone when a loud buzzing began near her feet. The sound ended when something struck her calf, sending fiery pain shooting through her leg. She stumbled backwards and fell, landing on her rump.

The blast of Devlin's gun right beside her nearly deafened her. Up on the sandstone boulders, a headless serpentine body thrashed and quivered in its death throes. The massive herd of buffalo kept moving calmly along.

Devlin dropped to one knee beside her. "Are you all right?"

She pulled up the hem of her riding skirt to reveal two bleeding puncture holes in her right calf. Sickening pain radiated up her leg. "That is a rattlesnake, isn't it? You once told me I wouldn't know trouble if it bit me my ass. I believe I'm in a great deal of trouble now, aren't I?"

Devlin's pale face confirmed her fears. He pushed her down. "Lie back and keep still."

She closed her eyes and dug her fingers into the dense grass between the stones. "Yes, of course. Do you know what to do? I'm sure you must. No doubt, you've encountered snake bites before. The first thing is to make a tourniquet. Then I believe you must cut the bite in a crisscross fashion, deeply enough to allow free bleeding. I shall try not to scream, but I may. Do not let me deter you. After that, I'm afraid you must suck out the poison."

"Mina?"

"Yes."

"When I said keep still, I meant your mouth, too." The sound of tearing cloth followed his words. She opened her eyes and saw him ripping his shirt into strips. He wrapped a strip around her leg and pulled it painfully tight.

Gritting her teeth, she said, "I'm sorry. I often babble when I'm upset."

"I've noticed."

"I try, but I can't seem to help myself."

"If you don't shut up, I'm going to gag you." The blade of his knife glinted in the sunlight.

"Wait!" She held up one hand.

"Mina, I've got to do this."

"I know, but I prefer you disinfect the blade. In my saddle bag you'll find a small black medical kit. There's a flask of whiskey in it."

His scowl deepened. "You told me you didn't have any whiskey."

"You asked if I had some to drink. I don't. It is for medicinal purposes."

"Hell, to think of all the times in the past few days when I could have used a drink."

"Then we wouldn't have it now, would we?" she shot back.

His silence proved he couldn't disagree with her logic. Instead, he went to her horse and returned with the bag. She opened it and pulled out the flask. After uncorking it, she raised it to her lips and took a hearty swig.

The liquid burned a path down her throat and pooled in the pit of her stomach. She coughed slightly, wiped her mouth on her sleeve, then handed him the flask. She lay back. "Pour it over the blade and then the wound."

*

Devlin stared at her in astonishment, not quite trusting his own eyes, then took a quick drink himself before dousing the blade.

"Hold still." His hand trembled, but he steadied it before he pushed the blade through her skin. Her scream pierced his heart. He had to steel himself to continue until the job was done.

When he finished the cuts, he sucked at the wound, spitting out the blood until he was sure he had removed as much poison as possible. But had he been quick enough? Grown men rarely died of snakebite, but Devlin had seen several children die after being bitten. Mina was such a tiny thing, but she was strong. It would depend on how much of the poison had gotten into her blood.

She opened her eyes and wiped at the tears flowing from their corners before meeting his gaze. "You must be honest with me, sir. Am I going to die?"

He pulled off the tourniquet. "Not if I can help it."

"If I should expire, I don't want you blaming yourself."

"I'll blame who I damn well please."

"I have asked you before to moderate your language, sir."

"And I've asked you to keep still. I'm going to make a poultice of ground snakeroot. It may take me a bit to find some. You lie quietly."

"Indeed, I shall, for I feel quite dizzy. I believe walking or riding will shortly be out of the question."

He gently stroked back her hair. "Don't worry. I'll take care of you."

She caught his hand, squeezed it and gazed into his eyes. "I know you will."

His chest tightened at the trust in her eyes. "It'll be okay, Mina."

"You are an excellent liar, but I believe you."

Devlin located a snakeroot plant nearby, ground it into powder between two rocks and mixed it with a little water from his canteen. After smearing the paste over Mina's wounds, he bound it in place with strips of his shirt. She remained quiet and that worried him.

Devlin knew his poultice would help, but the poison might overwhelm her. She needed a doctor. Her best chance was for him to head to Ellsworth. Hopefully, he'd meet a wagon train on the way and could beg help from them.

He wrapped her in her own blanket and gently lifted her to his saddle, then he swung up behind her. Her mare he left loose knowing she would stay close. The mules he tethered to his saddle horn with a longer rope.

He was forced to travel slowly, stopping often to check on Mina and make her drink. She was in pain. Her hands gripped the edge of the blanket with white-knuckled intensity, but she didn't complain. She merely accepted his canteen with a forced smile. For the first time since he'd met her, he wanted to hear her non-stop chatter.

Sometime later, he topped a ridge and saw the wagon ruts that cut a trail through the grassland. He turned his horse east toward Ellsworth. After another hour on the trail, he saw a circle of three wagons. Relief coursed through him. "Mina?"

She opened her eyes briefly. "Yes?"

"There are some wagons up ahead. You hold on, Lady Wilhelmina Smith. Do you hear me?"

"I shall, and thank you, Devlin. You have been most kind."

Any reply he wanted to make stuck in his painfully closed throat. He rode within hailing distance of the wagon train. Reining in, he called out, "Hello, the camp!"

He frowned when no one answered him. Something wasn't right. He hesitated, not wanting to approach within rifle range without an invitation. He called again. "Hello the camp! Can I come in?"

A figure moved away from one wagon. "You'd best keep on moving, mister," a man called out.

Devlin urged his horse closer. "I've got a woman here that's sick from snake bite. I need help."

"We got our own sickness to worry about and our own dead to bury. There's cholera here."

Cholera! Fear made Devlin's heart pound. The dreaded disease could wipe out a whole train or settlement in a matter of days.

"Much obliged for the warning." Devlin turned his horse to give the wagons a wide berth.

"If you're thinking of heading to Ellsworth, they got it bad there." The man advanced to within a few yards.

"What about the fort?"

"We saw twenty new graves on our way past. We didn't even camp there, but it didn't do any good. My boy and my wife came down with it two days later, anyway. My Beth told me I was a fool to sell our farm to go chasing after gold. I buried her and my boy out here in this godforsaken nothingness this morning. I hope she can forgive me."

Leaving the man still muttering to himself, Devlin rode away. Taking Mina to the town or the fort was out of the question now. Cholera would spread up and down the trail. He'd seen it before. He knew only one place where he could care for her. The dugout cabin was a day's ride to the northwest.

It was the one place he'd wanted to make sure she never saw, but if she died, he could at least bury her beside her husband.

Chapter Sixteen

The sun was setting the following day by the time Devlin saw the trees that marked the course of the creek where the cabin was hidden. Riding down into a dry gulch, he dismounted to check on Mina again. He had fashioned a travois using two long saplings as poles and a blanket to carry her. This time, she didn't open her eyes when he called her name. He touched her face. She was burning up.

"Mina, honey. Wake up." He shook her shoulders.

She woke and stared at him with red-rimmed eyes.

"Mina, I've got to leave you for a little while. Do you understand? There's a cabin up ahead, but I need to check it out before I take you within sight of it."

She swallowed with difficulty. "Did you call me honey?"

"No." It had been a slip of the tongue.

"Oh. I thought you did. It made me happy. Don't be gone long."

"I won't."

"Promise?"

"I promise."

She frowned at him. "If you break your word, I shall be exceedingly vexed."

He placed his canteen in her hands. "I wouldn't want that. I'll be back as soon as I make sure it's safe."

"Why are you running off without me, Artie?" Her words were a bare, harsh whisper. "Your father will suspect something if you keep this up."

Devlin frowned. "Mina?"

Muttered words he couldn't make out was her answer. He glanced around at the empty prairie, hating the idea of leaving her unprotected, but he was wasting time lingering beside her.

Making his way down the gully, he entered the stand of timber along the creek and cautiously started upstream.

*

A horse whinnied nearby. Mina opened her eyes. The setting sun coated the low clouds in the west with brilliant shades of red and gold. Her mare stood close beside her.

"It was most odd, Sabiha. I was dreaming about shoes. I had a pair once that were almost the same shade as those clouds. My leg hurts dreadfully. Did I break it? I broke my arm once. Do you remember? It wasn't your fault the dog startled you. I tried to be brave so Artie wouldn't worry. Not that he ever worries about me much. I'm like a little sister to him. Kendrick was the only one he loved."

She looked down and discovered she was lying on a stretcher made of coarse wool blankets. "It's so very hard to think. Was it a snake? I believe I'm dying, Sabiha. Vincent will be so sad. I didn't even find my fossil."

She raised her head and looked for Devlin, but he wasn't near. He'd told her something important, but she couldn't remember what. There was something she needed to tell him, too.

"Drat that man. Where is he when I need him?"

Her head lolled back onto the blanket. Sabiha stepped closer and lowered her nose to Mina's face. Mina raised one hand to stroke the mare's cheek. "If I die, you must tell Mr. Elder I have grown very fond of him. You must tell him I don't hold him to blame. I'm quite sure he won't believe you."

She giggled. "One, because you're a horse, and two, because he is determined to disagree with me. He's not at all like Artie. Artie was such a gentle soul. I remember when I first knew I loved him. I was twelve, and he gave me a beautiful blue hair ribbon."

Her eyes drifted closed. "I was a foolish girl."

*

Devlin found the cabin the same as he'd left it last fall. From the cover of the thick trees, he scanned the area. The creek had been high here, too, but it hadn't reached the timber walls. The recent floods had helped conceal the place by adding to the mass of logs and debris along the high bank that hid the building from casual sight.

Even the beaver had been busy since Devlin left. A new dam blocked the creek, forming a deep pool below the cabin. As far as he could see, only a few deer and raccoon tracks dotted the faint path leading from the creek to the rock overhang that sheltered the front door. He moved cautiously closer. Pushing open the narrow door, he stepped inside.

He waited for his eyes to adjust to the dim light. The scurry and squeak of pack rats in the log rafters were the only sounds he heard. Satisfied no hostile occupants, human or animal, had made themselves at home, he moved through the cabin and pulled the buffalo robe from the room's only window to let some light in.

The lean-to cabin had been built back into the hill. One side was a solid rock wall with a small stone fireplace jutting out of it. The other walls were logs chinked with earth and dried grass. The twenty-by-twenty-foot room held two rawhide laced beds along the far wall. A small table stood near the door. Cut stumps served as a pair of chairs. Artie's trunk and gear sat in the middle of the dirt floor.

They served as a stark reminder why he didn't want Mina here. But what choice did he have? With cholera up and down the trail, taking Mina to any fort or town was out of the question. Here, he had shelter and a place to care for her.

He dragged the trunk into one corner, raising a cloud of dust as he did so. He knelt beside the log wall, slipped his fingers in a notch and lifted the latch. A concealed door swung open. From the cavity behind it, he pulled out two whiskey kegs, then shoved the trunk in. After replacing the kegs, he closed the door. It was almost impossible to detect.

He pulled a buffalo robe from the second cot and took it outside. He beat it against a nearby tree until most of the year's accumulation of dust had drifted away on the wind. Taking the hide back inside, he spread it over the leather lacing of one bunk. It wasn't much, but it was all he had in the way of comfort. Perhaps later he'd have time to make a mattress of dried grass for her. If she lived that long.

No, he couldn't think that way. She would live.

Leaving the cabin, he worked his way back to Mina. She lay on the travois, but one hand now gripped her mare's bridle. He tried to pull her fingers loose, but she hung on tightly.

"Mina, let go."

"Promise you'll marry me?" she muttered.

Devlin couldn't hide his surprise. "What?"

"Promise you'll marry me when I grow up, Arthur," she mumbled.

Devlin pulled her hand again. Of course, she hadn't meant she'd marry him. Why did she have to talk about Artie now?

"Vincent doesn't approve of your bachelor's ways. He wants you to give up your expeditions and learn about the shipping business."

She tried to sit up. "Where are you going now? Why can't you stay here? Vincent isn't well. He'll miss you dreadfully when you're gone."

Devlin forced her to lie back. With a final tug, he got her fingers loose. "Mina, you aren't making sense. You're talking out of your head."

She fell silent, but he wasn't sure if it was a good sign or a bad one. Moving to his horse's head, he led the animal toward the shelter.

Outside the dugout, he slipped his arms gently beneath Mina. She cried out when he moved her leg. The sound tore at his heart. Her eyes opened, and he stared into their pain filled depths. "I'm sorry, Mina. I have to move you."

She bit her bottom lip and nodded slightly. He lifted her from the travois. A faint whimper escaped, but she suppressed it. Her face grew a shade paler, if that was possible. Moving as carefully as he could, Devlin carried her inside and laid her on the bed he'd made ready.

He knelt beside her. "I'm going to leave you for a bit to take care of the animals. Then I'll be back. Do you understand?"

"Yes."

"Good." At least she seemed rational for the moment.

He stepped outside and led the horses and mules upstream. A few hundred yards south of the cabin, a small trickle of water joined the creek from the bottom of a deep, narrow gully that cut back into the hillside. He led the animals through the narrow opening into a small box canyon.

The floor of the ravine where it widened out was covered in deep grass. The poles he and Artie had used to build a makeshift gate were lying where he had left them on the last day. Refusing to give in to the memory of those hours, Devlin forced himself to concentrate on making sure the horses and mules were secure. After that, he unpacked Mina's medical kit and pulled his saddlebags and bedroll from his horse. He'd return for her trunks and gear later. For now, he left them outside the corral fence.

Back at the cabin, he spread the contents of her medical kit out on the table. He located a small, corked bottle labeled laudanum. After mixing a few drops into a tin cup from his saddlebags, he kneeled beside her. Raising her head gently, he held the cup to her lips. She took a few swallows before pushing it away.

"Drink it all," he insisted.

"It tastes like you washed your socks in it."

"It's laudanum. Drink."

She did as he bid. When she had finished it, he lowered her back to the bed. "Mina, I'm going to change the bandage on your leg. I'm not going to lie. This will hurt."

She gave a slight, quick nod and gripped the edge of the bedding.

Bracing himself for the task, Devlin sat on the end of the cot, hoping the painkilling effects of the laudanum would last long enough to finish the job. He lifted her foot onto his lap and unwound the bloody cloth strips from her swollen and discolored leg. When the last piece came off, he sucked in his breath at the sight.

The flesh around the crisscross cuts was nearly black and oozed thick, dark fluid and pus. Infection on top of the venom spreading through her was certain to kill her. It would take more than his meager medical skills to save her. She'd need an iron will to live.

He stared at her pale, set face. She was doing her best not to cry, but tears squeezed past her tightly closed lids and left damp trails as they trickled down her cheeks. It twisted his guts that he couldn't ease her pain but giving her more laudanum in her weakened state might kill her, too.

She fixed her gaze on him. "Is it bad?"

"Not too bad."

"I thought we had already discussed this poor penchant you have for lying, Mr. Elder. Kindly stick to the truth. I deserve that much."

"All right, it's bad, and you said you'd call me Devlin."

"Is it infected?"

"Yes."

"In my kit, you will find a bottle of iodine and one of carbolic acid. You should alternate using them each time you change the dressing."

"I've had some experience with wounds."

"Have you? Of course. I wish you had not given me the narcotic. I feel most peculiar."

"Go to sleep, Mina. I'll take care of you."

"I know, darling. Sorry to be such a bother…"

Her words trailed away, and he waited until he was sure she was deep into the drug induced sleep before he treated the wound with the stinging iodine.

Chapter Seventeen

The low, banked fire cast a faint glow inside the small cabin as it heated a blackened pot suspended over the embers. Wood smoke scented the warm night air. Outside, the whir and chirping of cicadas rose and fell in their impatient nighttime songs. A breeze stirred a sigh from the leaves of the cottonwood trees hugging the creek. Inside the cabin, death hovered just beyond the shadows.

Devlin dipped the cloth he held into a basin of cool water and twisted it. His hands ached. His fingers were white and puckered, but he didn't pause. Folding the fabric that had once been part of Mina's petticoat, he placed it on her brow. She half turned her face away from him and muttered something he couldn't make out.

Rinsing a second cloth, he used it to cool the hot skin of her neck and slender arms. He marveled at how delicate she was, yet how such strength and determination lived in one small woman. But was she strong enough?

Pulling the blanket aside, he bathed her full breasts and down to her waist, not allowing his gaze or his hands to linger. When she shivered, he pulled the blanket up and tucked it close beneath her chin. He closed his fingers around her wrist. The fast flutter of her pulse left his throat dry with fear. Had he given her too much laudanum? Listening to her whimpering and crying out in pain was worse than torture. He didn't dare give her more.

He willed his strength into her. "You hang on, Lady Wilhelmina Smith. Do you understand? This time you're going to listen to me."

She didn't respond. Dread crawled across his nerve endings. He placed her arm under the blanket and turned his attention to her leg. Carefully, he pulled off the bandage and poultice of snakeroot. The angry red swelling made her skin taut and shiny. The wound looked bad. It wasn't draining. Knowing what he needed to do would cause her more pain, he steeled himself for the task. The poison needed to come out or she would die.

He rose stiffly from the stool by her bed and crossed to the fireplace. Lazy steam rose from the pot. Dropping in some cloth, he used a short stick to stir the bandages. Satisfied they were hot enough, he used the corner of his shirttail to lift the pot handle from its hook. Heat bit through the thin material. He hurried to set his burden on the table, then jerked his hand away and blew on his stinging fingers.

Using the stick, he lifted the bandages from the water, allowing them to cool slightly until he could just bear touching them. Moving back to the bed, he sat down and leaned his weight across both her knees. Then he placed the steaming cloth on her infected leg.

Her scream tore through the night. He held her down as she thrashed and struggled. One flailing arm hit his nose and brought tears to his eyes, but he didn't let go. Twice more, he changed the hot bandages and held her down as she writhed in pain.

The fourth time he laid a steaming pad on her skin, she went limp, her face deathly pale. The cloth on her leg turned pink as the wound broke open and the pus drained. He had succeeded, but was he too late? Had the poison spread too far?

Throughout the night and next day, Devlin kept close to Mina's side. Her fever climbed despite his efforts to cool her. He forced her to drink a weak tea made of boiled water, herbs and willow bark. Some of it she swallowed, but much of it trickled down her slack chin.

She was out of her head. He listened to her rambling mutterings and tried to make sense of them. Once he had to hold her down when she became determined to get up and search for her lost husband. Each time she called out for Artie, her distraught pleadings were like salt in the wounds of Devlin's soul.

As the second night gave way to the pre-dawn light, she grew calm and deathly still. Each breath she took was barely noticeable. Her fever burned steadily higher. He had done everything he could. She would live or die tonight. All he could do was watch. He dropped his head in his hands.

His mother's voice came to his mind. Once, years before, she had sung a Cheyenne prayer to ward off death when his little sister Namid lay gravely ill, stricken with lung fever. He had asked his mother why she didn't pray as the white men prayed.

"The Great Spirit will only hear prayers that come from the heart, my son. My heart is Cheyenne now. You must search inside yourself for the words that mean the most to you and speak those words to the Creator."

He had joined his mother in song that night. Namid survived and grew to be a pesky, inquisitive thorn in his side, much to his mother's delight. He hadn't seen his sister in years. After he left the tribe, he never spoke to God again. Not in English or Cheyenne.

His soul wasn't in any shape to be asking favors of a higher power, but Mina's was. She deserved better than to die this way.

He rose and walked outside. The stars overhead faded one by one as the night crept away to the west. Walking down to the creek, he pulled off his clothes and stepped into the cool water. Morning baths were the custom among the Cheyenne men of his tribe.

When he was done, he climbed the steep hill above the cabin and faced the dawn. Lifting his arms, he leaned his head back and let the morning wind caress and dry his body. From deep in his memory, he pulled forth the words his mother sang that night.

As the sun rose, Stone Warrior raised his voice and chanted a plea to the Great Spirit to spare the life of Buffalo Woman.

When the last phrase died on his lips, he dropped to his knees and sank back on his heels. Exhaustion pulled at his body, draining away his strength. The longing to lie down in the sweet grass and sleep was overpowering, but he could only truly rest by Mina's side.

At the cabin door, he paused. If she did wake, she wouldn't appreciate the sight of him standing over her naked. He went down to the creek and pulled on his pants but left his shirt off. Somehow, it felt right. Like the old ways.

When he returned to her bedside, he moved his cot close beside hers. Taking her hand in his, he lay down and closed his eyes.

*

Mina heard the faint twittering of birds and wished she could close her ears to the sound and fall back asleep. She was so tired. Her body ached unlike anything she'd known before. Her leg throbbed in pain with each beat of her heart. Then she noticed the scratchy hide beneath her and a musty smell mixed with wood smoke. She forced her puffy eyelids open. Logs and branches crisscrossed overhead.

Someone had put her inside a woodpile.

There were more logs stacked around her. A scrabbling, scratching noise caught her attention. Some kind of animal scurried overhead in the dim light. The humor of it made her smile. Sharing a woodpile with vermin meant she wasn't dead, didn't it?

Turning her head to locate her glasses, she found Devlin sleeping beside her. His face was softly out of focus, but she knew who it was. He held her hand in a gentle grip.

She should pull away, but she didn't. Instead, she relished the feel of her fingers nestled in his much larger hand. His skin was warm, callused and rough, the hand of a powerful man. The sight of him stirred her blood. Desires and yearnings she'd kept long buried stirred awake when she was near him. Despite the pain and exhaustion weighing her down, she wanted to feel his lips on hers.

Heat raced to her face as she tried to consider exactly what giving in to those yearnings would entail. Her marriage had been a pretense in every sense of the word, a ruse to make an old man happy, and spare him the humiliation and shame of knowing his son was a homosexual. Mina couldn't count the number of times she had tried to convince Artie his father would understand and still love him, but nothing she said had persuaded him.

He'd had more to fear than his father's reaction. It wasn't until the passing of the Offences Against the Person Act just four years earlier that England abolished the death penalty for homosexuality. Now, a conviction meant ten years in prison.

Artie claimed he could survive the scandal, but his father would be ruined. Mina knew it was true. And that dear man still waited to hear the fate of his only son. Vincent's hopes rode on her shoulders. She couldn't let him down.

Carefully, she pulled her hand free of Devlin's grip. His eyes shot opened.

She pushed a strand of hair away from her face. "I seem to have lost my spectacles. Do you know where they are?"

He swung his feet over the edge of the cot and sat up. Lord, he was outright handsome in the faint light, with a dusky growth of beard darkening the hollows of his cheeks. The sight of his bare chest sent flutters through her body. Once she had compared him to a wolf in a cage. Now, unhindered by the trappings of society, he looked even more like one. Free and untamed.

"How are you feeling?" His voice sounded gravelly.

"Perhaps a shade better than the snake."

Reaching over, he laid a hand on her forehead. "You're still flushed, but the fever is down."

Not for long if he kept his hand on her tingling skin. She brushed him aside. "Your ministrations have done wonders, sir. It appears I owe you my life."

She wanted him to take her hand again. Instead, she slipped it under the covers. And met only bare skin.

She lifted the blanket edge, peered under and screeched. Clutching the wool beneath her chin, she looked at him in outrage.

He leaned toward her. "What's wrong?"

"I'm naked! How dare you! You lecher! You beast!"

"A second ago, you were thanking me because I saved your life."

"That was before I knew you had gawked at my—my—"

"Breasts?"

She didn't have to pretend indignation. "My bosom! And while I was unconscious! That, sir, is despicable behavior!"

His wide grin chased away the wolf and replaced it with a boyishness she hadn't seen before. "You wouldn't let me look at them while you were awake, so what choice did I have?"

"Oh, you—you pervert!"

"They're mighty nice bosoms. I've rarely seen a finer pair." He choked on a laugh. "Although, once in New Orleans, there was this gal in a kind of window-box. She was out to here." He gestured with his hands.

"You're laughing at me! I'm lying on my deathbed, and you are making jokes at my expense. I demand you return my underclothes at once."

"Can't."

She glared at him. "What do you mean, you can't?"

"You were burning up with fever. I had to cool you down. I managed to get your shirt and skirt off, but I had to cut the laces of that contraption you were squeezed into. How do you women breathe in those things?"

"You cut up my corset?" Her voice shot up an octave.

"Yes, but you can relax. I left your drawers on."

The very idea of him manhandling her unconscious body left her faint and oddly breathless.

"Your consideration overwhelms me, Mr. Elder," she managed weakly. "Please be so kind as to wait outside while I dress."

"Not until I've had a look at your leg." He took hold of the lower corner of her blanket, then gave her a sly glance. "May I?"

Annoyed, but knowing she had little choice, she nodded. He folded the cover back, exposing her leg from the knee down and nothing more.

He rubbed a hand over his jaw. "I was afraid of that."

"What's wrong?" She wanted to look but couldn't see much without her glasses.

Finally, by pulling her arms out from under the material, she could hold it tight across her chest and rise on one elbow. She took one look, then sank back and stared at the wooden logs overhead. Even without her glasses, she knew it was bad.

She swallowed hard. "It looks ghastly."

"It looks better."

"That is better? Then why are you concerned?"

"Because I've got a suspicion you won't stay down unless I tie you to the bed."

She flexed her ankle and grimaced as the pain shot up her leg. "Have no fear. I won't be dashing about."

"Much as I'd like to believe you, I'm keeping your clothes for another day."

She scowled. "You wouldn't dare."

"Don't test me. You are to stay in bed today and tomorrow." He picked up her spectacles from the table but held them just out of her reach. "Agreed?"

"Oh, very well. But at least allow me to put on some nightclothes. They are in my trunk." She snatched the eyeglasses from his extended hand and settled them on her face. She glanced around. "Where are my things?"

"I moved your trunk to the lean-to at the back of the cabin."

"And my horse?"

"Safe in a small box canyon just south of here."

"I see. Well, if you won't allow me to get up, you'll have to fetch my things for me." She pulled the blanket up to her chin, resolving not to stare at his bronzed, well-muscled chest now sharply in focus. "You may go."

He touched his brow in a brief salute. "Yes, milady."

"And put on a shirt." She called after him as he stepped out the door. "And can you fix some coffee?"

Outside on the creek bank, Devlin gazed up at the heavens through the dappled leaves overhead. The grin he wore stretched even wider as he spoke to God. "*Ma'heo'o*, I give you many thanks for saving this woman."

"Mr. Elder," she called from the cabin, "since you're heating water for coffee, could you bring me some to wash in, and a towel and some soap? And something to eat. If you please, I'm quite famished. What do you have? Perhaps some biscuits would suit. Only if you have some already made, of course. Do you? Oh, and my hairbrush, bring it as well! I have an absolute rat's nest. It will take me hours to untangle it."

Propping his hands on his hips, Devlin couldn't hold back a chuckle. "Is it too late, Great Spirit, to ask that her tongue be lamed?"

"Mr. Elder, are you there?"

He grinned. "Yes, milady. I'm coming, milady. Don't fret, milady."

"There is no need to be snide, sir."

No, but there was every reason to be glad. Mina, bossy, annoying, and beautiful, was going to live. Devlin ran down the bank and gave a whoop of glee as he launched himself into the creek with a tremendous splash.

By late afternoon, he had stopped making trips out to her trunk and dragged it inside. He left it propped open beside her cot. At her insistence, he strung a rope across one corner of the room and draped several blankets over it to provide privacy. Standing outside her partition, he cleared his throat, and she bade him enter.

Twice during the day, he had looked in and seen her napping with an open book on her lap. Good, she needed rest, if she admitted it or not. Dark circles and hollow cheeks marred the beauty of her intelligent face. A reminder of how close he had come to losing her.

She sat upright in bed now, using the Cheyenne style backrest he'd made from woven willow branches. Her hair had been brushed into submission, tightly braided and draped over one shoulder. She was decently covered in a prim nightgown with the blanket folded across her lap. But he remembered exactly how she looked naked, right down to the mole on the side of her left breast.

Someday, when she was being particularly stubborn, he would mention it just to see the anger flash like lightning in her deep blue eyes. The thought made him grin. He stopped beside her feet.

"Yes?" She waited for him to speak.

"I thought I'd go check on the horses and mules. Is there anything else you need?"

She chewed the corner of her lip as she glanced around. "No. I am fine, thank you. Will you be gone long?"

"Half hour, maybe less."

"I regret I am a burden to you, Mr. Elder. I shall attempt to make amends as soon as I'm able to get up."

"You used to call me Devlin."

"I guess I did, Devlin."

"Stay out of trouble while I'm gone. I'll change the dressing on your leg when I get back."

She flinched and held up one hand. "Please. Take all the time you need with the horses."

"Not looking forward to my ministrations?"

"In a word? No."

He tipped his head to the side. "I'll be gentle."

"It throbs like the devil while I'm just lying here. Somehow, I don't believe it will improve with your questionably gentle tending."

"Throbs like the devil, does it? Why, milady, that's practically swearing."

"A lapse on my part caused, no doubt, by associating with low company."

He gave a bark of laughter. "I don't think it's smart to insult the doctor."

"More like witch doctor. What is the repulsive smelling stuff you have smeared on my limb?"

"Snakeroot, pounded up and mixed with things you don't want to know about."

"Thank you for sparing me the details."

He laughed again. He couldn't remember the last time he'd felt like laughing with any woman.

"Seriously, Mina, I came in to give you this." He pulled his gun from his holster and held it out to her, butt first.

She took it and slipped it under the blanket beside her. "I assume you'll take a rifle?"

"Yes. Just don't shoot me when I come back."

She gave him a sweet smile. "The thought never crossed my mind."

"Swearing and lying. Tsk, tsk, milady. What next?"

"Perhaps I'll try murder."

Amusement dropped from him like a stone. "I don't recommend it."

He spun away and left Mina staring after him, puzzled by the abrupt change in his demeanor. Her spirits, elevated by his adorable deep laugh, drooped and took her brief feeling of euphoria with it. She was as tired and wilted as a two-week-old bouquet of roses. Her leg hurt dreadfully when Devlin wasn't there to take her mind off it.

Witch doctor indeed. More like bewitching doctor. Her growing attraction couldn't be allowed to keep her from completing her mission, but when she made him laugh, her heart sang. Now with the cholera outbreak Devlin had told her about making returning more dangerous than staying, she could continue her search as soon as she could travel. Even Devlin wouldn't be able to argue with that logic.

Chapter Eighteen

After three days of forced inactivity, Mina decided Devlin had had his way long enough and announced her intention in a tone that dared him to argue. "I believe I shall get up today."

Crouched by the fireplace with his back toward her, Devlin grunted. The smell of roasting rabbit and wild onions enticed her growing appetite.

"Was that a sound of agreement or opposition, sir?"

"Does it matter?" He sounded annoyed.

She bit her lip. "Of course it does. I don't wish to appear ungrateful for your care, but even you must agree my leg is much improved. A little exercise will only strengthen it."

"How little?"

"A stroll around the cabin and clearing. Nothing strenuous, I promise."

He rose and eyed her from across the small room. "All right. After we eat."

She smiled. "Excellent."

"I expected you to be champing at the bit before this."

"I didn't wish to be a difficult patient," she said primly.

He rolled his eyes but wisely refrained from commenting and carried the pan to the table beside her. After dividing the portions of meat between them, he pulled over the wooden stump serving as a chair while she sat on the edge of her bed. Mina did justice to his well-cooked meal and offered to wash the plates after their meal was done.

He hesitated, but nodded and picked up his rifle. "Just don't fall in the creek."

"Where are you going?"

"To have a look around. With Standing Bear's band on the loose, it pays to be careful. Watch your step when you go down to the creek. Keep to the rocks and walk a slightly different path back so you don't leave a plain trail for someone to follow."

"You believe we are in danger, even here?"

"This ain't Hyde Park in London."

She glanced around the decrepit cabin. "How could I have forgotten?"

He turned away, but not before she saw a ghost of a smile tug at his lips. "Remember. You can walk to the edge of the clearing but no farther."

"I shall do as you bid," she agreed.

"Make sure you do."

"Or what? You'll take my clothes again?"

He looked over his shoulder. "Don't tempt me."

It was the look in his eyes more than his words that stopped her retort. Silence seemed the wiser choice.

Once Devlin was gone, Mina slipped his gun in her pocket and then carried the pot and plates to the creek, being careful to step on the rocks as he had instructed and using her sturdy parasol as a cane. The small amount of exertion tired her more than she cared to admit and made her leg ache like a rotten tooth. Setting the dirty dishes aside, she dipped her hands in the water, then used them to cool her cheeks and neck. The afternoon heat was stifling without the brisk breeze that normally made the cottonwood leaves flash green and silver as they fluttered.

After checking around carefully, she sat on a wide stone and pulled up her skirt to examine her leg. She unwound the bandage with care, regretting only briefly the loss of her finest muslin petticoat. The sight of the ugly wound took her aback. She would always carry a puckered scar to remind her of her time with Devlin. A scar on her leg to match the scar on her heart. Because try as she might to ignore her feelings, he had found a way into her heart. No matter how happy she was spending time with him, this interlude would end. He was a restless soul who wanted to wander the plains while she had a life waiting for her with Vincent.

Redressing her wound, she drew up her knees and rested her chin atop them. Going back to London, after she found what she was seeking in Kansas, meant she would never see Devlin again. Sadness crept in to tighten her throat and prick her eyes with tears. He was a scoundrel, a libertine, and possibly the best liar she had ever met. Should he realize how she felt, he would likely attempt to seduce her.

Her skin grew warm at the idea, but her pride and principles would never allow her to give in. In guarding Vincent from the truth about Artie, she had spent years pretending to be happy, pretending to be married, pretending not to care she didn't have children. Artie hadn't given her even that consolation. Now she had to hide her growing attraction to Devlin. The unfairness of it all stirred her anger. She picked up a flat rock and sent it skipping across the smooth surface of the water. It sank from sight, leaving only widening ripples to mark its passing.

Like the lies of her life, the ripples spread until they lapped at the far shore. Quietly, she waited until they died away. Her life had to be more than this, more than lies, even if those lies had been born of a need to protect the two men she loved.

The sun scorched her shoulders. She opened her parasol to block the bright rays. Unfortunately, she had no way of blocking dark thoughts from her mind. Happiness was not within her reach unless she turned her back on all she knew.

What kind of life could she have with Devlin even if, miracle of miracles, he should return her affections? Would he give up this untamed life and come with her to England? There would be precious little work for a frontier scout among her social set.

She raised her face to the slight breeze that found its way through the trees. The freedom of these plains drew at her heart and soul, but try as she might, she couldn't imagine raising children in the cabin behind her with its packed dirt floor.

She picked up a second rock, intending to sink it along with her disturbing thoughts, but her fingers found a subtle difference in the smooth contours.

She held the rock to the light, then dipped it in the water to bring out the image. The faint impression of a leaf lay perfectly pressed into the stone.

Her blood pulsed with excitement. Pushing her spectacles more firmly in place, she studied the stone closely. Tiny, unusually serrated edges adorned the tri-lobed leaf. She'd seen nothing like it in her years of studying fossils. It was possible she had discovered a new species of prehistoric flora.

She began examining the other stones around her. The third one she picked up contained the impressions of an ammonoid, a squid-like creature that lived inside a shell. Another stone contained the impression of a different leaf.

The wind grew still. Mina heard rustling in the tall grass beyond the creek and scanned the area but saw nothing alarming. Gripping her parasol tightly, she patted the pocket of her skirt. The weighty feel of Devlin's pistol reassured her.

She turned back to the stony ground. Her fossils must have washed from upstream. She studied the terrain again. Stepping carefully from stone to stone as Devlin had instructed, she made her way toward the next bend in the creek, keeping her eyes glued to the ground for traces of more treasures.

*

Devlin checked on the horses in their makeshift corral, happy to see Mina's mare hadn't yet found a way out. She was standing contently beside the two mules. When Devlin's horse moved to join the group, Sabiha laid back her ears and swung her rump toward him.

"Just like her mistress," Devlin muttered under his breath. Both Mina and her mare were happy to show the males who was boss.

Once he was sure the animals were secure, he made his way toward camp. At the edge of the clearing, he stopped short. The hairs on the back of his neck sent a tingle of warning. Something wasn't right.

He scanned the area closely, then he saw what was wrong. The plates Mina had taken to wash lay stacked on the creek bank. There was no sign of the woman who haunted his every waking thoughts and invaded his dreams.

Devlin slipped back into the cover of the underbrush. Carefully, he shifted to a better vantage point. Nothing moved in the clearing. He checked for signs a struggle had taken place but saw none. The sounds along the prairie creek were reassuring. Two squirrels chattered and chased each other in the branches overhead. Birds flew from treetop to treetop unconcerned. He was downwind of the cabin, and the only scent he could pick up was the faint aroma of wood smoke from the small fire he cooked with.

Where was Mina? Had the trip to the creek proved too much for her? Somehow, he doubted that.

Stealth, learned in a lifetime of living with the Cheyenne, kept him from calling out or dashing to the cabin. He took his hat off and laid it on the ground. Slowly, he worked his way around the clearing until he could move down the side of the cabin. A crack in the chinked wall let him scan a small section of the interior. Mina's cot was empty. No sound came from within. What he couldn't see was if anyone stood just inside the door waiting for his return.

Crouching, he crept forward. At the side of the door, he pulled in a deep breath, then launched himself against the wooden barrier. It flew back against the wall with a bang as his momentum carried him inside. He came up from a roll with his rifle aimed to sweep the spots he knew someone might hide. The cabin was empty.

Where the hell is she?

He left the cabin and strode to the creek. The plates lay unwashed. Mina had followed his orders about stepping only on stones, but he saw where several small rocks had been turned over. Their darkened bellies showed where they had nestled in the moist ground. He touched one. The dampness of the stone told him something had disturbed it less than half an hour ago. A deep, narrow hole in the earth had him puzzled for a moment until he realized it had been made by Mina's parasol tip.

Her trail was plain enough for a baby to follow. She had headed upstream alone. His blood turned cold at the thought. Artie's grave lay less than a mile away. Could she make it that far on her bad leg?

He knew the answer before the question finished forming in his mind. Mina could do anything she set her mind to. He crossed the clearing to retrieve his hat. After jamming it on his head, he took off after her.

Covering the rocky terrain with long strides, he considered what explanation he could give for why he hadn't told her about her husband's grave. He'd been foolish to mark it with the man's name. Telling her the truth was out of the question. His cowardly act had cost many more lives since that day.

Devlin pushed the thought to the back of his mind. He would have to live with what he'd done. In those first weeks and months, he had used whiskey to hold his nightmares at bay. He didn't have such luxury now. He needed a clear head to keep Mina alive.

A few dozen yards upstream, her trail turned away from the creek and into a wide, dry gully. The bleached white chalky walls rose three to four feet on either side. Around the third bend he spotted her crouched beside a pile of dirt.

She looked up at the sound of his boots crunching on the gravel. The sweet smile she sent him drove the harsh words he planned right out of his mind.

She held up a small stone. "Devlin, come see this. It's a shark's tooth. They're everywhere."

She struggled to her feet, leaning heavily on her parasol with one hand while she held a collection of rocks nestled in a fold of her skirt with the other.

"Mina, what are you doing?"

She beamed at him. "Finding fossils. This place is loaded with them. I've found at least three varieties of shells, the bones of a four small fish, shark teeth aplenty and two of the finest leaf impressions I've ever been privileged to see. Come look at them. This mix of sea and land fossils means this area was once a shoreline where forests pressed close to the prehistoric sea in the Late Cretaceous period. Who knows what other things I may find? Isn't this wonderful?"

"Wonderful," he drawled. He stood a few feet away, drinking in the sight of her happy and carefree as a toddler in a mud puddle.

"I'm so glad you found me. I simply can't carry all this with me. Can you take some back to the cabin while I explore further?"

"No."

She had already begun searching the gully walls, pulling at bits of stone and dropping any that didn't interest her. "But you simply must help me. I wish I had a basket or a bucket."

Sighing, he pulled off his hat and held it out. She looked at his offering with a bit of puzzlement, then laughed. "An excellent substitute, sir, thank you."

She began transferring the stones gathered in her skirt into his hat. When her skirt was empty, she shook it out and brushed at the clinging white dust with one hand. "Fossil hunting is dirty business."

"So is getting scalped. Aren't you forgetting something?"

She adjusted her spectacles and gave him her full attention. "What?"

"You're the smartest woman I've ever known. How can you be so stupid? You gave me your word you wouldn't leave the clearing."

She glanced around. "It appears I'm a liar."

"Yes."

Tipping her head slightly, she studied him. "Do you really think I'm smart?"

"You're being stupid today."

"Well, I had a perfectly good reason."

"And I had a perfectly good reason for insisting you stay near the cabin. Besides, you shouldn't be walking so far on that leg."

She glanced down. "It's hurting quite a lot, now that you mention it."

"I should turn you over my knee for the scare you gave me."

She grinned. "Were you worried about me?"

"No."

"You most certainly were." She looked pleased.

"I'm mad as a wet hornet." He thrust his hat loaded with rocks into her hands, then slipped his rifle sling over his head and let the gun hang across his back.

"Because I disobeyed you?" Her saucy tone showed she didn't fear his ire.

"No." He slid an arm behind her back and one behind her knees and swung her up into his arms, taking care not to jostle her injured leg any more than he had to. He was a bit surprised she didn't protest—or beat him senseless with her parasol.

"Then why are you angry?" She slipped one arm around his neck and held his hat and her parasol cradled on her stomach with the other.

"Because, besides carrying you, plus a ton of rock, back to camp, I'm going to have to wash the dishes."

She looked at him through lowered lashes. "Poor, Mr. Elder. I really am a burden to you."

"More than you know, milady."

"I hope you can find it in your heart to forgive me."

Her sly little smile made him wish he could make good on his threat to spank her pretty pink buttocks. Instead, he chose a more direct way to avoid the romantic pitfall he saw opening before him. He smiled back. "Why, milady, I believe you're flirting with me."

Her brows snapped into a frown. "I most certainly am not! I do not flirt."

Her offended tone nearly made him want to laugh. It was amazing how often he wanted to smile or laugh when she was near. He began walking toward the cabin. "My mistake then."

"Yes, I'm merely excited about my discoveries."

"That would account for your blush."

"I am not blushing. I've had a touch too much sun because I had to use my parasol as a cane."

"Yes, I see your complexion will soon be ruined."

Her gaze flew to his, sudden worry clouding her pretty eyes. "Do you think so?"

He schooled his features into stern lines. "You'll be as brown and wrinkled as a walnut inside of two weeks. By the end of the month, you'll be hideous."

Her eyes narrowed. "You're making fun of me."

"Could be."

She lifted her chin and looked away. "You, sir, are no gentleman."

"Never claimed to be."

She pressed her pretty lips closed on whatever remark she wanted to make, and he felt a twinge of regret. Life with Mina was never dull.

Back at the cabin, he deposited her on her cot. Ignoring her squeak of protest, he pulled the hem of her skirt high enough to check the dressing. "Your leg is swollen. Keep off it for the rest of the day."

She pushed his hand aside. "I can look after my wound from now on."

He straightened and watched as she quickly rearranged her skirt. "Fine, but pay more attention to it than those rocks."

"Fossils." She began removing them from his hat.

"Rocks." He took his hat back when she had emptied it onto her lap. Shaking out the dust, he tossed it onto his bunk in the far corner of the room.

She arranged her loot around the edge of her cot. The largest stone she picked up to scrutinize. "Fetch my writing utensils, my charcoal and my small set of tools, please."

Knowing he had lost her attention to some ancient leaf, he did as she asked. Keeping her mind occupied and keeping her off her leg and away from Artie's gravesite were his goals. If it took a hundred rocks a day to do it, he'd carry them in gladly.

*

For the rest of the afternoon, Mina cleaned her finds, made sketches of them and carefully categorized them in the pages of a blank journal she had unpacked from the recesses of her trunk. As she finished jotting down notes about the last leaf, she noted with surprise the light was fading. Devlin entered the cabin carrying an armload of firewood.

She adjusted her glasses. "Is it evening already?"

"Near enough. Are you done with your roc—fossils?"

"For now. Some of them need further cleaning. It would help to have a workbench and a place to keep them organized, but the limited space here prevents that. I really must pay more attention to what strata of earth I find them in. Today, I was simply overwhelmed with the thrill of my discoveries."

He stacked his wood to one side of the fireplace. "What do you have so far?"

Pleased at his interest, she launched into a description of the science behind classifying fossils. If he was bored with her lecture on the latest work by Professor Leidy or the early discoveries by European scientists, he didn't show it. He asked pointed questions, revealing his intellect and a good grasp of science. When she realized she had been rambling on for far too long, Mina fell silent.

"This bird fossil you hope to find. Do you have any idea where to look for it?" he asked.

"I only have Artie's map and the few details I pieced together from his journal entries. He was exploring an area of ground around a wide box canyon with a small stream. The fossil was imbedded in a slab of rock jutting out from the rim of a smaller gully on the eastern side."

"Hmm."

"I suppose you are going to tell me there are a thousand canyons like that in this area."

"No, I was thinking it sounds a lot like the canyon where I'm keeping the horses."

She leaned toward him. "Really?"

"Let me have a look at his map again."

She opened the lid of her trunk and pulled the thick oiled silk bundle from inside. Without hesitation, she handed it to him. "Could we be close to his campsite?"

He rubbed his chin as he studied the sketch. "I've heard this creek called Lodge Creek by some trappers."

Her finger tapped the page. "This symbol looks like a tent. It could be a lodge. It could even be this very cabin, couldn't it?"

"Take it easy. You're getting ahead of yourself."

"But we're close. I feel it."

"Maybe."

"I shall begin exploring the canyon first thing tomorrow."

"And if you find it, what then?"

She opened her mouth to speak, then closed it. Looking down, she smoothed the creases from her skirt. "Once I find the fossil, I will take it back to Vincent, and we will leave for London with all haste."

"With all haste? Will it be easy, Mina? Going back?" he asked quietly.

Was he asking if she would miss him? She couldn't let him see how much. "I don't know what you mean."

"Seems to me you like these plains."

Looking down, she nodded. "True, but Vincent needs me."

"When he's gone, what will you do? Will you finally live the life you deserve? Or will you find some other man who needs a model wife or nurse?"

She shook her head. "I wasn't a model wife."

"No? I think that's exactly what you were. Only it was a model you made to please others. Don't keep living your life for a sick old man and his brainless son out of a mistaken sense of duty."

Her chin came up. "What do you know about putting someone's wants and needs before your own? You're a drifter, a rootless man living by his own rules, little better than a savage. What do you know about duty?"

"Nothing." He tossed the map onto the foot of her bed and left the cabin.

Instantly sorry she had belittled him, she called out, "Devlin, wait!"

He didn't stop.

Chapter Nineteen

The next morning, an uncomfortable silence lingered in the little cabin. Mina saw no way to heal the breech with Devlin. His words about Vincent and Artie had touched a nerve. Try as she might, she couldn't put them out of her head.

She'd given up a chance to marry someone who loved her, a chance to have a home and children of her own. Did she regret those things? Yes, but she had made her choice out of love. Devlin didn't understand. Nor could she explain without revealing Artie's secret. She wasn't about to destroy her husband's reputation. Such information had a way of spreading and it would kill Vincent if he found out.

When the sun had risen halfway up the eastern sky, Mina gathered her parasol and placed her tools, a newly sharpened pencil and a sketch pad in her sturdy canvas bag. With the strap slung over one shoulder, she headed to the canyon where they kept the horses. Devlin followed, silent as a shadow with his rifle nestled in the crook of his arm.

Sabiha, at least, was happy to see her and greeted Mina with a low whinny and playful nuzzling. After spending a few minutes lavishing attention on the mare, Mina deposited her gear at the foot of the low eastern cliff and began a close survey of the area. There were fossils aplenty, ammonoid spirals, brachiopods, clams, snails, even a turtle shell, but not what she was after. Half a dozen smaller gullies emptied into the canyon. They offered Mina the best hope of discovering where Artie had been exploring. Devlin squatted near the corral entrance; his face impassive in the bright sun. Mina longed to apologize, but she wanted him to apologize first.

She chose the crevice closest to the front of the canyon. By noon, her exploration had yielded three fine fossil specimens of small fish but not one bird. Thrilled with her finds, she sketched them and made detailed notes about their discovery location before moving on. As hard as she searched, she found no indication Artie had explored there.

Some hours later, she emerged from the narrow confines of the fissure, miserably hot, covered in clinging, gritty dust from head to toe and feeling decidedly tired and irritable.

Devlin waited in the shade of a small tree near the corral's entrance.

Looking cool and composed, he raised a canteen to his lips, tipped his head back, then wiped his mouth on his shirtsleeve. "Find anything?"

"Not what I was looking for." She climbed through the pole fence with difficulty and came to stand beside him. "May I have a drink of your water?"

He turned the canteen upside down. Only a few drops trickled out. "Sorry. Gets mighty hot inside those arroyos, doesn't it?"

Mina resisted the urge to jab him with her parasol. That she had failed to take a canteen was her own fault, but she suspected he was happy to drive the point home. She straightened her spine, snapped her sunshade open and headed for the cabin.

*

Devlin watched her limp along and called her every kind of fool. She'd spent too much time in the sun today. She hadn't recovered enough for such a long outing. Irritating was too mild a word for her. He rose and followed along. After a few dozen yards, her steps slowed. She closed her parasol and used it as a cane the rest of the way.

Back at the cabin, she went directly to the creek bank, where a spring bubbled out of a rock ledge. She dipped her hand in the water and drank her fill. Sitting back, she pulled out her hanky, wet it and used it to mop her brow. Her trembling hands showed him how close to exhaustion she was.

Compassion slowly replaced the annoyance he felt at her stinging comments last night. He went into the cabin, opened the lid of her trunk and pulled out her soap. He ran his thumb across the smooth finish, then held the scented bar to his face and inhaled the delicate lavender fragrance. The scent would remind him of her long after she was gone.

Shoving aside the sobering thought, he pulled a towel from her trunk, took a blanket from her cot and went outside. She remained seated beside the creek.

She looked up as he stopped beside her. Her glasses had slipped a little way down her nose. Her intense blue eyes stared at him over the tops with guarded suspicion. He squatted down, took one of her hands and placed the soap in it. "You look like you could use a bath."

A tiny smile curved her lips as a sparkle sprang to life in the depths of her eyes. "Is that your way of telling me I stink?"

He smiled back. "I don't mince words, milady. When you stink, I'll tell you."

"Fair enough. It is uncomfortably hot today. Perhaps a bath would be just the thing. Only." She flushed, and he knew it wasn't the heat.

He rose to his feet. "I'll keep watch from up on the bluff. Don't worry. Those elderberry bushes will provide a good screen. How's your leg?"

"The wound is closed and healing. I don't think a brief stint in the water will hurt it."

"I'll trust your judgment. If you need anything, call out and I'll come down." He turned away.

"Devlin, I'm sorry about what I said last night."

At the sound of her hesitant apology, he stopped but didn't turn around. He drew a deep breath and let it out slowly. "Never be sorry for speaking the truth."

"I will say the same thing to you, sir. None of us leads a blameless life."

"Some of us carry more blame than others."

Without looking back, he made his way to the top of the bluff that sheltered the cabin under its overhang.

*

Mina moved into a dense clump of willows and elderberry bushes. She knew Devlin was right about the foliage blocking his view, but she still had a moment's hesitation unbuttoning her shirt. By standing on her tiptoes, she could just make out the crown of his hat at the top of the hill. Feeling somewhat reassured, she unlaced her boots and rolled down her stockings, then dipped one foot in the creek. It was refreshingly cool.

She parted some branches and glanced up the hill again. He remained in the same place. The lure of the still, shaded water proved stronger than her modesty, and she undid her shirt and slipped out of her skirt. Wearing only her muslin camisole and bloomers, she waded in.

The slippery mud of the creek bank squished between her toes. She had to grab hold of a nearby branch to keep from falling. Once she regained her balance, she ventured farther out. The water rising up her thighs sent a shiver of delight through her. Compared to the heat of the day, the pool felt almost icy. Once she reached a place hip deep, she took a deep breath and dove forward. The water enveloped her in a breathtaking rush of cool bliss.

Breaking the surface, Mina wiped her eyes and grinned with pleasure. She tried swimming a few strokes, but found it made her leg ache. She contented herself instead with drifting on her back and staring up at the flawless blue sky. Little by little, the aches and pains of a day spent in cramped and dirty quarters seeped away.

Knowing while she relaxed in the tranquil pool, Devlin was sitting out in the scorching sun and keeping watch finally prompted her to take up her soap and bathe. It was well she hadn't tarried, for barely had she climbed out of the pool and wrapped herself in the blanket, when his voice came from outside her leafy bower.

"Time to get out, milady."

"Indeed, I have already done so. It was most refreshing."

She emerged with the blanket clutched tightly in front of her. Feeling shy about being seen with her hair hanging in wet tentacles about her like strands of seaweed, she brushed past him and made her way toward the cabin. "I shall finish changing and keep watch from the hilltop while you bathe."

"It that *your* way of telling me I stink?"

She paused at the doorway and cast a look over her shoulder, trying with difficulty not to smile. "I'd rather not say."

He didn't. It hadn't escaped her notice that he came into the cabin each morning with dripping hair and his shirt clinging to his damp body.

When she came out of the cabin dressed in dry clothing, and feeling considerably refreshed, she joined him near the water. She carried a hairbrush in one pocket of her skirt and a rifle in her hand. Her hair she had confined by tying a scarf around it at the nape of her neck. It would take some time for it to dry, even in the hot afternoon air.

Devlin shed his shirt and Mina found herself again mesmerized by the sight of his bare torso. She reached out and gently touched the jagged scar on his shoulder. "What happened here?"

"A Kiowa knife."

"You say that so calmly. How old were you?"

"Fifteen. There was a raid on our village. They were after horses and captives. One of them had my—had a little girl. I pulled him off his horse, but not before he stabbed me. While we were struggling, my mother picked up his lance and ran him through. She saved my life."

"What a brave woman." Mina pressed her hand against the old wound. How close it had come to his heart. She could feel its steady beat beneath the warm skin under her palm. She shuddered to think she might never have known him. "What about these matching scars on your chest? What happened here?"

"Those are from the Sacred Sun Dance. You wouldn't understand. Are you going to keep watch from here while I bathe?"

"What?" She looked up and met his amused gaze.

He covered her hand with his own. His other hand went to the top button on his pants and slipped it open. "You might see more than you bargained for."

Jerking her hand free, Mina spun on her heels and headed to the top of the bluff, hoping he hadn't seen the blush rushing to her cheeks. Drat the man! He positively delighted in discomforting her.

Every time she felt she was getting to understand him, he outraged her sensibilities and left her feeling like an awkward schoolgirl.

By the time she reached the hilltop, her aching leg had replaced Devlin at the top of the list of dismal things about her current situation. She found where he had been sitting and settled down with his rifle across her lap. With one hand, she massaged her calf and waited for the pain to lessen as she scanned the countryside. She took particular care to avoid looking down at him. While she had waded and bathed behind a screen of bushes, she was certain he would not.

After peering out at the endless sea of grass and low hills for a full two minutes and seeing nothing of interest, her eyes were drawn to the creek below. If she moved closer to the rim, she could see more of the stream. Only to make sure no danger approached, of course.

She sidled toward the edge. When the tops of the trees on the opposite bank came into view, she stretched out on her stomach and wiggled forward. By carefully parting the tall grass in front of her, she soon had an unobstructed view of the creek and the naked man standing with his back toward her.

He stood knee deep in the water, working her soap into a lather in his dark hair. His shoulders and back were tanned bronze down to his waist. Below his waist, his skin was pale, but the contrast served only to enhance his masculine appeal. His buttocks and thighs were firm and taut. A flush heated Mina's body from head to toe.

The aspects of his male figure were even more attractive than the first time she had seen him naked. His form was quite magnificent. He could have modeled for Michelangelo's beautiful sculpture of David.

She adjusted her glasses and rose slightly. In doing so, she dislodged a small stone. It went clattering down the cliff face.

He paused in his ablutions. Mina ducked down, smashing her face into the grass. Mortified by her own audacity, she held her breath. It was a long minute before she dared to look. A wave of relief washed over her when she saw he had moved to deeper water and was rinsing the soap from his body.

Using extreme care, she crept backwards until she was sure she was out of sight. She sat up and glanced around. Nothing but cloud shadows moved across the nearby hills.

She loosened her hair and removed her brush from her skirt pocket. Grabbing a handful of hair, she ruthlessly pulled at the tangles. Perhaps by forcing her snarled locks into a semblance of order, she could force her wayward thoughts into order as well.

She tried, but all she could think of was how magnificent he looked and how much she wanted to look again.

Fifteen minutes later, she had removed the worst of the knots and was letting the breeze dry her hair when a voice behind her made her jump almost out of her skin.

"See anything interesting?"

She sprang to her feet and whirled to face Devlin. "I don't know what you mean?"

The wretched man was smiling. It was only a tiny crinkle at the corners of his eyes, but she knew full well he was laughing at her.

She raised her chin. "I saw nothing remarkable."

"Really? I thought from up here you might have had a pretty good view of things."

"The vista was quite boring, actually."

"You don't like grass?"

"Not particularly."

"Odd, because it looks like you were rolling in it." He gestured to the front of her blouse.

Mina looked down. Grass stains and dirt marred the front of her clothing. She brushed ineffectively at the marks. "I slipped and fell on the climb up here."

"You should be more careful. You might have had a nasty fall if you were close to the edge."

The wind blew her hair across her face. She tugged it aside. "I wasn't close to the edge at all. Thank you for your concern. Shall we go?" Without waiting for his reply, she headed back toward the cabin.

Over the next few days, Mina spent more and more time searching the canyons and gullies for fossils. She developed a plan which allowed her to work through the early hours of the day before the heat was too intense and then spend the afternoon hours inside the cooler cabin, cataloging and cleaning her discoveries.

Late in the afternoon, she would venture out again with Devlin to scout areas to be explored the following day. Of the bird with teeth, she found not a trace. But as more and more new fossils came to light under her eager searching, the need to find it slipped further back in her mind. Some of her finds were new species of plants and sea creatures. When she presented them to the Natural History Museum in London, she would insist they bore her name.

Devlin proved to be invaluable. His keen eye often found patterns and irregularities in the chalky ground she overlooked. Nine times out of ten, he could point out an area that would yield a prime specimen.

She only had to tell him once how to uncover and remove their fragile discoveries. After that, he worked well without her supervision, and she was free to move on to the next area without worrying he might ruin the find with a clumsy extraction.

One evening found them sitting side by side on a buffalo robe near the creek, enjoying the coolness of the evening and the songs of cicadas. Overhead, stars came out one by one as the twilight faded into night. She looked over to see him staring up into the sky. He sat with his hands locked around one knee while the other leg stretched out in front of him.

What was he thinking about? She longed to know but hesitated to ask.

"What?"

She jumped, startled by his voice. "I didn't say anything."

"You didn't have to. I can feel your eyes boring into the side of my head."

She looked down at her hands. "I'm sorry."

Searching desperately for a safe topic, she buried her fingers in the long hair of the robe. "How do the natives hunt these huge animals with only bow and arrow? With a hide so thick you wouldn't think an arrow wouldn't even penetrate it."

"They ride up beside them and aim for a spot just behind the front leg. A close, hard shot there will pierce the lung and sometimes even the heart if it isn't deflected by a rib. Other times they drive some of the herd over a buffalo jump. A drop off like where our cave was. The maimed animals are easier to kill."

"It sounds brutal."

"So is starving." He leaned back on his elbows and met her gaze. "Do you know who gave the buffalo to the Cheyenne?"

"I would say, God, but what would a Cheyenne say?"

"A long time ago, far to the north, a band of Cheyenne lived where a rushing river emptied into a large cavern. Times were hard. There was little food, and the people were hungry. Because they needed food, three of the bravest warriors decided to explore the cave. It was a dangerous thing to do, but those three warriors jumped in. Once inside, when their eyes could see in the dimness, what do you think they found?"

Mina turned to face him, eager to hear more of the story. "I have no idea. What?"

"They found another opening and when they went inside, they discovered a very elderly grandmother."

"Inside a cave, inside another cave under a river? How odd."

He rolled his eyes at her. "Who's telling this story? You or me?"

She waved one hand. "I'm sorry. Go on."

"The grandmother asked the men what they wanted. They told her they were looking for food for their people. There was seldom enough to eat and the children often went hungry. When she asked them if they were hungry now, they said yes. She brought out two pots. One was filled with buffalo meat, and the other held corn. She invited them to eat, and they did, but no matter how much they ate, the pots remained full."

"An old woman in a cave under the river had magic containers of food?"

He squinted at her. "Are you making fun of me?"

She grinned. "No. I'm just trying to keep my facts straight. Go on. It's a wonderful tale."

He lay back on the robe. "I think I'm done."

"No! All right, I'm very sorry. I do want to hear the rest of it. Please?"

"Are you going to interrupt again?"

"I'll be as quiet as a mouse. What happened next?"

"Because the young men were brave enough to jump into the cave, the old grandmother told them to take the pots back to their tribe. She instructed them how to plant the corn and how to harvest it. She also said buffalo would come soon. The men took the food back to the people, and the tribe ate their fill. And when they finished, a buffalo jumped up out of the cave, then another and another until soon they covered the whole prairie."

"That's a lot of buffalo from one cave." She tried to stifle a giggle.

"I thought you were going to be quiet."

"Sorry."

He gave her a hard stare but continued. "The Cheyenne planted the corn the way the grandmother told them, and they followed the buffalo out onto the prairie and hunted them. In the fall, they returned to the river and found a field of corn ready to be gathered in. Afterwards, there was always plenty of food for everyone. And they were forever grateful to the grandmother who gave them the corn and the buffalo."

"It's a wonderful tale. Tell me another one."

"It's getting late. We should turn in."

"Oh, just one more. Please? Please? One more."

He chuckled. "Now you sound like Namid."

"Who is that?"

His smile vanished. He sat up, staring into the night. "Someone I knew a long time ago."

Mina could tell by the sound of his voice the closeness they had shared was gone. She tried once more to keep him beside her. "I would like to hear more of your stories."

Rising to his feet, he said, "Maybe I should tell you the one about the woman who cut her husband into pieces and fed him to the rest of the family and how his head followed her around forever."

She grimaced. "That wasn't exactly what I hoped to hear."

"Not a good bedtime story?"

"No."

He reached down and drew her to her feet. "Are you afraid of ghosts?"

"I don't know. I've never met one."

He gave her a half smile. "The Cheyenne believe in ghosts, and they fear their supernatural powers."

"Do you fear ghosts?"

He let go of her hand. "Only the ones I've met."

He turned and walked away, vanishing into the darkness.

Mina got ready for bed, but sleep eluded her. She lay awake a long time listening for his return. In the small hours of the night, she heard him come in. The next morning, he was gone again when she woke.

For the next two days, he spent more and more time away from camp. She finally asked him where he had been, but his curt answer only puzzled her.

"Appeasing a ghost." When he didn't offer more of an explanation, she let the subject drop.

Several days later, Mina returned from checking on the horses to find him hammering long pegs into the cabin wall. On the floor beside him lay several rough-split boards.

"What's all this?"

He pushed his hat back and wiped the sweat from his forehead with his sleeve. "I'm tired of those rocks cluttering up the floor. Every time I turn around, I step on one. I'm making shelves so you can keep the damn things out of the way."

Mina stood speechless.

He lifted a board and settled it on the thick pegs, then tested them by pressing down. They held.

She clasped her hands together under her chin. "I don't know what to say. You did this for me? How?"

"I used a hatchet and a stone wedge. They aren't pretty, but they'll work."

"They're wonderful. Thank you so much. This will make cataloging my finds much easier. Can I be of some assistance?"

"No, this is the last." He lifted a second shelf and set it about a foot higher than the first one.

In no time, Mina had arranged her fossils according to plant or animal, sea or land creatures. When she finished, she stepped back and placed her hands on her hips. "Quite satisfactory, sir."

He merely grunted, but Mina wasn't fooled. He was as pleased with her praise as she was with his thoughtfulness.

Devlin pushed up the brim of his hat. "You've got quite a collection going."

"Indeed. Despite not finding Artie's bird fossil, I've amassed an astonishing number of what I believe are new species. When word of these discoveries gets out, paleontologists will flock to this area."

"You'll be famous."

Mina wrinkled her nose. "I very much doubt it."

"Why?"

"In point of fact, the credit for these discoveries would go to you."

"Why? You found them."

"Ah, but I am a woman. There are very few women in scientific fields, and those of us trying to earn a place in those hallowed halls are overlooked or dismissed. I have sent many fossils to the British Museum's Department of Natural History. My name is not listed on any of them. My friend Mary Anning made hundreds of fossil discoveries, but since she was a poor untrained worker, she sold her finds to men who then took credit and had new species named after them. It was grossly unfair."

"You mean like you are trying to do for Artie?"

Mina frowned at him. "It's not the same at all."

"You're doing the work, but you intend to give him the credit."

"The credit is his. He made the discovery. He simply couldn't recover the fossil. I intend to see he gets the credit due him."

Devlin grunted.

"What?"

"I don't see the difference. If you find it, you should get credit for it. Not your husband. Something tells me he was too stupid to recognize what a treasure he had."

"Sir, I can't allow you to speak ill of my husband."

"I'll speak however I damn well please."

"And I have asked you repeatedly not to swear, Mr. Elder."

"Well, we make a good pair then, don't we? You never do what you're told and neither do I."

Mina crossed her arms over her chest. "Now you sound like an argumentative child."

"Better to sound like one than to be one."

"How dare you!" She fought to hold on to her temper. Exchanging insults with the man wouldn't gain her anything.

She turned and picked up her sunshade from its place by the front door. "I shall be working in the eastern part of the horse canyon. Thank you again for the shelves. Good day." Sweeping her skirt aside, she flounced out of the room.

Irritating, odious man!

She fumed as she marched toward her latest digs. One minute he did something incredibly sweet. The next minute he ruined it with some demeaning statement. She couldn't decide if she wanted to kiss him or part his hair with a rock.

She made her way out to the next likely area she and Devlin had marked for exploration. A shallow gully just past the horse canyon ran eastward onto the prairie. Mina had wanted to explore the creek bed to the north, but Devlin had vetoed her idea as unsafe and convinced her to explore south of their camp. Because she believed he knew the area better, she'd agreed.

Later that afternoon, she stood in the bottom of a chest high gully and examined the wall where she detected the first faint marks of manmade tools. They were weathered to the point she couldn't be certain of their origin, but hope rose in her breast. Perhaps this was the area Artie had been exploring.

The day grew hotter, and she was thankful for the shade of her parasol. By wedging the handle in her belt loop, she could keep her hands free. The only drawback was the wide spokes of her sunshade caught on the gully walls when she stooped or squatted to work on the lower portions.

She was down on her knees working loose the most interesting slab of limestone imbedded with the fossils of many squid-like creatures when the sound of hoofbeats caught her attention. She tried to rise, but her open parasol became wedged between the narrow walls and prevented her from standing. Extracting the cumbersome article from her belt, she freed the spokes from the ground and stood. Immediately, she saw the legs of two horses standing in front of her. Tipping back her shade, she found a pair of fearsome-looking native men gazed down at her.

Chapter Twenty

The two men in front of Mina sat at ease on their horses. Were they dangerous? Wearing only buckskin breechcloths and leggings, they watched her with impassive expressions. Their black hair hung in long braids down their chests, but their broad weathered faces were free of the war paint Mina had been led to believe they wore.

She gathered her wits and tried to formulate a plan. She had her derringer in her pocket, but it held only two bullets. Her chances of disabling both men were slim. Her parasol might spook their horses and allow her time to escape, but the gully's narrow width and snaking course would prevent her from covering much distance before they had time to recover. The parasol's cloth dome certainly wouldn't block arrows or bullets.

As these thoughts and others raced through her mind, she noticed the men made no hostile moves. Indeed, the way the younger of the two smiled at her left her feeling most uncomfortable. He spoke in a language she didn't understand.

A reply in the same guttural tones came from behind her. She looked over her shoulder. Devlin came striding toward her. She had never been happier to see anyone.

*

Devlin leaped over the narrow gully Mina stood in. Ignoring her, he walked up to the men. In the tongue of his youth, he addressed the older of the two men in Cheyenne. "Walks Far, it is good to see you."

Walks Far returned his greeting. "Stone Warrior, it has been many seasons since you came among our people."

"I follow the way of the white man, now."

Walks Far nodded slowly. His impassive, wrinkled face gave no hint of his thoughts. After a moment, he said, "It was your choice to make. You will always be welcome at my lodge."

"My thanks. You are also welcome by my fire."

Gesturing to the young man with him, Walks Far said, "This is my grandson, Red Buffalo."

Devlin held his hand waist high. "I remember him, but he was only a small boy when last I saw him."

Red Buffalo sat up straighter on his horse and puffed out his chest. "I am a warrior now with many scalps of our enemies on my war lance. Soon I will take a wife."

Devlin didn't care for the way he looked at Mina.

She cleared her throat. "Mr. Elder, if I might have a word with you?"

Devlin ignored her.

The young warrior frowned at her. "The woman has no manners, Stone Warrior. She interrupts men when they are speaking."

"Mr. Elder, I require your assistance." She was struggling to get out of the gully but making little progress.

He said in English over his shoulder. "Shut up until you're spoken to."

"I beg your pardon?" Her shock was obvious.

Turning, he reached down, snatched her parasol from her grip, then grabbed her hand and pulled her up to level ground.

She seized her parasol and took it from him. "Did you just tell me to shut up?"

"I did. Don't make me tell you again."

"Of all the nerve."

The young brave snickered. Mina sent him a sharp look. The older man spoke in slow but respectable English. "Stone Warrior, it is good to see you have a woman. I will tell Namid. She will be pleased."

Mina spoke under her breath. "Who is Stone Warrior?"

"I am."

"Do you know these people?"

"Yes. Now shut up." He switched to Cheyenne again, leaving her in the dark.

Mina still glared at him and whispered. "Speak to me like that again, and you'll find the point of my parasol in a very awkward part of your anatomy."

She walked toward the Indians and held out her hand. "How do you do, gentlemen? Since Mr. Elder seems reluctant to do the honors, I shall introduce myself. I am—"

"My wife." Devlin grabbed her outstretched hand in a punishing grip.

"Your what?" She stared at him in disbelief.

He threw his arm across her shoulders and pulled her tight to his side. "She needs much discipline. Forgive her."

Mina opened her mouth, but he covered it with his hand and whispered in her ear, "Go along with me unless you want that young buck to think you're his for the taking."

When he lifted his hand from her lips, she cast a wide-eyed glance at Red Buffalo and then at Devlin. "He wouldn't dare."

"He would."

Mina held her peace. If what Devlin implied was true, she would go along with his ruse, but he would certainly hear her opinion of his treatment once they were alone.

The young man exchanged a few more words in Cheyenne with Devlin. Devlin shook his head. The young man wasn't pleased, but whatever they said seemed to amuse the older warrior. After a few more exchanges, they turned their ponies and rode away.

As they disappeared over the rise, Mina found her tongue.

"Exactly what was going on?"

"Red Buffalo offered to buy you."

"He what?"

Devlin began walking toward the cabin. "He offered two ponies. It's a good price. I was tempted."

Mina rushed to keep up with him. "You're joking."

"About his wanting to buy you? Or about being tempted?"

"I'm not sure I want to hear the answer."

Devlin nodded. "Smart woman."

"Are they from your mother's tribe?"

"Yes. Swift Fox's band is camped a day's ride to the north."

"Are we in danger?"

"From them?" He jerked his head toward the two figures growing smaller as they rode into the distance.

"Yes." She struggled to keep up with his long strides across the uneven ground.

"Not unless Red Buffalo decides to count coup on me by stealing you." He stopped, and Mina nearly collided with him. "I suggest you stick close to the cabin for the next few days, just in case."

"He really wanted to buy me? It's quite flattering in a strange sort of way. Is it the custom of the Cheyenne to steal brides?"

"He doesn't want you as his wife."

She stopped as the implication sank in. "Oh, I see." Then she ran to catch up with him. "Do you intend to visit the camp? I would welcome the chance to meet natives who are friendly."

"I'm not going to Swift Fox's camp."

"But you said yourself it's been years since you last saw them. Surely you don't want to miss this opportunity?"

He stopped and spun around so fast she almost ran into him again. He pushed back the brim of his hat. "We aren't going, and that's final!"

"You needn't yell at me. My hearing is quite good."

He turned on his heels and stomped away. As he did, Mina heard him mutter, "I should have taken the damn horses."

"I'm worth at least six!" she shouted. He didn't reply.

The old man had called Devlin Stone Warrior. The name suited him. Miffed, but deciding not to push visiting the tribe, she followed him back to the cabin.

The next day, Mina took a break from fieldwork and stayed at the camp. Not because Devlin had suggested it to prevent her from being kidnapped by an amorous young brave. No, it was because the cabin had become too cluttered to live in comfortably. It was time to engage in a bit of housework.

Hands on hips, she surveyed the single room with a critical eye. Her specimens, her tools and her clothes had spread out of her sleeping area and were taking over what little space remained. Devlin's things were neatly folded on his cot or stored underneath it. She found the contrast interesting. Although housewifery skills were not her strong suit, having had servants for much of her life, she had no aversion to setting her own mess to rights.

First, she turned to the shelves Devlin had made for her. She began by straightening out her collection but ended up with her fingers trailing over the surface of her gift. The wood was rough cut. She took care to avoid splinters, but no present had touched her heart more.

Devlin might make fun of her work, but here was proof he respected what she did. To hew out these boards, using only a small hatchet had taken hours of labor. His only purpose in building them was to make her work easier and display it for all to see.

Not that there was anyone to see what she had discovered. Hidden as they were in the wild, her finds could just as well have remained in the earth. Unless she found a way to transport her specimens and notes back to civilization, her work here would count for nothing. While there were fine fossils in her current collection, nothing was near the significance of Artie's bird.

Would Vincent be pleased with what she had accomplished? This extensive collection of fossils told a story of ancient times, but they also told how she was shirking her duty. Each day she spent extracting and cataloging her own discoveries was one less day she spent looking for Artie's find, but it was one more day she could spend with Devlin. She was happy in her woodpile, prospecting for fossils alongside a man she adored. It was what she had always hoped her life would be.

She cared deeply for Devlin, despite knowing nothing would come of it. The idea of leaving him was becoming unbearable. Almost as intolerable as the knowledge Vincent still waited for word about the fate of his son. He would be worried about her, too. She hadn't been able to send a telegram in weeks.

She couldn't let her heart's yearnings lead her astray. Having failed at all she had hoped to accomplish, there was no choice but to travel to Fort Harker, send word to Vincent, and return to Philadelphia.

Yet here on these barren plains, she'd found a glimpse of true happiness, a vision of what her life could be like. To remain would mean leaving Vincent to face the end of his life alone, a broken man with no one to care for him but servants, robbed of pride in his only son and deserted by the young woman he had rescued from hell.

Leaving the man she loved as a father to such a fate was unbearable. She had to put aside her feelings for Devlin and finish what she had set out to do.

With a sigh, she turned away from her specimens and surveyed the cabin. Her scattered clothes would be the best place to start. She picked up several shirts and spotted a gray skirt that had found its way onto the pile of firewood beside the fireplace. She vaguely remembered tossing it over the wood so the wet hem might dry properly. Two days ago or three? She picked it up. A small snake fell out of its folds.

Mina dropped the cloth and leaped back with a shriek. She covered her mouth with both hands, shaking from head to toe as the memory of the rattler froze her blood. Glancing toward the door, she tried to summon the will to run outside, but her legs refused to obey.

The reptile slithered across the floor. Her quick prayer it would go outside remained unanswered. The snake darted under Devlin's bed.

Little by little, her terror faded, and her common sense returned. "It is only a baby blacksnake. It is not a rattlesnake. Not a poisonous creature."

Speaking the words aloud helped to calm her nerves. "It can't harm me."

She pressed a hand to her heaving bosom. "Unless one counts being scared witless as being harmed."

Crouching, she peered under Devlin's cot. The snake lay stretched out beside his saddle bags. She straightened and took a step back as she gathered her calico skirt in both hands and hiked it above her knees. If the creature came after her, she didn't want it getting tangled in her clothing.

Devlin would kill it for her. She started toward the doorway but stopped. Black snakes were harmless. Devlin would laugh at her. Not out loud, of course, but he would laugh. Turning around, she faced his bed and squared her shoulders. She wasn't a spineless maiden who swooned at the sight of a harmless reptile.

Crossing to the fireplace, she pulled a long piece of kindling from the woodpile after carefully checking for relatives of her unwanted guest. She swung the stick with one hand, testing its strength. With her other hand, she kept a tight grip on her bunched-up skirt and petticoats.

Once armed, she approached Devlin's bed again. Crouching down, she could see the snake hadn't moved.

"All right, what is my plan of action?"

Perhaps she could prod the serpent into moving outside. She really didn't want to kill it, only to see it made its home elsewhere.

She poked her stick under the cot. The snake coiled tightly and hissed. She poked again. The creature struck her stick, biting in retaliation. Mina dropped her end and jumped back, frightened almost witless by a menace less than twice the length of her boot. Drawing her tattered courage close, she crouched down and grasped her stick again. "You're not poisonous. You can't hurt me, but you will get out of this cabin."

The snake remained defiantly coiled, unmoved by her threat.

What she needed was more room to maneuver. Grasping Devlin's bed by one corner, she shoved it aside, exposing her nemesis.

The serpent realized his cover was gone. In a flash, he wiggled toward the wall. Before Mina could stop him, he slipped through a crack and disappeared. Almost. A mere inch of his black tail remained sticking out from under the log.

Mina considered the situation. The log wall was built flush against the rock hillside behind the cabin. Obviously, the snake could go no farther. Grasping his cool, scaly hide and pulling him free looked like one option. Except, she couldn't bring herself to do it. She couldn't touch him. Not even with gloves. Where were her riding gloves in this mess? It didn't matter.

Moving the bed farther out of the way, she pondered her dilemma. Perhaps she could slip a cord or ribbon over the creature's tail and pull it out?

The absurdity of roping a snake's tail with one of her hair ribbons brought forth a nervous giggle. She would have to seek Devlin's assistance, after all. But what if the snake moved from this spot while she was out looking for Devlin? How could she sleep knowing the thing might lie coiled under her bed or look for more clothing to snuggle inside?

She sat down on Devlin's cot. How could she make sure the snake didn't escape while she was gone? As she stared at the wall, seeking inspiration, she noticed something odd. There was a notch in one log about three feet above the floor. The logs looked as if they had all been cut in a line a few inches past the notch. Intrigued, she moved closer, keeping one eye on the tail protruding near her feet. The smooth notch appeared manmade. After careful inspection, she inserted her hand inside. Her fingers touched the cool metal of a hidden latch. Excited by her discovery, she lifted the catch, and a three by three-foot section of the logs swung outward. She bent down to peer inside.

"What the hell do you think you are doing?"

Devlin's angry bellow startled Mina, causing her to bang her head on the low opening. Rubbing the tender spot, she glanced up to see his fierce scowl.

"I have asked you repeatedly not to swear at me, sir."

"What are you doing snooping through my things?"

"See what I've found. It's some sort of secret opening. What do you think it's for?"

"It's for hiding stolen whiskey."

His quick answer gave her a moment's pause. She adjusted her glasses as she studied his angry face. "Why would you think such a thing?"

"Because that's where I hid the whiskey I stole last winter."

Her mouth dropped open, but she snapped it shut. "You admit to stealing another man's property?"

"Sort of."

"Sort of! What exactly does that mean? Did you steal it or did you not?"

"The man owed me money and wouldn't pay, so I took his whiskey."

"You're a thief?"

"I'm a man who makes his own rules."

She gestured toward the dark space. "Is there any whiskey left, or did you drink it all when I was sleeping?"

His eyes snapped with anger. "There are two kegs in there, and they haven't been touched."

Banging the door shut, he glared at her. "Not that I haven't been tempted. If there's any woman on earth who could drive a man to drown himself in a hog's head of rotgut, it's you."

She rose to her feet and dusted off her skirt. "You were a drunkard long before you met me. Don't lay your weaknesses at my door."

"I've seen you tip back a drop, remember? If you get thirsty, help yourself. I won't stop you."

"The only time you have seen me take a drink was for medicinal purposes. I rarely imbibe."

"So you say. What were you doing moving my things, anyway?"

"I was chasing a snake."

That surprised him. "What kind of snake?"

"A blacksnake."

"Why chase a harmless blacksnake?"

"It made itself at home in the skirt I left drying on the woodpile. I took exception to its residence in my garments and tried to shoo it outside. It took cover under your bed."

She planted her hands on her hips and glared at him. "I shouldn't be surprised one snake would seek the company of another."

He pushed his bed into place against the wall. "Red Buffalo came back this morning and upped his offer to three ponies. If he comes back tomorrow, I'm going to let him have you for a lame mule."

Anger filled every pore of her body. "I may just go. His company can't be any worse than that of a drunken thief."

"Why I haven't strangled you yet is a mystery."

"And why I haven't shot you surpasses all understanding."

Standing toe to toe, glaring at each other, Mina became acutely aware of his nearness, of the heat from his body, the sound of his hard breathing. His scent, so masculine and earthy, seemed to crush her anger and sweep it aside.

A shimmering energy replaced it unlike anything that had possessed her before. She wanted him. Wanted his touch, wanted to run her hands through his hair, wanted to feel the strength of his arms around her and his body pressed to hers. Intense desire, sharp and almost painful, filled her.

Reaching up, she grasped his face between her hands and pulled him down until their lips met. Sweet, heady languor replaced the last bit of common sense she possessed as Devlin deepened the kiss.

Would he make love to her? The idea nestled into her mind and wouldn't budge. Did she want this?

He cupped her face gently and then slipped his fingers into her hair. She grew breathless when he let one hand slide over her shoulder and down her back. He pulled her tight against his body, and she knew he desired her.

Was it so wrong to want to know what love between a man and a woman was like?

The image of lying down with Devlin sent a curl of longing sweeping through her body. She began drowning in a rush of sensations. She slipped her arms around his neck and pressed her breasts against his chest, wanting to feel his skin against hers. But there was too much clothing between them.

He broke the kiss and raised his face, panting heavily. "I can't do this."

Mina ran her tongue over her lips to quiet their tingling. She dropped her hands and stepped back, stunned at her own audacity as shame swept away her desire. What on earth had come over her?

Devlin looked totally bewildered.

How could she have been so wanton, so lacking in decorum? What must he think of her? Clearly, he didn't desire her. She needed to get away. Rushing past him, she left the cabin, grabbing her parasol from its place by the door as she went.

*

When Devlin's reeling mind settled into some sort of order, he lifted a hand to his lips and let out his breath in a slow whistle. "If that's how she intends to win her arguments, I'm going to have to find more things to fight about."

With Mina, that shouldn't be hard.

He glanced toward the hidden room. His heart had dropped to his boots when he came in and saw her looking through the hidey-hole door. He had pushed Artie's trunk to the back wall of the small cave and set the kegs in front of it. She wouldn't have seen it unless she had taken a candle or lantern in.

He knew once she found out about the space, he wouldn't be able to keep her from exploring it. Telling her about the whiskey had been the only way he could think of to keep her curiosity at bay. She'd never search it after he'd suggested she might want a drink.

Although nothing was ever certain with her. Wasn't her kiss proof of that? One second, she was boiling angry, the next second, she was turning up his toes and other body parts with a kiss that made his head spin. Why?

Because she was a lonely widow, and he was the only man in sight? Was it odd to think she might seek comfort in his arms? That she might truly care for him was a foreign thought, yet on some level, he wanted to believe it.

He heard a shout from outside. The words were in Cheyenne.

Stepping out of the cabin door, he saw Mina near the creek bank. Her eyes sought his. He raised one finger to his lips. She nodded in understanding.

The shout came again from across the creek. Moving to where he could see through a break in the trees, he spotted the lone rider on the hillside. It was a Cheyenne woman. She sat on a small gray horse and seemed to scan the creek. She shouted again and then fell silent, waiting for an answer.

176

*

Mina moved closer to Devlin. "Is she calling us?"

The young Cheyenne woman shouted again, this time raising one fist in the air. Her horse shifted nervously.

"What is she saying?" When Devlin didn't answer, Mina glanced up. He was gazing at the young woman intently, a look of something between pride and pain etched on his face.

Mina turned her attention back to the visitor. It was hard to tell her age from this distance, but she had the carriage and mannerisms of a young woman, younger perhaps than Mina. Her long, black hair glinted in the sunlight as it blew freely in the wind. She wore a beaded buckskin dress that showed her slender figure to advantage.

Why did the sight of this woman affect Devlin so? How did he know her? They must have meant a great deal to each other at one time for the woman to come seeking him alone. Mina felt a flash of jealousy and a growing desire to see the woman's face up close.

The woman shouted the same phrase again. Mina turned to Devlin. "What is she saying?"

"She wants the trees and the wind to tell Stone Warrior he is afraid."

"Why does she think you are afraid?"

The girl shouted again, in English. "Stones and water, tell my brother he is a coward!"

Mina glanced at Devlin in surprise. "She speaks English. Why did she say brother?"

"Because that is my sister." He turned and walked away.

Chapter Twenty-One

Mina caught up with Devlin and grabbed his arm. "Oh, no you don't. She is your sister?"

"Yes."

"You left your sister behind when you left the tribe? How old was she? I don't believe this. I understand why your mother choose to remain, but after she died, your sister's place would have been with you, not with a tribe of savages."

His sudden, fierce scowl frightened her. "I've seen more savages in white settlements than I've ever seen among the Cheyenne."

She took a step back. "I'm sorry, that was wrong of me, but you know what I mean."

"Leave it alone. You know nothing about it."

She propped her hands on her hips. "Then enlighten me."

"It's none of your business, Mina."

"I'm making it my business. Having been abandoned as a child, I would have given anything to have a brother. Perhaps that's why I loved Artie. He became my big brother before he was my husband."

Devlin sighed. "It wasn't what I wanted. It was my mother's wish."

Shocked, Mina asked, "But why?"

"Because Namid is the daughter of Swift Fox. She's the reason my mother didn't dare stay among whites after we were rescued. Have you seen the way native women are treated by white men? Most treat their dogs better. My mother knew her half-breed child would be scorned and abused. It was for her unborn child my mother went back to the Cheyenne."

"I see." It made sense now.

"Do you? To the Cheyenne, a child's parentage doesn't matter. My sister was loved and cared for by everyone in the tribe. Would it be the same if she lived next door to your wealthy father-in-law in Philadelphia or in London?"

Mina studied his face. His eyes flashed with the anger burning inside him. He was a man torn between two races. A man who could join either side in the struggle unfolding around him but didn't want to choose. Understanding softened Mina's heart and made her want to reach out and comfort him. If only she knew how.

"I'm afraid you're right, Devlin. Your sister would not be treated with kindness by many people who claim to be civilized. All too often, they judge those who are different harshly."

Some of the anger dimmed in his eyes. "I promised to honor mother's wishes."

"Namid is a pretty name. What does it mean?"

"Star Dancer."

"Why does she say you are a coward?"

He jerked away. "How should I know?"

Mina thought she understood. "It's because you refused to go see her, isn't it? The old man, Walks Far, he said she wanted to see you, and you refused to go."

"So what if I did?"

She glared at him. "That, Mr. Elder, was extremely unkind."

"You know nothing about it."

"I know if I had a brother who refused to see me for years, I would be hurt enough to confront him and demand to know why."

"Not a Cheyenne brother and sister."

She folded her arms over her chest. "You expect me to be believe the Cheyenne are less fond of their siblings than whites?"

He sighed heavily. "Not less fond, but custom forbids a brother and sister to speak to one another once they become adults. A brother and sister can never be alone together. It's taboo."

Mina felt her jaw drop. "That's the most preposterous thing I've ever heard."

"Just because it's not your custom doesn't make it wrong. Is incest permitted in England?"

Mina pressed a hand to her chest. "Of course not. It's repugnant and immoral as well as illegal."

"There must never be a hint of incest between brothers and sisters in Cheyenne society, so they may not speak to one another. This is the way things are done."

"You're saying once your sister became an adult, you could never address her?"

"That's right. I can speak to her by posing a question to someone who is with her, like her husband, her friends, even her children, but we can never be alone together. That's why I couldn't take her with me."

Mina digested this new information. A lot about Devlin Elder made sense now. Caught between two cultures, he'd chosen to remain with his mother and half-sister, who could never be a part of the white world. Once his mother was gone, he still had a little sister to hold him to the Cheyenne people he admired and respected. Yet she would separate him from them in the end. Faced with a custom that made it impossible to speak to the only family he had, he'd chosen to leave.

She gazed into his angry, troubled eyes. "How incredibly sad that must have made you."

"Now you know why I didn't go to the village."

"Of course, but it seems you have forgotten one very important point in all this."

"What?"

She grinned. "You are not Cheyenne, therefore are not bound by their customs." She spun on her heels and headed toward the creek.

He caught up with her and forced her to face him by gripping her shoulders. "You forget Namid is Cheyenne. Cheyenne women are chaste until marriage. They are always chaperoned until marriage. It's amazing she would come here alone."

"Well, there's no reason I can't speak to her."

"Don't forget, they think you're my wife," he cautioned.

At the bank, she paused, then deciding she didn't care if Devlin Elder saw more than was decent of her bloomers, she hiked up her skirt and waded in. Fortunately, the water below the beaver dam was only knee deep, and she crossed without mishap.

On the other side, she shook out her skirt, raised her parasol and started through the trees toward Devlin's sister. As she burst out of the thick foliage, she startled the young woman, and her horse wheeled in fear.

Namid narrowly avoided being unseated but controlled her mount. Mina stood still to give the girl time to regain control of her horse and her composure.

Settling her sunshade on her shoulder, Mina moved forward slowly. "I beg your pardon. I did not mean to give you a fright."

The young woman threw back her shoulders. "I am not afraid."

"Of course. My name is Wilhelmina Smith."

"We-he-minta Smith?"

"You may call me Mina. Your brother tells me your name is Namid, and it means Star Dancer."

"Are you my brother's wife?"

"Well…"

"Are you the reason he won't come to our lodge? Is he ashamed for you to see his half-breed sister?"

"No. Of course not."

Namid looked over Mina's head. Mina turned to see Devlin standing at the edge of the trees.

"Tell him it is not he who needs to be ashamed," Namid yelled. "It is I who am shamed by my white brother."

Mina moved closer and placed a hand on the young woman's knee. "Please, your brother is not ashamed of you, and we would love to visit your village."

"Truly?" Some of the defiance left her pretty face, replaced by shyness and an uncertainty that tugged at Mina's heart.

"Truly. I've been absorbed in my work for far too long and in doing so, I have kept your brother here because he fears leaving me alone. I apologize."

Mina beckoned Devlin with one hand. "Come here. Come, come. It's my turn to say I'm sorry. Don't stand there gawking. When I am wrong, I admit it. This is, after all, only the second time I've been wrong since we met."

Namid smothered a giggle with her hand. "You speak much as my mother did when my father scolded her."

"A lesson I hope you learned well. A woman may be wrong, but her husband should never point it out. Men are wrong so often it is a wife's duty to set them straight whenever possible. Your English is very good."

"Mother and Stone Warrior made me speak the white tongue every day when I was young. Now, when the army or traders come to our camp, I speak for my people. Sometimes, Walks Far and I talk together. He complains the white words are like little children who run away and hide if he does not use them."

"Your brother also told me a Cheyenne man may not address his sister once she becomes an adult."

"This is true. But he may speak to those around me. He can look at me with pride when he sees me."

Devlin wasn't the only one hurt by the choice he'd made.

Mina smiled at Namid. "Among my people, a brother is free to speak to his sister any time he wishes, even when they are alone."

"That is not right." Namid scowled.

Mina nodded. "For your people, it is not. But for my people, it is fine. We will honor your customs when we visit. I will play chaperone, and Stone Warrior will speak to you with me here. I warn you not to expect too much. On his good days, he is not a talkative soul. I've known him to go a whole week with only a few grunts."

*

Devlin listened to Mina chatting with Namid and marveled at how she put his sister at ease. Another marvel was how his sister had grown from a gangly girl of twelve, all knees and elbows, into this beautiful woman. Was she seventeen, eighteen now? It didn't seem possible.

Her long hair shone blue-black in the sunlight. Her soft eyes were gray, the same color as his own, and wide set above a straight nose and high cheekbones. Full lips curved into a smile at something Mina was saying, showing straight, even teeth. Her chin was still slightly pointed and reminded him of how stubborn she could be. He remembered seeing her chin raised in defiance at Swift Fox or his mother more than once.

Mina beckoned to him impatiently. He moved forward, rubbing his sweating palms on his pant legs, unsure of what he should say to a sister he hadn't seen in five years and never expected to see again.

He stopped beside Mina. To his surprise, she took his hand in a tight grip. "I've told your sister we are pleased to accept her invitation to visit her village."

Some of the merriment faded from Namid's eyes, replaced by uncertainty as she looked down at him. The last thing he wanted to do was to cause her pain, but it was his duty to protect her.

"Hello, Cricket," he said, hoping to restore her smile. It worked.

"Hello, Skunk," she replied, blushed, and looking away.

This couldn't be easy for her. "You've grown up," he said.

"Did you think I would stay the same chattering child who earned your name for me?"

He gave her a faint nod. "I guess I did. Where is your chaperone?"

Namid glanced back the way she had come. "Her horse is not as fast as mine. She'll be here soon."

Devlin's face was grave. "You should not be out here alone."

"I am a woman now. I will take a husband and have children of my own. Red Buffalo is courting me. He is a fine warrior. He will join others and slay many of our enemies in battle," she stated with pride.

Devlin felt the hairs on the back of his neck rise. "Is Red Buffalo a Dog Soldier?"

"He wishes it. He talks of joining Standing Bear and his warriors soon."

Mina shifted closer to Devlin. He slipped his arm around her shoulders. His happiness at seeing his sister faded as uneasiness took its place. "Is Standing Bear at your camp?"

"Not for many weeks, but he may return soon. The white soldiers hunt him. Swift Fox fears he will bring their anger down on our village."

Devlin nodded. "Swift Fox is wise."

"Our mother's words made him wise. She told him the whites would come in numbers greater than the mighty buffalo. If the Cheyenne are not to be trampled, they must make friends with the whites."

"Your mother was right," Mina said.

Namid shook her head. "Many believe the whites cannot see the Cheyenne as friends, only as enemies. My father's council has kept our young warriors from joining Standing Bear, but I do not know for how long. The great iron horse approaches our hunting lands, and the white men kill many buffalo."

Mina pulled away from Devlin. "Then we must show your people whites can see them as friends when we visit your village. Don't argue with me about this, Devlin. I have made my mind up."

Devlin carefully weighed his options. Letting Mina have her way might be his best chance to keep her safe. Standing Bear wouldn't harm them while they were guests in Swift Fox's camp.

He nodded to Namid. "Sister, we will be happy to visit you. We'll break camp here and join you soon."

"Father will be most pleased. A splendid feast will be given for you and your wife. We camp at the meadow of many beaver ponds." Namid turned her horse and rode away.

Mina stared at Devlin. "You agreed much too quickly to visit the camp. What are you thinking?"

He took Mina by the arm. "Red Buffalo knows we're camped here. If he tells Standing Bear, he and his band won't waste time coming after us. We'll be safer as guests of my stepfather than out here with only two rifles between us. If Standing Bear returns to the village, he won't move against us while we're under the protection of Swift Fox."

"I don't understand."

He pulled her toward the cabin. "The Dog Soldiers need peaceful tribes to hide among, to care for their wounded and to trade for supplies. He'll abide by the rules of the camp because he needs their help. Standing Bear won't risk losing that just to see me dead. He's bent on revenge, but he isn't stupid."

Standing Bear's quarrel with him was personal. Standing Bear would see it took many days for him to die a slow and agonizing death. A swift kill was not his way. Devlin decided not to share that information with Mina.

He said, "It isn't safe here anymore. Now I know Red Buffalo wants to join the Dog Soldiers, that changes things. We need to move tonight."

"But we'll come back, won't we? What about my collection? What about my search?"

He stopped and forced her to look at him. "Think about how Buck's family died. Think about what Standing Bear's men will do to you if they find you. I might not be able to protect you, Mina. I can't take that chance. Not even for your fossils."

Mina paled at the mention of Buck's family, and Devlin was glad. She had to understand the risk.

He swept her into his arms and carried her across the creek. Outside the cabin, he put her down, wishing he could hold her longer, keep her safe forever in his embrace. Foolish thinking. "Pack only what you need. We'll have to travel fast. I'll bring the horses and mules up, but we can't take time to pack your trunks."

Mina watched him hurry away and went inside. She gathered a few of her clothes and packed them helter-skelter into her saddlebags. What to take and what to leave? Her books and journals she stowed in her trunk on the slim chance she could recover them in the future. The last thing she snatched up was Artie's journal from the foot of her bed. The rubbing of his bird with teeth fluttered to the floor.

Pausing, she picked up the drawing and carried it to the light streaming in the doorway. If only Artie hadn't thought of the fossil as a joke. If only he'd seen the value of his discovery and excavated it, his name would have gone down in the annals of science, and Vincent could rest easy knowing his son had done something important with his life.

How long she stood staring at her husband's artwork, she couldn't say. She didn't look up until the light was abruptly cut off. Devlin stood in front of her.

She searched his face. "It was a wild goose chase, wasn't it?"

He sighed. "It was something you felt you had to do. I'm sorry it turned out this way."

"I guess I always knew he must be dead. He never loved me, you know. Well, except as a friend, a sister, really."

"Then he was a fool."

"No, he wasn't made the way most men are. He loved deeply, but the one he loved was forbidden."

"You mean he loved another man," Devlin said.

Mina's eyes widened. "You knew?"

"You talked a lot when you were out of your head with fever. Among the Cheyenne, it's not seen as perverted. It's accepted."

She drew a deep, unsteady breath. "Then it's sad Artie wasn't born a Cheyenne."

"It must have been hard to learn such a thing about your husband."

"I knew before I married him. I discovered Artie and Kendrick together the night of my eighteenth birthday ball. My shock was nothing compared to what I knew Vincent would suffer. He adored his son, but he can be a hard man. Artie never lived up to his father's expectations."

"You're making excuses for him. He was a grown man."

"With a gentle soul. Vincent didn't understand. I wanted to protect them both. They had done so much for me. I was the one who blurted out that Artie had proposed to me. You should have seen how happy it made Vincent. I'd made my bed and didn't complain because it wasn't comfortable. Homosexuality was punishable by death in England until recently. Now the punishment is ten years' incarceration. Artie wouldn't have survived that. Vincent saved me from prison. I would have done anything to spare Artie the same fate."

Devlin lifted her chin with one finger. "Did anything include following your husband around the world and helping to keep his secret?"

"It was easier when we traveled. Quelling the rumors in town was more difficult. He loved Kendrick, you know. It was hard for them not to be together. After Vincent's stroke, I hoped Artie would stay to be near his father, but he couldn't."

"Why not?"

"It was Kendrick who had a genuine passion for scientific exploration. He had mounted an expedition to study the indigenous people of the Amazon. Artie couldn't bear to be parted from him for so long. Kendrick was killed when a group of soldiers overran the village where they were staying. When we received word, I remember thinking the charade was over at last. I was relieved by another man's death. How horrible is that?"

"But instead of going home, Artie came here."

"When his returning ship reached New Orleans, he wrote to tell us he'd met someone who convinced him to visit the tribes in Kansas, to make a scientific study of them in honor of Kendrick. I was so angry when I got his letter. Vincent needed his son."

"Artie expected too much of you."

She gave him a wry smile. "I was capable, and he knew it. He loved his father. He simply loved Kendrick more. I suspect the person he met became his new lover. Artie never saw evil in anyone. All I wanted was for Vincent to end his days believing his son's life counted for something."

"He's gone. What does it matter how?"

She frowned. "Of course it matters. I'm not willing to spend my life in this limbo, wondering if my husband found someone else and decided it was better to disappear than to tell me. If he's dead, his father needs to know."

"Dead is dead, Mina."

"I need to know the truth. Can't you understand?"

He walked to the door and stared outside. "I'm sorry."

She stared at her shelves and fossils. "All of this was for nothing. We'll never come back here, will we?"

He looked at her over his shoulder. "Never is a long time. Who knows? After you get back to Philadelphia and Vincent, you might return one day."

But Devlin wouldn't be here. She glanced at the cot where Devlin had nursed her, the shelves he'd made for her lined with dozens of her finds. He was in every corner, every inch of this place. She'd never come back to this if Devlin wasn't with her.

She turned away from him and tossed the sketch into the smoldering embers of the fire. In a second, the paper burst into flames, then slowly crumbled into ash. "I'm ready now."

"Mina, wait." Devlin caught her arm as she moved past him.

"Why?"

"What if you find out something about Artie and it changes what you thought about him?"

"I don't know what you mean?"

"What if he was involved in something he shouldn't have been?"

"Do you know something about my husband you haven't told me? What was he involved in?"

Turning aside, he picked up his saddlebags. "I heard rumors, that's all. I heard he might have been trading guns to the Indians."

"Preposterous! Artie would never become involved in something like that."

"I said they were rumors."

Mina tried to visualize timid Artie in the role of a gunrunner. "No. The idea is simply too ludicrous. What would be his motive?"

"Money? I don't know."

She studied Devlin as he gathered up his belongings. Why was he telling her this? "Perhaps I should ask what your motive is for slurring my husband's good name?"

Devlin scowled at her and picked up his bedroll. "Artie was a saint. He used a silly girl who thought she was in love with him to hide his secrets from his own father. And instead of thanking her, he took off with his lover and traveled the world, spending the money his doting old man lavished on him. Move over, Saint Peter. Make room for Saint Artie."

"How dare you?"

Devlin dropped his gear with a thud. "If Artie was such a noble fellow, why are you here digging in the dirt to find a rock he left behind? So you can prove to the world he wasn't an idiot."

"He wasn't."

"You should be safe at home, drinking tea and cosseting an old man you love like a father. You can't make a hero out of your sniveling coward of a husband."

Mina realized the nails of her clenched fingers were cutting into the palms of her hands. Slowly she opened them and smoothed the sting away on the folds of her skirts.

"I will say one thing for you, Mr. Elder. You certainly know how to make leaving this place easier. I wouldn't spend another night here with you if my life depended on it."

Charging past him, she tried to get away, but he grabbed her arm.

"Your life does depend on me. If you forget that, you're a bigger fool than he was."

"You can go to the devil." Mina jerked away before he could see the tears filling her eyes.

Chapter Twenty-Two

Devlin watched Mina storm out of the cabin. She'd never admit her husband was anything but a misunderstood martyr. Nor would she forgive the man who robbed her beloved Vincent of his only son. She'd want to see that man burn in hell, and she'd be happy to stoke the fire, even if it meant going there herself. In a way, Devlin was already in hell, craving the sweet touch of a woman he could never have. Looking after her day and night and wanting nothing but to kiss her, lay her down and make love to her until she cried out in ecstasy.

He could live with her anger, but he couldn't live with the thought of what Standing Bear would do if he caught her.

Until he was certain it was safe to return to Fort Harker, he had no choice but to take her to Swift Fox's village. Once there, he could leave her in his sister's care and slip back to the wagon trail. The settlers would pass along word of conditions at the fort. If need be, he could ride to the fort himself, but he didn't like the idea of leaving Mina for so long.

There was no telling what trouble she'd find.

The only hitch in his plan was if Swift Fox would give them shelter or not. Namid might believe the chief would welcome Devlin, but things had changed for both men in the last years. They stood on opposite sides of a growing divide.

Following Mina outside, Devlin watched her mount her mare and kick the horse into a gallop. She splashed across the stream, sending sprays of water in wide arcs. Once on the opposite bank, she rode to the top of the hill and pulled to a halt. After a minute, she snapped open her ridiculous sunshade and sat waiting, every inch the impatient aristocrat, leaving him to load the mules alone.

He made quick work of securing the few supplies they had left and pulled the cabin door shut, adding a few branches to hide the entrance. Then he swung aboard his pinto and headed after Mina. As he approached, she deliberately avoided his gaze.

"Well, Mr. Elder?" she snapped.

"Well, what?"

"Don't be obtuse. Which way?"

"North."

"Fine." She nudged her horse forward.

Devlin wished he knew for sure he was taking her to safety. He was trusting his gut. Not a simple thing to do when it came to the woman riding in stiff-backed anger a few feet ahead. She rattled his thinking, and that was dangerous for them both.

They rode until sunset. After making a cold camp and spending a sleepless night on the hard ground, Devlin was glad when late the next morning, they crested a small rise and saw the Indian encampment below them. The Cheyenne village lay on the far side of a small winding creek, where young cottonwood trees marked its meandering course between dozens of beaver ponds

Nearly thirty tepees were pitched in a circle that stretched several hundred feet across. The pale hide tents stood out creamy white against the backdrop of green summer grass. Feathers and strips of bright cloth fluttered from the tops of the lodge poles like pennants. In the center of the encampment, several cooking fires sent thin spirals of smoke drifting skyward.

It was like stepping back in time. Home lay before him.

A shout from a sentry on a nearby rise announced their arrival. He knew they were being watched. Within minutes, the young men of the village galloped toward them, screaming and banishing weapons.

"Stay calm. They won't harm us."

She pressed Sabiha closer to him. "I pray you're right."

Her steady nerves impressed him as a dozen men surrounded them. Tension simmered in the air. He saw hatred on many faces of the men he'd once called friends.

The group parted and one man, older than the others, rode up beside Devlin. Swift Fox's weathered face was lined like a crinkled sheet of parchment. His long braids were streaked with gray, but his dark eyes under thick brows remained sharp and assessing. Two eagle feathers dangled from a thin band of rawhide that confined his hair. He sat at ease on his chestnut stallion and held an iron tipped lance upright in one hand. More eagle feathers fluttered from leather strips bound to the wooden shaft.

Devlin spoke first in Cheyenne. "May we enter the camp of my mother's husband?"

"The son of my wife has been gone for many seasons. I see a white man now, not a Cheyenne boy."

"I follow the way of the whites, but I have not forgotten my Cheyenne family."

"The way of the whites is the way of our enemy."

The two men eyed each other for a long moment. Devlin spoke again. "I can never be an enemy of my mother's husband and the father of my sister. I come as a friend."

Swift Fox nodded once. "As a friend, you are welcomed."

The group of men surrounding them parted and allowed them to continue down toward the village.

As they entered the circle of lodges, the women and children of the camp clustered about them in a grinning, giggling group. Mina became the center of attention. The women patted her skirts, and the children jumped and shouted, pointing to her parasol. She pulled it closed.

Devlin's sister stepped forward and indicated Mina should follow her. Mina met Devlin's eyes, waiting for a sign from him. He nodded. She would be safe here.

*

Stepping down from her horse, Mina looked around, smiled and snapped the shade open again, much to the delight of her audience.

A tall youth came forward and reached for her horse. Mina clutched the reins tighter. She looked at Devlin. "Will she be safe with them? I recall you said it was acceptable to steal horses."

"It would be impolite to steal from a guest," he said. "The boy will take her to graze with the village herd. At night, she'll be tethered outside your lodge."

At his reassurance, Mina patted Sabiha's neck and gave the command for the mare to go with him. The boy led Sabiha away, but others near his age crowded around him. Only two of them dared touch the prancing white mare, but it was apparent they admired her.

Devlin got off his horse and whispered in Mina's ear. "I want you to go with my sister and do as she says. I must speak with Swift Fox alone. It may take a while."

"Can't I come with you?"

"Not this time. You'll be fine. Namid will take good care of you."

She searched his face. "I'm still angry with you, but I find I dislike the idea of letting you out of my sight."

It was odd how much she trusted him when he so often made her mad. He gave her a reassuring smile. "Go with my sister."

She nodded and followed Namid to a nearby tent. Stopping at the low oval opening of the lodge, she looked back once before stepping inside.

After giving his horse and the mules over to be cared for, Devlin followed Swift Fox to his lodge. Upon entering, Devlin politely waited for the chief to take his place. The smell of the smoke and herbs drying in bundles hung from the poles brought swift and poignant memories of his childhood.

He'd spent many nights by the fire in his stepfather's lodge, where he sat joking with other boys his age, including Standing Bear, telling stories of brave deeds they would carry out when they were old enough to go to war. Memories stirred of times spent watching his mother and sister tend the fire and fashion clothing from deerskins decorated with bright beads and porcupine quills. They were good memories from a time when he believed he knew where he belonged.

At the back of the tent, Swift Fox sat down on his bed of hides and blankets. When he had made himself comfortable, he motioned to Devlin and spoke in Cheyenne. "Come. Sit beside me." He motioned to his left side.

To be invited to sit on the lodge owner's left was a mark of honor Devlin felt he didn't deserve. Politeness, so highly valued by the people of the plains, prevented him from refusing. Devlin sat down beside the man who had been both father and teacher to him for many years.

"Swift Fox honors me by inviting me into his lodge."

"The sight of you after so long does my old heart good. I see much of your mother in you. Why have you come among us?"

"To seek safety for the woman I travel with. I must go to the white man's fort. I ask that she be allowed to remain here under your protection until my return."

Swift Fox nodded. "Namid tells me she is your wife."

An unfamiliar lump rose in Devlin's throat. He didn't want to lie to Swift Fox, but he had to protect Mina's reputation. Somehow, it was easier to voice his feelings in Cheyenne. "My woman is called Mina. She is dear to my heart, Father. All I cherish in this world I would give to keep her safe. Can you help us?"

It was the truth. Devlin loved her and wanted Swift Fox to know.

Swift Fox nodded and smiled gently. "A man does not know happiness until he holds the woman he loves. This is good. I will aid you and Mina."

Devlin blew out a breath of relief. "Thank you."

Swift Fox grew serious. "There are reports of sickness at the fort and white settlements. You should not go there. Stay with us. A strong hunter is always welcome in this camp."

"I must take Mina back to her people beyond the wide river. It's too dangerous for her here, but I won't take her to the fort until the sickness has passed."

"Your mother went back to her people, but she was not happy there."

"Mother knew happiness only here in your lodge. Mina has not lived among the people. She wishes to return home."

"All whites should return across the great river."

Devlin chose his next words with care. "They will not. More will come like a swarm of locusts. They cannot be stopped."

Swift Fox sighed heavily. "I fear war is coming. You have lived long with the whites. Are there men of peace among them?"

"Not enough. Just as there are not enough men of peace among the Cheyenne."

"Our way has always been the way of war. Kiowa, Shoshone, Blackfeet, Pawnee, all feared our lances. A Cheyenne boy does not become a man until he has fought an enemy. You fought many."

"If the Cheyenne are to survive, you must tell the people the way of the warrior is over."

"They will not heed me."

Devlin knew it was true. "Do you know where Standing Bear and his Dog Soldiers are?"

"Standing Bear has gone south seeking gold to buy more weapons."

"Who is selling him guns?"

"The old Métis."

Devlin's jaw tightened. Frenchie Dubois. He was surprised Standing Bear still trusted Frenchy after what had happened last time. "Where is Standing Bear getting gold?"

"He has not told me."

"To welcome him to your village may lead the white soldiers to take revenge on you for the things he has done."

"It weighs heavy on my heart, Stone Warrior, but he is my sister's son. Tonight we will have a feast in your honor, smoke the pipe, and speak of better times, you and I."

"I would like that."

After spending a quiet hour with Swift Fox, Devlin left the lodge and went in search of Mina. There was no telling what trouble she had gotten into by now.

She was easy to spot. His sister and her friends had lost no time in decking Mina out in a deerskin dress, matching leggings and beaded moccasins. Her blond hair, now hanging in long braids, set her apart from the other women gathered around one of the cooking fires.

As he approached, he saw relief cross her expressive face. Unfortunately, he knew it would be short-lived.

She extended her arms and spun around. "How do I look?"

"Like a true Cheyenne maiden."

"Ha!" She grabbed the two golden braids that reached almost to her waist and flapped them. "Not with hair this color. I can't believe how soft this dress is."

"It's doeskin. Who did you give your dress to?" He looked around.

"I believe her name is Running Horse. She admired it, and I let her try it on. I think she is still trying to figure out hooks and eyes."

"I hope it wasn't one of your favorites."

"It is, why?"

"Because if you gave her your dress, then it belongs to her now. She will view it as a gift."

"Oh, dear. And the woman who wanted to carry my parasol?"

"She's now the proud owner."

Mina's mouth twisted with mild annoyance. "Your sister failed to mention this."

"She knows only Cheyenne customs. She would assume you did, too."

"I'm glad I haven't opened my saddlebags."

"Take my advice and wear what you have on while you're here. Otherwise, you'll find yourself out of clothes in no time. My stepfather has set aside a lodge for us. I'm sorry, but these people must believe we're married."

"Well, I don't like it."

"How is it different from sleeping in the same cabin?"

She lowered her voice and hissed, "I had no choice then and no one knew. Now everyone will know we are sharing a dwelling."

"Believe it or not, it is the only way I can protect your reputation. As my wife, you will be treated with respect. Cheyenne women are virtuous. Trying to explain that we were only traveling together would place you in a class of women you don't want to be lumped with, understand?"

She crossed her arms over her chest and scowled. "Perfectly."

"Before you take a scalping knife to me, it will only be for one night. I'm leaving first thing in the morning."

Her eyes widened behind her spectacles. "Leaving?"

"I need to make certain it's safe to return to Fort Harker. I'm not taking you into the middle of a cholera epidemic."

"Shouldn't I come with you?"

"No. I can travel faster alone. Besides, it's easier to hide one horse than two. A man traveling alone will attract less attention."

She chewed her lower lip. "All right, I shall remain here."

"You will?" He couldn't hide his surprise.

She fisted her hands on her hips and glared at him. "I am perfectly capable of accepting a rational plan of action."

"You couldn't prove it by me, but I'm glad you're willing to be reasonable."

"How long do you expect to be gone?"

"If I cut straight south, I should hit the wagon road in two days. Hopefully, I'll meet up with a stagecoach or wagon train and get information about conditions at the fort. If not, I'll ride on toward Ellsworth. I could be gone a week, maybe a week and a half."

Worry clouded her eyes. "That is a very long time."

"I'll be back for you."

Mina reached out and laid a hand on his arm. Warmth spread through his body at her gentle touch. "It never crossed my mind you wouldn't. Please promise you'll take care."

"I will."

*

Mina struggled to keep fear out of her voice as she gazed at him. "Despite our differences, I would be quite upset if you were to get yourself killed."

A small smile lifted one side of his mouth, making her long to kiss him. "I'd be upset, too."

Gazing into his stormy gray eyes, she wondered what he was thinking. If only she knew for certain she was a free woman. If only she dared reveal the longings fluttering like trapped birds inside her when she touched him. "Devlin, I—"

"What?"

The words stuck in her throat. She was a coward, a spineless, sniveling coward. No, she was a married woman. "Nothing. Just take care of yourself."

That evening, as a crowd gathered around the fire in the center of the lodges, Mina found herself relegated to the group of women on one side. She ate her fill of boiled buffalo meat, flat bread and stewed dandelion greens with tiny wild onions. The cooked turnips she politely passed on, but she helped herself to a second bowl of the sweet, berry filled pudding the women pushed on her.

With Namid at her side to interpret, she answered questions and enjoyed the stories told by the men gathered on the other side of the fire. Devlin sat beside his stepfather. He looked out of place among the men in his linen shirt and dark pants, but it was easy to see the older man welcomed him. It was also easy to tell some of the younger men didn't.

Many times during the evening, Devlin sought her out with his eyes and gave her a brief nod, as if to let her know she wasn't forgotten. Each time, she felt herself blushing and hoped he didn't notice.

At a signal from the chief, Devlin spoke to the group, and Namid translated his words for Mina. He urged the council of elders to seek peace with the white men. There was dissent from all sides of the council. One man spoke up, saying Métis would bring more guns. They should fight and defeat the whites. His statement was greeted with cheers from the young men. The elders remained silent.

Mina knew the destruction the army could bring against these people and fervently hoped they would heed Devlin's words.

Later in the evening, the guests left until only the family remained in the lodge. The men went outside. Mina watched Namid lay out the sleeping mats the family used. Mina hated giving Devlin's rumor credence, but after hearing mention of guns, she had to know if Artie had been involved in the illicit trade.

"Namid, has a white man ever come to this camp with guns to sell?"

She nodded. "Yes, a few Métis have done this."

"Métis. Who are they?"

"The Métis are traders from French Canada. They come to trade for pelts, but they often bring whiskey. It makes our people foolish and trade away their hides for nothing of value. Father has forbidden the Métis from bringing it again. Red Buffalo and his friends grumbled about that. They like firewater. I do not."

"So no Englishman has come to trade."

Namid paused, then brightened. "Yes, one came with two Métis last spring. Red Buffalo said they promised many more guns."

Could it have been Artie? "Do you know this man's name?"

Namid shook her head. "The Métis speaks our language. I was not needed."

"Did you see him? What did he look like?"

Namid smiled. "He was a pretty man."

"Pretty like Devlin?" Mina asked.

"No, his skin was pale, his hair like fire."

"He had red hair. Did he have a mark on his cheek here?" Mina pointed to the side of her face where Artie had a small strawberry birthmark.

Namid nodded. "Yes."

Mina reeled with shock. Artie had been here, but he couldn't have been selling guns.

Devlin's sister stepped away to spread her sleeping mat, but Mina crossed the lodge and grabbed her arm. "Where is he? Where did the English man go?"

Namid frowned and pulled away from Mina's tight grip. "He left with the Métis. I never saw him again. Come. I will take you to your lodge."

Mina followed, but her mind was spinning. Artie had been among these people. He'd promised them guns to use in the fight against his own kind. Was the French-Canadian trader he traveled with his new lover? Was that why Artie's letters had stopped?

She pressed a hand to her trembling lips. Namid had to be mistaken. Vincent would die of shame if he learned Artie had become a criminal. A gunrunner. A man without honor. Vincent must never find out.

The lodge Namid led her to was empty when she went inside, but someone had laid a small fire. It glowed softly, making flickering shadows on the hide walls. She sat down on the sleeping mat near the back wall.

Try as she might, Mina couldn't understand how Artie could have changed so much. What madness had engulfed his mind? How could he sell guns to people like Standing Bear who used them to slaughter innocent women and children? Had Kendrick's death unhinged Artie's mind? No wonder he hadn't returned to the fort for his things. But it was possible he was still alive.

She blew out a long breath. He clearly didn't care about her since he'd embarked on this dangerous new life without a word. She meant nothing to him.

Old insecurities rose to torment her soul. Artie had abandoned her, just as her father had when he killed himself, without considering how it would affect her. The same way her mother had cast her aside as inconvenient. Mina wrapped her arms around herself. What was wrong with her? Why didn't the people she loved want her? Tears spilled down her cheeks at the pain of so many rejections. Why was she unlovable?

Turning on her side, she gave into grief and cried bitter tears until she was exhausted, and sleep overtook her.

A rumble of thunder woke her sometime later. It took several seconds to get her bearings as she stared at the lodge poles overhead. The fresh smell of rain scented the cool air. The plop, plop of drops hitting the hide walls made a soothing sound. A little rain found its way into the smoke hole at the top of the poles, making the fire embers hiss and sputter.

Mina raised her head. A lightning flash illuminated the outline of a man sitting cross-legged beside the open doorway, followed quickly by thunder. She knew who was there. A gust of cool wind found its way in, and Mina shivered.

A second flash showed her Devlin wasn't watching the storm. His eyes were fixed in her direction. Artie didn't want her, but Devlin did. She wanted him, too. Wanted to feel his strength holding her, his weight pressing her down. Slipping one arm out from under the blanket, she lifted the edge in an unspoken invitation. Would he reject her, too? She held her breath.

He rose and crossed to her. She shifted on the mat to make room for him. He lay down on his back beside her. Relief and something more filled her heart. She was falling in love with this man. Should she tell him, or would that make him retreat?

Rolling onto her side, she faced him in the darkness. Without a word, he slipped one arm around her and pulled her close.

Her befuddled mind didn't know what to do next, but her body seemed to know. She settled her cheek on his shoulder and let her hand slide across his shirt front as her leg found a comfortable resting place on his thigh. She felt his breath stop on a ragged gasp. Had she done something wrong?

She tried to move away, but his arm tightened around her.

"Stay," he whispered, his breath stirring the hair at her temple.

A wave of passion filled her and pushed away all thought. The feeling of his body against hers made her blood pound. His free hand covered hers where it rested over his heart and cradled it. His thumb rubbed slow circles on her skin. A wonderful, exciting warmth spread through her.

Snuggled against him, she felt his chest rising and falling with each breath and gloried in discovering how well she fit against his side. It was as if she had been made for him.

Lying in the darkness, she breathed deeply. The wind brought the perfume of the rain-washed grass to mix with the smell of the dying fire and the deep, masculine scent so uniquely Devlin's own. A sense of security settled over Mina like the softest down comforter. Nothing in her whole life had ever felt as right as this.

He lay still, as if waiting for her to make the first move. He didn't seem to realize she already had.

"Make love to me, Devlin."

"Are you sure, Mina?" He sounded almost frightened.

"Oh, I'm very sure." She needed to matter to someone. He might not love her, but he wanted her.

He stroked her hair. "I won't do this if you'll regret it in the morning."

"I have had a lifetime of regrets. This will not be one of them. I promise."

"What about your husband?"

She pulled her hand from beneath his and cupped his cheek, forcing him to look at her. "I was never his. I will be yours tonight, if you want me."

He groaned as he rolled over and stood up. She shivered in the cool air, missing his warmth. Didn't he desire her? Had she misread his intentions? Humiliation sent heat rushing to her face.

He held out his hand. "Come here."

"Why?" She could barely look at him.

"Darling, this will go a lot better with our clothes off."

She shot to her feet, keeping her gaze fastened to the floor. "I didn't think of that. I'm afraid I don't know how these things are done. That's not exactly true. I understand the mechanics of it."

He placed a hand beneath her chin and forced her to look at him. "I know how these things are done."

She swallowed hard and clasped her hands together. "Of course you do. You have experience. Many experiences, I expect. What do I do now? Do I take my own clothes off or do you? You may give me directions to make me more sensual in your eyes."

"You talk too much, woman."

"I know." She clamped her lower lip between her teeth.

"First things first. Where's your gun?"

"Here in my belt." She withdrew it with two fingers.

He took it from her and tossed it aside. "Did you get your parasol back?"

"No." Why would he want her parasol?

He looked around. "Did you adopt another dog?"

Mina smiled. Her embarrassment fled as she realized he was teasing her. She wanted to hold him and never, ever let go. She'd fought against it at every turn, but she had fallen head over heels in love with Devlin Elder.

Boldly, she stepped close and pressed her hand to his chest. She would have this night with him to remember forever. One by one, she undid the buttons at the top of his shirt. "I have no gun, no parasol, no dog, no soldiers, not even a dead buffalo to rescue me. I fear my virtue is at your mercy, sir." Heady desire made her voice low and tremulous.

"Finally." Devlin groaned again and pulled her hard against him.

Every inch of her body was pressed to his, but she needed more. She raised her face for his kiss, and he complied.

She loved the feel of his mouth on hers and the taste of him. His lips were soft and yet firm at the same time. His mouth moved to her cheek and nuzzled at her earlobe. She shuddered in his arms, not with fear, but with a burning longing to be taken by him.

His hands caressed her body from her shoulders to her hips. When he cupped her rump and lifted her against the bulge of his erection, they both moaned. His lips came back to her mouth. She couldn't get enough of him.

Her buckskin dress was in the way. She wanted it off, wanted his clothes off, needed to feel his skin against her skin.

As if he read her mind, he broke the kiss, pulled his shirt off and tossed it aside. Then he dropped to one knee in front of her. He gathered the material at her hips and slowly drew it upward. She shivered again when the cool air touched her heated skin.

"Raise your arms, Mina," he whispered.

Self-conscious, she crossed them over her chest. He rose to his feet. "Please, I want to see all of your beautiful body bathed in firelight. I want to look at you and know you want me, too."

She slowly raised her arms, and he helped her pull the dress off, along with her chemise. He dropped the clothing in a pile and simply stared. She was wearing only her white cotton bloomers. She crossed her arms again, but he caught her hands and held them wide.

"Dear God, you are the most gorgeous creature on the face of the earth."

"I'm short." She licked her dry lips.

"You are a petite goddess." He brought her hand to his mouth and kissed the inside of her wrist, but he didn't let her go.

"My bosoms are too large. Men prefer less endowed women."

"A jealous hag must've told you that because no man ever would."

"It was my maid."

"Mina, your bosoms are magnificent, but the most attractive part of you is your wonderful mind." He leaned forward and kissed the rounded top of breast.

Her knees went weak. She put her head back in silent invitation. He spread kisses up her chest to her throat and down to her other breast. He stopped just above her throbbing nipple and blew on it. She twisted her hands free, plunged them into his hair and pulled him forward. When he took her breast in his mouth, her body jerked and arched against him.

"Oh, please, more."

"You shall have much more, Mina, but I don't want to rush this. Not for you." His voice was husky with emotion and fueled her need to pull him closer. He stepped back, undid his trousers and let them fall to his feet. She did the same with her bloomers, and then they were both naked.

Staring at his superb body, she remembered how it looked, wet and glistening in the sunlight while he bathed. She had seen him only from a distance then. Now he was inches away, and he was even more resplendent in the firelight.

His wide shoulders tapered to slender hips. The evidence of his desire jutted out from the mat of curls at the juncture of his powerfully muscled thighs. He wasn't self-conscience in the least. He stood there easily and let her look her fill. How could she satisfy such a virile man? She knew nothing of what he wanted from her.

He lifted one eyebrow. "Like what you see?"

"Yes." Her heart fluttered so wildly she could barely breathe.

He walked past her and lay down on the bed. He rose on one elbow and held out his hand. "Come here. I have much more to show you. Unless you're afraid?"

He knew her so well. Her nervousness vanished. Her chin came up a notch. "Let it not be said I hesitated to add to my education, Mr. Elder."

She took his hand, and he gently pulled her down to lie beside him.

The storm raged outside. Flashes of lightning, rumbles of thunder and the hammering rain on the walls made vibrant background music as he wrapped the blanket over them both. Long into the night, Devlin made love to her with gentleness and care until she was writhing with passion. When he took her at last, she was ready for him, and together they found satisfaction in each other's arms.

Eventually, the storm moved on, and the thunder died away in the distance. Content, Mina lay curled with her back toward Devlin. His arm across her waist kept her encased in contentment.

She loved him. There was no doubt in her mind now. She loved him with her whole being.

Should she tell him? How did he feel about her? He'd made wonderful love to her, but men could make love without being in love. She drifted to sleep, thinking tomorrow she could gather her courage and tell him how she felt and ask if he felt the same.

When she woke in the morning, he was gone.

Chapter Twenty-Three

Devlin's absence continued over the following days. Mina threw herself into the activities of the camp, determined to learn all she could about the people he had grown up among. Keeping busy was the only way to dull the sharp edge of worry that gnawed at her. Devlin would be all right. He would return for her.

When he did, what then? She didn't dare think about the future. She loved him, but she wasn't sure how he felt about her. He desired her, yes, but did he care for her?

At night, when she was alone, heartache twisted deep in her chest as she lay on her sleeping mat, smoothing a hand over his side. She tried to regain the feeling of happiness she'd known, but it was no use. The warmth and scent of his body had faded. She tucked the memory of being loved by him into her heart for safekeeping.

During the day, the women of the village were amused by her attempts to manage the chores they took for granted. Although less skilled, Mina's dogged determination to learn soon earned their admiration. With Namid at her side, she gathered heavy bundles of wood, scraped hides with bone tools, even tackled cutting up and drying the meat brought to camp by the hunters. It was exhausting work.

None of the women seemed to mind. They spent the day in cheerful chatter and laughter. The old woman to whom Mina had given her parasol was frequently nearby, opening and closing her trophy and grinning.

The men of the village, when they weren't out hunting, enjoyed friendly camaraderie. Teenage boys played pranks on one another, but none generated hard feelings. Mina was soon treated as a friend and found herself the object of a few pranks by the young women. The camp was a cheerful place. She could see why Devlin felt connected to these people. They were far from savages.

Yet the memory of Buck's family never left her. It was impossible to reconcile those vile acts with the people she was coming to know and admire.

Not all Mina's blunders provided amusement. Once, she walked between the fire at the center of the lodge and Swift Fox. Namid chastised her for her rudeness. The following afternoon, Mina stopped to admire the intricate painting and feather work on Swift Fox's war shield. It rested, like others throughout the camp, on a tripod beside his lodge.

Mina reached out to touch the yellowed bear's claws dangling from the center. As she did, a woman began shouting at her. Startled, Mina spun around, knocking the shield to the ground. She reached down to pick it up, but the woman struck her hand and pushed her away. It wasn't until Namid appeared Mina learned why the woman was angry.

"You must not touch the shield," Namid hissed. She entered the tepee and returned with a blanket. With great care, she covered the shield.

"I'm sorry," Mina said. "I don't understand."

"A warrior's shield has much power. If it touches the ground, it must be covered and left alone. Long Nose, the medicine man, will decide for how long. Then the shield must be passed through medicine smoke before it can be used again. Let us hope no enemy attacks until after this is done. I would weep to see my father go into battle without the magic of his shield to protect him."

After that, Mina took great pains to go out only with Namid. From Devlin's sister, Mina learned many things about the Cheyenne. She learned the lodges belonged to the women, not the men. Although the women did not speak openly at the councils, much of what they decided was discussed between husbands and wives beforehand.

Even the dogs of the camp had their tasks. They provided alarm by barking if strangers approached and cleaned up the scraps left over from cooking. Most were thin, and Mina began keeping a few pieces of dried meat in her pocket to give out. Soon, she was greeted with tail-wagging friendliness by all of them.

"What are those little girls doing with the puppies?" Mina asked one morning as she and Namid joined a group of women carrying heavy skins of water back from the creek. Three girls of about seven or eight were squabbling over some puppies.

Namid smiled. "They are the babies. Each one wants the prettiest baby to be hers. See, now they have decided."

Several young boys joined the girls. As Mina watched, the boys took the mother dog and tied a pack to her back, along with a bundle of long sticks. The girls, after placing their puppies in miniature cradle boards, hoisted them to their backs, and joined the boys. Together, they marched out into the prairie a little way and came back to the center of the encampment. At a command from the tallest boy, they unpacked the dog and set up a small lodge.

"They're playing house," Mina exclaimed.

"Do white children play at being the mother and father?"

"Oh, yes, but we play with dolls, not with puppies."

One of the little girls came to Mina and offered her a puppy in a cradle. Confused, Mina glanced at Namid. "What does she want?"

"She is offering to let you play, too."

Mina grinned and took the pup to rock in her arms, crooned softly to it.

"Will you give my brother a baby soon?" Namid asked.

"What?" Mina looked up, shocked until she remembered her supposed marriage.

Namid seemed taken aback. "I am sorry. Is this not talked of by white women?"

"Women of the same family, yes. Strangers do not discuss it." Mina struggled to hide her embarrassment.

"But are we not women of the same family?"

"Yes, but you must give me time to get to know you better before we discuss such private matters." The thought of having Devlin's child flooded Mina with happiness and then unease. What kind of life they could have together?

"I wish to know many things about the marriage bed," Namid said. "Is it true a man can make you touch the stars when his body joins with yours?"

Mina glanced around, noting the children playing nearby and a group of women working hides in the shade of a tepee. She returned the puppy to the little girl, grabbed Namid's hand and pulled her toward the creek bank. Straining to keep her voice down, she said, "This is not a conversation we should have in public."

"No one here knows your speech except Walks Far and he is asleep in his lodge."

"Yes, of course." Namid's logic wasn't lost on Mina, but she simply could not instruct Devlin's sister on the joys of wedded bliss. How did she tell this child a man could make a woman rise to wondrous heights, then fall into a chasm of pleasure? More than once.

Namid frowned. "I only ask because Red Buffalo wishes to make me his wife. I know it would make my father happy. Only, I am not sure I wish it."

Reaching out, Mina cupped the young woman's face between her hands. "There are many things in this world I am unsure of, but I know this for certain. If you don't wish with your whole heart and soul to have Red Buffalo hold you in his arms, then he is not the man for you. You must do what makes you happy, Namid. Not what pleases your father."

"Is it so for you and my brother?"

Mina smiled as she recognized the truth. "Yes. When he takes my hand, my heart sings. No other man has ever made me feel as he does."

"Then I will wait for such a man, too."

Shouts from the camp caused both women to turn. A group of ten riders approached from the south. Mina shaded her eyes against the sun. "Do you know them?"

"It is Standing Bear and his Dog Soldiers."

A chill swept over Mina. The image of Buck's family flashed before her. For a second, she thought she would be sick.

She swallowed hard. "Which one is Standing Bear?"

"The brave on the appaloosa stallion. There are also two Métis with him," Namid added.

Artie wasn't among the riders, but Mina knew one of them, Frenchy Dubois.

As the band galloped into camp, Frenchy broke away from the group and headed straight for her. He yanked his horse to a halt and leaned forward in the saddle. The look in his eyes told her he had not forgotten their encounter.

He spat on the ground at her feet. "Ah, *Cheri*! I have waited for *zis* day."

Mina summoned all her inner strength and stood resolute. "I see you have not acquired manners since we last met. I look forward to giving you another lesson."

Frenchy Dubois grabbed his whip from the pommel of his saddle. Mina braced herself for the blow. She wouldn't give him the satisfaction of seeing her cower. Namid stepped between them.

"Get out of the way, squaw!" Frenchy struck Namid across her upraised arm.

At her cry, the village women came running. In seconds, Frenchy was being pelted with stones, bone scrapers and any tools or sticks they had handy. He threw up his arms to cover his head, screaming obscenities.

Standing Bear bellowed a command. The women stopped their attack, but not their shouting. He rode his horse into the melee, forcing the women back.

Mina paid no attention to the angry clamor. She pulled Namid aside. "Are you hurt? Let me see."

An angry red welt marked Namid's forearm and the side of her neck. "It is nothing."

Guilt flooded Mina. "His blow was meant for me."

"I could not let him strike my sister."

A swell of affection for Namid left Mina stunned. Recovering her voice, she said, "I can fight my own battles, but thank you for trying to protect me."

"It is what Stone Warrior would want."

"Perhaps, but it is not what I want."

The shouting had attracted the attention of the rest of the camp. Swift Fox parted the crowd as he crossed to where Mina stood with Namid. He examined his daughter before asking one brief question.

Namid answered quietly. He glanced at Mina, nodded, then turned and spoke to the crowd. Two men pulled Frenchy from his horse and dragged the man away. The rest of the people dispersed, leaving only Standing Bear sitting on his stallion a few steps away.

Mina studied him. He was a handsome man with wide shoulders and muscular arms, but his dark eyes stared at her with unblinking malevolence. She couldn't look away. His braids were bound with long strips of red cloth dotted with tiny white flowers.

Mina's stomach clenched as she realized it was the same material she had seen under Anna Murphy's mutilated body. Noting her gaze, his lips twisted it into a sneer. He stroked the cloth with one hand, then raised it to his lips.

Mina averted her eyes and prayed she wouldn't vomit.

"Why white woman in camp?" he demanded.

Namid laid a comforting arm around Mina's shoulders. "She is wife of Stone Warrior and welcomed as my sister."

His following words were in Cheyenne, but Mina guessed their meaning. He wasn't happy. Yanking his horse's head around, he rode across the camp to join his followers.

Mina gathered her scattered wits and turned to Devlin's sister. "Why is he here?"

"Perhaps to get more men to join him."

"I can understand his hatred of whites after the way they killed his family, but why is Frenchy Dubois traveling with him? It doesn't make sense."

"He is Métis. He may have brought guns. We will learn more at the council tonight."

Mina looked at Namid in shock. "Métis? Is he the man who came with Artie? With the red-haired English fellow?"

"One of them, yes. I do not see the other one, the one the Englishman liked. They were always together. Once I see them kiss."

Dread settled in the pit of Mina's stomach. Artie had chosen poorly if his new lover was an associate of Frenchy.

The appearance of Standing Bear eased one worry. Devlin had eluded them. She was sure Standing Bear would gladly display his scalp. Now the Dog Soldiers knew she was in camp, they might lie in wait for Devlin's return. How could she warn him? She could only watch, listen and pray a way presented itself.

"Where did your father's men take Monsieur Dubois? I wish to speak to him."

Mina wanted to know what he knew about her husband's disappearance, but could she trust him to give her the truth? It was unlikely unless it was of some benefit to him.

Namid pointed. "He's in a lodge on the edge of camp until my father decides his punishment. You may not see him. Do not worry. My father is a just man."

Mina scowled. "I worry the punishment won't be harsh enough. The man is a scoundrel. He needs to be taught a lesson."

Namid smiled. "He will not soon forget the day he dared strike a chief's daughter."

Later that night, Mina joined the other women seated near a campfire burning at the center of the circle of lodges. Nearly everyone from the camp was there. Once again, Namid served as her interpreter. When the Frenchie joined the group of men beside Standing Bear, Mina noted a bandage around his right hand.

She tugged on her friend's sleeve. "What happened to Monsieur Dubois?"

"My father made him hold a hot coal in his hand. The scar will remind him to think before he strikes another woman."

The two smiled at each other. Mina squeezed her friend's arm. "As you said, your father is wise."

Standing Bear addressed the assembly. Mina leaned close to Devlin's sister as she softly translated his words. It was no surprise Standing Bear pushed for all-out war. As leader of the Dog Soldiers, his word carried weight among some of the younger men. It was only when he spoke of soon having many rifles for his braves that Mina and Namid exchanged worried glances.

When it was Swift Fox's turn, he talked about making peace, of moving south and accepting the new lands offered to them. He spoke of all the battles that had been fought and lost and his wish that no more of his people die.

Which man would the people follow? Mina felt the uncertainty creeping through the crowd. Then someone on the council shouted a name and others echoed the call.

Namid leaned toward Mina. "They are calling for Kills Plenty. He is very old. The oldest of all our bands. He was once a great warrior and revered chief. Now, he has medicine dreams of much power. Many seek his wisdom, but he tells his dream only to a few."

Mina watched as they carried a small, ancient man with snow white hair to a place of honor beside Swift Fox. With his gnarled hands, gaunt face, and sunken eyes, it was easy to believe this man had seen a hundred summers or more.

He asked for the pipe and, after offering it to the four corners of the earth, he passed the smoke over his face and head with one hand. When that was done, he spoke.

Namid seemed mesmerized by his voice. Mina tugged on her sleeve twice and whispered, "What is he saying?"

"He is telling of a vision he had."

Namid fell silent. A murmur ran swiftly through the crowd as the old man continued.

"What did he say?" Mina asked.

"He saw the Cheyenne trampled underfoot by white men thicker than the buffalo."

Standing Bear leaped to his feet. Mina didn't need an interpreter to tell her he scoffed at the old man's vision. The Dog Soldiers cheered him, but Swift Fox demanded silence.

Standing Bear stormed out of the council and took some of his men with him. The arguments for and against war went on for another hour. When the meeting broke up, Frenchy and the other Métis man followed the remaining Dog Soldiers out of the lodge. As they passed behind the women, Mina heard the two exchange heated words spoken in French. She was able to catch most of it.

"I must follow them. They are planning something." Maybe she could learn where Artie was and if he was involved in the scheme. Rising, she pulled a shawl over her head to hide her light hair.

"Don't," Namid begged.

"I'll be fine." Ignoring her friend, she joined the others moving away from Swift Fox's lodge and worked her way closer to the men. When they entered a lodge at the outskirts of the camp, she walked past until she was sure she was out of sight and then doubled back. Sneaking close to the rear wall, she tried to hear the conversation inside over her thudding heartbeat.

The words she overheard chilled her to the bone. She had to stop them. But how? The thought was cut short when a hand clamped over her mouth.

A muscular arm circled her waist and lifted her off her feet. Despite her struggles, she was carried away from the camp and into the darkness.

Chapter Twenty-Four

Mina flailed wildly, clawing at her abductor's hands. Her heels found his shins, but the soft soles of her moccasins only caused him to stumble briefly as he carried her toward a stand of willow trees. Finally, mustering every bit of strength she possessed, she drove her elbow back into his ribs. His breath whooshed out in a grunt. His grip loosened. She twisted free. Whirling around, she tried to knee him in the groin.

He blocked the blow. "Stop it, Mina!"

The sound of his voice froze her. "Devlin?"

"If I say yes, will you quit trying to geld me?"

"Oh my God, you're safe." Mina launched herself at him, wrapping her arms around his neck, hugging him tight.

He stumbled backward a step as his arms closed around her. For a long minute, he held her close. It felt so good to be in his arms again. Unfortunately, it couldn't last.

"Mina, you're choking me," he whispered.

She loosened her hold and leaned back. "I'm so glad to see you. I knew you'd come back. Is it safe to return to Fort Harker? Do you know Standing Bear is in camp?"

"I saw him ride out half a while ago with five of his men. Keep your voice down. According to a stage driver I met, the epidemic has dwindled. I'm not sure how we'll get away from here with the rest of Standing Bear's band in camp."

"He and Frenchy are planning to rob an army payroll on its way from Denver. They're going to buy guns from Mexican traders with the gold. Standing Bear and some of his men have gone to set up an ambush. We must warn the army. Oh, Devlin, I've missed you." She threw her arms around his neck.

"I've missed you, too." He kissed her with a passion that made her head spin.

"Ah, we 'ave *ze* sweet reunion, no?"

Frenchy's amused drawl made Mina's blood run cold. Devlin whirled to face the man. With one hand, he pushed Mina behind him.

"*Mon ami*, do not worry I kill you now. I think perhaps I will not live long if I do *zis* here. Standing Bear, he want very much to kill you himself, but he has left on a little journey."

"What are you doing here, Frenchy?" Devlin demanded.

"I come to do business with *ze* Cheyenne. To trade trinkets for skins and hides."

"You mean to trade whiskey and guns. That's your real business, isn't it?" Mina couldn't hide her contempt.

"No! *Ze* army no like whiskey and gun traders. *Zey* make it very bad for such men. *Zey* hunt *zem* like dogs."

Mina moved from behind Devlin. "He's planning to buy guns for Standing Bear."

"But *zat* is what your husband did, *Cheri*. Yes, I know who you are. *Ze* proud wife looking for a lost fool. I know your husband. His stupidity, it almost git me killed."

"Artie's alive? You know where he is?"

"Stone Warrior gives you sweet kisses. Did he not tell you?"

"Tell me what?"

Devlin took a step toward the man. "Shut your mouth, or I'll shut it for you."

Something wasn't right. The tension between them wasn't about guns. "Devlin, what is he saying?"

"Nothing. Go back to the lodge, Mina."

Mina looked from one man to the other. Frenchy wore a smirk that sent her heart plunging to her feet. Devlin's eyes glinted with fury. His hands were clenched into fists.

She touched his arm. "I don't understand."

"I said go back to the lodge." Devlin's voice crackled with fury. She winced but stayed.

Licking her dry lips, she faced the Frenchman. "What do you know about my husband?"

"He was friend of Stone Warrior. Stone Warrior brings him and his guns to meet with Standing Bear."

Mina turned to Devlin. The moonlight drained his face of color and left it blank of any emotion. She recoiled from the idea forming in her brain. It couldn't be. "You never came with Artie to the Chalk Hills. You told me."

Frenchy's soulless laugh terrified her. She wanted to run and hide. Something hideous was happening, and she didn't know how to stop it.

"He bring your man to *ze* hills. And when *ze* guns your man 'ave are no good, he shoots him in *ze* head."

She flew forward and struck Frenchy across the face. "You lie! Devlin would never do such a thing."

Frenchy's eyes glinted with anger as he rubbed his jaw. "Tell her, Stone Warrior. Tell her how you shoot her man when he lay on the ground begging for his life."

Laughing, he turned and walked back to the camp.

Mina's mind fastened on the horrifying image and wouldn't let go. Artie pleading for his life as someone raised a gun to his head. She pressed a trembling hand to her lips. But it couldn't have been Devlin. Not this man. Not the man she loved. It was unthinkable.

She stared at him, waiting for him to deny it, to say Frenchy was lying. Only he didn't. He stared at his feet.

"Tell me it's not true," she whispered.

"It didn't happen like he said."

"Not like he said. What does that mean? It happened? You shot my husband? You killed him?" A frightful roaring filled her ears. She couldn't draw a breath.

Images of Artie flowed through her mind. The way he had hugged her the day Vincent brought her home from prison. Artie making her laugh at his silly jokes. How handsome he'd looked in his Bedouin robes. The way he smiled when he went exploring the streets of Peking with Kendrick at his side.

She tried to focus on Devlin, but Artie's image swam before her eyes. She racked her brain for some sort of explanation. "Maybe it was an accident. Tell me it was an accident, Devlin."

He looked away, unable to meet her gaze. "It wasn't."

She staggered back a step and pressed her hands to her mouth. "No, don't say that."

He reached for her. "Mina, please. Listen to me."

She struck his hand away. Revulsion pulsed through her. She shivered uncontrollably. "You knew. All this time you knew he was dead, and you let me go on hoping and searching. Why?"

Anger sent new strength through her quivering muscles. "What kind of cruel thrill did you get from it? My God! To think I let you kiss me. Let you make love to me."

She rubbed her mouth with the back of her hand so hard her teeth scraped her inner lip, and she tasted blood.

Devlin stepped closer. "Let me tell you what happened."

She struck his cheek as hard as she could. "You bastard. What makes you think I'd believe a word that comes out of your mouth? We've been together for weeks and all this time you knew he was dead."

She pressed her hands to her pounding temples as tears streamed down her face. "Oh, my God! How could you?"

Whirling around, she raced away from him, away from the heartbreak and pain. Tears blurred her vision as she ran. Why, why had she believed in him? Why had she loved him?

How could she have been so stupid, so gullible? Shame burned in her breast. She had kissed him, made love with him, and all the time he'd been lying to her.

She reached the lodge Swift Fox had given them and stopped just inside. The bed she'd shared with Devlin lay in front of her. Fresh tears stung her eyes. The joy she'd felt in his arms only a week ago turned to ashes in her mouth.

Namid was there tending the fire. She looked up and rushed to Mina's side. "My sister, why are you crying?"

"I can't stay here." Mina pressed a hand to her lips to hold back the painful cry building in her heart. She began untying her saddlebags from where they hung on one of the tent poles.

Namid stood beside Mina. "What is wrong?"

"I can't speak of it. Please, I need to go."

"Is it your monthly woman's time? Do you need to go to the lodge of women only?"

Mina stopped fumbling with the laces of her pack. It was foolish to think she could simply leave camp. Devlin or the others would come after her. She looked at Namid. "This woman's lodge. Can Devlin go there?"

"No! No man may enter it."

"Then, yes, I must go there. Quick, before he comes."

Namid brought a blanket and laid it over Mina's shoulders. "I am sorry there is no baby for you. Do not weep. The spirits will bring you a child when the time is good."

Mina leaned into her embrace. Let Namid think she cried because she wasn't pregnant. What was one more lie? It was kinder than telling her friend her brother was a murderer.

Namid led Mina to a small lodge set apart from the rest of the camp. Thankfully, it was empty. Mina sank to the floor and pulled the blanket close. When Namid left, Mina lay down and fought back her tears.

She never wanted to see Devlin again. Never wanted to hear his voice. Never wanted to feel his kisses or the sweetness of his arms enfolding her.

Stop it! It was all a lie. He doesn't care about me.

She pulled the blanket up to her chin and rolled onto her back. She wanted to go home. Vincent would be worried since she hadn't contacted him. How would she tell him about Artie's death? That his son had become mixed up in smuggling guns? Had Artie changed so much?

She hadn't seen him for more than a year before he disappeared. A year could change a lot of things. A single minute had been enough to send her world crashing around her ears.

Thoughts of guns made her recall Frenchy's plan she'd overheard. The army was moving a shipment of gold from Denver to Lawrence, Kansas. They would reach Fort Hays in four days, but half of Standing Bear's Dog Soldiers would attack the convoy before it got there. None of the men in guard detail would suspect the Indian scouts they'd hired were Frenchy's men. If only she could warn them. But how?

It would take days to reach Fort Hays. Provided she could find her way to the fort across the trackless grasslands.

She was alone, without supplies or maps. What chance did she have? Yet to give in and stay put seemed like the coward's way out when Standing Bear was already on his way to the ambush.

Mina sat up as a new thought occurred to her. There were supplies at the cabin. From there, she could ride south and find the stage road. Then she'd send word to the fort with the first wagon or stage heading west. It wasn't much of a plan, but it was all she had. She couldn't stay here. She had to do something.

Outside, an owl hooted. The lonely sound chipped away at the last of her self-control. Artie was dead, and Devlin had killed him.

Pillowing her head on her arms, Mina gave in to her grief and wept deep, soul-wrenching sobs. The man she loved was a murderer.

*

Outside the women's tent, Devlin settled cross-legged in the dew laden grass and listened to the sound that tore his soul to shreds. Whatever hope he'd cherished of a life with Mina was gone. Blown into nothingness.

He endured the pain of her weeping because he deserved it. Tipping his head back, he let the wind dry the moisture that welled up in his eyes.

There had been so many chances to explain her husband's death, but he'd let them slide by, hoping she would never find out. At first, he'd kept silent because her family had the power and the money to hunt him down. Later, he didn't tell her because he didn't want to hurt her. Now, even if she listened to his side of the story, it wouldn't matter. She hated him. He couldn't blame her. He hated himself.

Sometime later, when the moon had set, the sound of Mina's crying died away. He hoped she slept, hoped she'd gained that temporary release from her sorrow. Tomorrow, she would still hate him. He'd never see her eyes brimming with delight while she showed him some new fossil. She would never kiss him again. He'd never hold her in his arms and make earth-shattering love to her while they listened to the sound of the rain.

He rubbed one hand over his weary face. What he needed was a bottle of whiskey. Only, there wasn't enough whiskey in the world to drown the pain in his heart.

If he couldn't drink himself into a stupor, the next best thing was to seek his own bed. The bed where Mina had lain in his arms for one sweet night. That memory was all he had now. All he would ever have. Rising, he walked slowly back to his tepee.

A few hours later, his fitful rest ended when he heard a cry of alarm outside. Rising, he rushed out with the others.

A woman ran up to Swift Fox. "An evil spirit has visited our camp."

"Why do you say this?" Swift Fox demanded.

"The Dog Soldiers' shields and others are lying on the ground. The dogs never barked. It must have been a spirit."

Devlin turned and saw Swift Fox's shield still hung on the tripod beside the tepee, but Sabiha wasn't among the other horses.

Damn the woman! He never should have let her out of his sight.

He caught Namid's gaze and motioned for her to check the women's lodge. When she emerged a few seconds later, she shook her head.

Brave to slip through the camp and lay down the Dog Soldiers' shields to prevent them from pursuing quickly. Foolish because where would she go? She'd need supplies if she was trying to reach Fort Harker or Fort Hays.

She'd go back to the cabin. It was his best chance of finding her.

An argument broke out among the Dog Soldiers, bringing the sentries in to find out what was happening. It might be his only chance. He moved to where his horse was tied and freed the pinto. Namid appeared on the other side of his animal. She patted the horse's neck. "Beautiful one, tell your master I will go to other side of camp and shout that our enemy is coming. Your rider must go protect his brave wife."

Devlin smiled. "Fine horse, tell my sister she is truly our mother's daughter."

She giggled and faded back into the shadows of the lodges. As soon as he heard shouts and running feet, Devlin walked quietly out of camp with his horse, mounted when he was sure he was far enough and then rode into the night.

Chapter Twenty-Five

Devlin didn't know how much of a lead he had, so he pushed his horse hard. His sister's plan wouldn't work for long. Once they realized he wasn't in camp, the men Standing Bear had left behind would be after him. Mina had a head start but by how much?

His gut told him she would go to their cabin. She was impulsive but far from stupid. Unfortunately, Red Buffalo could lead the warriors straight there.

As his horse raced on, Devlin looked back frequently. The horizon remained free of riders. After a few hours, he started to believe his luck was holding and slowed his horse to a walk to rest it, but he didn't stop. It wasn't until he crested the last rise late in the afternoon and saw the tree-lined creek below that he allowed himself and his mount a brief respite. He dismounted and walked the winded animal down toward the trees. What if Mina wasn't there?

When he reached the creek, he saw Sabiha standing near the cabin door. Relief caused the muscles of his body to betray him. He leaned on his tired horse's neck to keep from falling. Now he'd found her, he was reluctant to go further. The idea of confronting her hatred chilled him to the bone, but they had little time.

He allowed his horse to drink before crossing the water. Outside the cabin, he paused. Was Mina more likely to shoot him if he entered unannounced or if he called out? The risk was about equal.

At the door to the cabin, he stopped and looked in. Mina sat on the floor with Artie's trunk open and all its contents scattered about her.

She looked up from reading one of Artie's journals. "I opened your secret panel hoping to find a cache of supplies or guns."

He took a step inside, tense and uncertain. At least she wasn't shooting. "I keep some hardtack and pemmican in there."

"I found it." She tilted her head to one side as she stared at him. "Why did you keep his things?"

"I'm not sure. Guilt maybe."

She gestured to one book lying on the table. "He really was trying to smuggle guns. The crates he told the army contained his excavating tools and equipment had false bottoms. There are even details of how much it cost to have them built. That's why you made me open mine. You wanted to be sure I wasn't smuggling, too."

"I swear to you, Mina, I didn't know what he was doing."

She gave him an odd smile and nodded. "I know. Artie kept meticulous notes, even of his illegal activities. What a foolish boy. He wrote in here his guide didn't suspect his true purpose in staying here."

He came in and sat on the end of his bed. "I wasn't his guide the first time he came out here."

"Yes. That name is recorded as Indian Jim. He didn't bother to learn the man's full name. For someone who wanted to save the natives, he was as guilty of demeaning them as anyone else."

She closed the book on her lap and looked around. "He met Andre Laurent, an associate of Frenchy Dubois, in New Orleans. Laurent told him about the Sand Creek Massacre. Artie and Kendrick witnessed a similar slaughter in Brazil where Kendrick was killed. Artie was deeply affected. I believe he hoped to help the native people here. The guns were all at Frenchy's urging."

Devlin nodded. "Frenchy found a wealthy, naïve young man and used him."

"My foolish, foolish husband. Was he really so guileless?"

"Artie made his own decisions."

Mina's eyes held a faraway look, and Devlin wondered if she even heard him.

"My poor Artie. He used his own money to buy the guns and bring them here. He was never interested in hunting fossils. It was a ruse until the exchange could take place in case someone from the fort came out to check on him."

She frowned at the book. "It was Standing Bear, I'm sure, but he doesn't refer to him by name."

"Nothing can change what happened, Mina. Leave these things and let's go."

"Artie had two sets of journals. Did you know? One as a cover for his science and one with his true dealings. Isn't that bizarre? I didn't know my husband at all."

Devlin moved to crouch beside her. This calm reciting of details alarmed him. He was more prepared to deal with her anger. "Mina, we must leave. The Dog Soldiers will be after us. We don't have much time."

She focused on him then. "I'm not moving until you tell me exactly how he died."

"I shot him."

She closed her eyes briefly. When she opened them, pure determination glared out at him. "Why?"

"Don't make me do this."

"I had a lot of time to think on the ride here. When I stepped inside this room, I realized the man who saved my life, the dear man who made those shelves for me, who made such tender love to me, he isn't a man to kill someone in cold blood. Tell me what happened."

"What difference does it make?"

"It makes a difference to me."

Devlin looked into her beautiful blue eyes and called himself every kind of fool. Then he grabbed the thin thread of hope she offered. If she understood, maybe someday she could forgive him.

"I jumped at the chance to work for your husband last summer. I really liked him. He seemed harmless enough, just an odd character with too much money and not enough sense. Why else would he want to dig up fossils? One day, about two weeks after we got here, Frenchy showed up. When the two of them went off together, I knew something wasn't right."

She opened the book in her lap. "He mentioned that in his next-to-last entry. They set a time and place to meet with the buyer. Artie's major concern seemed to be how to keep you from finding out. When Frenchy offered to kill you, Artie began having serious second thoughts. Too little, too late."

Devlin pushed his hat back. He recalled the day with perfect clarity. "Artie insisted I go hunt for fresh meat. We weren't low on supplies. I didn't find any sage hens. What I stumbled across were three burned out wagons. The settlers had been tortured and scalped."

"Standing Bear?"

"Him or some of his men. I high tailed it back here to warn Artie but ran into their war party. I had a good horse, so I made a running fight, but wasted a lot of lead. They dropped back after I hit a couple of them. They didn't know I was almost out of ammo."

Devlin fell silent, thinking of the day and wishing he'd made other choices.

"But you always keep one bullet, don't you?" Mina asked quietly.

He nodded. "Yeah, I had one bullet left. I knew what the Dog Soldiers would do if they got their hands on me."

She paled at his words and looked down. "I remember their handiwork, too."

Devlin wished there was some way he could spare her knowing what came next, but the time for lies and half-truths was past.

"To shake the war party, I rode into the canyons north of here. There was a storm coming. All I had to do was to hide and pray the rain washed my tracks away. After a while, I thought I'd lost them, but I couldn't be sure. I was trying to make it back to the cabin when I heard yelling. I crept as close as I could. That was the first time I saw the guns. They were scattered on the ground beside Artie's crates."

"So he handed them over. I had hoped he changed his mind."

"I don't know what was wrong with the guns, but it was obvious they didn't work. Someone sold your husband defective ones. Standing Bear and Frenchy were arguing."

"And Artie?"

Devlin closed his eyes. "He was already staked to the ground."

"He was being tortured?" She pressed her hand to her lips.

Devlin forced himself to go on, to bring back those horrible moments. "I think he must have been unconscious for a while, because he suddenly began screaming and screaming. I'll spare you the details of what they did, but no man could survive after that."

"Oh, dear God!" she whispered.

"There were ten of them. I had one bullet. What choice did I have except to stay hidden and hope he'd die quickly? I swear, Mina, it was too late to save him even if I'd had a hundred men with me. Only, he didn't die quickly. He just kept screaming."

She moaned as she rocked to-and-fro.

Devlin hated what he was doing to her, but she had a right to know the truth. "Finally, I couldn't stand it. I took aim at Artie. Standing Bear was leaning over him. I made a choice. One I've regretted every day since."

"You shot Artie?"

"I let Standing Bear live. If I'd made a different choice, Artie would still be dead, but maybe Buck's family would be alive. Maybe a lot of people would still be alive."

*

Silence settled over the cabin. Mina opened her eyes to see Devlin rise and turn toward the door. His shoulders slumped. He leaned against the door frame as if too tired to stand unaided.

She had the truth at last. The whole horrible truth. It was ghastlier than anything she had imagined. Little by little, she understood what Devlin had been living with, what it had done to him.

"How did you escape?" The strength in her voice surprised her.

He wiped a hand over his face. "Dumb luck. I knew my horse couldn't outrun ten fresh ones. As I rode down the gully, I saw a badger den under a lip of rock. I got off, slapped my horse and sent him running, then I crawled into a hole like a trapped animal and waited. It began raining heavily. It must have washed away any signs of me. I lay in that hole for the rest of the day and all night. Twice I saw the legs of their horses go past as they tried to track me. The next day, I crawled out, buried your husband and marked his grave with his name and the date. It was the least I could do. Then I walked to Fort Harker."

Mina rose to her feet and replaced Artie's journals in his trunk along with a few of his clothes, his favorite blowgun and some artifacts he'd brought back from the Amazon. Softly, she closed the lid. "I'm glad his grave is marked. Thank you for that and for telling me the truth. I expect we should go."

He looked at her as if he didn't quite know what to say. She wasn't up for more conversation, either. Every emotion in her had been rung out until she was empty as the fossils on her shelves.

She left the cabin without looking back. Devlin held Sabiha's head as Mina mounted. She looked down at him. "I'm glad you didn't let him suffer longer."

*

Devlin met her gaze and nodded once. It wasn't exactly forgiveness, but it was something. Tired but oddly cleansed, he mounted his weary horse. Together, they rode across the creek and headed south. They had gone

221

less than two miles when a war whoop split the air, quickly followed by others. A dozen riders rushed at them from a rise a quarter mile ahead.

Devlin hauled his horse's head around. "Head back to the cabin. We can make a stand there."

Mina kicked Sabiha into a run. Devlin stayed right behind her. Relief surged through him as the trees along the creek came into sight. A second later, more riders burst from that cover, cutting them off from safety.

They had no choice but to make a run for it northward through open country. Mina leaned low over Sabiha's neck to help her mare and to make herself a smaller target. Devlin turned to fire at the warriors gaining on them.

"Why aren't they shooting at us?" she yelled.

Devlin threw off another round as his gut clenched with fear. "They want us alive."

Mina knew what he meant. She urged Sabiha to greater speed, but Devlin's horse began faltering. Mina drew back to stay beside him.

"What are you doing?" he yelled. "Get a move on."

The wind whipped her hair into her face. "Your horse can't keep up."

"Don't worry about me. Go."

"I'm not leaving you." His horse stumbled and almost fell. Mina cried out, but his horse kept going.

Devlin threw a glance back, then pointed off to the right. "Head for that bluff. Maybe we can hold them off."

She turned toward a lone mound that rose out of the flat plains. Scarred by dozens of eroded gullies, it looked as if a giant animal had clawed away at the sides.

They made it as far as the foot of the rise before Devlin's horse fell. Devlin rolled clear. Mina yanked Sabiha to a stop and turned back. Devlin gained his feet and raced back toward his fallen mount. Gunfire splattered the ground at his feet, but he kept going and tried to get his saddlebag, but it was wedged under the horse.

He turned and ran to Mina, leaping on Sabiha's back behind the saddle. "Into that canyon."

Mina guided her mare into the closest gully cutting down the side of the hill.

"Get down and take her to the top," Devlin yelled.

Mina slid off and began leading her mare upward. Devlin knelt where he was and fired off three rapid rounds. A moment later, he was behind Sabiha, urging her uphill. The gully snaked back and forth, providing cover, but it was tough going between the narrow high walls.

Clawing and stumbling their way upward for fifty yards, they made it around the next bend and found a dead end. There was nowhere to go.

*

Devlin's face told Mina they were trapped. He positioned himself on a ledge of rock and began firing downhill. After a few rapid shots, he stopped. "They're going to make their way above us. We'll be sitting ducks if they do."

"Can't we make a run for it?"

"Not on one horse. We wouldn't get a mile."

"Sabiha is fast. There isn't a horse anywhere that can catch her."

"With one rider, maybe. Not with two." From the cover of the ravine, Devlin fired again. An advancing brave toppled from his pony.

Crouching down, Devlin searched his belt for more carriages. He found only two. He met Mina's gaze. His face was pale and streaked with dirt, but there was no panic in his eyes.

She fumbled for her derringer in the pouch at her belt. "I have two bullets in here."

"They won't fit my gun. The rest of my ammunition is out there in my saddlebags. I can't hold them off with these, Mina. They'll rush us soon."

"What are you saying, Devlin? That it's hopeless?"

He nodded mutely and watched the color leach from her face. A strange calm settled over her features. "Then I must ask you for a favor, Devlin Elder. The same favor you granted Artie. I don't think I can do it myself."

"No!" The cry tore from his throat, driven by the depths of his love. He pulled her into his arms and held her against him. Tears blurred his vision.

She rested against him for a moment, then pushed back and looked into his eyes. "I should also mention I love you, Devlin Elder, with all my heart and for all eternity."

He gazed at her beautiful face. "I don't deserve your love. But I'm not letting you die here. There's one chance for both of us. You can get away on Sabiha."

"I won't leave you."

He grasped her by the shoulders. "They won't kill me, but they will make me watch while they rape and torture you. They'll keep me alive until Standing Bear returns. That may be several days. Get to Fort Hays and bring back help."

"They'll torture you."

"I'll survive until Standing Bear gets hold of me."

He dragged her toward the mare. "Stay low until you reach the bottom. I'll give you as much time as I can."

"I'm not leaving you." She tugged at his hand, trying to break free of his grip.

He held her close and whispered against her hair. "Live for me, and you will save us both. Do you understand? I owe it to Artie to save you. I can face anything if I know you're safe."

She tried to press the derringer into his hand, but he shook his head. "Keep it in case you need it and use it."

Nodding, she tucked it into her belt and cupped his face in her hands. "I'll come back."

"I know you will."

Then he helped turn the horse in the narrow confines of gully and pulled off the saddle to lighten the load. He lifted Mina to the mare's back. Sobbing, she tried to cling to him, but he pulled her hands free and pressed them to the horse's mane.

"Go now. They don't know I'm empty. It'll take several seconds for them to realize what you're doing."

A clatter of rocks sent him spinning around. He shot the warrior ready to leap down on them. The brave crumpled to the ground and lay still.

Turning to Mina, Devlin said, "Go."

"I will always love you. Devlin. Don't die."

"Dying is easy," he said. "Living takes courage. Show me some courage, Lady Wilhelmina Smith."

He slapped the horse's rump to get Sabiha moving. Mina looked back, and Devlin knew he would remember her tear-stained face for as long as he lived. Maybe by saving her, he could put Artie's ghost to rest.

But he had to live long enough to give her a good head start. Racing back to the top of the ravine, he called out in Cheyenne, "My brothers, can you hear me?" he yelled.

"I hear you, white man. You are no brother of mine," someone shouted back.

"My mother sat in your chief's lodge! She cooked his food and made moccasins for his feet! How am I not your brother?"

"Your mother was a slave. You are whelp of a slave. Standing Bear wishes to kill you himself. Maybe I make your woman my slave. If she doesn't please me, I kill her slowly."

"I have killed many braves today, but it is the blood of Standing Bear I want. I claim the right to face him in combat," Devlin shouted.

He looked down the gully. Mina had reached the bottom. Soon she would be in sight to the men above him. "Go with God, little one," he whispered, then he stood up and gave a keening war cry.

*

Mina's breath came in ragged gasps. Wrapping her fingers tight in Sabiha's mane, she slammed her heels into the mare's flanks. Sabiha broke into a run and charged out into the open. She listened for sounds of pursuit and tried desperately not to look back.

Remember him as you last saw him. Looking so damn brave.

Yet, she couldn't help herself. She had to know. She reined to a stop and spun her horse around. Devlin was being dragged down the slope by two braves. Standing Bear wasn't among them, but Frenchy Dubois was. One brave rushed at Devlin with his hatchet raised. Mina thought they were going to kill him before her eyes, but Frenchy stopped the man.

Devlin said Standing Bear wanted to kill Devlin himself. They would hold him captive and wait for their leader to come. Then they would torture Devlin. He would die a horrible, slow death and there was nothing she could do. Unless she could bring help.

A shout from one brave sent several of them running toward their ponies. She recognized Red Buffalo in the group. They'd seen her. She raised her hand in a salute, hoping Devlin would see, then whirled Sabiha and raced away.

Tears streamed down Mina's face, but she held back her sobs. Devlin was depending on her. After a mile, she chanced a glance behind her. Three braves were pushing their ponies hard. Red Buffalo had a good horse. He pulled ahead of the others, but she knew he couldn't catch her. She slowed Sabiha to give her a chance to regain her wind, but Sabiha tugged at the reins, ready to keep running.

"Okay baby, I know you want to go, but it's a long way to the fort."

The mare settled into a steady gallop at Mina's calming words. Yet every drum of her hooves was like a stake pounding into Mina's heart.

I'm running away. I've abandoned him.

What could she do? He had given everything for her. She couldn't let his sacrifice be in vain.

She glanced back. The Indians had closed the distance to perhaps a half a mile. She bent low over Sabiha's flowing mane. "Let's show them what we're made of."

The mare shot forward, and Mina stayed low, letting the mare find her own way, jumping small gullies that cut through the grass and tuffs of brush blocking their way. After another mile, Mina looked back. The riders had fallen back, but not as far as she had hoped. They would not give up. They knew the land, and she didn't. Anywhere ahead of her, a creek or deep ravine could block her path and make her lose her precious lead. She could try to make it to the wagon trail, but she couldn't run Sabiha day and night. The mare had already covered miles.

Off to her left, a dark green line of trees signaled the course of a creek, and she recognized the area. It was the creek where their cabin stood.

She checked Sabiha as a sudden thought struck her. At the cabin, Devlin had something that might make these braves abandon the chase. He had two full kegs of whiskey. Could she draw the men following her there without getting caught or killed in the process?

She had to risk it.

Riding into the water, Mina turned the mare downstream. The mud churned by the horse's hooves drifted ahead on the current. They would think she was trying to throw them off her trail by sticking to the water, but she would make sure enough signs pointed the way.

Splashing along the shallow creek bed was easy riding, but she couldn't run Sabiha here. The gap between her and the men behind would narrow.

Mina almost missed the faint trail that led to the cabin until Sabiha turned toward the bank on her own.

"Oh, you good girl. You remember the way."

The mare scrambled up the bank, leaving hoofprints in the soft mud. Once they reached the grassy glade in front of the dugout, Mina jumped off and pushed open the cabin door. Inside, she rushed to open trees secret panel and wrestled one keg into the middle of the floor.

Was it enough? Would they know what was in it? She couldn't do anything more. Time was running out.

She needed some kind of weapon. Anything! Her notes and specimens lined the walls and shelves Devlin had so painstakingly made for her. Tears blurred her vision. She squeezed her eyes shut and forced them away.

Again, she searched the room and spied a knife with a broken tip lying on the stone hearth. She grabbed it up, amazed at how wonderful the weight of it felt in her hand. So far, she had her derringer with two bullets and a knife.

Now, what else? Think. He said you're the smartest woman he's ever known. Prove him right.

In the corner, Artie's trunk caught her attention. She threw it open and pulled out its contents: clothes, his journals and personal items. She dug to the bottom, hoping to find something she could use.

"Damn it, Artie, you were a gunrunner! Why couldn't you leave a rifle that worked and a hundred rounds of ammunition?"

Disappointment weighed her down until she saw the woven reed case. His blowgun. Artie had written extensively about its use by the natives of the Amazon. Did he still have the darts and poison he'd mentioned?

She pried the case open. The blow tube, twelve darts, and an unbroken amber vial marked with skull and crossbones remained intact. It wasn't much, but it was something. Tucking the case under her arm, she started to close the trunk and then stopped.

Let the braves think she had come here for a reason. Let them wonder if she'd found a gun. Maybe they'd think twice about following her. With one last glance around, she hurried out the door.

Outside, she mounted and urged Sabiha up the hill behind the cabin. At the top, she dismounted and swept out their tracks with a branch. On the hilltop, she crept back to the edge and lay down where she had a view of the cabin below. She didn't have long to wait.

Through a break in the trees, she saw three mounted men appear around the bend in the creek. They moved boldly, scanning the trees and creek bank, obviously unafraid of the lone woman they trailed. They moved up the creek and out of sight past the beaver dam. Long minutes passed. Had they missed her tracks? She craned her neck, trying to catch sight of them without giving her location away. When they didn't appear again, she glanced around nervously.

Could they have seen her? Were they even now sneaking through the long grass to catch her unaware? She gathered herself to make a run for her horse.

Just as she thought she couldn't wait a second longer, she glimpsed movement in the trees below. Red Buffalo had left the creek and was making his way toward the cabin on foot. Then she saw a second and a third man. They converged on the door with caution.

When the first one disappeared inside the cabin, she nearly collapsed with relief. Now, if they would only take the time and open the keg.

Red Buffalo came out and searched the ground outside. He knelt, and she knew he'd found Sabiha's shod hoof prints. Her plan had failed. She inched back from the edge. A shout from below stopped her. The other two braves came out rolling the keg between them and laughing.

An argument ensued. Mina could only guess by their gestures what was going on. Red Buffalo wanted to keep after her. His two companions soon dissuaded him. Using a hatchet, they chopped a hole in the keg's top. The contents sloshed out. Soon, all three were drinking from the cask with their hands.

So much was being wasted. Would there be enough left?

Red Buffalo wised up and went into the cabin, returning with two tin cups. How long would it take them to get drunk and pass out? She wanted to leave, but if she were spotted before they were incapacitated, they could renew the chase. Sabiha needed rest. Mina had sacrificed her lead for this crazy plan. It had to work.

After nearly an hour, they were sitting on the ground and clumsily passing the cups around. Red Buffalo staggered into the cabin and emerged, rolling the second keg in front of him.

Another argument ensued. One brave obviously wanted to open the keg. He waved his hatchet in wide circles over his head. Red Buffalo shook his head. After a while, they brought their horses into the clearing. They made a sling from one of her dresses and secured the second keg to a horse. Red Buffalo mounted his animal, and his companion hefted the open keg up for him to hold. Then they rode out much less silently than they had crept in.

Her plan worked. Mina rolled to her back and stared at the cloudless blue sky, relief making her lightheaded. Were they taking the whiskey back to the others? If so, by nightfall, the entire group might be drinking. Maybe downright drunk. If Devlin was still alive, could she sneak into their camp? Could she free him and not get captured?

Or should she ride on to bring help? Could she reach the fort in time to save Devlin? He was being tortured even now. She closed her eyes and pounded her fist into the dirt. "Oh, bloody hell! I must save him."

Carefully, she descended to the cabin, hoping to find something to aid Devlin. She already knew there was nothing inside, so she went to the lean-to at the back. Her crates were still sitting inside, waiting for her to fill them with fossil specimens and ship them east. A moment later, she spied the long poles of the travois and harness he'd made to carry her here. An idea formed. Maybe she could ship herself into their camp.

If Devlin wasn't dead, he was going to kill her for this.

Chapter Twenty-Six

Stripped naked and staked spread-eagle on the stoney ground, Devlin's body was a mass of bruises and painful cuts his captors gleefully inflicted each time they walked past. The tight ropes at his wrists and ankles cut into his flesh. The burning agony was nothing compared to what lay in store. He didn't struggle. Instead, Devlin hoarded his strength to sing his death song when the time came.

The blood red sun dropped behind the butte where he had hoped to make a stand. It would be dark soon. The Dog Soldiers had made camp out in the open, unconcerned with discovery.

Frenchy came over and squatted beside Devlin. "These braves want to build a fire on your belly to laugh at your screams as it burns through you."

Devlin spit at him.

Frenchy laughed. "Standing Bear wishes to do this himself. Maybe he will cut you open and pull out your guts so coyotes can feast while you watch. You make him very mad when you kill zat white fool before Standing Bear finished 'aving his fun."

Pulling a knife from his waist, Frenchy drew a thin line from Devlin's breastbone to his belly button with the tip. Devlin gritted his teeth against the searing pain and forced himself to lie still.

"You are brave, *mon ami*. Will you be so brave when I take zat blond-haired whore on ze dirt beside you? She will like it, I promise. You 'ave many days to watch us before Standing Bear comes. It will be fun, no?" With a laugh, Frenchy stood and went to join the others by the fire.

Please, God. I don't care what they do to me. Just let Mina get away.

Several hours later, he heard horses coming into camp. He raised his head, straining to see in the dark. Two warriors rode in and stopped beside the small fire. It was plain they were drunk. They could barely stay on their mounts. Mina wasn't with them.

Frenchy pulled a keg from Red Buffalo arms, and the brave toppled to the ground. Other braves surrounded the remaining man, shouting and laughing as they unloaded another whiskey keg. Devlin smiled. His cache had been discovered.

He'd stolen the whiskey from two traders bent on using it to cheat friendly Cheyenne and others out of their hides and horses. Whiskey was the single worst ill white men had introduced to the tribes. Even in Swift Fox's band, few men would resist the drink, though Swift Fox forbade it. The Dog Soldiers immediately opened the keg. Everyone wanted their share.

Frenchy cursed and pulled the Red Buffalo to his feet. "Where is ze white woman?"

Red Buffalo struck Frenchy's hand away. "Her horse is too fast. We cannot catch her. But she leads us to the firewater. I bring it back to share with my friends." He threw his arms wide, then sank limply to the ground.

Devlin let his head fall back. Tears of relief slipped from the corners of his eyes. *Good girl, Mina. I said you were smart, but I didn't know the half of it.*

She'd led the men to the whiskey and gotten away. He could face death knowing she was safe, and his debt to Artie repaid.

Frenchy tried to keep the others away from the kegs, but his efforts were futile. Soon, they were dipping their hands in to scoop up the potent brew. Devlin closed his eyes. Distracted guards increased his chances of escape.

A brutal kick to his ribs drove the air from his lungs. Gasping and coughing, he looked up to see Frenchy glaring at him.

"Your woman, she git away, but you are not so lucky. Maybe you live till Standing Bear comes. Maybe not."

*

Using the rawhide bedframe from the cabin and her knife, Mina fashioned a sling beneath the travois to lie in and covered the frame with a buffalo hide, draping it over the sides where it hung nearly to the ground. It would hide her, but it also blocked her view except for an inch or two around the edges and a gap at the front where she could look out. Using a long, leather strap passed through Sabiah's bridle, Mina stretched it under the horse to her hiding place beneath the travois, allowing her to guide her mare.

On top of the litter, she had tied her and Artie's trunks and secured the heavy hide to the wooden poles with leather thongs so it couldn't be pulled off by the vegetation she passed or by the men she prayed would take her horse and travois into their camp without looking under it.

Sabiha was her Trojan horse. Mina hoped the braves would take her into their citadel.

What she could do once in their camp was another story. Mina headed Sabiha toward the last place she had seen Devlin.

She could see her horse's legs and a short way directly in front of Sabiha, but little else.

Armed with a derringer, her carefully sharpened knife, a blowgun and twelve poison darts, Mina guided Sabiha across the dark prairie.

If Devlin was alive. If she could locate the camp without being discovered. If they were drunk. If she could get close. If… if… if.

Only one thing was certain in her mind. Should she get close enough to Devlin, she would end his suffering and then her own life. The dart for Devlin was in her blow gun. She might only have one chance. Should she be unable to use her gun, she had a second dart for herself hidden in her sleeve, the tip carefully covered with a hollow reed.

Her plan had more flaws than a dictionary had words. The only thing in her favor was the moonless night sky.

Long grass and weeds scraped her face and arms as she hung inches above the ground. She had buffalo hide covering the underside of her sling, too, so she could duck from sight if she needed to, but while she was driving, she had to have her arms and head out.

Her first glimmer of hope came when she caught sight of a riderless horse standing a few yards ahead of her. As she approached, she saw one brave from the cabin where he had passed out and fallen to the ground.

At least she knew she was headed in the right direction. Leaving him, she continued north until she saw the faint glow of a fire in the distance. The Dog Soldiers hadn't moved. They were camped at the base of the bluff where she'd left Devlin.

Soon, she had worked her way to within several hundred yards of the renegades' campfire. She dropped one end of the guide rein, pulled it through Sabiha's bit and back into her hands. It had to look as if the horse had wandered this way alone. "Walk on. Allow him," Mina whispered, wanting Sabiha to go with the first person who approached her.

Her well-trained mount continued forward. After another hundred feet or so, Mina heard voices. They had been spotted. She could hear them coming closer and tried to remain calm, to slow her breathing, but her heart was about to jump out of her throat. Taking her pistol out, she held it to her temple. She would not make Devlin suffer more by watching her torture.

The toes of the men's moccasin clad feet gathered around her. Sabiha sidestepped nervously as one of them approached her.

Instead of leading the horse on, he merely held her while his companions argued loudly. One of them jumped on the travois. Mina flinched. She heard him open the trunks. He must be looking for more whiskey. She heard pushing and shoving. One man was knocked down. She saw the back of his head as he landed near her where the buffalo hide didn't quite touch the ground. If he turned his head, if he looked her way. Her finger tightened on the trigger.

He shoved himself up, and the argument continued until the brave holding Sabiha began walking forward with unsteady steps. He led her mare to where a group of horses stood and tied her there, leaving Mina with a limited view of the camp.

She couldn't believe her luck. The renegades were staggering around, yelling and drinking. Her plan had worked better than she'd dared hope. Everything depended on the men becoming drunk. If even one of them remained sober and on guard, her plan wouldn't simply fail. She would die without helping the man she loved.

Straining her eyes, she searched for Devlin. Then she saw him. He lay staked to the ground a dozen yards beyond the fire. Was he alive? Her pulse hammered in fear. She couldn't tell. If only he would move.

Then she saw Frenchy leave the fireside and go toward Devlin. He paused beside the captive and delivered a kick to the side of Devlin's head. Mina pressed a hand to her mouth to keep from crying out. Laughing, Frenchy pointed toward her. "Your woman, I think she is dead. Her horse comes here for company. *Zis* is too bad. I wanted to kill her myself." Laughing, he staggered back to his companions.

He would pay for that one day, but at least she had proof Devlin still lived. She studied the layout of the camp. Devlin was too far away to hit with a dart or a bullet from her derringer. She would have to wait for the whiskey to do its work or use her riskier backup plan.

Carefully, she unwrapped Artie's blow gun. She had already dipped the darts in the dark, foul-smelling poison. Now, she prayed Artie's research was correct because he'd written the poison would incapacitate a grown man in seconds.

*

Devlin tried to focus on Sabiha. Why would Mina have taken the time to load her trunks? To save her damn fossils? Where was she? Was she dead? He hoped it had been quick. If not, he didn't want to know.

Both Devlin's eyes were swollen, and his sight was blurry from kicks to his head, but he thought he saw movement under the travois. He blinked and shook his head to clear his vision. Small fingers lifted the edge of the hide a fraction, then the tip of stick protruded from underneath.

What the hell? No!

His breath froze in his lungs. She couldn't be under there. What was she trying to do? Get herself raped and killed while he watched?

He glanced at the drunken men staggering around the fire. None of them seemed to have noticed. He dropped his head back to the ground. Staring in her direction was a sure way to draw attention to her.

He'd thought she was safe. He'd given his life so she could escape. Instead, she was fifty feet away from her worst nightmare. And his.

One guard who hadn't been drinking strolled by with a gun cradled in his arm. He was headed toward the horses. Devlin called out an insult, hoping to draw him away. The man laughed and kept walking.

A few feet from where Mina was hiding, he stopped and swatted at something on his thigh. Turning to the others, he took a couple steps in their direction, fell face down in the grass and lay still. Was he drunk? Only seconds ago, he'd seemed sober enough.

The tip of the stick disappeared under the travois. Mina must have Artie's blow gun. How many men could she take down before someone noticed her? He pulled at his bonds with renewed strength, but it was no use. He couldn't help her.

The night wore on and the men wound down as more and more of them passed out. A second warrior approached the travois with staggering steps. He dropped to his knees and keeled over a few feet away. How many darts did she have? How many more braves were out beyond the firelight? He had no way of knowing.

When the last dancer toppled over, Frenchy walked among them, kicking some and cursing. He'd been drinking, but he wasn't drunk. He

234

shouted in the darkness. No one answered. He kicked one more hapless brave and began walking toward Devlin.

He paused and squatted with his hands on his hips. "I don't get to ride your woman, but I get to ride her fancy horse. Or maybe I kill it? She liked her horse, no? You want I should send it to the next life to find your whore? Maybe I do that. Maybe I slit its throat while you watch."

He rose and staggered toward the mare. A red feather appeared in the grass by his feet. He kept walking. He drew his knife and tried to grab Sabiha's bridle. The mare snorted and rose straight up in the air with her hooves flailing. One struck the side of Frenchy's head. He dropped like a rock, a dark stain spreading in the grass. Sabiha settled to the ground and snorted. She shook her head and side-stepped away from him.

Mina slipped from beneath the buffalo robe and raced to Devlin's side. She was alive and unharmed. They might just get out of this.

"Of all the hare-brained, crazy schemes—" He stopped because his face was being covered with kisses in between incoherent babbling.

"Please don't be mad. Thank God, you're alive. Did they hurt you? Of course, they hurt you. Look at you. Can you ride? Oh, my God, oh, my God. I killed those men."

"Mina, stop." He wanted to kiss her too, but he wanted his hands untied so he could strangle her.

"I don't know what I would have done if you'd been dead. Are you angry with me? Please don't be mad." She kissed his neck and his bare chest. "I was going to kill myself."

"Mina, stop!"

She pulled back. "I'm sorry. Did I hurt you?"

"Stop crying and untie me. We need to get out of here."

"Of course."

Pulling a knife from the waistband of her doeskin dress, she cut the ropes binding his hands and feet. With her help, he sat up and began rubbing the raw flesh to bring some feeling to his numb fingers. The pain of his blood rushing back made him catch his breath. They didn't have time to waste nursing his wounds. There was no telling how long before some of the men returned to their senses.

He surged to his feet, but he would have fallen if she hadn't held him up.

"Look what they did to you." She touched the cut on his abdomen.

He grabbed her hands. "You insane woman! What were you thinking?"

"Well, while I was loading the poisonous darts into the blowgun, I kept thinking, don't prick yourself, Mina. That is a stupid question, Devlin. I wanted to save your life or end your suffering if I couldn't free you and then end my life, too. Because I don't want to live without you."

"You foolish, beautiful woman." He kissed her, then pushed her toward the horses, expecting a shot to ring out from the darkness at any moment. "We need to get out of here."

He crossed to where her first victim lay and began pulling the pants off the brave's body. He hurriedly put them on. "We have to reach Fort Hays and tell them what Standing Bear has planned. Once the army learns where the Dog Soldiers have been getting their guns, they can put a stop to the trade."

"What should we do with him?" She pointed to where Frenchy lay moaning in the dirt beside Sabiha's feet.

"We should turn him over to the authorities, but we'll travel faster without him. Besides, I think Standing Bear will happily deal with him for letting me get away."

She nodded. "I shall cherish that vision. Can you ride?"

He glanced down at his bloodied torso. "It looks worse than it is. We'll take three horses each and trade them out as they tire. Gather any canteens, rifles and what ammunition you can find quickly. We're not going to stop until we reach the fort. We'll scatter the rest of the horses to make it harder for them to follow us."

They chose the best-looking animals and were soon underway. Mina led Sabiha and another mare while she rode a blue roan stallion. Her euphoria at rescuing Devlin was soon swallowed up in the grueling ride.

Afterwards, she would recall little of their flight across the plains. They pushed the horses hard until daybreak, then stopped to rest briefly beneath a lone tree on a small creek. The two previous days and nights without rest took their toll on Mina. At times, she fell asleep, waking only to catch herself before she fell off her horse. How Devlin managed she never knew, but each time they stopped to rest, he was there to help her down, to offer her water from his canteen and bites of hard biscuits.

The rests were never long enough. It seemed each time she laid her head on the ground, Devlin roused her and urging her up again. They dropped the spent horses and rode the fresher ones, but all the animals were lagging by the end of the first day and night.

Finally, two long days after they started, Mina aboard her tired mare stumbled up to Fort Hays with Devlin at her side a little after noon.

Their arrival generated a considerable commotion. It wasn't until she was standing before the tent of the fort commander that she realized what a bizarre picture she must present. No wonder these men were staring at her. Her beautiful doeskin dress was covered in dust. One sleeve was ripped, as was her neckline, letting the garment hang off her shoulder. Her lips were gritty with dirt as she tried to speak.

She rubbed her face knowing it did little good and glanced at Devlin. He stood beside her bare-chested, coated with dried blood, and obviously on the verge of exhaustion. A more disreputable looking pair would be hard to find.

The commander exited his tent, his displeasure clear at having his noonday meal interrupted. "What is the meaning of this? Who are these people?" he barked at the young private beside them.

Tired beyond measure and annoyed at being dismissed by a military popinjay, Mina drew herself up to her full height. "You may address your remarks to me, Captain. I am Lady Wilhelmina Smith of Silsby Hall, Bedfordshire and London. This is my guide, Mr. Devlin Elder of Fort Harker. We have important information that must be relayed to the military commanders along the stage route to Denver as quickly as possible. After that, I shall require lodging, a hot bath and some food. Is there a woman here who can act as my maid? I fear I shall require the loan of some clothing, as well."

No one moved. They stood as if transfixed. Mina propped her hands on her hips and stomped her foot. "Do not stand there gaping like fools! Send for a courier at once to relay this information!"

The captain's eyebrows shot up. He bowed slightly. "Forgive my manners, Mrs. Smith. I am Captain James Hubbard. Won't you and your guide step into my tent? We are rebuilding the fort after the flood this spring. I fear these tents are the best we can offer. Private, send for Lieutenant Baker's wife at once."

"Yes, sir!"

As the young man hurried away, Mina turned to Devlin. "You should see a doctor. Some of those cuts look infected."

"I will once we tell Captain Hubbard what we know."

"Yes, of course."

"This way, Mrs. Smith." The Captain held back the flap, and Mina proceeded inside.

Once they had made their report and answered all the captain's questions, Mina allowed herself to be led away by a sympathetic, middle-aged wife of one of the fort's officers.

*

Devlin watched her go with mixed emotions. Mina was safe, and he thanked God. It slowly became clear to his exhausted brain that she had all her answers now. He knew what had to happen next. She would go back to Vincent in Philadelphia and then Silsby Hall in Bedfordshire or London. She would go home.

Even in buckskins, she was every inch the lady who gave orders and expected them to be obeyed without question. Who else would require a maid to attend to her and expect servants to do her bidding? She didn't belong here in the dust and blood. This was his life, not hers.

She had called him her guide. And that was all he was. A lady might dally with a servant, but she was still a lady. He was nothing more than one of her servants. A guide hired briefly, but no longer needed. Somehow, he had forgotten that.

Only he would never forget the feeling of her body beneath him, of sinking into her warmth and finding heaven in her arms. Mina said she loved him, and he believed her, but he couldn't allow that. If she wouldn't leave him when her own life was at stake, she wouldn't leave him now that they were both going to live. It was up to him to make her go home.

"She is a remarkable woman," Captain Hubbard said with an appreciative gleam in his eyes. Devlin wanted to punch him.

"Is she married?"

"Widowed."

"You don't say. A wealthy family, I take it."

"Yes."

"I wonder if she'll be staying long?"

Devlin gritted his teeth. "I have it on the best authority that she will leave for Philadelphia as soon as possible."

"Whose authority?"

Devlin swung his steely gaze to the man. "Mine."

The captain drew back. "I see. We'll be mounting a detachment to track down Standing Bear and his band first thing tomorrow. I'd like to offer you a job as a scout. The Army pays good wages."

"Sure, I'll give you a hand after I've had some rest. My business with Mrs. Smith is finished."

*

Mina was fretted over and pampered with a cup of strong tea and a delicious slice of warm kidney pie. After that, she was allowed a bath in a brimming copper tub. Mrs. Baker exclaimed over the state of her hair and saw to its washing herself.

Mina fell asleep but was roused and forced to leave the lovely bath. Someone dried and dressed her like a child. She wore a soft, if overly large, cotton nightgown and was hustled into a narrow bed.

Her last thoughts were of Devlin. Only when she had been assured he was being looked after did she allow herself to relax. They were alive. They were safe. What now? She fell asleep with her question unanswered.

It was bright inside the canvas tent when Mina opened her eyes again. A bugle call sounded nearby. She sat up on her narrow cot and stretched stiff muscles. A few minutes later, Mrs. Baker bustled in.

"Goodness sakes, child. I thought you'd never wake up."

"How long have I been asleep?"

"Since yesterday afternoon. How are you feeling?"

"Exhausted."

Mrs. Baker chuckled. "I'm not surprised. I hear you're lucky to be alive."

"Where is Devlin? I mean, Mr. Elder?"

"He was just here asking after you. I told him I'd send word when you were awake. Can I get you anything?"

"A cup of your wonderful tea, if it wouldn't be too much trouble." Maybe some tea would lift the fog that hung in her brain, slowing her thinking.

"No trouble at all," Mrs. Baker said with a smile. "I've cut down a skirt and one of my blouses for you. You're such a tiny thing. Mrs. Dalton kindly lent you one of her corsets and some underthings. You'd be swimming in mine, for sure."

"Please thank Mrs. Dalton for me."

"You can thank her yourself. Captain Hubbard has asked the wives to plan a small supper party for you this evening. If you're feeling up to it? It's rare we get a female visitor, let alone a noble woman from England."

The last thing Mina wanted to do was mingle with a bunch of strangers, but she smiled meekly. It was easy to slip back into the dutiful society woman she'd once been. "That would be lovely. Let me get dressed and tidy up."

When she emerged from the Bakers' tent half an hour later, she felt decidedly odd in her borrowed clothes. She missed the freedom afforded by the buckskins she'd grown accustomed to. She turned to Mrs. Barker. "Where are the things I was wearing when I arrived?"

"Those horrible heathen clothes? I had them burned."

A stab of loss followed the woman's words, but Mina held her tongue as a polite guest should.

Across the parade ground, she spied Devlin leading a horse and walking toward her. A rush of joy filled her heart. She couldn't control the grin that spread over her features. He was dressed in dark pants and a faded trooper shirt. Somewhere he'd found a new black hat and shiny boots. He looked wonderfully handsome.

Her feet itched to run to him, but she knew such brazen behavior would be frowned upon by Mrs. Baker and the other women gathering near. Mina turned to the group. "If you'll excuse me, I must speak to Mr. Elder."

Before any of them could reply, she hurried away. Reaching him, she held out her hands. He took them briefly, then let them drop. He glanced around, then looked at his boots.

Something was wrong. Mina crossed her arms over her chest to ward off a sudden chill on the hot summer afternoon. "I hope you've recovered from your ordeal, Mr. Elder."

"A little iodine and some sleep did the trick. How are you?"

"It's amazing what a hot cup of tea can do. Mrs. Baker has made me her pet project. I'm feeling positively civilized in my borrowed finery."

She bit her bottom lip. "They burned the dress your sister gave me. I was upset, but what could I say? They are trying so hard to be kind to me. I see you found some clothes as well."

Mina forced herself to stop babbling. What was wrong with him? Why wouldn't he look at her?

On the other side of the parade ground, a bugle sounded, and a company of men formed up. It was then she noticed the bedroll behind Devlin's saddle. Her throat went dry. "Are you going somewhere?"

He looked at her then. "I've agreed to guide a troop to hunt down

Standing Bear. Word came early this morning that he attacked the supply train and made off with part of the gold. If he isn't stopped before he gets those rifles, hundreds more may die. I had the chance to kill him once and didn't take it. Look how many people have died because of me."

"You mustn't blame yourself."

"Maybe I won't if I help now."

He seemed to fade away before her eyes. What was wrong? "I shall worry dreadfully about you, but if you feel you must go, I will remain here until you return. I'm sure I can occupy my time. Perhaps I'll hunt more fossils. Close to the fort, of course. Fossil hunting is what I do best."

Devlin met her gaze. His eyes were hollow and guarded. "You aren't staying. You're going back where you belong."

"I beg your pardon?" She wasn't sure she'd heard correctly.

"There's a stage going east the day after tomorrow. I've purchased a ticket for you."

She laid a hand on his arm. "You don't have any money."

He looked at his horse. "The Captain gave me an advance on my first month's wages as a scout."

"You're staying on, then?"

"Yes." He turned to mount his horse.

This wasn't right. He acted as if he wanted to get away from her. She grabbed his arm. "Darling, what's wrong? Why are you acting this way?"

"Did you forget that I nearly got you killed? Have you forgotten what I did to Artie?"

"Of course not."

This wasn't the place for such a conversation. People were watching them. She moved a step closer and lowered her voice. "You love me. I love you. I don't want to go back east."

He looked toward the column of riders forming up. "I'm sorry, Mina, I have to go. You belong in England. I belong out there. Go home. Live a safe life. Find someone to love, someone to have children with."

"I want to do those things with you, Devlin."

He shook his head. "Your beloved Vincent is waiting for word of his son. He's the reason you came. The reason you need to go back."

Mina racked her brain for something to say, something to make him change his mind. She couldn't lose him now. "But you love me. How can you send me away?"

He looked her in the eyes. "You're so naïve. It wasn't love, milady. It was lust. Look, it shouldn't have happened, but it did. I'm sorry."

She took a step back as her heart dropped. "You don't mean that."

"I warned you I'm the wandering kind. Sorry if you expected more. Goodbye." He tipped his hat, mounted his horse and rode away.

It took every ounce of pride she possessed not to run after him. She stood in the center of the dusty parade ground watching as he joined the troop, and the men rode out together. She remained standing, staring after him until the column disappeared down the trail. He never looked back. Little by little, she noticed the scorching sun on her shoulders, the smell of dust and horses, someone shouting orders.

"Mrs. Smith, are you all right?" Mrs. Baker's kind voice beside her made Mina realize how tired she was.

"No."

"Perhaps you should lie down. You'll feel better after a little more rest."

It wouldn't help. She'd never feel better again. Devlin didn't love her. He'd said it to her face without flinching. He didn't want her.

What a fool she was.

*

Devlin hated himself. He'd broken her heart and his own. Watching the love in her eyes die as she gazed at him had been more painful than any torture Frenchy inflicted. Devlin's fingers ached from his tight hold on the reins. The slightest movement of his hand would turn the horse around. He could ride back to Mina. Back to tell her he was a liar, that he loved her more than life itself.

He'd endured loss and pain before but nothing like this. A black hole yawned before him, ready to swallow his soul. Life without Mina wouldn't be worth living. He'd never see her smile, never hear her endearing laugh, never hold her close again, and it was his fault. Driving her away was the only way to keep her safe. He knew that. Somehow, saying he broke her heart for her own good didn't ease his self-loathing.

All he hoped for now was to end Standing Bear's reign of terror. Maybe he'd get killed in the process.

"How soon do you think we'll cross Standing Bear's trail?" the soldier beside him asked.

"When we cross it," Devlin snapped and rode ahead, not wanting to speak to anyone. Too bad he didn't have a bottle of whiskey to drown his sorrows in.

No, even that wouldn't help.

Chapter Twenty-Seven

Mina's hired carriage stopped in front of the familiar three-story brick mansion on the outskirts of Philadelphia. She wasn't glad to be back. Instead, she dreaded the coming meeting with her father-in-law. She had tried to send a telegraph telling him of Artie's death, but never found the right words. In person, she'd find a way, and hoped it would make it easier for Vincent to hear.

Stepping out of the carriage, she shook the wrinkles out her dark blue dress. The long train ride had been just as horrible coming east as it had been going west. Worse really, because each mile carried her farther away from the man she loved. The man who didn't love her. Why couldn't she put him out of her mind?

She had stopped briefly in St. Louis to buy suitable clothes, widow's reeds. The black dresses were as much for her lost love as for Artie, but no one must know. She glanced at the pointed toes of her new shoes and longed for the comfort of her moccasins. Those days were gone. Never again would she know the freedom the vast plains offered. Maybe with the width of the Atlantic between them, she wouldn't feel the pull of Devlin on her heart. Maybe.

Adjusting her spectacles, she stood for a moment in front of the house. Vincent would be waiting for her. It should have felt as if she had come home, but it didn't. Home was wherever Devlin was. Somewhere out on the windy prairie she had left behind. She prayed he was safe, even if he didn't want her.

Squaring her shoulders, she climbed the broad front steps and pulled the bell. A few seconds later, the door opened. She smiled at the surprise on her butler's face.

"Lady Wilhelmina?" Stanley stood wide-eyed with shock.

"In the very tired flesh. Would you be so kind as to have my bags brought in?"

"Of course. Welcome home. Mr. Vincent is going to be so happy to see you. We were worried about you out there with those heathen Indians raiding and scalping. You should have let us know you were coming."

"Didn't you get my message? I sent a wire from Salina." It was a lie.

"No. Mr. Vincent has been very worried."

"Then I shall see him at once."

"He's in the study. I'll tell Mrs. Worthington you're here. She'll have the maid make up your room."

After thanking Stanley, Mina handed over her gloves and cape. Then she walked down the wide hall to the study at the rear of the house. The smell of beeswax and lemon polish permeated the air. Everywhere the woodwork and brasses gleamed, giving the fine home a cared for air. It seemed Mrs. Worthington had been a good choice for housekeeper and nurse.

Outside the double oak doors of the study, Mina hesitated. Vincent still harbored the hope that Artie was alive. It would be her task to crush his hope with the truth.

At least some of the truth.

She tapped on the door and pushed it open. Inside, light flooded the room from the tall, mullioned windows offsetting the somber tones of the rose damask walls and oak bookcases. Vincent was seated behind his desk, his head bent close to the lace cap of Mrs. Worthington, who was seated in a chair beside him. He glanced up, and a look of pure joy spread across his face. "Mina!"

"Hello, Vincent." The sight of him brought tears to her eyes. He struggled to rise, and she rushed to his side, throwing her arms around his neck. He held her in a crushing grip with his good right arm.

"Is it really you? My God, I've been worried out of my mind."

Mrs. Worthington muttered some comment and left the room. Mina loosened her hold and gazed fondly at the handsome silver-haired man she loved so dearly. "I sent a wire before I left Kansas, but it seems my message has gone astray."

"Never mind. Let me look at you. Why, girl, you're as brown as a nut."

She chuckled and sat on the corner of his desk. "I lost my parasol to a Cheyenne grandmother. Do I look a total disgrace?"

He cupped her face with one hand. "You look beautiful."

Mina's happiness faded as she stared at him. How did she begin? "I'm so sorry, Vincent. I'm afraid I bring sad news."

The light faded in his eyes. "Artie?"

"It is as we most feared."

"He's dead? You know for certain?"

"I spoke to the man who buried him. There can be no doubt."

He seemed to shrink before her eyes into a sad husk of a man. "Do you know how it happened?"

She dreaded this moment. Taking a deep breath, she closed her eyes so she wouldn't see his pain. "He was killed in an Indian attack."

"I've been reading terrible stories in the newspapers. Did my son suffer?"

"I was told he died instantly from a single gunshot." The half-lie slipped easily off her tongue. Nothing would be gained by revealing the awful truth.

Vincent covered his eyes with one hand for several moments, then reached out and patted her hand. "We can be grateful for that, at least."

She nodded without speaking. For a few minutes, they sat together, the muted ticking of the clock the only sound in the room.

Vincent roused. "Thank you, my dear, for traveling all that way and hunting down the truth. I know how much you loved my son. You are a daughter to me. I want you to know nothing will change that. You must be exhausted after your journey."

"I'm fine. Don't worry about me."

He patted her hand. "I'd like to be alone for a while. Do you mind?"

"Of course not." She kissed his cheek. He had taken the news better than she expected. Rising, she crossed the room to the door.

"Mina?"

She paused with one hand on the knob and looked back.

"Were you able to find the fossil he discovered?"

She swallowed hard. "No, I'm sorry."

"It was only a slim hope."

"Yes, I'm afraid it was."

"Would you ask Mrs. Worthington to step in?"

"If you want, I can inform the staff about Artie."

"I'd like to tell Martha myself."

"All right." Mina left the room. Outside, she found Stanley hovering a discreet distance from the door. He approached with obvious reluctance.

"Milady, is there any news of Mr. Arthur?"

"Sad news, I'm afraid. My husband is dead."

"I'm sorry, milady. I surely am. Poor Mr. Vincent. He'll take this hard. I'd best go get Mrs. Worthington. She'll know what to do."

"Vincent wishes to tell her himself."

Stanley bowed slightly. "I understand."

"We will need to get out the black crepes and cover the door knocker."

"Mrs. Worthington will see to it, milady. You should rest. She'll take care of everything."

As the elderly man turned away, Mina wondered if her place as mistress of the household had been usurped in the past two months by the worthy Mrs. Worthington.

Over the next few days, Mina came to realize exactly how true her assumption was. Mrs. Worthington never indicated Mina wasn't the one in charge, but each time Mina voiced some request or issued an order, Mrs. Worthington had already taken care of it.

In the mornings, the woman took Vincent's breakfast tray to him personally and remained with him while he ate. Once, while passing his room, Mina swore she heard laughter inside.

As Vincent recovered from the news about his son, Mina was pleased to see how much stronger he appeared than before she'd left. He used a cane to walk now instead of being pushed about in his wheeled chair. On nice days, he took short walks in the gardens at the back of the house. Mrs. Worthington, some mending or stitching in her lap, sat on the garden bench and kept an eye on him or strolled beside him.

From the window seat in her room, Mina watched but didn't join them. She didn't feel like company, and no one bothered her. Perhaps the household thought she was in mourning. At any rate, she kept to her rooms, and no one intruded on her privacy. She was surprised when Vincent announced his desire to remain in Philadelphia for an extended period, but she didn't mind. England was too far away.

Day after day, night after night, she thought constantly about Devlin. Was he all right? Had he found Standing Bear? She scanned the western papers every day for some hint but saw nothing.

Vincent held a private funeral for his son, with only a few close friends in attendance. When it was possible, he could have Artie's remains transported the family plot here. Standing beside the empty grave, Mina mourned her lost husband, brother and friend, but more than that, she mourned her lost love. To go on living without Devlin seemed a task too hard for her to accomplish. In a thousand years, if someone excavated her body, they would find more than bones. They would surely find her heart because she knew it had turned to stone.

Fall came and still she stayed in her rooms. The cloudy September skies reminded her of Devlin's eyes. The rain brought back memories of their night together as they lay in each other's arms. She missed him. Missed his rare smiles and his wit, even his scolding. Life without Devlin was empty. It shouldn't be. He didn't love her.

Then, almost a month to the day after she had arrived, Mina rose from her bed to see the sun shining outside. Something was different. Standing at the window, she realized her life would go on. She was done hiding. Either she could stay in Philadelphia with Vincent, or she could go out and make her own life, but it wouldn't be in England. There were fossils to be discovered in this new country, and she wanted to find them.

The choice, once so difficult to imagine, was simple. She would go west and fund her own dig. Professor Leady might help her gather a team. Smiling, she turned from the window and promptly threw up in her wash bowl.

Mina cleaned her face and put the startling episode down to the fish stew she had had last evening.

Looking down from her window, she saw Vincent and Mrs. Worthington enter the garden. Mina dressed in a gray gown, not her black one and went out to join them. As she approached the housekeeper, Mina noticed for the first time that Mrs. Worthington had changed, too. Gone were the gaunt cheeks and dull, downcast eyes of the woman Mina had hired. Martha Worthington presented the picture of a pretty, middle-aged woman with lively eyes and a faint blush to her cheeks.

She was gazing with rapt attention across the garden. Following her line of sight, Mina saw Vincent had stopped to converse with Mrs. Worthington's son, who worked as a gardener at the estate. Mina went to join her.

"Vincent has made amazing progress, Mrs. Worthington. You must tell me your secret." Mina sat beside the woman on the wooden bench.

"It's nice to see you up and about, Mrs. Smith. I'm afraid your father-in-law's recovery is no secret. It's just fresh air, exercise and making him do for himself."

"Do for himself?"

"Begging your pardon if I'm speaking out of turn, but he doesn't need to be coddled."

Slightly affronted, Mina said, "I didn't realize I had coddled him."

"And that was the trouble. He needed to stretch himself, needed to find out what he could do even if he failed the first, second or fourth time. When we love someone, it's very hard not to rush in and do for them."

She was looking not at Mina, but at Vincent making his way toward them. Mina noted the woman's heightened color as Vincent joined them. Was something going on between them?

The next afternoon, intending to tell Vincent of her decision, Mina opened the door to the study and discovered her father-in-law and Mrs. Worthington in an embrace. She stood dumbfounded until they noticed her.

"I beg your pardon," was all she could think to say.

With an embarrassed cry, Mrs. Worthington hurried from the room, her hands pressed to her cheeks.

Mina waited for an explanation. Vincent busied himself behind the desk and avoided looking at her.

"Vincent, is there something you'd like to tell me?"

He looked at her with a sad smile. One that reminded her of Arthur. "Despite what you are thinking, I assure you your place is here. This is your home. Nothing and no one will ever change that."

It was the perfect opening to tell him of her decision, but she was interrupted by a knock at the study door. Stanley opened it and announced, "Constable Monroe, to see you, sir."

Vincent nodded. "I've been expecting him. Show him in. Mina, you may want to stay and hear this."

A tall, dapper man with shining brass buttons on his uniform doffed his helmet and stepped forward. "I thought you would like to know, sir, a man has been arrested for the murder of your son. The wire came from Salina, Kansas, just this morning."

Mina took a step toward him. "Standing Bear has been captured?"

"No, Madam. He escaped, but a gunrunner by the name of Dubois was taken into custody. He gave up his former accomplice and told the sheriff in Salina he witnessed the murder of Arthur Smith by Devlin Elder and led the authorities to your husband's grave."

"Sniveling, stinking, no-good pile of buffalo dung! I can't believe it." Mina paced across the study floor and back. She noticed both men staring at her in open astonishment.

"I'm sorry if I appear overwrought, gentleman. He's a dastardly villain and a liar."

"Elder?" Vincent asked.

"Oh, he's a liar, too. A skilled one, but I meant Frenchy Dubois." A sudden thought struck Mina.

Devlin *was* a good liar. A very good liar. How many times had he proved that?

So why had she believed him when he said he didn't love her? It wasn't true. He did love her. He'd sent her to safety the only way he knew how. And she was going to make him admit it. "I need to have a word with Mr. Elder. Is he still at Fort Hayes?"

"He's in jail. Elder confessed," the constable added.

"He what?" Mina groped behind her for a chair and sank onto it.

"When he was arrested, he confessed."

Closing her eyes, she whispered, "Devlin, what have you done?"

She felt a hand on her shoulder and looked up to see Vincent's worried face. He addressed the police officer. "What will happen to Mr. Elder?"

"He's being hanged a week from tomorrow."

"Hanged?" Mina shot to her feet. "Over my dead body."

She headed for the door, yanked it open and shouted, "Stanley!"

He rushed into the room. "Yes, Miss. Is everything all right?"

"It most certainly is not. Send a cable to Sheriff Wilson in Salina, Kansas. Tell him to delay the execution of my husband's murderer until I arrive. I wish to witness it. Send a hundred dollars to cover any expenses or trouble my request may cause. That should convince him to wait. Make sure you get a reply. Then secure me a ticket on the next train to Kansas. Have Sabiha loaded along with my riding gear and have our attorney attend me at once. Tell him it's a matter of life and death. Go, go!"

"Yes, milady." Stanly bobbed his head and hurried away.

"Mina, what has come over you?" Vincent demanded.

Crossing to him, she took his hand. "Vincent, I'm in love with the most wonderful, most noble, sometimes stupid man that ever lived. I will not let him throw his life away. Artie was killed by a renegade named Standing Bear and by Frenchy Dubois. I won't let Devlin die in some preposterous attempt to ease his conscience or to free me of my affections for him. I must save him from himself, so I'm going back to Kansas."

"My dear, you can't go running off like this."

She kissed his cheek. "Yes, I can. I love you, I always will. Have a wonderful life. Make an honest woman out of Mrs. Worthington and tell her I said I'm done coddling you. She'll understand. Now, I must hurry."

"Mina, please," he called as she headed for the door.

She stopped and looked back. "You want me to be happy, don't you, Vincent?"

"Of course."

"Then don't try to stop me. Oh, and you must do me one more favor. Have the bulk of my money transferred to a bank in Salina."

"All of it?"

"Half. I'll send for the rest when I get settled."

"Settled where?"

"I have no idea. Isn't it exciting?" She blew him a kiss and raced up the stairs to pack.

*

Inside the familiar narrow cell, Devlin sat on his cot with his back propped against the wall and opened a letter from Buck. It had taken nearly a month to reach him, having been addressed to him at the ranch, but it had been forwarded when his arrest was reported in the newspapers.

Devlin,

I hope this letter finds you well. Caleb and I had made it safely to Denver and on to Cañon City, where we located Anna's sister. Caleb is learning to get along with four cousins.

Soon as I saw how many young ones the Newcomes had, I knew there'd be a place for the boy. His aunt and uncle were happy to take him in. Mrs. Newcome is a real fine lady, but her husband is a stuffy fellow. I hope you don't mind keeping an eye on the ranch by yourself for a while. I'd kind of like to stay and see Caleb get settled in. The boy has had a hard time of it. Luckily, Caleb's uncle tolerates his dog, cause that boy doesn't go no place without his Taffy.

I was wondering if Mrs. Smith ever found the bird bones she was looking for. Tell her I met an old mountain man that swears he saw a graveyard of giant bones in the southern mountains beyond Cañon City. He claims some of them was

taller than a man on a horseback. Course, he's drunk a lot, and
folks don't take stock in everything he says. I don't either, but
I thought Mrs. Smith might like the tale.
*   Your friend,*
*   Buck*

Devlin laid the letter on the coarse blanket covering his cot. He would have to write Buck and let him know he wouldn't be able to look after their place and ask him to write to Mina. She'd want to know they were both safe. Would Wilson let him pen a note before he was hung? From the high, barred window, the sounds of the scaffold being finished filled the air. His sentence was being carried out tomorrow morning.

One day to live, and all he could think about was Mina.

For the thousandth time, he considered writing to her, but he knew he'd never be able to get the words in his heart down on paper. Besides, what could he really say? *I love you, darling, but by the time you read this, I'll be dead.* It was best to let her think he had drifted out of her life.

"Elder, you got a visitor!" The sheriff's bellow boomed in the small space.

Looking up, Devlin couldn't believe his eyes. Mina stood beside Wilson, looking demure in a black dress, matching hat with a black veil and a black parasol hooked over one arm. She held a large bible clutched to her chest and looked every inch the grieving widow and even more beautiful than he remembered.

"If you don't mind, Sheriff, I wish to have a few minutes alone with my husband's murderer. I simply must hear in his own words how my Artie died."

"I don't think that's wise, madam."

She sniffed into a hankie she carried, then placed a hand on Wilson's arm and leaned toward him. "I should heed your words. Heaven knows you tried to warn me about this villain before and I refused to listen. It is only by the grace of God I am alive today."

The sheriff patted her hand. "This is too hard for a woman like yourself."

She dabbed her eyes. "No. It is my Christian duty. Has he asked for a man of the cloth?"

"A preacher? Him?"

"I thought as much. I have come to hear my husband's last words and offer my forgiveness to Mr. Elder. By doing so, perhaps I can help him turn to God in his final hours."

Devlin had no idea what she was up to, but he was willing to go along with it if it meant he could spend a few minutes alone with her. He stood and gripped the cold bars. "Let her try to save me, Wilson. This should be fun."

"Ain't nobody gonna get your black soul except the devil himself."

"Please, Sheriff," Mina pleaded. "Only a few minutes. What harm can it do? Let me attempt to save his soul so some good may come of this terrible tragedy."

"All right, but I'll be close by."

"The thought is a comfort, sir. Bless you."

Mina watched the sheriff leave. As soon as he closed the door behind him, she threw herself against the bars and wrapped her arms around Devlin's neck.

"Oh, my love, I was afraid I would be too late."

He kissed her, cursing the bars holding them apart. The joy of seeing her again and the pain of knowing she would watch him die almost broke him. "Mina, what are you doing here? Why did you come?"

She pulled back a little and frowned. "What a stupid question, love. I'm here to get you out of jail. This is my first prison break, of course, so if you have any useful information, I'm open to suggestions."

"You can't be serious."

She reached down her bodice and extracted a Colt revolver. "So far, this has been much easier than I expected. The sheriff really should have searched me. Sabiha is tied up outside. There's two weeks' worth of supplies in the saddlebags. My attorney said once you cross into the Oklahoma or Colorado territories, you're a free man. Kansas law doesn't extend outside the state. Even for murder. Also, he doesn't know I'm breaking you out of jail. We shall, of course, return one day to clear your name and see both Standing Bear and Frenchy hang for what they did. I swear it."

"Mina, I confessed."

"Why? I know you wanted me to forget about you, but this is rather drastic."

"I needed to tell the truth. All of it. I was sick of hiding what I'd done."

"My lawyer is pushing for a mistrial. Your conviction won't stand. If you had asked for a proper lawyer in the first place, none of this would have been necessary. But we don't have time for legal maneuvers now, so I'm getting you out of here. Unless you are determined to hang after all I have done for you?"

"I didn't think I would hang for a mercy killing."

"You shouldn't. It's a grave miscarriage of justice."

Devlin bowed his head. He had one more confession to make. "Mina, before we met, I spent some time with Wilson's wife. I'm sorry. She told him about us. I think he rigged the trial. The judge is her cousin. All the men on the jury were Wilson's friends."

Her eyes narrowed. "How many of their wives did you sleep with?"

He heard the anger in her voice. "A few."

"Well, I'll not let you hang for it so long as it doesn't happen again. Now, I'm going to get you out of here."

He looked up then. "My beautiful, brave, foolish, Mina. I can't let you do this. If you get caught, it will mean prison for you."

"Nonsense. I do not intend to be seen as your accomplice. That's why I'm not coming with you and why there's only one horse outside."

She pushed the gun through the bars. "I am nothing but a distraught, unbalanced widow who came here intending to shoot the man who killed her husband. Can I help it if you lured me close and disarmed me? Of course not. I'm a weak woman."

"This is the craziest scheme I've ever heard."

"Stop objecting and listen to me. You will hold me hostage at gunpoint. I will scream for help. Do be careful. The pistol is loaded."

She hiked up her skirts, extracted a roll of bills from her garter and pushed them through the bars to him. "I hope it is enough."

Speechless, he could only stare at her.

"Take it, Devlin. Now is not the time to have principles! I have plenty of money. Get used to it."

Reaching between the bars, he cupped her face. "When I said I didn't love you, I lied."

"I know. I believed you at first, then I remembered you are an excellent liar. Don't ever lie to me again."

"I won't. I love you more than I can ever tell you. More than my life."

Leaning forward, she kissed him with a sweet, stirring strength that promised a future he hadn't dared dream about. Pulling away, she turned and wrapped his arm around her neck. "We'll talk about this later." Then she screamed.

The door burst open, and Sheriff Wilson charged in, his gun drawn. At the sight of Devlin holding a pistol to Mina's head, he came to a skidding halt. "What the devil?"

"Open the cell door, or I swear I'll kill her."

Sobbing, Mina squirmed in Devlin's hold. "Do as he says. Please! Don't let him kill me. I beg you, sheriff, help me."

Damn the little hellcat, she was putting on a good show. Devlin tightened his grip, cutting off her pleading with a squeak.

"You heard the lady. Drop your gun." He pointed the revolver at the sheriff and motioned for him to comply.

Reluctantly, Wilson did. "How'd you get a gun?"

"You can thank this scheming gal. She didn't intend to save my soul. She came here to put a bullet in me."

Mina pulled his arm away from her neck a fraction. "I only wish I had succeeded, you miserable scoundrel! Hanging is too good for you. I wanted to see you beg for your life!"

"Mrs. Smith, I'm sorely disappointed in you," Wilson moved to unlock the door with the large key that hung on his belt.

"Step back," Devlin motioned him over. When Wilson did, Devlin shoved Mina, and she went flying into the man's arms. She wasted no time wrapping her arms tightly around his neck and sobbing loudly.

Sliding out of the cell, Devlin tipped his hat and smiled, then motioned for the two of them to get in. They did, moving slowly, with Mina crying like an abandoned child and clinging to Wilson.

*

As Devlin shut the cell door and locked it, Mina realized he had failed to mention which way he would go. To Oklahoma or Colorado? How would she find him again? She looked at him wide-eyed.

Devlin touched the brim of his hat. "I wish I could stick around to see how this turns out, but I'd best be going. Thanks for the gun, milady, but take my advice and give up trying to kill folks. Go do what you do best and don't forget to write."

He laughed and strode out of the room, pulling the door shut behind him.

Wilson shook the cell door. "I'm going to kill that bastard when I see him again."

She might never see Devlin again. Mina's knees gave way at the thought, and she sank on to the cot. The crackle of paper caught her attention. She pulled a letter out from beneath her thigh and stared at it for a long second. *Don't forget to write.*

A tiny smile tugged at the corner of her mouth. She shot a covert glance at Wilson. He had gone to the window and started shouting for help, paying her no attention. Quietly, she slipped the letter into her pocket.

After a most uncomfortable hour spent in the cramped cell with Sheriff Wilson alternately bellowing for help and fruitlessly shaking the bars, they were released when the evening deputy came to bring Devlin his supper.

Almost at once, Mina was forgotten as the men set out to round up a posse and pursue Devlin. She wasn't worried. Sabiha was faster and had more endurance than almost any horse alive. Devlin would get away.

She walked across town to the train station and sat down on a bench outside on the platform. Pulling the envelope from her pocket, she read Buck's letter, making note of the return address in Colorado. Then she placed it in her bag and walked into the depot.

A bald, middle-aged man in a striped vest and a black conductor's hat waited behind the counter. "May I help you?"

"I'd like one ticket to Cañon City, Colorado, please."

"The train only runs to Fort Hayes, ma'am. After that, you'll have to take the stage to Denver and then another one down to Cañon City."

"That will be fine."

"Will you be wanting a round-trip ticket?"

Mina smiled. "One way, please. When a person decides to do what they do best, there is no need to look back. I shall only look forward."

Chapter Twenty-Eight

The Rocky Mountains soared high behind the rugged foothills hemming Cañon City. A dusting of light snow topped the hills. It would be gone when the warm afternoon sun hit it, but the changing leaves and the smells of autumn signaled winter was on its way.

Devlin drew his tired horse to a stop in front of the house he hoped belonged to young Caleb's aunt and uncle. He pushed his hat back with one finger and glanced around, wondering if he remembered the address correctly. The town wasn't big. He'd find the family, eventually. The two-story home in front of him with its fresh paint, large front porch and lace curtains at the windows looked out of place in the rugged western town. It was the sort of house that would suit Mina right down to the tip of her parasol.

Had she understood what he'd tried to tell her? Was she waiting for him? He prayed she was. That hope had sustained him for weeks during his five-hundred-mile ride.

The town's wide dirt main street boasted a handful of one and two-story false-fronted businesses. Most of the houses were little more than cabins tucked behind the main thoroughfare. He looked back at the imposing house. A yellow dog sat up on the porch and growled at him. It was Taffy. He was in the right place.

"Dev, you made it!" Buck rushed past the dog down the wide front steps.

Dismounting, Devlin clasped his friend's hand. "It's good to see you, Buck. Is Mina here?" He held his breath, waiting for his friend to answer.

"She got here three weeks ago. Wish you'd gotten here sooner." Buck's smile became stilted.

The hairs on the back of Devlin's neck prickled.

Sabiha whinnied loudly and tugged at the lead rope tied to his saddle horn. He had purchased a second horse from Swift Fox when he stopped briefly at the village to see Namid and explain where he was going.

"Can you take care of the horses, Buck? I want to find her."

Buck rubbed his palm on his pant leg before unhooking Sabiha's lead rope. He wouldn't make eye contact with Devlin. "I know where she is. I'll take you there as soon as you get yourself settled."

Something wasn't right. Buck was too nervous. "I want to see her now."

"You can't. Not till after four o'clock."

Devlin reached the end of his patience. He'd been on the move, dodging Army patrols and Indians, camping in makeshift hideouts and traveling mostly at night for the last five weeks. He needed to see Mina.

"Where the hell is she?"

Buck sighed. "In jail."

Devlin's stomach clenched in a hard knot. Had they discovered she helped him escape? "For what?"

Buck began leading the horses to the barn at the back of the property, and Devlin followed. "There is a group of women in town. They've been causing a ruckus, what with marching in the streets and carrying signs. Mina says they're suffragettes. They want the right to vote and to be equal to men. Seems Kansas just gave women the right to vote in school elections and the women here want it, too. Can you believe that?"

It sounded like a cause Mina would champion. "So, why is she in jail?"

Buck unsaddled Dev's horse. "They had a rally a few days ago. Then a fight started between some men. The women were all arrested for disturbing the peace. Mina is sort of their leader."

Devlin closed his eyes. Of course she is. "Will I have to break her out?"

"There ain't no need. They're getting a hearing at four o'clock. I think the judge will let them all go. In fact, I'm sure of it."

"Why?"

Buck jerked his thumb toward the house. "The Right Honorable Judge Henry Newcome is tired of trying to wrangle all his kids without his wife."

Devlin frowned at Buck. "Caleb's uncle is a judge?"

"Yup, and he's been looking more peaked by the day. Five kids are a lot to handle. I'd say he's nearly at the end of his rope. Mina talked his wife into joining her cause. He had to give Mrs. Newcome the same sentence as all the others. He's not happy with Mrs. Smith."

"Neither am I." Devlin clenched his fists. He had been dreaming about their reunion for weeks on his lonely trek across the prairie. Longing for the moment she would race into his arms, and he could kiss her senseless. And where was she? Locked up. Still, he had to see her.

Was she right about his wanted status outside of Kansas? He had passed the new territorial prison being built just outside of town and didn't want to be its first inmate.

Pulling off his hat, he slapped some of the dust from his clothes. "What time is it now?"

"About three, I reckon."

"Then I have an hour to enjoy the sight of her behind bars. Which way is the jail?"

"Three blocks that way," Buck said and led the horses into the barn.

The jail was easy to find. The small, squat building with barred windows and heavy wooden shutters sat between a pair of busy saloons. Hitching rails in both directions were crowded with horses and mules. The sound of raucous voices and piano music spilled onto the street.

Devlin passed by the swinging doors of the saloon without breaking stride. He would give his eyeteeth for a drink of whiskey, but he wanted to see Mina more than he wanted to cut the dust from his throat.

Hell, he needed to see her more than life itself.

The city constable sat to the side of the door with a shotgun resting casually across his knees. A group of five angry men stood in front of him, demanding to see their wives.

"Court is in session over the Paradise Saloon. You can go on up. Your wives are there already."

When the men walked away, Devlin approached the constable. "I'm here to see Lady Wilhelmina Smith."

"She's the only one I got left." He rose to his feet and pushed open the door. Devlin entered the tiny space and saw her seated at a cot in one of the two cells at the rear of the room. Relief sucked the strength from his muscles and sent the sting of tears to his eyes. She was so damn beautiful. She wore a frilly pale-yellow dress with yards of white lace edging the ruffles. Her hair was up in a riot of curls. She was reading. Her spectacles had slipped down the bridge of her nose. She didn't glance up.

"Hello, Mina."

Her gaze shot to him. Her eyes widened with shock. "Devlin?"

The joy in that one breathy word made him forget everything but the need to hold her.

She jumped to her feet. "You made it."

"Did you doubt me?"

"Never."

She took one step toward him and crumpled to the floor.

*

Mina opened her eyes and tried to bring the world into focus. A strange man with black hair and a neatly trimmed beard was leaning over her. He had a stethoscope in his ears and held the cold metal bell on her chest. She pushed his hand away.

He leaned back with a frown and spoke to someone over his shoulder. "I find nothing wrong with her."

"Then why did she faint?" It was Devlin's voice. She hadn't dreamed it. He was here.

The bearded man handed her glasses to her. "Is there a chance you could be pregnant?"

Drat! Mina clasped her lower lip between her teeth. She harbored that suspicion, but this was not how she planned for Devlin to find out. She wanted to tell him when they were alone.

"That is an indelicate question to ask in mixed company, doctor." Eliza Newcome scolded. Mina's new friend pushed her way into Mina's field of vision. "Can you sit up, dear?"

Mina nodded and did so gingerly. The brief dizziness vanished. She looked over the surrounding people until her gaze settled on Devlin. His face was pale gray beneath the stubble of his beard. His eyes, his beautiful eyes, brimmed with worry. She smiled tenderly at him. "I'm fine. Will everyone please go away? Except you, Mr. Elder. I would like you to remain."

Judge Newcome took a step forward and glared at Mina. "If this is some ploy to avoid appearing before me, it will not work. You are going to stand trial for your crime of inciting a riot, Mrs. Smith."

Eliza waved him back. "Don't be an ass, Henry."

The outrage on his face was so funny, Mina had a hard time

suppressing a giggle. Devlin looked ready to hit the man. Henry Newcome drew himself up to his full height of five-foot-four. "Eliza, have you forgotten my position in this community?"

She sighed heavily. "I'm sorry, dear. Don't be a pompous ass."

His face flushed scarlet. "I shall amend your sentence to three months in jail if you speak to me in such a manner again."

She rose and patted his chest. "No, you won't. I daresay the house is a wreck, and you haven't had a decent meal since I left. If you return home without me, the children will revolt in the most calamitous fashion possible. You will not have a moment of peace for three months, while I shall enjoy the respite. Now, stop huffing. There's no reason you can't pass sentence on Mina right here. She does not have to go to your courtroom, which is nothing but a room over a saloon. You have every bit as much authority in here as in there, do you not?"

"Well—yes."

"Good. The rest of us were sentenced to time served. Mina does not deserve a harsher punishment."

"I released your friends to the strict supervision of their husbands and fathers. Mrs. Smith has neither to keep her in line. She is a disruptive influence on the women of this community. I sentence her to one year in jail."

"A year?" Mina gasped and sank back against the wall behind her cot. She pressed a trembling hand to her chest as she stared at Devlin.

The doctor took hold of her wrist. "Everyone clear out. This excitement is not good for my patient."

Judge Newcome and the others muttered their disapproval, but they all headed for the door. Only Devlin remained, standing stoically outside her open cell door.

She cast an imploring glance at the man beside her. "Please, Doctor. May I have a few minutes alone with Mr. Elder?"

The doctor glanced from her to Devlin. "A few minutes."

The instant the man closed the outside door behind him, Devlin crossed the space in three quick strides and gathered her into his arms. "Mina, darling, I've missed you so much."

Then he was kissing her with all the pent-up passion she had dreamed of, and she was kissing him back.

He stopped to catch his breath and tucked her head beneath his chin. "God, you feel good. You smell good. I want to rip your clothes off and make love to you until we both die."

She clung to him as tightly as she could and pressed her trembling lips together as tears slipped from the corner of her eyes. "That may have to wait a year."

"You couldn't stay out of trouble for a month?"

"Don't lecture me. You're wanted for murder." A sob slipped out as she teetered on the verge of breaking down completely.

He kissed her forehead and then each of her eyelids. "Don't cry. I love you with my whole heart and my whole soul. I've waited my entire life to find you. They won't keep us apart for a year."

She leaned back to gaze at him. "I don't deserve you."

He gave her a wry smile. "Probably not, but who else is going to put up with you?"

Pulling her close again, he held her tight and kissed her gently. When he drew away, he gave her a shaky smile. "Mina, I have a plan. I'm getting you out of here."

Mina wanted him to kiss her again, but that would have to wait. "A jailbreak? It's risky, but it could be done."

"No. Not a jailbreak." He shook his head. She had the feeling he was laughing at her.

Taking her by the shoulders, he made her sit on the cot and dropped to one knee in front of her. "Lady Wilhelmina Smith, my darling Mina, will you marry me?"

She couldn't have been more shocked if he suggested she dance nude in the street. "I beg your pardon?"

"I love you. I will always love you. Please say yes."

The light dawned on Mina. "Oh, I see. You're doing this so as my husband, the judge can release me into your custody. Brilliant. I wish I had thought of it."

He gave her a little shake. "Do you remember in Salina when I told you I would never lie to you again?"

"Yes. Isn't it odd how many of our conversations have taken place in jails?"

He brought her hand to his lips and pressed a kiss to the back of it. "I spoke the truth then, and I'm speaking it now. When I thought I was going to hang, all I wanted was to kiss you one more time before I died. For the past weeks, all I thought about was finding you and holding you in my arms. I want to marry you because I love you and for no other reason. I'm tired of feeling lost and alone. I'm incomplete without you.

When you're with me, I know where I belong. Please, say you'll marry me."

Tears welled up in her eyes. "That's the sweetest thing anyone has ever said to me. Are you sure? You're not the marrying kind."

"I am now."

She studied him intently. He was an excellent liar. How could she be sure? "This is not because the doctor made you think I'm pregnant, is it?"

"No."

"You're sure?" Her voice quivered ever so slightly.

"Absolutely positive." He tipped his head to the side. "Are you?"

How would he react to the truth? Clenching her hands together, Mina looked down. "Well, as fate would have it, I am. Are you upset?"

He leaned back but remained on one knee in front of her. "Surprised, yes. Upset, no. Give me a minute, okay? You're really having a baby?"

"That normally follows a woman being pregnant." She bit her lower lip as she waited for him to say something else.

A worried frown creased his brow. "I don't know how to be a father. I know nothing about kids, Mina."

He would make a wonderful father, but he wouldn't take her word for it. She had to help him believe it. "You knew your sister when she was a baby, and when she was growing up, didn't you?"

He thought for a bit. "Yeah."

"You held her when she cried and your mother was busy, didn't you?"

"Sometimes, sure."

"What do you remember about that?"

"She was so tiny. I thought I might break her, but the first time she smiled at me it was like the sun came out."

"I imagine you kept her from stumbling into the fire or into a creek when she got older."

Devlin nodded. "She was a fearless little thing. You couldn't take your eyes off her for a minute."

"Did you like her?"

A slow grin spread across his face. "I liked her a lot. Despite how much trouble she was, I loved her and still do."

Mina smiled at him tenderly. "That's what fathers do."

"So, we're gonna have a baby? A family. Yeah, that's good." His smile widened. "Namid is gonna be overjoyed when she finds out."

Mina looked away. One last hurdle remained. "Aren't you going to ask me if I'm sure it's yours?"

"What? The thought never crossed my mind. Why would it?"

"Well, because we weren't married. I was a woman of lose morals. I seduced you. Sort of. You may think I have seduced other men."

He chuckled heartily. Mina glared at him. "Don't laugh at me, sir. I'm capable of seducing many men."

His smile disappeared, replaced by intense sincerity shining in his beautiful eyes. "Milady, I don't doubt you could sweep a thousand men off their feet as beautiful as you are."

Mollified, Mina cleared her throat. "A thousand may be a bit of an exaggeration."

Devlin cupped her cheeks. "You don't give your heart easily, darling. That you gave it to me is a miracle I've thanked God for every day since we've been apart. I could never doubt your loyalty."

"Thank you." The last of her doubts faded away.

Crushing her close, he kissed her until her head was spinning. Her body grew hot with desire as his lips trailed kisses down her neck to her the top of her breast where her gown impeded his progress. He drew back and kissed her nose. "I don't want to wait any longer to marry you. I'm going to find a preacher."

Panting heavily, Mina pulled her neckline up to a more modest position. "An excellent idea, darling. Oh, wait, the judge can marry us more quickly." She had waited long enough for the man she loved with all her heart and soul.

Devlin scowled. "I thought a judge imposes fines, sentences men to hang, or sends them to prison."

"Every judge, justice of the peace or captain of a ship can marry people. All we need are two witnesses. We don't have to be married by a preacher."

"Don't women want a proper wedding with flowers and such?"

"I had all that with Artie." She laid her hand over Devlin's heart. "What I want is to be held in your arms forever."

"Judge Newcome it is." Devlin kissed her, then opened the front door. The group was still assembled. He motioned for them to come inside. Mina saw Buck had joined the crowd and waved to him. When everyone was inside, Devlin said, "Your Honor, I would like to marry Mrs. Smith as soon as possible."

"That's great!" Buck yelled.

The judge didn't share his enthusiasm. "You believe it will make me commute her sentence as I did the others. I think not."

"Henry." His wife's voice carried a stern warning.

He frowned at her for a long moment, then gave a quick shake of his head. "Our local minister has gone to Denver on business. He'll be back in six days. The wedding can take place when he returns, but Mrs. Smith will remain in jail until then."

"That won't work." Devlin's tone sent chills down Mina's spine.

"Well, that's the way it has to be," the judge said firmly.

Mina heard the ominous click of a gun being cocked. The constable slowly raised his hands.

Devlin's pistol was pressed to the man's side. "Lay your gun on the desk, close the shutters and step outside. Judge, you stay here."

Mina stared at him, aghast. "Darling, what are you doing?"

Buck's mouth dropped open. "Are you loco?"

Devlin motioned for the constable to obey him. When the man stepped outside, Devlin barred the door. "She said yes, and I'm not waiting six days to be with my wife. Judge, you're going to do the honors. Buck, you're a witness."

"I'll be the other witness." Eliza pressed both hands to her cheeks. "How romantic."

Mina smiled at Devlin. "Quite foolhardy, but yes, very romantic."

Henry crossed his arms and shook his head. "I refuse."

Eliza took her husband's hand. "No, you don't. You will marry these two, and then we'll go home, where I will show you how much I love and admire you, kitten."

"Eliza! I've told you not to call me that in front of others." He glanced around. "Besides, this man is committing a crime."

She smiled gently. "It's a crime of passion, and no one has been hurt. Do this for me, please Henry?"

"No!"

"Please?" she pleaded. "I'll make pork chops for supper. I know how much you like them."

Mina could see Henry wavering. "Oh, very well. What is your name, sir?"

"Devlin Elder."

"Take her hand."

Mina jumped to her feet and flew to Devlin's side. He gripped her hand with his free one, but he didn't lower his gun.

The judge gave his wife a stern look. She smiled brightly. Withdrawing a Bible from his desk, he took a deep breath. "We are gathered here to join this couple in the bonds of holy matrimony. Do you, Devlin Elder, take this woman to be your lawfully wedded wife, for—".

"I do."

Henry scowled at him. "There is more to the question, sir."

"That's my answer. Keep going."

Mina squeezed his fingers again. She was so happy she thought she might burst into fizzy bubbles like a shaken bottle of champagne.

Henry turned to her. "Do you, Wilhelmina Smith, take this man—".

"I do. I do."

"Oh, for heaven's sakes. Then, by the power vested in me by the Territory of Colorado, I pronounce you husband and wife. You may kiss the bride and pick up your marriage certificate at my office tomorrow. I'm going home. Eliza, come along." He reached for her.

She shoved his hand away. "And Mina's sentence is commuted to time served?"

"Yes, anything to get my life back to normal."

Eliza kissed his cheek. "Thank you, kitten."

Devlin nodded to Buck, who opened the door. The constable was still outside, but he stood back when he saw the judge and his wife coming out. Buck tipped his hat and stepped out, too.

Devlin holstered his gun. Mina dashed to the door and lowered the bar into place. Turning her back to it, she faced the most exciting, rugged, wonderful, romantic man in the world. And he was all hers. "I'm so happy you're here, Devlin."

He crossed to her and took her hands in his. "Truthfully, I expected to find you hunting fossils. Not waiting in jail."

"It isn't as enjoyable without you listening to me babble about species and preservation methods."

He grinned and kissed her nose. "I like learning about your passion, and I adore the way you babble."

"I'm eager to learn more about your passions." Mina couldn't believe she'd said that out loud as a blush heated her cheeks.

"Making love to you is my new passion, wife." He groaned and tried to pull her close.

She put one hand on his chest, then stepped away as a newfound boldness took hold. "This cot is quite comfortable, husband."

Interest flared in his eyes. "Is it? Come here, Mrs. Elder. We're not married until I kiss you."

She sauntered past him to resume sitting on the cot. "My dear Mr. Elder, I hate to contradict you, but we are not legally wed until our union is consummated."

He began unbuckling his belt as he walked toward her. "God, I love how smart you are."

She lay back and held out her arms. "I know. Never let it be said I hesitated to add to my education. Show me more, darling."

His gun belt hit the floor. "Gladly, milady."

Author's note:

A fossil bird called Ichthyornis was discovered in Rooks County, Kansas by geologist Benjamin Franklin Mudge in 1872. It was the first bird with teeth ever found.

About the Author

Pat (Patricia) Stroda was born on the edge of the Old West between Abilene, Kansas and the Santa Fe Trail in the Kansas Flint Hills. As a child, she found a cavalry spur in the pasture of her family's farm and became hooked on tales of the Wild West that happened near where she grew up. Having inherited the story-telling gene that runs in her family, she turned that gift into a second career after she left nursing and became a *USA Today* and *Publishers Weekly* bestselling author. She writes under the pen names of Patricia Davids and Hope Navarre.